JONAH K.

Dr. Bob Bell

Non Nocere Press

NON
NOCERE
PRESS

*This book is dedicated to all healthcare providers
who demonstrate their commitment to reconciliation
through the services they provide.*

Best wishes,

CONTENTS

Endorsements

Dr. Bob Bell's riveting and dramatic story has the reader living in the fast-paced mind of a heroic trauma surgeon. He captured the misogyny and biased treatment women surgeons face in a way that is both triggering and empowering. **Dr. Carmen Quatman, MD, PhD, Orthopaedic surgeon-scientist**

With "Jonah K.", Dr. Bob Bell firmly establishes himself as a master storyteller. Bob weaves an inspired fictional tapestry, representing both the best and worst of the human condition. From the tragic legacy of residential schools and the crushing politics of academic healthcare, characters emerge full of courage, passion and resilience. This is a brilliantly written third book from a talented novelist. You won't forget these intriguing individuals or this stirring story. **Paul Alofs, Former CEO Princess Margaret Cancer Foundation and award-winning author**

Dr. Bob Bell is probably the only author today who can turn acute insights on the general topics of human nature, history, politics, capitalism, and specific topics of healthcare delivery, into page-turning stories that are both compelling and inspiring. He does so once again in his third novel titled "Jonah K." **Keith Ambachtsheer, Former Chair Princess Margaret Cancer Foundation and award-winning author.**

Weaving extensive research and an original, compelling story, Dr. Bob Bell has written an important and relevant novel that, at once, advocates, educates, and engages the reader. This is a very good and worthy read! **Anne Golden, Former CEO United Way Toronto and former CEO Conference Board of Canada.**

A great read. The story eloquently portrays the fate of multiple characters who rise out of their painful pasts to build a new chapter in their lives. **Dr. Anil Chopra, Vice-President Medical Affairs, University Health Network.**

Bob Bell offers another gripping and highly engaging novel. This time, the novel is Canadian to its core. In addition to highlighting what a modern medicine has to offer, Bell tackles several current Canadian issues, from the injustice and intergenerational impact of the residential schools, exploitation of native peoples and lands, racism, to the delivery of healthcare in the Canadian North. The characters are engaging and the story line is very moving. You will shed some tears. It is an uplifting and optimistic story showing what could be possible. **Dr. Mary Gospodarowicz, Former Cancer Program Medical Director, University Health Network.**

In "Jonah K.", Dr. Bob Bell's latest fiction, he once again tells a story that entertains and informs. Young Jonah's journey from a remote Indigenous community to the Toronto corporate scene and back to his roots is packed with great characters. From their perspective, we understand the inequities Indigenous people face in health care delivery. **Rita Burak, Former Director University Health Network.**

"Jonah K." is very relatable to the real world of health care (including sexism/misogyny, and northern community health care challenges), relationships, business and indigenous trauma. Fantastic that proceeds of the book will be provided to the Indigenous Health Program at UHN. **Tracy MacCharles, Former Ontario Cabinet Minister.**

Bob Bell's latest novel is a fast moving and riveting story that touches on so many of the current key issues of our time. Woven into a great tale are the well-researched details of the Canadian health system, broad aspects of corporate finance, and the hopes and dreams of indigenous communities in the north. We are treated to an insider's look at orthopedic and trauma surgery, the development of the legal cannabis industry, the role of hockey in the north and the tragic consequences of the Residential schools of the last century. We see both the dark side and the joy of sex and romance. Exciting, uplifting and even educational! You won't be able to put it down. **Dr. Michael Baker, former Physician-in-Chief, University Health Network.**

The breadth and depth of the characters, the rich historica educational context (cannabis, diamond mining, urban/ remote healthcare, indigenous culture/experience, racism and sexism), and the twists and turns make this a compelling novel. This story is not just entertaining it is also deeply emotional and storyline against a backdrop of exploitation, inequality, and suppression. **Ken Deane, Healthcare Leader.**

Bob Bell has written another page turner with a strong plot and characters. He raises profound questions about the well-intended paternalism of central planning experts - particularly in indigenous communities. **Will Falk,**

Healthcare Leader.

"Jonah K." grabs you from the first page and is tough to put down. Dr Bell weaves a wonderful and engaging story with multiple intriguing sub plots and rich characters. The book deals deftly with the long-term impact of Canada's dismal record regarding First Nations, the excesses of the mining industry, life in 'the North', and, as only a medical doctor can, integrates seamlessly into the story both front line medical procedures and broader health policy issues. "Jonah K." is a must read. **Stephen Bear, Former Director Princess Margaret Cancer Foundation.**

Dr. Bell explores the multi-layered dynamics of some highly socially relevant topics in a wonderful set of interwoven stories contained in the successful life of Jonah K. Complex human dynamics – equality, respect for our indigenous communities and leading to human growth and understanding. **Tom Wellner, CEO Revera Living.**

Bob Bell's third novel, "Jonah K." explores the complicated relationships between indigenous peoples and Canada against a backdrop of topics as Canadian as it gets, from hockey, to resource extraction, to health care in remote communities, to hierarchies that are often dominated by men. Jonah K should be on everyone's reading list. **Mark Rochon, Healthcare Leader.**

In his third novel, Bob Bell has managed to intricately display his story-telling abilities. He has woven a tale of a successful, honourable and bright Indigenous man and his ability to rise above the horrors of the aftermath of the residential school system through hard work, education and the kindness of others. The reader is taken on a varied educational journey involving the intricacies of orthopedic surgery, the struggles of female doctors in a male dominated profession, the complexities of an Indigenous community trying to survive in the face of an overbearing mining conglomerate, and the inordinate problems facing the health care system in its attempts to address service to an outlying community. Easily readable and tenderly written. **John Mulvihill, Former Board Chair, University Health Network.**

It is an interesting and easy read about the issues around healthcare and Indigenous People. A positive plan of the problems and solutions. Hope is key. **Lionel Robins, Former Chair, Princess Margaret Cancer Foundation.**

We know when the book ends that the story does not. It is a Canadian story, our story – one which too many of us knew but did not feel. Bob Bell ends that. Read this, learn, feel our history and future promise, and be inspired. **Ronnie Gavsie, Healthcare Leader.**

"Jonah K." Is another fast-paced and intriguing novel from Dr. Bob Bell. The reader is transported on a fascinating journey from Toronto's boardrooms to Canada's far north and provides insights into Indigenous life, diamond mining and of course, health care. **Krista Sereno, Healthcare Assistant.**

Jonah K. is a fascinating character deserving of your attention! **Peter Jacobsen, Attorney.**

A highly intriguing modern thriller that reflects our history. The author has deftly and intricately created characters that keep you wanting more. **Kim Baker, Healthcare Leader**.

Bob has taken you into the legal, healthcare and indigenous domains in "Jonah K." A great read! **Linda Haslam-Stroud, Healthcare Leader**.

Once again, Dr. Bob Bell's unique blend of medical expertise, political insight and commitment to social justice culminates in a story with something for everyone. "Jonah K" is an exploration of relationships, loyalty and betrayal; and reminds us that our collective and personal histories shape our futures. **Lori Marshall, Healthcare Leader**.

CHAPTER 1

The Moment. October 29, 2017

By Sunday evening Jonah Kay had become accustomed to being ignored. Sitting beside his best friend David Morton, Jonah observed with ironic detachment as the decisive moment that characterizes most business negotiations finally arrived.

Francis Wells, the lead American investment banker, had been generally silent for the past two days. Meanwhile, junior bankers on both sides of the polished boardroom table had traded competing PowerPoint presentations with widely different estimates of how much International Brands should pay for its potential investment in CannWeed. Now, with only six hours left to get a deal, Wells was taking over the negotiations, speaking slowly, his words aimed at CannWeed's CEO.

"David, you know that my client, International Brands, is the largest adult beverage company in the world. Their balance sheet is primed for investment, and they believe that cannabis drinks are going to be a high growth product in the future. We respect what you have done in growing CannWeed. But we both know you need four hundred million dollars urgently – yesterday. And that's what we are offering as our partnership contribution."

The New York banker exemplified bespoke, polished assurance. His perpetual tan was highlighted by his crisp white shirt and the slim tailoring of his suit showed his devotion to the tennis court at his Florida estate. Francis Wells continued, pacing his comments in a slow drumbeat directed at David Morton.

"I repeat, David, we respect what you have accomplished as CEO of CannWeed. But the valuation you are placing on CannWeed is far too high. The deal we are proposing will provide two hundred million dollars for you to get ready for Canadian cannabis legalization and the new products that we want to develop with you. We have told you that we will go as far as four hundred million in total including cash to help you pay off some debt and to deliver the reward that you and your investors deserve."

Here he paused, staring at Morton for long seconds before continuing. "But, if you continue to insist that our investment in CannWeed is worth eight hundred million – then, David – you are simply whistling Dixie. We have another option – you know that. And we have only six hours left to get this deal done before we start exploring that next option."

Looking around the boardroom from his chair at the gleaming hardwood table, Jonah could see the disconsolate faces of CannWeed's six Canadian investment bankers. They were rigid in their seats, their tension reflecting the reality that their payment for three months of hard work would be lost if this deal did not close. Jonah could see David Morton's round face beginning to redden in response to Francis Wells' direct comments. Jonah knew David was approaching the risky moment when he would begin to bargain in anger.

The five American investment bankers on the other side of the table sat casually with the relaxed arrogance of brokers who knew they enjoyed a crucial advantage. The Americans were certain that the opposing Canadian side needed this deal more than they did. Jonah silently reflected that he was the only person in the room who knew the Americans were wrong.

As CannWeed's chief lawyer, Jonah had been quietly observing the deal making which had started Friday evening with a dinner in the hotel adjacent to the Toronto bank tower where they were now meeting. All day Saturday and Sunday the investment bankers from either side had swapped dueling presentations arguing differing perspectives of what CannWeed was worth.

The CannWeed bankers emphasized the new revenue that would likely flow to the company the following year when the Canadian government had promised to legalize marijuana. They used these cash flow projections to show that International Brands' investment in CannWeed should be valued at about eight hundred million dollars.

Jonah had correctly predicted to his friend David that the Americans would respond that these revenue numbers were entirely speculative. The International Brands American bankers insisted that they didn't really care about revenues from the Canadian market and simply wanted a partnership with CannWeed to develop cannabis beverages for the future American market. They wanted to test these products in Canada to be ready for the legalization of pot in America and insisted their investment in CannWeed should not exceed four hundred million dollars.

Jonah admired the well-practiced script that Francis Wells was following. He had kept his powder dry Saturday and most of Sunday. He was now determined to lower the boom on the Canadians and close the deal at the terms his client wanted. His unspoken message was clear. *"You're playing in the big leagues where I control things, David. I know just how much your company is worth to us and it's about half of what you think it should be."*

Jonah checked his watch. It was six p.m. on Sunday evening. The two companies' agreement to negotiate would expire at midnight. And Francis Wells thought he had the Canadians bent over a barrel. He hadn't budged from his opening offer of four hundred million, and he knew CannWeed desperately needed this investment.

Jonah understood why Francis Wells was so confident. If David refused his offer, then International Brands would immediately turn to Premium Bud, CannWeed's major Canadian cannabis competitor, and do a deal with them. During these negotiations, CannWeed had opened its books to the American bankers and International Brands now knew everything there was to know about CannWeed's business. It would be devastating to CannWeed if the Americans walked away to do a deal with Premium Bud, taking knowledge of CannWeed's business plans with them.

Over the four weeks leading up to this final weekend negotiation, CannWeed and International Brands had come to agreement on most of the terms and conditions that would define their potential partnership – how many seats International would get on CannWeed's board, the amount of money needed for investing in cannabis production and new products, the management structure of the potential new company. But they were still very far apart on how much International Brands should pay to invest in CannWeed. And time was running out as the midnight deadline for their negotiations approached.

Jonah could feel the tension as he placed his hand on David's forearm. After CannWeed invested to expand pot production and develop new products, after they paid off some of the bank loans that were strangling the company and paid their investment bankers' fees – after all that, four hundred million dollars would give David and CannWeed's investors just about nothing in return for the years of risk and hard work they had contributed to CannWeed's rapid growth. Four hundred million would be a devastating outcome for Jonah's best friend.

It was time. Jonah had hoped that he would not need to intervene, but intervention was clearly going to be necessary.

Holding David's arm, Jonah leaned in close and whispered

discreetly in his friend's ear. Jonah could feel David's forearm muscles relax and the CEO took a deep breath as he turned to the New York banker.

"Francis let's take a five-minute break. These are going to be our last few hours together developing this partnership. Let's make sure we spend the time wisely." David turned to Jonah who nodded before the CEO continued.

"To make sure that we are on the same page, let's get on a videoconference with Norman to ensure that we are still aligned."

Jonah saw a slight smile appear on Francis Wells' face across the table. Norman Ridgely was the CEO of International Brands. He was back home in Connecticut, leaving these negotiations to his bankers. Norman Ridgely and David Morton had discussed this investment in person on several occasions over the past few weeks. They had agreed that, if they could settle on price, it made sense to create a partnership through an International Brands investment in CannWeed. Now they were at the make it or break it moment of determining whether they could agree on a number for that investment.

Jonah knew that Francis Wells would think that David asking to speak to Norman at this late stage was a sign of weakness. Francis would expect that David was going to make a last-minute plea to Norman to increase his offer beyond four hundred million dollars. Francis would be certain that Norman would firmly refuse David's request to raise his bid. And then Francis would present International Brands with their new cannabis products at a bargain price. Or Francis would move on to do a deal with Premium Bud.

As Jonah retreated with the CannWeed team to their private conference rooms peripheral to the boardroom, the Canadian investment bankers clustered around David. Closing the conference room door behind him, David looked around at the bankers. "Okay guys, I need the room. Just me and Jonah."

The bankers regarded each other with surprise. This was

unexpected. They knew that David was running out of time. Midnight was fast approaching. Unless they could convince him to drop his price and close for the four hundred million bid that International Brands was offering, this deal and their fees were about to evaporate. This was not the time for their client to be planning tactics with a junior lawyer, especially not this very junior native Indian lawyer that they didn't know or trust.

They understood that David and Jonah had history and that Jonah had been representing David for the past four years while CannWeed had grown rapidly through acquisitions. But this was crunch time – exactly when David needed to listen to their deal making expertise – not unpredictable counsel from some untested Indian lawyer.

The lead Canadian banker protested, "David, we need to strategize about the call we are about to have with Norman. This is really our last chance, and we really need to dial back how much we are demanding here. Four hundred is a very good offer."

David stared back, slowing shaking his head. "I need to talk with Jonah. Then he and I will speak to Norman alone."

The lead banker flushed. "David this is really very irregular. I need to insist…" But David had walked to the external door of the conference room and was holding it open, ushering the bankers to the corridor where chairs lined the walls.

"Sorry, guys, I need a small team approach right now."

Closing the door, he turned to his friend. "Do we have photos?" Jonah nodded. With that, David strode back through the boardroom and knocked on the other side's door. As the American team answered, David entered the room and suggested, "Francis, I think that you and I should speak to Norman alone. I'm only bringing Jonah with me to the call."

The New Yorker was surprised. He was accustomed to working with David's Canadian investment bankers on a variety of cross border deals. Those bankers talked his language. Not in his league, of course, but reasonably good and generally knew their place. But he could not figure out this lawyer who was representing CannWeed.

Francis knew Jonah was from one of the big Toronto corporate firms. But he was far too junior to be working on a big deal like this and he looked like a native Indian, for God's sake. Long, straight black hair in a ponytail, dark, deep-set eyes. Dressed like a corporate lawyer but certainly did not resemble a buttoned-down mergers and acquisitions attorney.

Hearing Francis sigh, Jonah was sure that the banker would think that this request for a call was a last desperate ploy from the Canadian Pot King – the nickname that Jonah had overheard Francis and Norman using for David. Francis was probably expecting David to make an emotional plea to Norman. After Norman rejected the Pot King's final entreaties, Francis planned to finalize the deal that everyone knew CannWeed needed.

Jonah also knew that Francis would be thinking that if David was stubborn and refused to close at four hundred million, then he would simply move on and do a deal with Premium Bud. Jonah recognized Francis's fees would increase if he needed to negotiate with a second target. Jonah knew that these circumstances meant the American banker could squeeze David very hard to achieve a favourable price for his client.

Francis motioned the other American bankers to depart, leaving him, David and Jonah sitting in front of a large video screen. As Norman appeared on the screen from his home office in Connecticut, David provided welcoming remarks and reminded him that he had previously met Jonah when they visited him in New York. "Norman, Jonah has some information to share with you that we think is important for this last stage of our negotiations. Jonah, over to you."

Jonah nodded and fixed his eyes on the video screen's green light so that he would be looking directly into the International Brands' CEO eyes on his screen in Connecticut.

"Mr. Ridgely, you probably don't know that I come from an Indigenous community in northern Ontario. Tobacco has a special place in our culture. Many of our band council leaders have also supported legal medical marijuana dispensaries on reserve for years before Canadian legalization of recreational cannabis was even imagined." Jonah could see Norman nodding in puzzlement, obviously wondering what this was about.

"I have been careful to keep our community leaders aware of what CannWeed is doing with our current medical cannabis production and our corporate strategy for future legal recreational product. However, our main competitor, Premium Bud, has not been as straightforward, even though their main production facility is adjacent to one of the largest First Nations reserves in the province. And my colleagues on reserve have been concerned that Premium Bud seems to be producing and selling far more medical cannabis than they are licenced for by Health Canada." Jonah raised his hands to emphasize excess.

"You know Norman, every gram of Canadian medical cannabis production is strictly licenced by Health Canada." Jonah paused to ensure that Norman was following.

"Norman, I have a photograph to show you and Francis." Jonah opened the envelope he had carried into the room and pulled out two identical eight by ten glossy photographs. He pushed one across to Francis and held the other up to the screen for the CEO in Connecticut who leaned forward to peer at his computer screen.

Norman stared intently and then exclaimed. "What the hell am I looking at? What is this all about? Francis, what's going on here?"

Francis was looking at a photo of about ten police cars and cars with "Health Canada" logos sitting in a parking lot near the entrance to a large building. A sign next to the building entrance clearly read "Premium Bud Production."

The American investment banker looked at David Morton.

"David, what are you showing us?" David shrugged and tipped his head to Jonah who continued.

"Gentlemen, it appears that Premium Bud has exceeded its legal quota for medical marijuana by cultivating in unlicensed premises at their main production facility. We assume that they are selling that unlicensed product illegally. These photographs were taken when Health Canada and drug enforcement police officers made a surprise inspection of Premium Bud facilities late last week." Jonah waited to ensure Norman and Francis were paying attention to his next comment.

"Health Canada has scheduled an announcement along with the police in Ottawa tomorrow morning and I expect that they are going to suspend Premium Bud's production licenses for medical marijuana. Since their production reports are part of their investment disclosures, they will likely face enforcement actions brought under our securities laws as well. And if they are selling product illegally as I suspect, there may be criminal charges brought against management and their board."

"What the hell." Francis was looking at the photos. "How the hell did the cops know to raid Premium Bud now – just when we are in talks with CannWeed?" He looked up at both Jonah and David. David shrugged.

"And how did you manage to get these photos? How did you know just when...?" And then the investment banker stopped without completing his sentence.

Jonah leaned forward to speak to the International Brands CEO over the video link, ignoring Francis Wells. "Mr. Ridgely, we admire your leadership of International Brands and definitely think that a partnership between CannWeed and International would be good for both companies. We know that you think that if you cannot do a deal with us, you can turn to our competitor, Premium Bud. However, I think that your expectations will change with tomorrow morning's announcements about Premium Bud. After that announcement CannWeed is going to be the only company that you can partner with in the only wealthy western country where recreational pot is going to be legal about a year from now." Jonah stopped to take a sip of water and waited, looking at the video screen, allowing tension to build in the room.

"Mr. Ridgely, I suggest that we should extend our negotiations until midnight tomorrow night. I will draft something that we can both sign, agreeing to an extension of negotiations. That's not a big deal if we both agree. Tomorrow, your team will need to confirm what I have told you. I can promise that at 10 o'clock tomorrow morning there will be a joint announcement by Health Canada and the police in Ottawa." He then paused again for the most important part of his message.

"Thereafter, Norman, you will know that CannWeed is the only company in the world that will have licenced capacity to develop the new cannabis products that are important to International Beverages' future. And Norman, you are going to lead your company into these huge growth markets through your partnership with David." He turned to look at the now speechless American investment banker and then returned his gaze to the CEO over video.

"Gentlemen, should I draw up some paper extending our discussions for twenty-four hours?" He looked at his friend. "David would that be okay with you?" The CannWeed CEO could barely suppress his smile as he nodded.

Francis looked at Norman who was silently nodding on the screen.

A resilient response to setbacks was part of what distinguished Francis as the best in his business. He knew that when you have been severely injured in negotiations, the appropriate reaction is to ignore your wounds and move on. Francis sighed and nodded.

"Okay, gentlemen. Jonah, please draw up an extension and with Norman's agreement, I will sign on behalf of International." Norman continued nodding on the screen.

Francis Wells went on. "Why don't we reconvene tomorrow morning at eleven a.m.? I am sure that we will all be monitoring this ten o'clock announcement in Ottawa." He took a last look at the photo. "I suppose you want this back?"

Jonah put his hand out and Francis handed the photo over. The banker looked at David and Jonah. "Maybe you could leave me to discuss the situation with Norman."

David rose from his chair and walked out of the conference room and across the boardroom with Jonah following. The Canadian CEO entered CannWeed's conference room and closed the door. He then opened the conference room's outside door and stuck his head out into the corridor where his bankers were sitting. "That's it, folks, we are done for the night."

There was a palpable groan as the bankers leapt to their feet. "Ah shit, David, did they pull their offer? You didn't turn them down without us there, did you?" A smile broke out on David's face.

"No, no, relax guys. Jonah just convinced them that we needed a bit more time to come to agreement. We're extending the negotiation deadline twenty-four hours to midnight tomorrow night. Let's get together tomorrow morning – say just before ten." He continued smiling but closed the door leaving the bankers staring at each other in the corridor. They could hear David laughing inside the conference room.

Then they thought they heard him say, "Well you did it, you son of a bitch. Dammit all, you did it."

CHAPTER 2

The Break. October 30, 2017

As she scrubbed her hands at the operating room sink, Dr. Brynn Allard wondered whether it was a good idea to start complex emergency surgery just two hours after her heart had been broken and her life disrupted. She was on call for orthopaedic trauma at St. Bartholomew's Hospital in downtown Toronto. That morning she had returned to the hospital after a busy night of surgery and only three hours' sleep, planning to start a hip fracture surgery that had been delayed from yesterday's operating room schedule.

Her fiancé, Brian, had been working an overnight shift at St. Barts emergency room and she called as he was leaving the ER to let him know that she was doing a surgery and would likely not be home until the afternoon. She promised to wake him when she returned to their apartment.

When she learned on arrival at the OR desk that her case was again being delayed for a neurosurgery emergency, Brynn was upset for her patient, but also secretly pleased. She quickly walked the short distance home to the apartment she shared with her fiancé, enjoying Toronto's crisp fall air, hoping that

Brian would still be awake, looking forward to climbing into bed with him. She was disappointed to hear his deep breathing as she entered the bedroom, recognizing that he had already fallen asleep. Undressing quietly, she went around to her side of the bed where he had left his cell phone on the covers. Brian always programmed his phone for a long delay before his screen shut off and his last active screen was still glowing.

Brynn picked up the phone to transfer it to her night table. However, as she moved it, she came face to face with a text and attached photo showing her naked fiancé. Knowing that she was going to regret this moment forever but unable to stop herself, she scrolled up to find a topless picture of one of Brian's emergency room physician colleagues. Both photos were accompanied with passionate text describing a longing to be together.

Brynn sat on the edge of their bed scarcely breathing. The reason for Brian's recent reluctance to discuss wedding plans suddenly became achingly obvious. The pressure of advancing two intense professional careers was always a challenge in their developing relationship. But Brynn loved Brian and wanted to live her life with him.

As she sat in the dark, tears started silently but instantly became wracking sobs. She felt impossibly naïve as well as desperately hurt. She'd seen it happen before in the hospital's social pressure cooker. Her fiancé was having an affair with someone she knew on her hospital's staff.

Her sobs woke Brian and he rolled over and sat up when he saw the tears streaming down her face. Unable to talk, Brynn held up the phone which Brian grabbed from her. Brian started to mutter some obscure excuses and turned to sit with his back to her, his legs hanging over the side of the bed.

Then for the next fifteen minutes he talked without stopping. He admitted that he no longer loved her, couldn't say why, but told her that he and his colleague had fallen in love and that he was planning to leave Brynn.

Brynn's shock and despair were rapidly being replaced by

anger when her cell rang. She choked back her tears and answered the call. It was her resident in the trauma room at St. Barts. A young man had crashed his motorcycle and suffered a nasty fracture of his shoulder and upper arm. The break was badly displaced, and the patient had suffered both nerve and artery damage from the injury. Brynn knew immediately from the description that this man could lose his arm without expert and quick treatment.

Brynn announced on the phone that she would be there soon and walked to the washroom trying to control her sobbing. She washed her face, dressed quickly, and walked past Brian who remained seated on their bed. Before leaving their apartment, she stopped and turned back looking at the bedroom door.

"Brian, I'm going to do a case. I want you gone when I return. We'll need lawyers to work on separating what we own. But right now, I just do not want to see you. I want you out of my life immediately."

She closed the apartment door softly but firmly and slowly walked to the elevator, half expecting and hoping that Brian would run out into the corridor and announce this was all a terrible mistake. But as she paced down the corridor and waited for the elevator, her apartment door remained closed. She realized that the life she was enjoying while riding up this same elevator an hour ago was gone forever.

Thirty minutes later, Brynn finished her five-minute surgical scrub and took self-inventory to determine whether she should be doing this surgery. She was on a week of trauma call, and she knew that her two St. Barts partners who could manage this type of surgery were both out of town. Two Toronto hospitals managed severe trauma, but Brynn had talked to her colleague at the other trauma centre before her fateful walk home this morning. She knew that the other hospital's trauma team had several cases in the OR that day. Brynn really had no one to ask to take over the case.

And besides, what would she say if she were to call

a colleague? "I need help. I can't operate because I just discovered my fiancé is a cheating bastard." She would never live that down. Bad enough that the entire hospital would soon know through the effective institutional grapevine that her fiancé was sleeping with another doctor on St. Barts staff. Asking someone to cover her surgery would just inflate her humiliation.

Looking in the mirror over the scrub sink, Brynn could see that her green eyes were reddened. However, she was wearing goggles to protect her from eye splatter in the OR, and she doubted that anyone would recognize her distress. She took a deep breath, realizing that the best thing for her at this moment might be a surgical challenge to take her mind off the disruption in her life.

Walking into the OR, Brynn paused by the computer to review the x-rays while her resident and a medical student finished painting the damaged arm with surgical iodine to sterilize the skin and covered the extremity with sterile, waterproof paper drapes. Brynn had examined the young man outside the OR before he went to sleep. He had difficulty lifting his thumb and wrist off the table which indicated that the important radial nerve was damaged by the fracture.

Brynn knew that this weakness was due to nerve bruising and would likely be temporary. If she could fix the bone without causing further damage, the nerve would probably recover to normal over the next few weeks. The artery damage was more worrisome.

The young man's pulse at the wrist was absent. The vascular surgeons had taken an angiogram x-ray that showed that the normal flow of blood that carried vital oxygen through the main artery to the hand was blocked at the site of bone fracture. The hand would live for the next hour or two, but this was a real surgical emergency. Brynn knew that this reduced blood and oxygen flow would result in the young man losing his hand and arm if she didn't do her work very quickly and very well.

Brynn was a slender woman standing about five foot five inches in height. She was accustomed to her orthopaedic surgery colleagues towering over her, and Walter, the resident trainee helping her today, was no exception. Walter was well over six feet in height and his shoulders showed his commitment to the weight room. He was a senior resident. He deserved to start this case and do as much of the surgery as he could manage. After all, in the future he might be faced with treating the same injury if he were working in a community hospital as opposed to a downtown trauma centre like St. Barts.

But Brynn worried about Walter. She had previously learned working with him in the OR that he tended to overestimate his skills and often tried to use his strength to overpower situations that were better served by more careful surgical approaches.

Starting the surgery, Walter stood on the outside of the patient's injured right arm at the level of the shoulder. Brynn stood farther down the table towards the patient's elbow and the medical student leaned across the body from the left side of the table, ready to hold retractors that would help expose the bone fracture.

The vascular surgery residents entered the OR as Brynn's team started operating. "You guys gotta fix this fast," the chief resident said sharply. "That vessel has been blocked for at least three hours. His hand is going to be dead if we can't get in there soon to restore blood flow."

Walter started the skin incision from the patient's collar bone running diagonally to the outside of the arm at the point where the shoulder deltoid muscle attaches to the humerus arm bone. Unfortunately, Walter's incision went too deep and cut into the large cephalic vein that runs down the front of the arm. As blood filled the wound he exclaimed, "Dammit, that vein's not in its usual position."

Brynn remained silent. The vein was exactly where it was supposed to be.

After Brynn helped him stop the vein bleeding, Walter dissected along the front edge of the large deltoid muscle to expose the fracture. The deltoid is usually bulky in healthy young men, but this deltoid was massively swollen from the trauma. This was not going to be easy.

Walter was getting nowhere in exposing the bone fragments, and minutes were ticking away. The vascular surgeons were waiting impatiently for the orthopaedic surgeons to stabilize the bone so that they could repair the damaged artery. The vascular surgeons could not repair the artery first because the orthopods would inevitably disrupt their delicate artery restoration while putting the bone fragments back together.

Realizing that he could not identify the normal anatomy in this very damaged upper arm, Walter put down his instruments and tried reverting to strength. Feeling the fracture deep to the muscle with his left hand he took the elbow from Brynn and started to pull on the fracture, hoping to pull the bone ends back to their usual position.

"Whoa, Walter, take it easy," Brynn cautioned. "Remember the radial nerve is close to that fracture, and you can trap the nerve between the bone ends pulling it like that."

Brynn immediately moved up between Walter and the patient's arm. "Walter, I think you better let me take over. We need to be quick here."

Brynn could feel Walter's resentment as she squeezed past him to take over the operation. She quickly extended the incision farther down the arm and identified the radial nerve below the fracture then started tracing it up through damaged muscle to the site of the fracture. At this point the senior vascular surgeon arrived in the room.

"Brynn, how's it goin'?" he asked. "This guy's hand's gonna die if we don't fix that artery soon."

Walter grunted. "We'd get this done a lot faster if we just pull the fracture straight and put a plate on it, for Chrissake." Blood from the injured muscles was pooling on the OR floor and the constant drip was a metronome counting the seconds ticking away.

But Brynn had already gone to the place where she retreated when under surgical pressure. Time was moving slower for her, and she could barely hear comments being made by the other surgeons in the room. Dissecting gently while rapidly moving tissues aside, she focused intently on the radial nerve, tracing it up to the fracture site. Sure enough, the nerve was caught between the bone ends of the fracture.

"Look Walter, see how that nerve is trapped between the bone fragments? If we just pull on the bone without retracting that nerve out of the fracture, he will never move his hand again."

Without lifting her eyes from the surgical field, Brynn placed a small retractor on the nerve and gave the retractor handle to the medical student to gently pull the nerve away from the bone. "Gimme a clamp," she asked the scrub nurse.

With the nerve now safe, Brynn gently passed a metal clamp around the broken bone below the fracture site. "And now a Homan retractor please."

She took the second straight retractor without taking her eyes from the surgical field and used it to lift the massive deltoid muscle off the bone above the fracture line. She gave the second retractor handle to Walter. "Hold this muscle back gently, Walter".

And then, nearly miraculously, with the nerve safely out of the way and the muscle now held away from the bone, the two bone ends glided together. However, the fracture immediately fell back to its displaced position when Brynn took her clamp off the bone. "Okay, Walter we are going to need to apply the bone plate to the top of the fracture and then pull the lower fragment back to the plate to hold the humerus together."

"An eight-hole clover leaf plate with self-locking screws," said Brynn, keeping her eyes focused on the fracture site. The nurses had a selection of sterilized metal shoulder fracture plates ready, and immediately passed Brynn the device she had requested.

"Give Walter the drill. Walter I'll hold the plate in place on the shoulder. Be cautious when you drill and stay out of the joint, please." But Walter plunged the drill through the plate and into the bone far too rapidly. Brynn could feel the drill penetrate through the bone into the shoulder joint. "Walter, be more careful, will you? Keep that drill out of the joint."

Walter scoffed in response but placed the next five screws more carefully, tightly attaching the plate to the top of the fracture and the shoulder. Brynn then examined the radial nerve, carefully holding it out of the way while she again pulled the bottom bone fragment back flush with the metal plate. Now she was able to attach her clamp to the plate holding the two ends of the fractured bone perfectly aligned. "Okay Walter, I'll hold the clamp, you start drilling screws through the plate into the bone below the fracture."

Fifteen minutes later the bone was back together, held entirely straight by the metal plate with the fracture line barely perceptible. Brynn kept a careful watch on the radial nerve to ensure that Walter did not place his drill or screws through the exposed structure. For the first time in over an hour, she lifted her head from the surgical field to look at the vascular surgeons.

"You guys should start scrubbing. We're just about done, and the arm is nice and stable for you to repair the artery."

The lead vascular surgeon looked at the clock. "Brynn that was just over an hour. That's the fastest that I've seen anyone put a nasty fracture like that back together. Nice work."

Brynn held the wound open for Walter to stop small areas of bleeding and to wash the blood out of the surgical field. Then the vascular team was scrubbing in, and the orthopods stepped away from the table.

Brynn immediately felt drained. "Walter I am going to see the patients I operated on last night, then head home for a nap. Can you check this man's pulse when the vascular guys are finished, please? Gimme a call and let me know how he's doing, okay?" Brynn looked at her resident and student. "Thanks guys. That went better than it might have. I appreciate your help."

Brynn took off her bloody gown and gloves and headed to the surgeons' dressing room to change into some fresh scrubs prior to making rounds. As the door to the surgeons' room slowly swung shut behind her, she heard Walter talking to the medical student.

"She's such a goddam bitch. I coulda done that case by myself if she only let me do what I needed to do." As the dressing room door silently closed, Brynn's tears could not be restrained any longer.

CHAPTER 3

Azo. October 31, 2017

Azo had been declared Canada's best restaurant three years running since Chef Bruno Patolli opened his flagship eatery in a historic Toronto building. The tasting menu generally ran to eleven or twelve courses with an emphasis on Bruno's molecular concoctions that were Instagram ready for his foodie patrons.

David Morton had been bringing potential investors and future partners to Azo since Bruno opened. The CEO of CannWeed was also a small but early investor in the restaurant. Although reservations for Bruno's dining room generally had a waiting list of at least two months, David was always accommodated whenever he called. Bruno appreciated his early supporters.

Azo had a single, small private room that was fully booked at least four months in advance. The party that had reserved this space for Tuesday evening was told that there had been a booking mix-up and that their group would be accommodated in a divided area of the main dining room. The account manager who had reserved the room to entertain his clients grudgingly accepted his demotion from the private room when Bruno apologized personally and offered a future complimentary dining experience for two to make up for his team's oversight.

When David and his entourage arrived, Chef Bruno greeted them himself and helped to seat the initial party of ten in the private dining room. He then supervised the opening of the Charles Heidsieck vintage champagne bottles as the kick-off to David's party. When he called asking for the favour of the private room, David had confirmed to Bruno that the transformative deal he had mentioned to Chef on a prior visit was now closed and Bruno congratulated him warmly at the door. Bruno's staff loved David for his free spending, high tipping habits. David Morton was probably Azo's best customer.

Jonah entered the room about two glasses of vintage champagne behind David's arrival. He had been hard at work for the past thirty hours. Following Monday morning's announcement of the suspension of Premium Bud's medical marijuana licences and the concurrent description of securities actions and criminal charges against Premium Bud's management and directors, the tone of negotiations between CannWeed and International Brands had changed dramatically. Francis Wells had instructions from Norman Ridgely to get this deal done and David Morton had managed to extract just over eight hundred million dollars for the International Brands investment.

Jonah worked closely with the Canadian investment bankers past midnight Monday and all day Tuesday, structuring the International Brands' cash for shares investment. Jonah ensured that David was able to tender most of his founders' shares as part of the deal and when David signed back the International Brands offer just before midnight Monday, he was suddenly a wealthy man. Although he had ceded control of the new CannWeed board, David remained CEO of the company he had started. Norman Ridgely personally reassured David on another videoconference on Monday that David's role in the company was secure and that his continued involvement in CannWeed was an important reason for International's investment.

Jonah spent Tuesday meticulously documenting and papering the deal working closely with International Brands' corporate counsel, who he was now escorting to Azo for the celebration dinner. Jonah had a firm understanding of Canadian tax codes and had assistance from his firm's accountants and tax lawyers to ensure that David was going to keep his newfound wealth with modest tax liability.

Jonah's firm would be submitting a large fee for their work on this investment deal. He received a congratulatory call from the firm's managing partner early Tuesday morning. Jonah smiled as he listened to the top lawyer telling him how important Jonah was to the firm. The man had never spoken to Jonah before this call.

Francis Wells had flown home Tuesday afternoon after ensuring that there were no issues with papering the deal. He had casually asked his Canadian banker colleagues about "this guy Jonah Kay" before leaving. The Canadian bankers, who were delighted but puzzled about the dramatic change in International's estimation of CannWeed's value, told Francis that Jonah was a junior partner at his law firm. They understood that Jonah had been hired and made a partner as a condition of David Morton originally bringing CannWeed's corporate business to the firm. They also quietly suggested that this might be an example of affirmative action since all major Canadian law firms had a commitment to diversity in hiring and Jonah was Indigenous.

As Jonah entered the private room at Azo, he was immediately greeted by an ebullient David Morton. David and Jonah were the only people in the dining room aware of the content of the videoconference with Norman Ridgely held Sunday evening. The two of them had agreed with Francis Wells that they should keep that video meeting and its impact on their deal entirely confidential. So, guests at the table were puzzled when David leapt to his feet on Jonah's arrival and grasped the lawyer in a prolonged embrace complete with whispered commentary, a jocular slap on the back and a final hug. Most of the guests put the warmth of that welcome down to the fact that David was working on his third glass of the excellent champagne. The entire room heard David's loud whisper that, "We wouldn't be here without you buddy."

David had saved a seat for Jonah at the opposite end from his position at the head of the table. Jonah pulled out the seat to his right for the International Brands' corporate counsel who had walked with him to the restaurant, an attractive woman who appeared to be in her early fifties. On Jonah's left, David had seated the most junior Canadian investment banker working on the investment. Natalia was just turning thirty, a bit younger than Jonah and her brunette elegance inevitably turned heads when she entered a room. Natalia had played striker on her university's champion soccer team and maintained her fitness despite putting in the gruelling hours required for investment bankers.

Natalia was part of the contingent of bankers that David had ushered out into the hall before his video conversation with Norman Ridgely Sunday night. Like the other bankers, Natalia was curious as to what happened that evening. The bankers assumed they had experienced an incredible stroke of good luck when charges were announced against Premium Bud on Monday morning. Natalia recognized the importance of the extension of the negotiation period that David had attributed to Jonah on Sunday night and was eager to discover from the lawyer just what had happened on that videocall with Norman.

David stood at the head of the table and raised his glass. "Tonight, I am excited to celebrate the future of a wonderful partnership between two great companies. Next year the cannabis market is going to explode in this country. International Brands and CannWeed are going to lead that new market, first in this country and then around the world." David paused and looked at his guests.

"I am delighted that the deal teams from both companies were able to make it here tonight to celebrate our mutual success." Although Francis Wells had flown home earlier, three of the American bankers had stayed to dine with David along with International's corporate counsel who had arrived with Jonah. William Dahlin, International's Chief Operating Officer, had flown in from New York for the dinner and was seated next to David. The rest of the guests included five members of the Canadian banking team.

"I know how hard you've worked for the past few months through our negotiations and now closing the deal. Please join me in raising your glasses and drinking a toast to what we have all accomplished together." David drained his glass before sitting down to applause from around the table. But no sooner was he seated than he motioned the wine waiter to fill his fourth glass of champagne and immediately returned to his feet.

"Bruno's kitchen is going to provide us with a wonderful meal this evening and we have selected some great vintages to accompany the various courses of our dinner. I plan on enjoying myself tonight and after this toast I will avoid making potentially embarrassing remarks as I am going to carefully sample every drop of wine that comes to this table." His guests chuckled appreciatively. David had worked long and hard for this deal and deserved his celebration.

"But before I devote myself entirely to my cups, I would be remiss if I did not thank my best friend, Jonah Kay. But for Jonah we would not be enjoying Bruno's fine fare this evening. Jonah, thank you for everything you have accomplished – here's to you, my friend." And David again raised his glass, holding it out to Jonah at the other end of the table and then drained most of the bubbly before sitting. The rest of the table turned to Jonah while politely sipping and again applauding.

Jonah knew a few words were in order and stood glass in

hand. "David, we are extremely happy that you have achieved this partnership that is going to guarantee CannWeed's success in an exciting new market. I personally know how hard you have worked to get us here tonight, and I am proud to have played a small role in your success." Raising his glass to the International Brands counsel sitting to his right, Jonah concluded, "Like you David, I am excited to start working with our new colleagues from International Brands. As Bogart would have said, I think this is the beginning of a beautiful friendship."

As Jonah sat, the lead Canadian banker stood to pay tribute to David. Rather than listening to her boss however, Natalia leaned toward Jonah. The table was designed for ten people and seating twelve meant that Natalia was right at the end of the table, close to Jonah's chair. As she leaned forward Jonah could feel her leg pressing against his thigh. Her perfume was subtle and her red dress fit her tightly, the colour complementing her dark hair and hazel eyes.

"Jonah, I've been to quite a few of these deal celebrations. But I never remember such a fuss being made about the merger lawyer at any of these events. Usually, you guys are too busy with paper to even get to the deal dinner. When you are here, the client and us bankers generally just treat you guys like technicians. It's the bankers who usually get credit for doing the deal, not the lawyers. But David Morton certainly recognizes your role in achieving this agreement. Quite unusual." She dropped back in her chair as her boss droned on congratulating David. Her leg remained tightly applied against Jonah's left thigh.

"We haven't formally met, my name is Hillary Vanstone, International Brands' corporate counsel." The lawyer to the right of Jonah leaned forward to shake Natalia's hand and as she did, her leg contacted Jonah's right thigh. Jonah realized his interesting position at the table as he enjoyed Hillary's elusive perfume. Likely twenty years older than Natalia, she was an archetypical New York professional woman, fit, and sophisticated.

After Natalia introduced herself, Hillary continued. "I agree with you Natalia. International Brands has doubled in size through various acquisitions and partnerships since I've been counsel and I have been to many deal celebrations. But I never remember the lawyer getting as much appreciation as Jonah seems to be receiving. What's your secret, Jonah? I need to learn from you."

Just then Bruno arrived with five servers to explain the first course. His tasting menu was usually described as French-Asian fusion. The first course presented a Beau Soleil oyster nestled in foam contained within a shell and studded with sturgeon roe. The shell was positioned on a plate alongside a small bowl of sea urchin oursinade. These delicacies had been selected to accompany the champagne which Bruno ensured was topped up in everyone's glass.

Jonah had accompanied David to Azo on several occasions while deals were being considered during CannWeed's rapid expansion. Generally, as the tasting menu began, business conversation would momentarily cease for the moans that inevitably resulted from Bruno's unique molecular cuisine.

Natalia responded as expected, slurping the oyster, and then closing her eyes with an audible sigh when tasting the sea urchin thick, soupy delicacy. Her attention to Jonah's contribution to the deal had faded under Bruno's magic spell. But Hillary was persistent, delicately savouring the oyster and taking micro-spoonfuls of the oursinade. Jonah remembered David's comment about New York women when they were leaving an Upper East Side resto while raising money to sustain CannWeed's growth. "Did you see those women eating at the next table, Jonah? The way New York women stay so skinny is that they just don't eat. They take tiny bites, chew forever, and send half their food untouched back to the kitchen."

Holding her spoon above the delicate oursinade bowl without dipping it into the delicious creamy treat, Hillary continued, "Jonah, I was surprised when Francis told us that Norman intended to extend negotiations for twenty-four hours on Sunday evening. Now that the deal is done, I can say that our plan had been to conclude negotiations by midnight Sunday. We had authorization to go a bit higher than four hundred million and the plan was to make that small increase in our offer around ten-thirty that evening. When we left Francis alone on that call with you and David that plan was set and seemed to be working." She took a tiny sip of champagne, and the waiter removed her oursinade dish with suspicion. More than half the delicacy remained in the small bowl.

Hillary looked at Natalia who was talking to the New York banker on her left about her experiences diving for sea urchins in the Mediterranean Sea. Seeing that the younger woman was not paying attention, the New York lawyer continued. "We all know that last minute changes in negotiations could result in securities agencies taking a hard look at approving deals, especially if some unusual information became available at the eleventh hour. Francis was understandably but uncharacteristically silent about that conference call – especially after we heard about Premium Bud's problems the next morning." Hillary raised the linen napkin to blot imaginary foam off her lips.

Jonah examined those lips carefully. He had been working continuously over the past eighteen months as David achieved the scale for CannWeed that would make his company a perfect partner for an international beverage company. Jonah and David had operated around the clock, developing relationships with the myriad of small weed producers serving the Canadian medicinal market to extend CannWeed's production.

David's family was reasonably well off, but he did not have the capacity to expand CannWeed without outside financing. He and Jonah had alternated between closing deals taking over smaller producers and finding the investments and financing that would support the next merger. Jonah had no partner in his life and in the past year he had little time to either start a relationship or even to focus on an affair.

And now, with their strategy of achieving a big international investment accomplished, Jonah looked carefully at Hillary's lips and imagined a very immediate fling. He knew from comments at the deal table that the lawyer was divorced with two children in college. He could feel that his left leg was no longer in contact with Natalia's thigh as she rotated to speak to the tablemate on her left. And Hillary had turned towards him in her seat so that her thigh was now firmly pressed against his.

Jonah considered his words carefully. If regulators knew how he had learned about the timing of the raid from his cousins living on the reserve next to Premium Bud's production facilities, CannWeed's deal with International might be brought under a harsh spotlight. The regulators would have been even more concerned if they learned how the authorities had been tipped to inspect Premium Bud's operation. "Hillary there was no magic to the final stages of this deal. On Sunday evening I simply suggested to Norman and David that this transaction was too important for both parties to rush to conclusion. Having been at this for several weeks, I thought that it wouldn't hurt to wait for another twenty-four hours to see if we could get to a number that satisfied both parties. I could see that David was getting upset with Francis' comments about what CannWeed was worth. When David gets insulted, negotiating can get very hostile very quickly. I thought it would be best for everyone to sleep on it overnight."

Hillary showed a half smile that Jonah could not disregard. "Francis didn't say much but did bring our team back together at eleven o'clock Monday morning, just after the Ottawa announcement about Premium Bud. It almost seemed to us that he had advance warning about the raid on Premium Bud's facility. Of course, neither he nor his team would say anything. The bankers' fees are dependent on the deal closing without regulatory mishap, so they'll be as silent as those oysters we just slurped."

She took another millilitre of champagne from her glass that was being removed to prepare for the wine pairings appropriate for their next course. As she wiped her lips again and laid her napkin back on her lap, Jonah could feel her hand momentarily pressing on the inside of his thigh. Then her hands were both on the table and she continued. "No one is going to disclose anything here Jonah. This deal is the right thing for both companies and in the long run, it really doesn't make much difference whether it closed for four hundred million or a billion. We both know that someone gets richer based on that number and it's not you and it's not me. But Jonah Kay, I have a strong suspicion that Francis and Norman learned something about Premium Bud in that videoconference on Sunday night. I'll never mention it again, but since we are going to be working together closely in the future, I think you need to know my interpretation of events."

Jonah was closely examining Hillary's face and then glanced away briefly to Natalia who was surrendering to the champagne and the next wine pairing. She was raising her arms to emphasize her remarks to her tablemate about the differences in New York and Toronto investment banker compensation. Jonah noticed as she lifted her arms how her red dress emphasized her fitness. Natalia was gorgeous and this dinner would be a perfect opportunity to start something with this lovely young woman. Looking back at Hillary, Jonah could see the subtle lines around her eyes that emphasized the difference in her age from Natalia's. But as usual, the younger woman's appeal couldn't arrest his fascination with the older woman.

"Hillary you are giving us way too much credit here. And too little credit to the Health Canada inspectors who are very careful about how they regulate our medical cannabis market. They're aware that all pot companies want to ramp up production of medical cannabis to get ready for the legalization of the recreational market. They've stepped up inspections to ensure that we are obeying the limits on our production. I would say that Premium Bud was just unlucky – and stupid – to be caught exceeding their licences. And we were just fortunate that the news came out when it did."

Hillary's hand briefly went beneath the table again and pressed again on Jonah's leg as she adjusted her napkin and offered a co-conspirator's smile. "Well, Jonah, I can see that butter will not melt in your mouth. Have it as you will, but I have a sneaking suspicion that these circumstances were all linked together somehow." She removed her hand, tilted her head lower and smiled up at Jonah.

Jonah knew that she would be staying in the hotel next to the bank tower for at least the next two days while they worked together preparing the securities documents describing their new partnership. And thereafter, he and Hillary would likely be working together in both New York and Toronto as their companies' relationship deepened. Jonah briefly considered whether a fling in Toronto and or New York would be harmful to their professional relationship and decided that would be something he could work out as things progressed – or not.

He knew that he would tell David if he started an affair with Hillary. David liked to give the impression that he was emotionally clueless about what was happening around him. But Jonah had learned long ago that David knew everything about affairs of the heart and other anatomical regions that went on in his circle. And he and David had shared all secrets since they were teenagers.

Jonah regretted the serial infidelities that David had committed eventually resulting in his divorce from their mutual school friend Corinne. And Jonah was straightforward with his counsel now that David had thrown himself back into the very active and chatty wealthy Toronto dating pool. More than once, Jonah had reminded David that appearing either lovesick or predatory with women considerably younger than himself would impact both his and CannWeed's reputation. David would usually either pout or rebel when Jonah attempted to constrain his love life. But David also trusted his friend's judgement.

David would know if Jonah started something with Hillary and would provide his usual teasing about Jonah's taste in cougars. But both men knew how and why Jonah's attraction to women of Hillary's age had developed. And neither had much idea what to do about it.

Bruno's team was picking up the small empty bowls that had held rich sauce surrounding four impossibly delicate tortellini. Jonah noticed that Hillary had only consumed one and a half tortellini. On his left side, Natalia was sending back every plate scraped clean. Hillary discreetly mentioned to their waiter that he should only bring her a small "tasting" slice of the A5 Wagyu beef tenderloin when the final dinner course was served. Hillary wanted to avoid sending back an embarrassing large piece of ridiculously expensive meat to the kitchen and the waiter appreciated her warning.

Glasses were being changed on the table to accommodate the Bordeaux that David had selected to accompany the next courses. Jonah had avoided the wine all evening, limiting himself to the champagne for toasting. As a child he had experienced alcohol's destructive effects and generally avoided drinking, even in high school and college when he was running with a very party-oriented crowd. At social events today, Jonah would generally nurse a white wine Perrier spritzer. Tonight, it would be criminal to waste the fine vintage Bordeaux that David was serving his guests and Jonah covered his glass with his hand as the sommelier circled the table with the carafe.

Natalia was enjoying the wine selections as well as Bruno's kitchen creations. Jonah realized that she would likely be receptive to just about anything he suggested this evening. Her beautiful face was flushed, and she returned his smile readily. However, as the evening progressed, Jonah decided that he would offer to walk Hillary back to her hotel just as he had accompanied the lawyer to the restaurant. He expected that he might not be walking farther than her hotel this evening.

The Bordeaux was inspiring International Brands' COO William Dahlin to stand and add his toast to the good wishes being expressed for the new partnership. As Hillary turned to listen to her boss, Jonah took the opportunity to check his cell phone for messages. His phone had been turned off most of the day. His office knew where he was and would call him on a secure landline in the bank boardroom if he were needed. But as he scrolled through his phone calls, Jonah was startled to see several calls and three voicemails from Auntie.

He pushed back from the table, jumped up and moved to a quieter corner of the room with both Natalia and Hillary watching him with concern. Checking his voice messages, Jonah was horrified when he heard his auntie's voice. "Jonah, call me right away. Uncle has had a terrible accident."

CHAPTER 4

Moose. October 31, 2017

Just after noon on Tuesday, several hours before Jonah heard the frightening voicemail left by his auntie, nurse Suzanne Cormier was preparing to evaluate Uncle Samuel's leg in the Emergency Room of Wiichihinan Hospital. This hospital in the community of Moose served people living along the James Bay coast nearly nine hundred kilometres north of Toronto.

Suzanne was a newcomer to the Wiichihinan ER nursing staff and what she had heard about Samuel's leg from the transferring nurse in Port Muskek Hospital concerned her. She had graduated from nursing school in Toronto only months previously and had initially worked in a series of casual jobs in big hospitals in the centre of the city. Two weeks ago, she had arrived in Wiichihinan Hospital to fill one of the multiple vacancies in the ER nursing staff.

After her initial gradual exposure to patients as a graduate nurse in the well-staffed, cathedral-like hospitals on University Avenue in Toronto, her orientation to Wiichihinan was hectic and disconcerting. The Chief of Nursing took only twenty minutes to walk Suzanne through the entire facility.

"This is the surgical/obstetrical unit. A couple of our GP's do Caesarian sections if needed but we don't really do much surgery here anymore. We used to have a couple of surgeons come occasionally to operate, but they stopped coming two or three years ago and now we airlift anyone who needs surgical care out to Toronto or Kingston." Suzanne hurried to keep up. She was learning that everyone at Wiichihinan was constantly walking and talking fast while multi-tasking.

The Chief Nurse ended her tour in the ER. "We've got twelve stretchers, with two acute resuscitation rooms. You'll see that we often overnight patients for observation – or simply to give them a place to rest when they are waiting for a return airlift to their communities along the coast."

Suzanne's first five shifts were classified as "orientation" and she was expecting a senior colleague to work with her. However, most of her fellow nurses in the ER had little more experience than Suzanne and most shifts were short-staffed so that she was left to manage on her own as soon as she started.

Suzanne was well-trained despite her lack of experience. Most of the patients coming into the ER had worsening medical conditions – asthma, heart failure, diabetes – and Suzanne had plenty of experience from Toronto in managing these chronic diseases. However, her trauma experience was limited, and she had never looked after an injury like Samuel had suffered.

Jonah's Uncle Samuel was being airlifted by helicopter into Moose from up the James Bay coast at Port Muskek. Port Muskek was said to have a hospital, but the small facility was really a combination of six nursing home beds, a few overnight observation beds, and a nursing clinic. However, the nurses who worked in the Port Muskek clinic had experience and knowledge well beyond the usual scope of nursing practice.

Four remote nursing stations like Port Muskek that served communities along the James Bay coast were visited by physicians from Wiichihinan Hospital once a week but most of the time the nurses were on their own. And some of the injuries that came into their clinics would have tested fully trained trauma surgeons. Samuel had been brought to Port Muskek by friends who had found him in the bush after his wife Mary reported him missing Monday afternoon.

Samuel Sunderland was an experienced trapper who had been setting and baiting his marten boxes as winter approached. He was returning along the creek bed that he used to gain access to the dense underbrush where the martens roamed through the winter. The side of the creek bed had been undermined by rushing water during the spring run-off and Samuel's four-wheel drive vehicle collapsed the track at a particularly high and steep part of the creek bank.

Samuel was a taciturn individual and did not tell anyone what he felt as the vehicle rolled over on him during its rapid descent to the creek bed. Fortunately, water was low and he was not at risk of drowning when trapped by the tumbling four-wheeler that came to a stop in the middle of the creek. His head had avoided threatening stones during the rollover. But his right leg was trapped under the vehicle as it headed toward the slope, and Samuel did recall the snapping noise as his shin bone was shattered.

Samuel had spent many nights in the bush while tending his traplines. Usually, he would overnight in one of the utilitarian bush dwellings that he had built over the years. These huts provided shelter and a fireplace as well as a supply of warm blankets that he had stored in the camps. On occasion he had been forced to stay outside in deteriorating weather when getting to a camp in a blizzard became problematic. Samuel knew how to build a winter camp quickly and understood how to look after himself in the bush in any weather.

But he had never experienced being trapped and injured. He was soaked by the creek, freezing cold and wedged under the four-wheeler. Any movement increased the pain coming from his right leg and the vehicle was too heavy to dislodge.

With considerable pain and effort, he was able to twist and retrieve the satellite phone from the saddle attached to the damaged vehicle. Turning on the handset he was relieved to see a weak signal and dialed his wife. No answer. It took two attempts to locate Mary at her friends' and the signal kept fading in and out.

"Mary, I had an accident."

"Gee Samuel, where are you?"

"My four-wheeler rolled over. I am going to ping you my location."

"Are you hurt, Samuel?"

"Yeah, my leg's busted pretty good. Tell Charlie and Bill to get here as soon they can."

"Oh, gee Samuel. I'll get them right now and call you back."

"Mary don't call unless you can't get them. Show 'em the GPS location I'm gonna ping you and they'll know where to go. Charlie's been up here with me before. Don't call me 'cause I don't wanna waste the battery in case they have trouble finding me."

He heard Mary's deep sigh. "Oh, gee Sam, this is terrible. Okay, I'll call Charlie and Bill."

Samuel turned off his phone and settled into what he needed to endure until the boys found him. He ensured that his ping went through to Mary showing his GPS location and then turned off his phone. And took a deep breath.

Mary was airlifted to Wiichihinan Hospital from Port Muskek with her husband after his initial treatment at the Port Muskek clinic. Suzanne introduced herself to both Mary and her husband after the chopper emergency medicine team unloaded Samuel onto the Wiichihinan ER gurney. The ER doctor on call had done a quick trauma check on Samuel to satisfy herself that his injury was limited to his leg. She then gave Suzanne quick instructions to open the dressing that had been applied to Samuel's leg at Port Muskek while she attended to other patients.

Suzanne felt more anxious than she could ever remember

in her short nursing career. She had read the notes sent from the Port Muskek nurse that described an "open, 3B comminuted fracture of the proximal tibia". She vaguely knew this meant a terrible injury to both the shin bone and the skin and muscle of the leg just below the knee, but she had never seen this kind of trauma.

She turned to Mary and her husband. The thin walls of the ER did not stop the sounds of chaos penetrating into every exam room. Suzanne shrugged her shoulders apologetically to excuse the wails coming from the teenager who had been treated with opioid inhibiter in treatment for her overdose.

"Mr. Sunderland I am going to start a new IV in your arm to give you some painkiller and antibiotics. I'll wait for the painkiller to take effect and then we are going to remove the dressing so the doctor can look at your leg."

Samuel grunted. Mary was holding his hand and gently rubbing his arm. Mary looked up at the young nurse. "Thanks for looking after him. He doesn't say much at the best of times, and he had a very bad night."

After receiving her husband's distress call, Mary had located Charlie who contacted Bill. The two cousins were part-time trappers and Charlie had worked with Samuel for years while learning his craft in the rugged James Bay bush where martens were plentiful. After assisting Samuel for several winters, Charlie took over a trapline from an Elder who was finding it harder to get around. Bill often joined him in setting boxes and harvesting the furry animals from the traps.

Charlie knew Samuel's trapping grounds well but also knew it would be too risky to look for him at night. The track along the creek bed was treacherous even in full daylight. After receiving Mary's call on Monday, the two trappers drove their truck and trailer up the dirt road north of Port Muskek to the point where Samuel would take off into the bush using his four-wheel all-terrain vehicle to run up beside the creek bed. They were reassured to find Samuel's truck and trailer pulled off to the side of the road at the start of the track along the creek bed.

Night had already fallen, and the boys bedded down on a mattress in the back of Charlie's truck after unloading their two four wheelers from his trailer. They were up before dawn and started up the creek at first light. They located Samuel by mid-morning. It took the two of them to roll the all-terrain vehicle off his leg after giving Samuel a couple of shots of rye before lifting the ATV.

The trappers used wooden splints to stabilize Samuel's leg before loading him into a trailer they pulled behind Charlie's ATV for the ride back to the Port Muskek nursing station. It was a tight fit and the bumpy track along the creek was tough on Samuel. The wooden splints had been changed by the nurse for a fresh bandage and plastic splint in the Port Muskek clinic. It took some time to arrange the helicopter medevac from Port Muskek to Wiichihinan and this dressing had now been in place for several hours and needed changing and inspection.

Suzanne marvelled at Samuel's stoicism as he lay quietly on the stretcher. He had received little opioid pain killer during the transfer even though more had constantly been on offer. Suzanne had noted this in many of the older Indigenous patients that she was treating in the ER. They seemed to have a very high pain tolerance – or their upbringing and culture discouraged voicing complaints about pain.

Suzanne had looked at Samuel's x-ray sent to their computer system from Port Muskek. She was no expert in interpreting fractures, but she could see that the top of the tibia was badly broken with multiple fragments readily evident. The x-ray invoked an involuntary shudder from the young nurse as she wondered what she would see after unwrapping the dressing.

"Mr. Sunderland that painkiller we injected should have taken effect by now. Are you feeling more comfortable?" Samuel grunted.

"Samuel, answer the nurse. She is trying to help you." Even in this distressing situation, Mary was insistent on politeness.

"It's okay. Do what you gotta do."

Suzanne had prepared a dressing tray with bottles of saline to irrigate the dressing and then the fracture. She had read that the most important thing they could do prior to transporting Samuel south was to reduce the bacterial concentration in the wound through dilution with saline as well as giving large quantities of different antibiotics to protect against a variety of bacteria. If infection started in the bone after this kind of fracture, Suzanne knew that amputation could be the eventual outcome.

"I am going to take off the dressing now Mr. Sunderland." Suzanne's dressing scissors made short work of the gauze bandage holding on the dressing. "Tell me if I hurt you".

The nurses in Port Muskek had irrigated the wound and covered the broken bone with wet gauze. Suzanne put on a surgical mask and called the doctor over to look at the wound. As the doctor approached, Suzanne completed removing the gauze with the forceps and scissors held in her gloved hands. "I'll re-dress the wound after you see it, Doctor."

As she removed the gauze, Suzanne's first impression was the smell. It had now been about twenty-four hours since Samuel's fracture. His open wound had been exposed to creek water overnight and bacteria were flourishing in the rich environment of damaged bone and muscle. Suzanne felt the room spin and steadied herself to remove the rest of the gauze. She had only worked with this doctor once before and she didn't want to appear a neophyte.

But Suzanne couldn't help an involuntary gasp as the final dressings were removed. The calf was swollen and deformed with the fracture, and skin was missing over the front of the leg from the kneecap to well below the knee. Suzanne and the doctor could see shattered bone fragments extending down at least ten centimetres from the knee.

"Let's get ready to irrigate. We'll just let the irrigation run off the stretcher. Put a basin under the table." Suzanne could hear the concern in the doctor's voice. She was only a few years older than Suzanne but had worked in Wiichihinan ER since completing her training.

"Suzanne, use that hundred cc syringe to irrigate for eight litres of saline, then I'll stabilize the leg while you re-dress the wound. Then we will get a flight arranged to Toronto. He needs to be in the OR as soon as possible."

Controlling rising nausea from the smell and the sight of the leg, Suzanne squirted the bone fragments and torn muscle and skin with the saline. Remembering her nursing duty to focus on her patient and family, not just on the injury, she looked at Samuel and Mary.

"How are you guys doing?"

Mary smiled in return. "I think I am doing better than Sam right now, huh, Honey." She hadn't stopped holding his hand or rubbing his arm. Suzanne could feel her support and their closeness as a couple.

Sam grunted again and sniffed. "It don't smell so good, Doc. It sorta smells like a creek bed."

Suzanne felt her nausea fading and realized it was her job to offer confident but truthful reassurance. "I'm a nurse, not a doctor, Mr. Sunderland."

She noticed the deep creases in his face and could imagine the conditions that face had encountered in his life in the bush. Then he smiled and his warm brown eyes connected with her. "Well, it don't mean much to me what they call you. You seem to know what you're doin'."

Suzanne returned his smile. "Am I hurting you with this irrigation?"

Sam shook his head. "It's okay. Whad'ya think? Am I gonna lose it?"

For a moment Suzanne didn't know how to answer. And then she knew the right thing was to support Sam and Mary until they could ask that question of someone with more knowledge.

"To be honest, Sam – can I call you Sam?" He nodded. "I'm no expert, but I know they can do amazing things with broken bones these days and I know we're sending you to Toronto as soon as a plane can take you. I trained in those downtown hospitals, and they do some remarkable things there."

Mary enquired. "Can I go with him in the plane?" Suzanne nodded as she completed the irrigation. She called to the doctor who came over. Suzanne had gathered dressing materials for the leg, and they planned on changing the soiled splint that came from Port Muskek as well as applying a fresh dressing.

The doctor was even smaller than Suzanne, but she had clearly pulled on a few legs in her time. She held Samuel's foot under traction while Suzanne pulled away the remaining old dressing and splint and applied fresh protection to the fracture.

Samuel had been holding his breath during the ordeal and slowly released his breath as the two women laid his leg gently on the stretcher. Then he looked up at his wife.

"They may be little ladies, but they are pretty mighty, eh, Mary?" Then he looked again at the doctor. "So, you're gonna get me a free trip to Toronto, huh, Doc?" He looked back at Mary. "Mebbe we can see Jonah while we are there, whad'ya think Mary?"

As Suzanne cleared away the soiled dressings, she smiled to herself about how close Mary and Samuel seemed despite the desperate circumstances that brought them to Moose. She was nonplussed that they would think about visiting this Jonah at such a difficult time for Samuel. Jonah obviously must be special to them.

Suzanne felt a faint swell of satisfaction as she injected the final doses of antibiotic into Samuel's IV. She had managed this case without embarrassing herself despite never seeing a compound tibia fracture before. In the short time she had been in Moose she was constantly taking on responsibility for patients that would have been considered well beyond her skills had she remained in Toronto. And she was pleased to be proving to herself that she could manage it.

CHAPTER 5

St. Barts. October 31, 2017

Jonah ignored the looks of startled pedestrians as he ran the twelve blocks to St. Barts ER from the Azo Restaurant. He had apologized to his tablemates when he interrupted William Dahlin's speech congratulating David, explaining that he had a family health emergency and telling David that his uncle had suffered an accident. David knew Mary and Samuel from hockey games during high school and college and recognized what they meant to Jonah.

"Jonah, I'll come with you to St. Barts, no problem."

But Jonah was recovering from the panic caused by his auntie's voicemail. He managed to connect with her cell phone on the third try and learned to his shock that she and Uncle Samuel were both recently arrived in St. Barts Hospital ER a short distance from Azo Restaurant. They had been transported from Wiichihinan Hospital by plane, arriving in the ER just a half hour before Jonah connected with his aunt. Jonah assured David Morton that he would be fine and apologized again to the table before launching out of the restaurant, running at full speed despite his dress shoes, corporate suit and the briefcase he was carrying. As he passed people on the sidewalk, they instinctively turned to see who was chasing him.

Nearing the hospital and following the street signs for the ER, Jonah slowed to a trot and tried to gather his thoughts. Although Jonah was entirely at ease in the boardroom and the courtroom, hospitals terrified him. He had been in the St. Barts ER on two different occasions after injuring his knee on the hockey rink. Each time he had undergone a painful examination by doctors who twisted his injured knee. He then had to lie inside a claustrophobic MRI tunnel while images of his knee were obtained. He knew that he was lucky on both occasions that the examination and MRI confirmed minor strains rather than tears in his knee ligaments. But these experiences had unnerved him.

Jonah also knew his fear of hospitals originated from a darker place – a memory he tried to bury. He knew that Toronto hospitals were nothing like the nursing station at home, but both the smells of disinfectant and the sense of powerlessness and loss of control were similar. Those feelings washed over him as he entered the waiting area of St. Barts ER.

Perhaps it was the assertiveness resulting from Jonah's legal training that caused him to over-react aggressively to his feelings of helplessness and vulnerability. He approached the triage desk and declared loudly that his uncle had been transferred here from Moose and that he needed to see him immediately. The triage nurse was experienced and realized that anxiety can often provoke belligerent behaviour. She confirmed from the computer records that Samuel Sunderland had been admitted to the ER over an hour ago. She asked Jonah to take a seat while she checked with his nurse to see if Mr. Sunderland could have a visitor.

Rather than sitting, Jonah started pacing back and forth in front of the triage desk. Although he had not been sweating much during the run from Azo to the hospital, he was now starting to perspire profusely. His thoughts raged. He couldn't lose his uncle; the man was just too precious to him. Other patients sitting in the ER waiting room looked at Jonah with some trepidation. He was walking back and forth in front of the triage desk, muttering under his breath. Despite his corporate suit, he appeared out of control.

The triage nurse returned from checking on Uncle and looked at Jonah with concern, turning to check that the security team was available if needed. Confirming that she did have security back-up, she motioned Jonah over to her desk as she sat behind the heavy plexiglass divider that protected her from viruses and people.

"Are you here to see Mr. Sunderland?" When Jonah nodded, leaning forward to hear her through the thick plastic, she continued. "Your aunt and uncle are expecting you. You can go into Room …." She then paused and motioned the agitated man to sit in the chair in front of her where she usually took histories from ER patients on arrival. He was wide-eyed, breathing heavily, sweaty and disheveled despite his briefcase and expensive clothes. ER nurses are experienced with the unusual responses that hospital emergencies can engender and she immediately understood that Jonah was far from his best.

"Sir, I can see that you are very upset. Are you worried about your uncle?" Jonah made eye contact with her, somehow grateful for the question. He nodded and she continued. "The nurse told me that he has a nasty leg injury but is otherwise okay." Jonah's eyes were pleading for more good news.

"He needs treatment for his leg but really, I think that you may be over-reacting to the circumstances here tonight. Sit with me for a moment and try and get your breathing under control and calm down. Your uncle is going to be okay, and it won't help him at all to see you in such a state." She smiled at Jonah. "I bet you've had some bad experiences in hospitals, am I right?"

Jonah nodded, unable to trust himself to respond. He wasn't sure if he would scream or cry if he tried to speak so he just sat there without speaking. The nurse pivoted on her rotating chair to turn to a water cooler behind her and filled a paper cup and handed it to Jonah. He gulped the water in one swallow, and she smiled and filled another cup that he sipped more slowly.

"Are you feeling a bit better?" Jonah managed to croak, "Yes. Thank you. For the water."

"Okay, you can go in through these doors behind me, and you'll find your uncle in exam room three. Ask anyone for room three if you can't find him." She smiled at him again. "You know, many people feel how you do when they come to the hospital. Try and stay as calm as you can and remember that your uncle needs you. It won't help him if you're all agitated and upset."

Jonah nodded and mumbled his thanks again. He readily found room three and rushed in to see his aunt and uncle talking to a young, red-haired nurse. He ignored the nurse and put his arms around his auntie, feeling his eyes filling with tears. His guilt was overwhelming – he should have been back in Port Muskek with his auntie and uncle who had done so much for him. But then his tears were choked to a stop by his uncle's sardonic greeting, "Hey Jonah, nice of you to finally arrive." It was like he was welcoming a late guest to a backyard barbeque. Jonah caught his breath and leaned over the bed to hug his uncle. "Uncle I am so sorry that I wasn't there to help. Please forgive me."

His uncle smiled his craggy grin. "Jeez Jonah, if I had to wait for you to get there from Toronto, I'd still be lying in that creek bed. If I need a lawyer, I'll sure call on you, but if I need to get rescued from a creek, I think I'll call on Charlie and Bill." Jonah buried his head into his uncle's shoulder and hugged him hard. His uncle hugged him briefly, then lightly punched him the ribs. "Jeez, Jonah, are you gonna crawl into bed with me?"

Jonah choked out a strangled laugh and stood up, gradually gaining control with deep breaths. He looked at the red-headed nurse and wondered briefly why someone so young was looking after seriously injured patients like his uncle? He then realized that she was probably a student nurse. Probably the hospital sent the student nurses in to practice on Indigenous patients like his uncle. They probably thought that Indians were useful for beginners to practice on.

Jonah looked at her again. She looked no more than twenty years of age. He blurted out, a sense of outrage overcoming his fear and anxiety for his uncle. "Are you the student nurse? Where is your supervisor?"

The nurse looked at him in surprise. "I'm sorry, what did you say?"

Jonah was now starting to lose control again. "I know that these hospitals think that they can practice on Indians. Where is the real nurse?"

Jonah's aunt gasped. "Jonah Kataquit, where are your manners. Your uncle has had excellent treatment all day, don't you be so rude."

But Jonah realized he needed to take control for his uncle's sake. His auntie held politeness above every other value. And right now, his uncle needed an experienced nurse, not some student. "Auntie, you just don't understand. Unless we insist that Uncle gets good care, they are going to send all the students to look after him."

The red-headed nurse looked at Jonah with a puzzled expression. "I am sorry, I am not sure that I understand what you are saying. You think I am a student nurse sent to look after your uncle because he's Indigenous?"

Jonah nodded. "Yeah, we know all kinds of stories about hospitals sending students to practice on our people."

The nurse smiled. "Well, you will be happy to know that I am not a student nurse. In fact, I am not a graduate nurse, either. I was just about to introduce myself to Mr. and Mrs. Sunderland when you came into the room and started accusing me for some reason." She looked at Jonah with sympathy. "I can see that you are very upset about your uncle's injury. I get it, but believe me, we do not practice on anyone in this hospital."

Jonah looked at her with suspicion. "So, are you a clerk or something? When is the doctor going to see my uncle?"

The nurse smiled again. Jonah thought that she looked even younger when she smiled. "My name is Dr. Brynn Allard. I am the orthopaedic trauma surgeon on call." She looked at Samuel. "Mr. Sunderland, looking at the records sent to me from Moose, you have suffered a very nasty injury to your leg that requires surgery immediately. I am not going to undress your wound again to examine it here in the ER, there is no point to that – the situation is well documented in the notes from Wiichihinan Hospital. I need to examine and clean up your leg with you asleep in the operating room. I have reviewed the x-rays your doctors in Moose sent to our computers and I'll need to stabilize the fracture in your knee and shin bone tonight. With more than twenty-four hours since the time of your injury, it's essential we get you to the OR as soon as possible. It really is an emergency with the bone exposed and contaminated by your wound."

Jonah took a step back like she had slugged him in the chest. "Emergency surgery tonight? Wait a minute, where's your boss? If my uncle is going to the operating room tonight, he needs the best person available."

His aunt gasped. "Jonah you are being very rude."

She looked at Brynn. "I am so sorry Doctor, please forgive my nephew. He has good reason to hate hospitals and I know that he is very frightened for his uncle. He is not usually rude like this." She clucked her tongue at Jonah.

"That's alright, Mrs. Sunderland. I understand that everyone gets upset with emergency situations like this." She looked at Jonah. "What is your name, sir?" Jonah responded. "Well, Mr. Kay, I am afraid that I am the boss here. I am the surgeon on call for orthopaedic trauma until this coming Friday at five pm. There is only one other surgeon like me in the city right now and he's already busy with cases in his OR at our partner hospital uptown. So, like it or lump it, I am the right person to look after your uncle."

And now, Jonah made a comment that crossed the line for Brynn. "Well, I would really prefer if a man surgeon would look after my uncle. Don't you have a man around who can do this surgery?" His aunt sighed. "I am so sorry Doctor. What is wrong with you Jonah?"

But then Jonah climbed deeper in the hole he was digging. He could see that the red-headed surgeon's complexion was starting to turn the colour of her hair. And he blurted out. "I am a partner at" and named his law firm. "You don't want our firm checking on your credentials, do you?" Jonah regretted the words even as he was saying them. He knew he must sound like a pretentious ingrate. But he knew he needed to protect his uncle.

The room was silent. Brynn was barely controlling her emotions. These last few days had been awful. Her fiancé Brian was gone when she returned to her apartment after fixing that terrible arm fracture on Monday. She had not heard from Brian since then. She did see his lover in the ER earlier today and the woman had avoided Brynn completely. Brynn supposed that the next time she would see Brian would likely be in the ER when he referred a fracture case to her.

But then she remembered that she would not be returning to the ER after Friday. The Chief of Surgery had called her into his office this morning to confirm that the two new Orthopaedic trauma surgeons St. Barts had recruited would be taking Brynn's fracture call from now on. The hospital was instituting a policy of sub-specialization for all its surgeons and Brynn would now be limited to her primary specialty of doing hip and knee replacements. Brynn enjoyed doing fracture surgery and knew that she was good at it. With her extensive experience, she was likely better at trauma than these two newly trained surgeons.

Brynn knew that her income was going to drop by at least forty per cent when she stopped doing fracture surgery. But even more important, looking after trauma patients provided her with a variety of clinical challenges that she really appreciated. You never got bored with the urgency of fixing broken bones. Each case was a unique, different challenge that Brynn enjoyed. She knew that she was going to go crazy with the repetitive practice of only replacing arthritic knee and hip joints.

Brian was now gone from her life. Then the day after learning about Brian, she was told by her Chief that the practice that she had worked so hard to build was going to be much less satisfying. And now this goddamn lawyer was accusing her of racism and threatening to sue her if she didn't get a man to do his uncle's surgery. Suddenly all the events of the past few days just collided for Brynn. She could feel the blood rushing to her face and knew that she was likely crimson. She could feel hot tears starting to surface. She held her breath and bit her lip. She was damned if she was going to cry in front of this prick. But then she felt a hand gently grasping her wrist.

It was her patient, Samuel.

"Dr. Allard, allow me to apologize for my nephew. He has had some very bad experiences in hospitals. He's not acting himself."

"But Dr. Allard, that doesn't mean I forgive him for how rude he's been to you tonight." Samuel turned to look directly at Jonah. "For the first time in many years, Jonah, I am ashamed of you and how you have acted here. You are going to apologize to Dr. Allard right now here in front of me."

Brynn looked at his weathered face and saw the stern look that was aimed at his nephew. Brynn's tears thankfully failed to materialize, and she could feel her angry breathing subsiding as her diaphragm started working again. She looked over at the lawyer who was staring back at his uncle. "But Uncle, we need to make sure that you get the best care possible. This is important and we don't know this doctor at all."

"Jonah Kataquit, you stop this right now. You don't know

anything about how good a surgeon Dr. Allard is, and I'm embarrassed that you suggested that she isn't so good because she's a girl. And accusing her of practicing on me because of who I am, where I'm from! Jonah, what's the matter with you?"

Brynn looked at this grown man getting dressed down by his uncle. Jonah was looking at the floor, but Brynn could see that he was a good-looking guy. Long straight hair in a ponytail so dark there were blue highlights displayed in the hospital fluorescent lights. His eyes were pools, widely spaced and sunken above maxillary ridges that seemed carved. He was well-dressed despite being in a bit of a sweaty mess. Feeling herself coming back under control thanks to Mr. Sunderland's intervention, Brynn was curious about how the nephew was going to respond.

She was surprised. "I'm sor... I'm sorry, Dr. Allard. It's just... it's that my uncle means so much... so much to me and I feel so guilty that I was not... not there to help him." And then he raised his eyes from the floor to look at Brynn and she could see tears in his eyes. "I am sorry to upset you, Uncle. Doctor, please, please just take good care of him."

Brynn watched as Jonah's auntie now reached over and took his hand. Brynn couldn't help but feel a bit of envy at how nice this family was. "Gee, Jonah, I'm sure that Uncle is gonna be okay and Dr. Allard is gonna take good care of him, aren't you Dr. Allard?"

Brynn managed a thin smile. She had experienced enough emotion in the past few days to last her for three lifetimes. "Yes, Mrs. Sunderland, I will take very good care of your husband." The surgeon looked at Jonah who was appearing sheepish, looking at the floor and softly gasping while wiping moisture from his eyes and face. "So, now that we have settled that I am going to be Mr. Sunderland's surgeon, let me tell you all what we are about to do when we get him up to the OR."

Brynn explained that she was going to wash out the wound thoroughly and remove any contaminated tissue. She was going to reconstruct the fracture which had extended into

Samuel's knee joint using some screws to hold the knee joint surface together. And then she would place some threaded pins into the bone above and below the fracture and link the pins together with an external frame that would stabilize the tibia. Because of the risk of infection from the creek, she would not attempt to close the wound today. Instead, she would place a plastic wrap over the wound with suction attached through the plastic to drain out fluids and infection. That suction would induce the wound to start contracting closed.

She would expect to take Samuel back to the OR for a second operation within two to three days to clean the wound again and apply another plastic membrane suction device. And depending on how the wound looked at that second operation, she would either recommend a third cleansing or would do an operation to close the wound, likely by transferring some muscle over the open bone defect. But that would be in the future and now she was going to get the bone cleaned up and stabilized just as fast as possible. "I am going to call the OR right now and see if I can take Mr. Sunderland right up there."

Then she felt Samuel's hand softly on her wrist again. "Thanks Doc, I know you'll do your best. And please don't hold it against Jonah. He's really a pretty good guy despite acting like an idiot here tonight."

CHAPTER 6

Losing Lilly. December 12, 1988

Jonah was five years old when, on a December afternoon, he came home from school to find his mother cold and still in her bed. There was never a day thereafter, as a child or a man, when he did not think of his mum. But he needed to rely on his Auntie Mary and Uncle Samuel, who raised him after her death, to help him remember her.

For two or three years, Auntie made a point of talking about Lilly on the twelfth of each month following her death on December twelve. She was more willing to talk to Jonah about her sister than Uncle Samuel, but she would quickly become emotional and tearful, and usually she would stop before she could finish her story, unable to go on. While Uncle was more reliable when he chose to speak about Lilly, his taciturn nature made it challenging to get him to talk about his sister-in-law.

Mary would always look off in the distance remembering her sister as she told Jonah about his mother. "Jonah, even when she was very young, just a child, your mummy was so beautiful. She was really just too pretty. I knew it when she started school. I was in my last year when she started. When she arrived at school, you could see she was not the same as the rest of the kids." Jonah had seen pictures of his mother from her early days at the residential school. It seemed that there were more school pictures of her than any of the other children and he could understand why. Her shimmering hair, high cheek bones, deep set eyes, and long limbs marked her as a child who was different from the rest.

Mary worried that the nuns would take special interest in Lilly. Lilly told her that the nuns called her "their little angel." Mary had seen what could happen to pretty little girls when they became attractive teenagers at residential schools. And she knew that the special attention that Lilly might receive from the nuns would isolate her from other children. The nuns' favourites were resented by the other students.

"Jonah, I should have been there for your mummy," she often said. "I left the school the year after Lilly started, and I worried so much for her. She had no family at the school to look after her after I left."

Over time, Jonah listened to similar stories from other survivors of the infamous James Bay Residential School. Friends of his aunt and uncle, some of his friends' parents – most of them had been torn from their parents at an early age to attend schools that taught them to reject their families, their language, and their culture.

Kids who were loners and kids who were different – like Lilly – had the worst experiences. The nuns, the brothers and the support staff could always pick out the weak ones or the solitary ones. Kids who could not rally support around them were especially at risk.

Jonah's auntie never spoke much about her own time at residential school. When he tried to ask her about it, she would simply say, "Jonah, I had Samuel." Mary and Samuel were both from Port Muskek, but their families were not close, and they met after they were taken to the James Bay Residential School.

By fifteen, they were inseparable. They supported each other through the worst times at the school. Lilly was not so lucky.

Jonah knew that his auntie and uncle had married shortly after leaving the school and Samuel moved into Mary's parents' home in Port Muskek. Despite his youth, Samuel rapidly became a leader in the community. Samuel was at home in the bush and kept their table supplied with pickerel, trout, goose, and sometimes a moose. Samuel was known for his understanding of where martens ran through the James Bay bush and year after year he proved to be the most productive fur trapper in the region.

With his experience in the bush, Samuel developed a woodlot business that provided firewood to the Port Muskek community. He was also handy with construction and would always bid on projects whenever the reservation council found funding and materials to build new homes in Port Muskek. The men who worked with him readily responded to Samuel's job offers and increasingly relied on Samuel for employment. With the profits from his various business activities, Samuel could afford a used truck as well as the snowmobiles and all-terrain vehicles that were essential to his activities in the bush.

Jonah loved his time in the wilderness with his uncle. In addition to learning trapping, fishing, and hunting, Jonah found he could learn about his mother while sitting around campfires with Samuel. He was about ten or eleven when, sitting outside their fishing camp one late summer day, his uncle started to talk about Lilly.

"Jonah, the people in that school hurt your mother real bad," he said. "She never told us exactly what happened to her. There were bad men in that school, and they hurt her. And the nuns didn't protect her. When she came back from the school, she was afraid of her shadow."

Samuel did not yet tell his nephew that Lilly was pregnant when she returned to Port Muskek after the residential school closed in 1976. Fifteen at the time, she was unable or unwilling to say who had assaulted her. In some ways fortunately for her, she suffered a miscarriage and lost the baby. Jonah later learned from town gossip that Lilly became pregnant again at age seventeen. Like the first time, she would not say or did not know who the father was and again she lost the baby.

Young men in Port Muskek were certainly interested in Lilly, but, at seventeen, she was terrified by their advances and rarely left Mary and Samuel's house, where she had moved after the residential school closed. It broke Mary's heart to see how her beautiful little sister had been so badly damaged by her experiences at the school. When Mary tried to learn about the father of Lilly's second pregnancy, Lilly would break down or withdraw. Mary assumed that she must have been raped again on one of her rare absences from their home.

Jonah knew that his aunt and uncle had helped to care for him from the start when Lilly gave birth to him just after turning twenty-one. Lilly could not or would not comment on the father. Although Jonah would sometimes wonder about his father as a teenager, he was far from the only fatherless child in Port Muskek. Jonah was fortunate that his Uncle Samuel had served as a surrogate dad from his earliest days.

Jonah and Lilly lived with Mary and Samuel for the first three years of Jonah's life. Mary told Jonah that she and Samuel had never wanted Lilly to move out of their home. Samuel was active with Council and had been able to enlarge their house with an extra bedroom that would accommodate Lilly and her baby. But Jonah learned that his mother and Mary did not always agree on how he should be raised.

As he approached his teenage years, Jonah became more persistent questioning why his mother had decided to move out from Mary and Samuel's house. In explaining how his mother was changing during his early years, Mary recounted an event that had increased her concerns about her little sister.

"Jonah, after you were born, your mother was acting more and more quiet, never wanting to talk about anything. And then one day I saw her coming out of the shower with a towel wrapped around her and blood on her legs. I asked her why her legs were bleeding, and she turned away, but I lifted her towel and could see that her legs were cut. I was so shocked. We both started crying and sat there in the bathroom holding each other. She told me that she had no idea why she needed to cut herself. She had been stealing Uncle's razors to hurt herself."

"I remember her telling me, 'Mary, what am I going to do? I have terrible thoughts. The only way I can stop the thoughts in my head is to hurt myself with cutting. I am such a terrible person, and I am scared I am gonna hurt Jonah.'"

"Your mummy was hurt so badly at that school and felt so terrible about herself. I would try and tell her how good and beautiful she was, but she could never believe me."

It was Samuel who told his nephew about Lilly's drinking. "At first, drinking made your mum happier and not as frightened by other people. That wine relaxed her with people, I guess." He shook his head. "But then when she was drinking, she would become angry and argue with her sister – your auntie. If we suggested anything to her about you when she was drinking, she would get mad at us and say we were trying to steal you from her."

As Lilly increased her drinking, arguments between the adults became more and more common in their small household. Samuel did not explain to his nephew that the drink made her lose her fear of men in the community. She began staying out later and sometimes overnight with men her own age and older. Mary often suggested to Lilly that she and Samuel would always look after Jonah if Lilly wanted to stay out with her friends at night. But that just made Lilly angrier.

Mary was near tears as she recounted one particular argument. "She got so mad at me Jonah. She said, 'You are just so perfect Mary. You're just like the nuns – you know everything, and you always know better. Me, I'm just trash to you. The only way I can get away from you being so perfect is to leave this house and be alone with my friends. And I know that you want to take Jonah away from me. You don't think I can be a mother to him. Well, he's mine, not yours. You want to take my son away. That's not gonna happen.' Jonah, I was just so worried about you. I wasn't trying to steal you, but your mummy wouldn't listen to that."

From his earliest memories, Jonah considered his auntie and uncle to be second parents to him. He and his mummy were close, but he remembered that she was sometimes sleepy or had headaches and at those times he could rely on his aunt and uncle. Sometimes he would go into their room and crawl into their bed if he woke during the night and his mother was not in their room. Samuel and Mary had never had their own children and Jonah sometimes felt like he was their boy as well as his mummy's.

Jonah could not remember when Lilly finally insisted that she and her boy would move out of Mary and Samuel's house. Samuel assisted her taking over a small, construction trailer that had been fitted out with heating and plumbing for some visiting workers. The wooden prefabricated building rested on a poured concrete foundation that was at risk of flooding during spring run-off. Jonah remembered the smell of mould in that home.

Jonah remembered that Lilly would frequently leave him with Mary and Samuel when she went out with friends. And as time went on, Lilly would delay picking up her son, sometimes for several days, as her social life expanded. Jonah learned much later that Lilly developed a reputation for promiscuity in Port Muskek that deeply troubled her sister and brother-in-law. She was also associating with young men who were introducing drugs including cocaine and various pills to Post Muskek.

A year after Lilly and Jonah moved out of Mary and Samuel's, the spring waters again threatened their small trailer with flooding. Samuel insisted that the two of them should move in with him and Mary until the waters receded. Lilly finally agreed. Years later, sitting by the campfire with Jonah one evening, Samuel described this visit.

"We hadn't spent time with your mum for a while. Auntie and I were shocked by how she had lost so much weight and had been doing that crazy cutting everywhere on her arms and legs." Jonah had seen the scars but did not realize where the wounds came from.

His uncle continued. "She smelled a lot like that cheap wine she was drinking, and she had a lot of pill bottles." He shook his head. "But Jonah your mum was still by far the prettiest girl anyone had ever seen here."

Lilly still maintained the innocent beauty that had defined her for better or worse since childhood. But Mary and Samuel could see that beauty starting to fade with the abusive lifestyle her sister was pursuing. Her skin was becoming sallow, and she had lost a tooth from either trauma or decay.

When Jonah was four, Lilly began dating a young man who was known to be the main supplier of illegal drugs to Port Muskek. It was obvious that she was using cocaine. She was desperately thin and covered with self-inflicted scars that were now very evident. Jonah spent more and more time with Mary and Samuel but was devoted to his mother. And when sober, she was very close to her boy, gentle and attentive.

With time, especially after police enquiries into physical and sexual abuse against students at the James Bay Residential School became public, Jonah would learn that he was not alone as a child at risk in the Port Muskek community. In the communities along the James Bay coast, multiple generations of adults had suffered systematic trauma as children in this infamous residential school. Public disclosure of police records made the James Bay school notorious across Canada as one of the worst examples of genocide directed against Indigenous Peoples by the government and the church.

This long-time abuse was now inflicting its intergenerational impact across the James Bay community. The harm done to adults who had attended the school was being visited on the youngsters whose parents were psychologically and physically traumatized by the mistreatment they had suffered as children.

Samuel and Mary tried to make sure Jonah still had a childhood despite his mother's difficulties. Samuel bought skates for Jonah on his third birthday and a hockey stick for his fourth. As a boy, Samuel had enjoyed playing hockey on the river when he was home from school at Christmas and was one of the better players in the games organized by the religious brothers at the residential school. The brothers were brutal when playing with younger children and Samuel had learned to be evasive by staying away from the brothers' attempts to crush him on the ice. From his first time on skates, Jonah demonstrated speed and agility and Samuel enjoyed taking his nephew out on the hockey rink. For Jonah even his earliest days on skates seemed like moments of freedom from his worries for his mother.

At the age of five, Jonah began attending the local school. The school was a twenty-minute walk from their trailer across the Port Muskek community for Jonah. For the first few days, Lilly walked Jonah across town both ways. But then she repeatedly failed to meet him after school. As Jonah consistently walked home unaccompanied, people noticed. Several of the town folk told Mary and Samuel their concerns about Lilly's deteriorating ability to look after her son.

Mary and Samuel were torn about whether they should be more insistent that Jonah should live with them. On the increasingly rare instances when Lilly was sober, she was a warm and loving mother to her young son. And Jonah didn't ask to leave her. He made excuses to his auntie for his mother's absence – explaining she was tired or had a headache.

That winter, Uncle Samuel began taking Jonah to the hockey rink after school almost every day. Port Muskek had two outdoor rinks, one of which was used for hockey. The rink opened in early December and remained solidly frozen until spring. Before dinnertime, the rink was reserved for families teaching young children the basics of skating and puck handling. After an hour or more of hockey, Samuel would usually take Jonah back to his home for dinner.

Jonah always looked forward to the days when Mummy let him go to Auntie Mary's for dinner. Sometimes Mummy was too tired to make dinner and then he would usually eat some crackers or peanut butter on bread to fill his tummy. But after a few nights of dinner at Mary and Samuel's, Mummy would cry and tell him that he loved Auntie more than Mummy. He stayed home with her those nights, and they would eat snacks on the couch and watch cartoons or read stories together.

On the most important day of his life, Jonah walked home from school on his own. Uncle Samuel had promised to pick him up for hockey later. Jonah was cold walking in the December chill with a north wind starting to blow. He hurried home to find the front door was open and the trailer cold. He saw that the fridge door was open with the light on. He knew Mummy sometimes went into the fridge for her bottles and forgot to shut it.

Jonah closed the fridge and went into the bedroom to say hello to his mummy. She was asleep on her bed, lying on her side. Jonah took off his coat and carefully crawled onto the covers to avoid waking her. He cuddled up against her and lay there for a moment. Slowly, he realized that something was wrong. Her hand was icy cold. He thought that she should get under the covers to warm up and he tried to wake her. He tried to rock her back and forth to wake her, but she rolled like a stiff rag doll. He shook her head, but her mouth was tightly clenched, and no sound came out.

Jonah knew that he needed to do something. He went out the front door and started to walk the twenty minutes to Auntie Mary's house. He was so muddled that he forgot his winter coat and was wandering in the near dark cold wearing only a shirt. A neighbour saw him from her kitchen window. She ran to the front door, calling to him, "Jonah, where are you going? You're gonna freeze Honey, where's your coat?"

Jonah just kept on walking. He was confused about why Mummy wouldn't talk to him and afraid she was angry at him.

The neighbour called to her husband to check on Lilly and then ran out into the street to collect Jonah. He was already chilled and trembling violently. She brought him back into her house and wrapped him in a blanket, asking him if he would like a hot drink. Just then her husband ran back into the house. "We gotta call the cops," Jonah heard him say. "Lilly looks real bad."

The provincial policeman arrived within ten minutes of the call. Fortunately, it was the good officer who had recently arrived in Port Muskek. His older partner had been in Port Muskek for three years and was due for a transfer soon. The younger officer was much more friendly than his older colleague. He joined the neighbour going into Lilly's house and came out shortly after shaking his head.

The policeman backed his station wagon up to Lilly's door. He and the neighbour carried her out of the bedroom and laid her in the back of the police wagon, covering her with blankets. The neighbour's wife put Jonah beside her in the back seat of the wagon and they set off to the hospital, leaving their older daughter to get dinner on the table for the kids.

When they arrived at the nursing station, the husband ran in and returned with the nurse, who checked Lilly in the back of the police vehicle. Jonah could remember vividly that the nurse shook her head after briefly attending to his mum and then brought out a rolling gurney and helped the policeman place Lilly on the stretcher. The policeman, wife and the nurse conferred after they rolled Lilly inside the nursing station. Jonah recalled that the nurse said that she would keep him in the nursing station while they tried to locate Jonah's auntie and uncle. They had already tried Mary's phone but there was no answer.

Jonah later learned that Mary was visiting a friend for tea, having made a stew and fresh bread for dinner earlier in the day. She knew that Samuel was going to play hockey with Jonah, and she would be heading home soon to warm everything up for their arrival after the rink.

They left Jonah in the nursing station and dropped the neighbour's wife at home to look after her kids while her husband and the police officer set off searching for Samuel. They just missed Samuel at Lilly's house. Coming to pick up Jonah for hockey, Sam was surprised to find the house cold and empty. He figured that Lilly and Jonah had probably gone to his house, so he set off for home. But on arrival, neither Mary nor Lilly was there. Samuel next drove over to the hockey rink to see if Lilly had mistakenly taken her son to meet him at hockey. He had just turned around from the rink and was starting to head home when the police wagon approached him honking and flashing its lights.

The two vehicles stopped on the road facing in opposite directions and rolled down their windows. Lilly's neighbour spoke first, leaning across the police officer who was driving. "Jesus Sam, I'm glad we found you. Something terrible's happened. Lilly's gone."

"Gone, gone where?"

"Oh, for Chrissake, Sam, she's dead. We took her to the nursin' station and she was cold and stiff. She musta been gone for hours. And there was a bunch of pills around her bed."

"Oh, Jesus. Where's her boy? Have you seen Jonah?"

"We took him to the nursing station. He's okay, but I think he discovered his mum dead for cryin' out loud. Poor little guy."

Samuel stared out his truck window, silently shaking his head. He later told Jonah that he and Mary had been afraid this might come to pass. "Okay, I'll go get Mary and get over there to the nursing station. Thanks for what you guys done, eh."

The three men were all shaking their heads in disbelief as they rolled up their windows and drove off in different directions. Samuel arrived at his home just as Mary was walking up the drive. Samuel jumped out of his truck and ran over to his wife and put his arms around her.

"Sam what is it? What's wrong?"

"Oh Jesus, it's Lilly, Mary. I just met one of Lilly's

neighbours who was looking for me with that nice young policeman. They told me that they picked up Lilly and took her to the nursing station. And Mary, oh Jesus, Mary, they said that she was gone."

"Gone, whattya mean gone, Sam?"

"Mary, they said she was dead." Sam hugged her, but she pushed him away.

"Sam, where's Jonah?"

Samuel nodded. "They said that they took Jonah to the nursing station too and that he was okay. I came here to get you before going to the nursing station to get Jonah. I needed you with me."

Mary nodded silently. She climbed into Sam's truck, and they set off to get their nephew.

Jonah could always remember his relief leaping up to hug Auntie when she and Uncle entered the nursing station waiting room. The place was chaotic with screams coming from the back clinic area where patients were assessed. The nurse was obviously tied up with an urgent problem. Samuel and Mary sat on either side of the little boy who was cold and shivering. The waiting room was never well heated. Samuel took off his coat and wrapped it around Jonah.

"Auntie, Mummy came here a while ago. She was asleep and I couldn't wake her up and the police brought us here in their wagon. I want to go home. I'm hungry Auntie. But I don't want to leave Mummy."

Samuel and Mary looked at each other at a loss for what to say. Auntie put her arms around Jonah. "Here, son. Let me give you a hug and warm you up." Then she looked at Samuel again. The noise in the backroom had quieted down. "Sam, why don't you go back and ask the nurse what's happening?" Sam nodded and walked tentatively back through the door that led to the examination areas of the clinic.

Mary and Jonah could hear Sam talking to the nurse. And then the two of them walked back into the empty waiting area. The nurse walked over to the entrance and locked the door and then pulled over a chair and sat in front of Jonah. Samuel sat back at Jonah's side. Mary was still hugging the boy.

Jonah remembered the nurse taking his hands in hers. She seemed nice but she looked sad and tired. Jonah did not know that she had only been in Port Muskek for ten months and was feeling drained and worn out from the experience. There were supposed to be four nurses in town looking after nearly two thousand people, but since she had arrived there had never been more than two nurses on duty at any time. She was exhausted from working 60-hour weeks and frequently facing impossible situations like she was currently about to deal with. She was thirty-one but felt like she had aged ten years in the ten months she had been here.

"It's Jonah, right? My name is Nurse Darlene." Darlene thought to herself, "*The boy is beautiful. Looks like his Mum but innocent with those deep eyes.*" Darlene had been horrified when she examined Lilly's remains to see all her scars and wounds. What trauma that poor girl must have suffered. How terrible that abuse must have been to make her give up this beautiful child.

"Jonah, I am afraid that I have bad news for you. Your Mummy came in here very, very sick and I am sorry that she was too sick for us to help."

Jonah was nodding. "She's asleep, right? Is she going to wake up tonight or do we need to stay here until she wakes up in the morning?" He looked up at his auntie. "Maybe I should stay home from school tomorrow to be with Mummy."

The nurse and Mary looked at each other. Both were holding their breath, trying to hold in the tears. Mary heard Samuel sniffling. And then Samuel just lifted the boy onto his lap and enveloped him in his arms. "Jonah, you are gonna come home and stay with me and Auntie for a while. Your mummy is very sick, and she is gonna have to stay here. But me and Auntie are gonna give you some dinner and you are gonna stay at our place tonight."

Jonah smiled at his uncle. That was good news. He was

cold and so hungry, and Auntie always had good food. But then he frowned. "But what about Mummy? We can't just leave her here alone. I should stay with her."

With that, both Darlene and Mary started sobbing and Jonah looked at them with puzzlement. "What's wrong Auntie?" Neither the nurse nor Mary spoke through their tears. Samuel held Jonah close as the little boy sat on his lap. "Oh, jeez, Jonah. Your mummy won't be coming home. Not tonight. She's gonna stay right here. But we are gonna go home and eat."

"Can I say good night to Mummy before we leave, Uncle?"

At that, Jonah was even more puzzled because his uncle started crying as he looked at the nurse, saying, "I think it's probably best that Jonah says good night, huh? What do you think, Darlene?"

Darlene rubbed the back of her hand over her eyes and shrugged her shoulders. "If you think that's right. I just don't know. But give me a minute. I'll call you in." She left to arrange Lilly for her son to see for the last time. She called them in, and Lilly was lying under covers up to her neck. Jonah looked at his aunt and uncle. "Why is she sleeping so much? She's always sleeping today." They didn't answer and Jonah shrugged. He walked over to his mother and stood on tip toes to kiss her cheek. "Good night, Mummy. I am going to dinner at Auntie's, and I'll see you in the morning I guess."

Jonah took his auntie's hand and turned to leave, looking up at Mary. "I guess we should go and let her sleep. It's just so cold in here, Auntie. Her cheek is freezing. And hospitals always smell so bad. I wouldn't be able to sleep in this bad smell."

They walked back into the waiting room with Jonah's hands held by his aunt and uncle. Darlene watched them leave, leaning against the doorframe between the exam and waiting rooms. Samuel paused at the exterior door to open the lock that Darlene had closed.

"Shall I just leave it unlocked?" he asked, looking over his shoulder at the nurse who nodded through her tears.

And then the three of them headed out to Samuel's truck in the parking lot. But before the door swung shut, Darlene could hear Jonah's soft voice asking, "Auntie, Mummy's not coming home, is she?"

CHAPTER 7

The Tournament. March 22-24, 1996

T he only positive memories that Samuel Sunderland took from the eleven years he spent in the James Bay Residential School were his love for Mary and his enjoyment of hockey. His commitment to his wife had not abated during their eighteen years of marriage. Hockey however had been left behind as he focused on supporting his family with his work in the bush, in construction and his progressive involvement in Port Muskek politics.

Jonah's fulltime arrival in Samuel's household after Lilly's passing reinvigorated both these passions for Sam. He and Mary had longed for a family but after years of trying without success they were resigned to living without children. The responsibility for raising Jonah brought them together even closer with common purpose. Although Jonah was not related by blood to Sam, the boy's presence in Sam's life since birth had engendered a commitment to the child that could not have been stronger if Sam had been his birth father.

Having a boy brought new meaning and purpose to all

Sam's activities. Although Sam and Mary wanted Jonah to have opportunities that they and Lilly had never experienced, it was important to Samuel that Jonah understood the land that gave his people identity and meaning. Jonah was only five when Lilly passed but Sam immediately began introducing him to the James Bay bush that was so important to Sam's sense of self as well as his livelihood. By the time he was six, Jonah was enjoying joining his uncle on fishing and hunting expeditions while staying out in the bush for days at a time, learning about the animals, the plants, the water and the land that surrounded and supported their community.

Samuel was also pleased that having a son reconnected him to hockey. The residential school had always been provided with used skates and donated sticks from the south. The religious order brothers who instructed at the school were happy to play a very rough brand of hockey while teaching the younger children to play the game. In residential school hockey, Samuel had learned from an early age to always skate "with his head up" to avoid being dumped to the ice by a school brother's rugged body check.

Samuel had bought Jonah his first skates and stick while Lilly was still alive. Now he and Mary developed an enjoyable routine as winter arrived in early December. By then Samuel would have returned from time in the bush setting the marten boxes on his trapline and stocking the freezer from the fall hunt. Samuel would leave for his growing business and political duties early in the morning and then would pick Jonah up after school going directly to the rink for an hour or more of hockey before dinner. And if Jonah completed his homework quickly, he and his uncle would often return to the ice after dinner. Port Muskek had one ice rink reserved for hockey as well as ice that was usually kept cleared and flooded on the river by the lower reaches of the town.

There was no organized hockey for boys until age nine. That meant that younger children like Jonah would spend endless hours on the ice, being instructed by friends and family members while playing long pickup games that encouraged skating and puck handling skills.

One typical evening Samuel leaned on the boards of the rink with another residential school survivor watching the boys play. The man's son was on the ice with Jonah.

"So, that's Lilly's boy, eh, Sam? Good lookin' little player that, huh? Terrible what happened to his mum." Samuel nodded. Small talk was never his forte.

"Jeez, Sam, do you remember how those brothers at the school would treat us on the ice? I was scared to death whenever I put on skates. Between checking us when we were fifty pounds lighter and carving us up with their sticks. Those guys were just mean."

"Yeah, I guess we learned to skate better trying to get out of their way," Sam responded.

"Our kids are sure lucky today, huh, Sam? Compared to us going to that damn place. I guess kids like Lilly just never got over it, huh?"

Samuel taught Jonah the art of using the edges of his skate blades to carve the ice in achieving power, speed, and agility. The skates quickly became extensions of the boy's legs, and he developed the acceleration and quick manoeuverability that are foundational to hockey skills. Samuel had never developed the "soft hands" that characterize creative goal scorers. Jonah however walked around throughout the year bouncing a tennis ball on his hockey stick, developing the instinctive feel that allows great scorers to keep the puck attached to their sticks and shoot without warning.

Jonah's abilities set him apart from boys his own age and he inevitably played with older boys in the informal games at the rink or on the river. And after playing his first game in organized hockey at age nine and scoring every time he was on the ice, he was immediately elevated to the eleven and twelve-year-old league. Even though Jonah was three years younger than many of the boys he was playing against, he led the league in scoring in his first year of organized hockey.

The next year Samuel and the Elders organizing hockey in Port Muskek thought hard about whether Jonah should join the thirteen- and fourteen-year-old team that travelled on the ice road to play in other coastal communities. Jonah was doing extremely well in school and had accelerated a grade so that his classmates were all a year older than him. Mary and Samuel were pleased that Jonah needed no coaching or persuasion about schoolwork. When he wasn't on the ice during the long winter months, he would be curled up on the couch reading. By age eleven, the local librarian was ordering in a variety of fiction and non-fiction books to satisfy Jonah's voracious reading habits.

Mary was initially reluctant for Jonah to play on the travelling team. "Sam I just don't know about Jonah playing with those bigger boys. He could get killed out there."

Jonah was listening to his auntie and uncle discuss his hockey future from his bedroom. It was so exciting to imagine playing hockey in different rinks in towns along the coast. He had never been out of Port Muskek, and he had heard that in Moose they actually played in an arena, just like the professional teams. He was eager to experience what playing indoors would feel like.

"I know how you feel, Mary. Sometimes I just look away when he's carryin' the puck out of his own end or goin' into the corners against those big boys. But you know he has been playin' against bigger kids for years now and he sure has his wits about him when he's on the ice."

Somewhat reluctantly they agreed that Jonah could join the Port Muskek travel team. Samuel had seen how rough play in that league could be and knew that Jonah would be smaller than all the players, many of whom were into puberty and their growth spurts. But Samuel had carefully watched Jonah play with older boys and saw he had an uncanny sense of where opponents were on the ice to avoid contact with them. And, although many of the boys were older and bigger than Jonah, their recent growth often left them a bit clumsy. Jonah's skating quickness allowed him to elude boys sometimes thirty to forty pounds heavier while the puck seemed glued to his stick.

With Jonah joining the youngest travelling Port Muskek team, that team leapt to the top of the league standings. This was most unusual. The top teams in the James Bay league generally came from Moose, which was twice the size of Port Muskek. Hockey scouts for the semi-professional junior teams and the National Hockey League kept a close eye on local player development around James Bay, especially after a forward from Moose led the NHL in scoring while playing in California. James Bay players had a reputation for toughness and durability that was a reminder of the rough style of hockey that their fathers learned at the residential school.

Mary and Samuel followed Jonah's out of town play whenever possible. Mary remained concerned about Jonah playing with older boys but after a couple of years without any injuries she accepted the risk. Throughout December and early January, the boys would play in the Port Muskek house league. But by mid-January, once the ice road opened from Port Muskek through the other James Bay communities to Moose two hundred and fifty kilometres away, the travelling teams would be off every other weekend, usually playing at least two games a weekend in each of the towns along the coast and welcoming other teams to Port Muskek on alternate weekends.

The season culminated in the Moose Tournament in mid-March just before the ice road closed. During Jonah's James Bay hockey career, the Moose arena was the only enclosed facility in the James Bay league. Fans in other communities watched their teams play on outdoor rinks, often in minus thirty-degree weather. In March, the top teams in all age classes would play off in the relative comfort of the arena in Moose. This represented a much-anticipated luxury for the James Bay hockey mums and dads who could for once watch their kids play without risking frostbite.

Jonah was thirteen, playing with boys fifteen and sixteen

years of age in his second tournament in Moose. This year the tournament was particularly special, because for the first time ever, four teams from southern Ontario were taking the train to Moose to compete against the best four teams from James Bay. This unusual event engendered a carnival atmosphere along the coast and all hockey families were planning to drive down the winter road for this year's tournament.

One of the guys working for Samuel at the woodlot had a younger boy who hoped to play for the travelling team in the future. "Me and my boy are gonna spend the weekend staying with my cousin in Moose to watch the tournament, Sam. Maybe I could leave early on Friday?" Sam nodded.

"How's Jonah feelin' about the tournament, Sam? It's gonna be special with those boys from the south comin' up, huh? Do you think they're gonna kill our boys?"

"Ah jeez, I dunno. Jonah's pretty excited but I told him not to get his hopes up too much. Those boys down south play in arenas all year around, even in summer. They got power skating coaches, skill coaches and they're all trying to get them hockey scholarships to go to American universities, you know? I told Jonah he should just play his best and see what happens."

The tournament started on Friday with the championship games on Sunday for the best southern and northern teams. Samuel and Mary took their pick-up down the ice road which would shut down two weeks later. Sam had recently bought a new used truck with a double cab and drove the five hours to Moose with Mary and Jonah in the front and three players whose parents couldn't afford transportation in the back. The back of the pick-up was full of hockey gear.

Jonah was billeted with players' families in Moose and Mary and Samuel stayed with cousins. The Sunderland name was prominent in coastal communities and Sam had lots of relatives, all of whom greeted each other as cousin. Mary and Sam were known for the hospitality they gave to visitors to Port Muskek and they were welcomed wherever they travelled along the coast.

Mary and Sam were at the arena Friday morning to get good seats behind the Port Muskek bench. It was luxurious to be able to sit rather than stand beside the boards. The temperature in the unheated arena was around zero but having a thermos of warm coffee and sitting on a blanket that could be wrapped around your legs, protected from the inevitable northern wind blowing down from the pole – well this hockey viewing experience was magnificent compared to what they were used to.

The boys were going to play two games on Friday and one on Saturday against the other James Bay teams. The second game on Saturday would pit each James Bay team against a southern team. And then Sunday morning, the best two northern and southern teams would play off with the morning's winners facing off in the afternoon to play in the first "North-South" championship.

David Morton was a fifteen-year-old defenceman on the Royal Georgian College team. He was missing three parties in Toronto this weekend and was disgusted finding himself in this creepy place. His coach Shawn Ketchum was also the headmaster at RGC and had convinced school parents that travelling to play Indigenous teams would be a good experience for the RGC team as well as the teams they were playing against. David had smuggled a flask of vodka in his equipment and was sharing it with his RGC roommate in their billeted bedroom Thursday night.

"What the fuck are we doing here in this dump," Dave whispered to his bunkmate as they passed the flask. "I had a date with Corinne this weekend for crying out loud and you know how hot she is. And we take a two-day train trip to come to the Arctic because Mr. Ketchum is such a bleeding-heart pussy." His roommate muttered his agreement.

David continued taking another pull on his flask. "Those guys better keep their heads up. I'm gonna be scalp hunting when we play these Indians."

Jonah's team readily won their first two games against

James Bay teams with Jonah getting three goals in the first game and two in the second. Following the second game, the eight teams gathered in the Moose high school gym that had been set up as a cafeteria to feed the boys. Despite the best attempts of the coaches to get the boys to mingle, there were clearly two solitudes in that gym. The southerners were from private schools around the Toronto area whose parents had paid for this expensive trip to the north as an experience for their boys. The southern students all knew one another, and their side of the hall was raucous.

The James Bay side was subdued. The boys looked at the private school boys' clothes, their shoes, their watches with envy and disbelief. The sophistication and obvious wealth of these boys from southern private schools made the northern boys realize they were from different worlds.

Mary and Samuel picked up Jonah and some teammates after the dinner to return them to their billets. Mary was happy the boys were getting the experience of this tournament, but the four Port Muskek players were unusually quiet as they got into the truck. "How did it go guys," she wondered.

"It was okay, Auntie," Jonah responded. "But you wouldn't believe the stuff those guys have. Their hockey equipment, their clothes, their shoes. They're just so rich."

Samuel responded from behind the wheel. "Well, their shoes aren't gonna help 'em on the ice, Jonah. We'll see how you do tomorrow."

The first game on Saturday matched Moose against Port Muskek and it turned into a tight contest. Both goalies were walls, shutting down nearly every scoring attempt. Jonah's linemate got a goal in the second period on a nice feed from Jonah in the corner. Moose matched that tally in the third and the teams went into overtime, tied one each. Jonah had been the victim of several acrobatic saves by the Moose goalie. But with less than a minute remaining in the first overtime period, Jonah caught a bouncing puck to the left side of his opponent's goal with a perfect one-time shot that beat the goalie on his stick side. Jonah was mobbed by his teammates in celebration of completing the James Bay part of the tournament undefeated.

Their next game on Saturday afternoon was disastrous. They were playing RGC who had completed their round robin against southern teams undefeated. The tone of the game was set in the first five minutes when Jonah took a pass at centre ice in full flight and sped across the RGC blue line. Approaching the defenceman skating backwards in front of him, Jonah threw him a head fake to the left and then accelerated to his right to go between the defender and the boards.

David Morton was the RGC defenceman and had seen this move before. Ignoring the head fake he kept his eyes on Jonah's chest as the smaller kid attempted to surge past him along the boards. Carving the edges of his right skate deep into the ice as he continued skating backwards, David pivoted toward the boards, catching the much smaller player with his hip against Jonah's belly and then his elbow to the boy's head, smashing him face first into the boards. The arena was silent as Jonah fell stunned, face down on the ice. Players gathered around him as the RGC team smirked and gave David quiet support for his hit.

David was given a two-minute penalty for elbowing. Jonah struggled to his bench and sat out most of the remaining first period. He returned for some of the second and third periods but with their best player and leading scorer injured, Port Muskek was no match for the southerners and the game ended with RGC winning five to zero.

After the game, Samuel checked on Jonah in the dressing room. Jonah assured him that he was feeling better and came out of the dressing room to join his uncle and three teammates in the parking lot. Mary had been so distressed by the hit on Jonah that she had not been able to stay at the game and was taken home by Sam's cousin. As Sam was walking to his truck with his arm around Jonah's shoulder, the RGC coach came wandering over. He had clearly been waiting for Jonah to emerge from the dressing room.

"Hi, my name's Shawn Ketchum, I'm the RGC coach. How's your son doing? That was a dirty hit that David put on him. David's known for that in our league down south and most players wouldn't try to go around him like your boy attempted."

Sam looked the coach up and down. He had on colourful winter gear designed for survival on winter mountain tops. Sam was dressed in an old, stained parka he used trapping. "I dunno, Coach. Jonah dropped his head, huh, Jonah? You put your head down, you pay the price. The hit wasn't that dirty. We're used to that. But your boy sure got him good. Anyway, I think Jonah's gettin' over it, huh, son?"

Jonah nodded. "Yeah, I was stupid. I thought I could get past him along the boards and didn't see the elbow. Won't happen again."

Sam squeezed his shoulders affectionately and looked up at Ketchum. "He learns pretty fast this one. He's my nephew, not my son, but I guess he's like my son. That is when he's not lying on the ice like a dead fish like he was today." A rare smile crossed Samuel's face and he gave Jonah's shoulders an extra squeeze. "Well, we'll see what happens tomorrow. Maybe if we beat Moose tomorrow morning, we'll meet you guys in the final. I think our boys are hopin' for a rematch." And he held out his hand to Shawn and shook firmly before loading the Jonah's gear into his truck.

As he walked away to his ride, Shawn Ketchum smiled to himself. If David had landed that hit playing in their private school league down south, Shawn would be threatened by lawsuits from opposing team parents. And here, the family jokes about their kid looking like a dead fish on the ice. Shawn shook his head.

The second game between Moose and Port Muskek on Sunday morning was a repeat of the cliff hanger played on Saturday. This time the goalies luck deserted them as the game turned into a shootout in the third period. Port Muskek eventually won six to five on a final goal with less than a minute left. Jonah showed no ill effects from the prior day's collision and was at full speed throughout the game, scoring twice.

RGC had easily defeated the second-place southern team before the two northern teams played and the RGC players and coaches were in the stands watching Port Muskek and Moose play. The RGC players were noisy spectators, cheering and booing loudly. Shawn Ketchum reminded them on several occasions that they were guests and to tone it down, but the boys were having a good time and enjoyed their exuberance.

The final for the championship would be the boys' sixth game in three days. Accordingly, the match was scheduled for seven p.m. to give the players extra time to rest. It seemed the entire town of Moose as well as the visiting families from the James Bay communities had tickets to the game and the arena was packed with standing room filled shoulder to shoulder. During warmup the RGC players were loose and having a good time. They were certain after their five to zero win over Port Muskek on Saturday that this game was going to be an easy victory and that they would return to Toronto undefeated from this unusual trip to a strange place.

On his second shift, Jonah took a pass from his defenceman and accelerated across centre ice. The defenceman Dave Morton was skating backwards ten feet in front of Jonah as the smaller boy darted across the blue line, closing in on David.

David sneered at Jonah as he saw the smaller boy starting the same head fake to his left. David had seen that move yesterday and ignored it. And he ignored it again now, keeping his eyes glued to Jonah's chest. And then, just as David expected, Jonah put on a spurt, dropped his head, and sprinted to pass David between the defenceman and the boards.

'Just like yesterday', thought David. 'This kid obviously has limitations'. He had shown the kid that no one could pass him like this and here he was repeating the same stupid move that got him crushed yesterday. He almost felt sorry for the little

Indian. But knew that this was the other team's best player. Not only was he going to drape the kid all over the boards, but he was also going to repeat the elbow to the head. And probably this time, the kid would be gone from the rest of the game. David started to rotate from the hips to put a little extra momentum into the elbow as well as the body check.

David waited patiently until Jonah was irretrievably committed to his move toward the boards. The kid's head was down, and he was trying to outrun the defenceman. David knew that the smaller player was faster than him. But there was no way his speed would allow him to get through the rapidly narrowing space the kid was aiming for between David and the boards.

Relishing the impending contact, David carved his right inner skate blade into the ice and accelerated off that edge, holding his breath as he drove towards Jonah, anticipating the contact against the boards.

But as he pushed off his right skate blade, the gap between his feet widened by six inches. Suddenly, glancing down, David was shocked that the puck was no longer being pushed toward the boards but was sliding between his feet. And Jonah, instead of driving head down to the boards on his right, had somehow accelerated to his left toward the center of the ice. Leaving the puck unattended, he circled David moving left, just as David was pushing off to Jonah's right. Then Jonah reached his stick back to retrieve the puck from between David's feet and in one motion put it in the top corner of the net over the RGC goalie's shoulder.

There was a moment of stunned silence and then the Moose arena exploded. No one remembered seeing a goal quite like that in the kids' league. It was like something on a professional highlight reel. And it put their boys up one to nothing!

As the applause continued, David spun around from facing the boards. At first, he wanted to take a run at the kid. He had never been beaten like that before. But, despite his usual sarcastic arrogance, David Morton was at heart a decent guy who appreciated the underdog. As Jonah passed along the Port Muskek bench, accepting the line of hand slaps from his teammates, David skated up behind him and muttered, "Nice move Chief. Try that again and I'll fuckin' kill you."

And was surprised again when Jonah turned to him and responded with a smile, "You'll have to catch me first, Paleface."

Jonah got two more goals that game, but his efforts could not make up for the strength of the entire RGC team and the southern team ended up with a five to three victory. Both teams had played a lot of hockey over the past three days and Jonah took his time showering and changing after the game. He emerged from the arena leg weary and exhausted, ready to sleep for a long time before returning to Port Muskek tomorrow.

He was surprised walking out into the parking lot to see Uncle Samuel deep in conversation with the RGC coach. They were standing under a light beaming down from the overhanging roof that protected the entrance to the arena. As Jonah approached, his uncle motioned him over.

"Jonah, you met Coach Ketchum yesterday, remember? He has something interesting to discuss with you."

Shawn Ketchum looked down at the player. "Jonah, I have just been talking to your uncle about a scholarship that we give out once a year to a hockey player from somewhere outside Toronto who combines excellent hockey skills with good marks and a deserving attitude."

Jonah looked over at his uncle, puzzled, as the coach continued. "We will have to check out your school performance with your teachers Jonah. But your uncle tells me that you are at the top of your class even after accelerating a grade. If that checks out with your teachers, would you be interested in coming to school at RGC and playing on my team?"

The boy looked back and forth between the coach and

his uncle. "But where would I live? Uncle we don't have any cousins in Toronto, do we?"

Samuel smiled. "Well, yeah, we probably do have some cousins in Toronto. You know we got Sunderlands most places we wanna go. But listen to what the coach has to say about where you would live, Jonah."

Shawn Ketchum smiled at Jonah. "Jonah, RGC does have a boarding dormitory where business people and diplomats going overseas can send their boys while they are abroad. But I was saying to your uncle that since you have never been away from home, maybe living in the boarding dormitory would be too big a leap for you."

"I am the principal at RGC in addition to being the hockey coach. My wife Evelyn and I have a beautiful house on campus with plenty of room. Just like your aunt and uncle," he said looking over at Samuel, "we don't have any kids of our own. We would promise to take very good care of you and make sure that you get properly and safely introduced to Toronto and everything it has to offer."

Jonah was speechless. He looked at his uncle who responded. "Jonah, Coach Ketchum is gonna check with your teachers to make sure that you could handle the schoolwork down south. From what I've seen watchin' you study and read, I don't think that is going to be a problem." He reached up to scratch the back of his head thoughtfully under his hat.

"You and me will need to have a long talk with your auntie, though." He turned back to the coach. "My wife Mary was Jonah's mother's sister and when Jonah's mum passed away, Mary promised herself that she would always look after this kid."

He looked up at the coach. "But with this opportunity you are offering, I think I'll be able to convince Mary. Especially with what you said about Jonah living with you and your wife." Sam could not have understood the irony of his last comment. He stamped his feet against the cold. "We should all get inside somewhere warmer. Coach thanks for what you've offered tonight. You got my number, and I hope we talk again soon."

The two men shook hands and then the coach reached down to shake with Jonah. "It was a pleasure to meet you and watch you play Jonah. I hope that we can work something out that will let you play for me at RGC next season."

Jonah was speechless as he walked slowly toward his uncle's truck. They were going back to the cousin's home, and he was sure that there would be lots of conversation about this offer. But Jonah could not imagine just how his life was about to change as a result of this weekend.

Change in ways that offered tremendous opportunity. And change that would result in remarkable confusion.

CHAPTER 8

Brynn's Rounds.
November 2017

Several days after Samuel's precipitous arrival at St. Barts, the trapper was sitting up in bed with his leg elevated on a sling. Dr. Allard had taken him to the operating room the night that Samuel and Mary had arrived in Toronto, shortly after meeting him in St. Barts ER. After the surgery she met Jonah and Mary in the post-op waiting room. They both leapt from their chairs when she entered the small room to report what she had found in the OR.

"Mr. Sunderland has a very nasty fracture of his upper shin bone extending into his knee joint," she told them. "The upper end of his tibia, or shin bone, was shattered and the skin over the front of the shin was damaged by the fracture, meaning that the bone is exposed without skin coverage."

Mary couldn't help blurting out, "Will he lose his leg, Doctor?" Jonah put his arm around his aunt.

"It's really too early to say for sure, Mary. But I am hopeful. There was a lot of contamination and obvious bacteria growth in the muscle and bone, but I think we removed and cleaned most of the infected tissue. By the way, the folks at Moose and Port Muskek really looked after him well, irrigating the wound and starting big doses of the right antibiotics. I am impressed that they closely followed best practices." Brynn was a bit surprised. The treatment and documentation of care that Samuel had received in James Bay was first rate and the staff had recognized the severity of his injury and rapidly transferred him.

"I could not close the wound because of the infection. You will see when he comes to his room that he has a big metal frame on his leg. We call that an external fixator. Fortunately, I was able to reconstruct his knee joint. I managed to put the bone fragments that comprise the lower end of the knee joint back in place and held them securely with three large screws that are buried under intact portions of the skin and muscle. Then we placed threaded pins in the bone above and below the fracture and stabilized it by clamping those pins to the external metal frame. You'll understand better when you see him."

She lifted her hands, palms up, to emphasize it was difficult to conceptualize what she was describing without seeing Samuel's leg. Brynn was fatigued and irritated. That had been a very tough trauma case, and she knew that she had provided textbook treatment. Getting the knee joint fracture back to its normal position and fixing it with those three screws was difficult but she had repaired the knee perfectly. The case reminded her that she was a very proficient fracture surgeon and she loved doing this trauma work. She could not believe that St. Barts stupid new policy was going to stop her doing the trauma surgery that she enjoyed.

On the night of that first surgery, Brynn continued to explain at length what Mary and Jonah could expect. She looked at Sam's nephew appraisingly. He had been a total prick when she first met him, accusing her of racism and telling her he wanted a male surgeon to look after his uncle. But he had obviously calmed down now. She knew that she shouldn't be having these thoughts so soon after that bastard Brian. But Sam's nephew was a very good-looking guy. He looked like a movie star out of an old western – the handsome, silent Indian who accompanies the white hero. She immediately cancelled that image in her mind as she realized what a stereotypical, racist thought it was. And he sure had not been silent when she first met him.

"Since the wound can't be closed yet, I covered it with a plastic wrap that is connected to suction to drain away any infected fluid. I will need to take him back to the operating room later this week to clean the wound again and after that we will again re-apply the plastic wrap and suction. Then perhaps next week if everything is looking clean, we will try and close the tissues over the bone- probably by transferring some muscle from the back of his leg to cover the damaged bone. I applied the external fixator in a way that will enable his subsequent surgeries."

Brynn could see that Mary's eyes had clouded over with all this medical detail, but the nephew was following every word closely. He had great, deep-set eyes that were emphasized by chiselled cheek bones. He was over six feet tall – lean and sinewy. What was she thinking?

"Doctor, I assume my uncle will need to stay in Toronto for the follow-up that he will need and maybe some therapy?"

Brynn nodded. This guy was thinking ahead as she might expect. She remembered vividly that he told her he was a lawyer when he threatened to sue her because she was a woman. "Don't worry," she said to Jonah, "our social workers will organize a placement for him here in Toronto. I believe that there are some group homes in Toronto for people from James Bay who need to be here for medical care for a while."

The lawyer was shaking his head no. "Doctor, I will arrange for my Auntie and Uncle to rent an apartment or hotel suite close to your clinic for as long as they need to be here."

At that moment, Brynn's phone went off, calling her about another patient. She said her farewells, telling Mary and Jonah that she would be checking on Samuel in the recovery room but that he should be fine.

Two days later Brynn returned Samuel to the operating room to provide further cleansing to the open wound. After that surgery she told Mary and Jonah that the fracture and wound were looking good, and that Sam should soon be able to get the muscle transfer operation to close his leg wound.

On Sam's first weekend at St. Barts, Jonah was sitting with his uncle in his hospital room Saturday afternoon, reading some documents from his new colleague Hillary in New York related to the International Brands/CannWeed investment. With Jonah's rapid departure from Azo Restaurant at the celebration dinner, Hillary Vanstone, the International Brands chief counsel, had gone home to New York sooner than she might have if Jonah walked her back to her hotel. However, everything seemed to be going well with the response to the deal and neither firm was expecting resistance from shareholders or regulators. The stock market had expressed concern about the amount International Brands had paid for its stake in CannWeed and International stock had dropped after the deal was announced. CannWeed shares on the other hand shot up after International announced the premium they were paying for their share of the Canadian pot company.

After Sam's initial surgery, Jonah had called one of the partners who led the health law and medical malpractice issues in his firm and asked him to check out Dr. Brynn Allard's professional reputation. His colleague returned a glowing review. She was known as a rising star in the very strong Toronto constellation of orthopaedic surgeons. "Jonah, her primary specialty is total joint replacement for knee and hip arthritis. She has apparently done some interesting research on the response of bone to the various metals used in joint replacement implants and is considered the international expert on that topic. She is also known to be a superb trauma surgeon which I learned is unusual for a woman in her speciality. Your uncle is certainly in excellent hands with Dr.

Allard, Jonah."

Keeping Samuel company in the hospital was easy. Sam loved reading crime books and thrillers and Jonah had loaded up a supply of his favourite authors. Samuel was never talkative at the best of times and he and Jonah would spend long quiet hours in the hospital, Jonah working on legal files and Sam reading.

They both looked up as a tall young man entered the room dressed in scrubs and introduced himself as Dr. Redfearn. He explained that he had taken over Dr. Allard's trauma practice and would be taking Samuel back to the OR next week to close his wound with a muscle flap.

Jonah and Samuel looked at each other. Jonah waited for his uncle to speak. He thought that he knew what Sam would say. Jonah was right.

"Nice to meet you Dr. Redfearn, but my doctor is Dr. Allard. She's been looking after me since I arrived at St. Barts and she's been doin' a pretty good job, I think." Jonah waited to see how the new doctor would respond. The answer was arrogantly.

"Mr. Sunderland, Dr. Allard is no longer doing fracture surgery at St. Barts. The hospital has decided that all fracture surgery must be undertaken by trained trauma specialists. I have three years of training at the Seattle Trauma Center, and I am much better qualified than Dr. Allard to look after you."

Jonah looked at his uncle, then stood up in front of the new surgeon. "Look Dr. Redfearn, I am sure that you are very well trained and excellent at what you do. But as you heard, my uncle feels that he should remain under Dr. Allard's care. I don't want to make a fuss. But I will complain if my uncle does not get the care he deserves from the surgeon he wants."

Redfearn looked at them both, obviously considering his options. And then wheeled around and left Sam's room without a comment.

Late Sunday morning, Jonah and Sam were following their usual habits in Sam's room – Sam deep into a thriller and Jonah going through a briefcase of documents he had brought with him. Mary had gone to church and Jonah had promised to keep Sam company until she returned.

Jonah looked up as a woman entered the room. At first, he didn't recognize her because every time he had seen Dr. Brynn Allard, she was wearing scrubs, a lab coat, and a surgical cap. But now she was dressed in civilian clothes, in a shortish green dress that complemented her wavy, reddish hair. Jonah was struck by her as she entered the room. She was a good-looking woman, about five inches over five feet, standing with confident presence, hands on hips in front of Samuel.

"So, first you didn't want me as your surgeon and now I hear you don't want my colleague Dr. Redfearn either. What's with you guys anyway? Don't you know this is publicly funded healthcare in Canada? Do you think you get to pick and choose who's going to look after you?" Brynn delivered these remarks with an easy smile that defused her comments and sat down beside Jonah.

"How you doing, Mr. Sunderland? Feeling okay, no fever, not too much pain?" she asked Samuel as she sat.

Samuel scratched his chin. In the presence of this beautiful young woman, he realized he needed a shave. "Well, I would be doing better if my doctor wasn't deserting me."

Brynn smiled again and reached out to hold Samuel's hand. "Now don't you worry. Dr. Redfearn's a bit uptight, but he is very well trained and capable. He will do a good job for you Sam."

"Yeah, well that's exactly what he told me, Dr. Allard. Told me that I was lucky to have him offering me his services. But jeez, Doc, you're my surgeon." Sam looked over at Jonah.

Jonah cleared his throat. "Dr. Allard, first of all, please allow me to apologize again for the fool I made of myself when we first met. I was impossibly rude, and my aunt and uncle have been reminding me ever since what an idiot I was. Unless you forgive me, I may never hear the end of it."

Brynn lifted her hand with a smile and passed it over Jonah's head like a magician. She had a lovely smile, Jonah thought. "Consider yourself forgiven."

"Whew, thanks, I'll let my aunt know when she arrives." Jonah smiled in return. The hospital's grimy windows could not stop the sun from highlighting the surgeon's greenish eyes. Jonah could see latticed flecks of blue in the irises.

"Doctor, you won't be surprised that I have checked you out and discovered that you are eminently well-qualified to look after my uncle. Having operated on him twice, surely you are the right surgeon to care for him until he is discharged?"

Brynn grimaced momentarily. "Look, I am delighted to look after Samuel. He seems like a pretty nice guy even though he doesn't say too much." She looked at Sam and grinned. "And I really appreciated the way he came to my defence in the ER when his rather rude nephew was accusing me of racism and trying to fire me." She rotated to face Jonah. "But the hospital has decided in its wisdom that I will not look after trauma patients any longer and that Dr. Redfearn will take over my trauma practice. There's not much that I can do about that."

Jonah carefully considered his next words. "Doctor, would you be upset if I brought an injunction against the hospital on my uncle's behalf, insisting that you continue to care for him?"

Brynn stared at Jonah for a long moment and then broke out laughing. "Oh, my God, you lawyers are so pathetic. Weren't you threatening me with legal action if I did look after Sam when I first met you?" She turned to face Sam.

"Mr. Sunderland is your nephew always this aggressive? How do you put up with him?"

Samuel just shrugged. "I hear he's really good at what he does, Doc. But I don't understand him any better than you do."

Brynn stood up and Jonah glanced at her legs. "Okay, you guys, I don't think anyone needs to sue anyone here. Let me talk to Redfearn. I will look after you as my last official trauma patient Sam. It will be my pleasure!" And with that she bowed to Sam and left the room.

Samuel watched her leave. "That one's a pistol, Jonah. You should find out if she has anyone. I didn't see a ring on her finger."

So, Brynn took Samuel to the OR for his muscle transfer and then his skin and bone grafting operations. All this surgery turned out well and two weeks later, Sam was healing and ready to go home to the apartment that Jonah had rented close by the hospital.

Mary was already staying there and told Sam that he would be impressed. It was a big apartment on the thirty-eighth floor of a tall apartment tower, and Mary said they had a wonderful view of Lake Ontario. Brynn had told Samuel that he would need to see her every three weeks to ensure his fracture was healing and strongly suggested that he stay in Toronto to do physio since physiotherapy services were apparently limited in James Bay.

Sam was getting ready to be transferred by ambulance to the apartment the next day. He was getting up with a walker pretty well but still needed to elevate his leg after walking to prevent swelling. Jonah was coming to the hospital after work each evening to give Mary a break from visiting. On this evening, Jonah's friend David Morton had also dropped in to entertain Sam as he had been doing frequently since Sam was admitted. David was describing to Sam how the famous Sunderland network of cousins had helped him out on a recent business deal when Dr. Allard came in on her evening rounds to see Sam and write his discharge orders for the next day.

She had come from clinic and was wearing a dress under her lab coat. As she bent over to look at her patient's wounds, David turned to Sam appreciatively. "Sam you old dog, you did not tell me that your doctor is gorgeous. Aren't you going to introduce me, Sam?"

Brynn stood up and turned to Sam. "You know Sam, I am never sure what response I am going to get from your visitors when I see you. Sometimes they are trying to fire me, sometimes they are hitting on me." She reached out her hand to David. "I am Dr. Brynn Allard, Sam's surgeon."

David smiled back, shaking her hand. "Doc, seriously,

thanks for taking such good care of Samuel here. He's a pretty important guy."

"So I understand." Brynn looked back to Sam. "Your appointment is set to see me in three weeks Sam. And your physio will see you three times weekly until our first out-patient visit. It's time to get your knee moving and important to start strengthening your quadriceps muscle. I have written some suggestions for the physio as to what's safe for you to start with, and we'll update that advice each time I see you in clinic." Then she looked over at Jonah.

"You know, you have told me so many times that you're going to check me out, that I decided to investigate YOU with my friend the hospital lawyer. And she told me that you are apparently famous in Toronto legal circles right now for doing some sort of pot deal that everyone's talking about in Canada's business world." She turned to David. "So, I looked up the story in the business pages which I never read. And I think that it was your face in the picture accompanying the story. I think they called you the Canadian Pot King or something like that."

She turned back to Sam. "Did you know these guys are famous drug dealers Sam? Shame on you for hanging around with these criminals." She smiled and left a card on Sam's bedside table. "Sam, this is my office number. Call me any time if you have any problems. See you in three weeks." And left to continue her rounds.

David whistled appreciatively when she reached the corridor. "Holy smoke Sam, she is hot. Jonah, you didn't tell me about Dr. Allard. She's something else."

"David, I've been telling Jonah that she is a firecracker, but he just doesn't pay any attention." Sam shook his head. He couldn't figure out his nephew. He seemed to have plenty of women, but they were always a lot older than him, not the kind you would settle down and start a family with. This Dr. Allard would be perfect for Jonah, but she was probably already taken.

David looked at Jonah, listening to Sam's comments. He understood why Samuel was encouraging Jonah to pay attention to Dr. Allard. And he also knew why that would never happen.

CHAPTER 9

Evelyn. September to December 1996

L ooking back on it, once he understood what grooming meant, Jonah recognized that she had been grooming him from the moment he arrived. He doubted that she had planned it. It probably evolved moment by moment for her. Like steps in a journey, one leading to the next. He couldn't hate her for it. But it certainly had impacted his life.

The board of governors that hired and fired the headmaster at Royal Georgian College were responsible for developing the strategic plan for the boys school. And, after the usual consultations and deliberation, they declared that the school's goals would be characterized in two words – excellence and diversity. Both Jonah and Coach Shawn Ketchum were examples of that strategy.

It was easy to recognize how Jonah checked both boxes. He had demonstrated his excellence in the Moose hockey tournament RGC had participated in last winter. When Shawn talked to Jonah's teachers after the tournament, he found that Jonah was well-liked and a successful and motivated student. Jonah's personification of the diversity element of RGC strategy was obvious. Not only was he from the James Bay Indigenous community but Shawn discovered that his mother had been severely traumatized by her experience at the James Bay Residential School and had died, likely from drugs and alcohol, as a young woman.

Jonah exemplified intergenerational trauma resulting from the residential school system. Shawn Ketchum thought it would be fitting if Jonah could now benefit from attending one of Canada's best schools.

The RGC board was supporting their "Excellence and Diversity" goal by providing scholarships for children who exemplified the strategy. A recent scholarship had been given out to the son of Laotian immigrants whose designs had been responsible for two technology start-ups by his fourteenth birthday and another scholarship was supporting a violin prodigy from the Somali community.

The typical RGC student was very white, and their families were very wealthy. They had to be rich to afford the annual tuition that RGC charged. Considerable wealth was concentrated in RGC families in Toronto, and it was not unusual for a student to represent the fourth or fifth generation attending the school. The school was proud of this heritage in general but wanted to introduce some wrinkles. That strategy was supported by Jonah's scholarship.

In a different way, Shawn Ketchum also fit the strategy of excellence and diversity. Shawn was from a hardscrabble mining town in northern Ontario, far from the privileged society in downtown Toronto that supported most of his students. Shawn attracted attention from an early age with his goal scoring skills in hockey. Most of his teammates competed for roles in the junior hockey leagues that gave players their best chances to play in the National Hockey League. But Shawn had different ideas. He refused offers to play junior and instead accepted a scholarship to a New England college where he became a legend. Playing a starring role as a freshman,

Shawn led the college to three national championship games, winning the last two.

Shawn had enrolled in the college's education faculty and after his undergraduate hockey days were done he stayed at the school supporting himself with teaching and coaching jobs while he completed his master's degree and doctorate. His thesis investigated teaching methods in Boston's inner city school system. Shawn's research recognized the importance of introducing Black cultural themes in curriculum for Black schools and had a major impact on inner city school teaching methods.

Although his research had focused on education in disadvantaged communities, following completion of his doctorate Shawn accepted a job in a private New England prep school, combining teaching with coaching hockey. He progressed rapidly to serve as the junior school director and was seen as a rising star in the North American private school universe. When the headmaster position at RGC became available, the RGC board successfully recruited Shawn to return to Canada.

Shawn's wife was a Canadian who he had met while she was studying in Boston. Evelyn was from the prairies where her family owned and farmed land. She was younger than Shawn, had completed an economics degree but had not started her own career.

The Ketchums were childless, and Evelyn had time on her hands as they settled in Toronto. However, Shawn's Headmaster responsibilities provided Evelyn with a useful role. Shawn was responsible for fundraising and developing donors to support the costs of maintaining the RGC campus which was located on prime real estate in central Toronto. And Evelyn became a willing partner assisting Shawn's donor activity. She engaged in every aspect of the school's social activities, organizing the celebrations and parent groups that contributed money to the school.

Jonah, Mary, and Samuel flew from Port Muskek to

Timmins and then on to Toronto to arrive at RGC for the first time late in August. Jonah's scholarship paid for a return trip home at Christmas and also paid for Mary and Sam to visit Toronto twice a year during hockey season to see their boy play. Shawn and Evelyn met the three of them at the airport. Evelyn in particular made them feel immediately welcome. She was exceptionally gracious, and Mary was entirely impressed.

"Jonah, you know how worried I was about you moving to Toronto without us." RGC had reserved hotel rooms for the two nights before Mary and Sam would leave Jonah to start his new adventure in the big city. "Well, meeting Mr. Ketchum and his beautiful, charming wife – Jonah I am now feeling much better about you staying here. I know that she is going to take very good care of you, and it's so nice that you will be staying in her home." Jonah later promised himself that Mary would never know how ironic her words were.

After two days of Toronto sight-seeing with Mrs. Ketchum while her husband attended to school duties, Mary and Samuel returned to the airport for their trip home. Even Samuel shed tears saying goodbye to the nephew who had become his son and Mary was devastated to be leaving her sister's boy behind. Although he knew that he would miss his auntie and uncle, Jonah was exhilarated by the new adventure he was about to begin. He had been amazed by the scale of Toronto and thrilled by the beautiful waterfront, museums, and art gallery he had visited in the past two days. And his fourteen-year-old sense of excitement was racing when Evelyn promised that they would make a trip to the local theme park before school started.

She was good to her word. Shawn was busy the week before school started, orienting new teachers and welcoming new students and their parents. But, after a bit of coaxing Shawn agreed that Evelyn should take Jonah to the amusement park. Jonah was fascinated by the size of the park – it seemed bigger than all of Port Muskek – and the thrill of the rides. Jonah was surprised that Evelyn acted almost like a teenager, seemingly lost in the excitement taking Jonah on the rides. She was giggling and laughing, sometimes running between rides holding his hand. Jonah was a bit embarrassed when her skirt inevitably flew up on the roller coasters, but Evelyn didn't seem to mind. Jonah couldn't quite believe how lucky he was, coming to this great new city and living with these wonderful, friendly people.

Jonah was living in a room down the hall from Shawn and Evelyn in the large, heritage house on campus that was reserved for the headmaster and his family. It was a short walk to classes and to the well-appointed hockey arena on campus that had been built with generous donations from some of Toronto's wealthiest families. Hockey was THE establishment sport in Toronto. Even though Toronto's professional baseball team had experienced far more success than the long-suffering hockey Maple Leafs, wealthy Toronto was passionate about the winter game.

Deserting its gritty origins on the frozen ponds of towns and villages across rural Canada, hockey had become a rich child's sport in Toronto. The expense of renting ice and buying equipment put hockey beyond the reach of the city's burgeoning immigrant community. Hockey was typically played by wealthy white kids, while most brown and black kids focused on soccer and basketball.

Jonah settled comfortably into his first weeks of school which he found challenging but manageable. The second week of September marked the start of hockey training. As a sophomore who was the same age as most freshmen, Jonah typically would be playing for the junior team. But Coach Ketchum knew that Jonah's skills and experience had likely prepared him for the older senior team.

On the first day of practice, Jonah discovered his locker was next to David Morton's. Jonah was getting his equipment on when David made an ostentatious entry to the locker room. Carrying his hockey bag over his shoulder, he swaggered toward his locker, sharing high fives, barbs, and hugs with his teammates. It was obvious to Jonah that David was a popular guy on this team.

David towered over Jonah. He was sixteen and had already reached six feet whereas Jonah was only now starting to grow and fill out. David threw his hockey bag back into his cubicle and stared at Jonah.

"Well, shit. If it ain't the Chief. I heard you were coming and here you are. Come back for some more punishment, huh?"

Jonah felt intimidated just being in this beautiful, incredible hockey palace, sitting with these guys who clearly were accustomed to the surroundings they played in. But damned if he was going to show how just out of place he felt. He was tying his skates as David sat beside him and he imagined what his Uncle Samuel would probably say at a time like this.

He went on tying his skates for a moment and then slowly turned his head to David, channeling his uncle's deadpan style. "Good to see you again Paleface. The coach asked me to come down and give you some skating lessons." And returned to tying his skates.

David sat silent for a moment and then burst out laughing. "Shit, that's right you called me Paleface when we were playing you up in that crappy arena you call home. I called you Chief and told you I was gonna mess you up and you called me Paleface." He started laughing again and stood up.

"Hey guys, you gotta meet – what's your name again?"

"Jonah Kataquit."

"Ah, nobody will be able to say that." Turning to the locker room, David announced, "Guys, you gotta meet Jonah Kay. You guys that went up to the North Pole last year for that crazy tournament, you remember he scored a hat trick against us in the final game after I damn near killed him the day before."

He sat down and started getting undressed. "Well Jonah, enough of this chief and paleface stuff. We'll catch shit if the coach hears us saying that. He freaks out on anything that sounds like racism. My name's David, David Morton." The two boys shook hands and David continued.

"Jonah Kay, you got a lot to learn coming here from the Arctic but I cannot think of anyone who could be a better teacher for you than me, baby. Welcome to Toronto, Jonah Kay, I am gonna show you what it's all about!"

An hour and a half later David was retching in the toilet while Jonah was showering and getting dressed. As he returned to his locker and slumped down, David looked at his teammate who appeared much better than he was feeling. "Shit, every year I hate starting practice. Ketchum always makes us do those gassers at the end of workout and I'm just out of shape. I spent the summer up at our cottage and didn't work out much. What about you, Jonah? You looked pretty good out there. Were you skating all summer?"

Jonah laughed. "This is the first time I have put on skates since the last time we played you guys in March. There is no such thing as summer ice where I come from. But I helped my uncle at his woodlot all summer, getting ready for fall and winter sales, so I stayed in pretty good shape. Man, that ice surface here is amazing. I have never skated on ice like that before."

David looked at Jonah. "Are you telling me that you spent the summer chopping wood?" Jonah nodded. "Oh Christ, I can see I am gonna need to do some work to catch up to you, man. Wait for me here while I have a shower and we'll go up to dinner together."

The team ate together in a dining facility in the arena every night after practice while watching hockey film and getting instruction from Shawn Ketchum and the coaching staff. Practice started every night at four o'clock after classes and they were headed home by six thirty. It was surprisingly like the schedule that Jonah was accustomed to in Port Muskek, and he managed it readily.

Coach Ketchum was keeping a close eye on Jonah, looking for evidence of homesickness. Shawn realized that Jonah was making a huge cultural leap coming from Port Muskek to RGC, but he was pleased the boy seemed very comfortable with his transition. And David Morton was taking Jonah under his wing.

Shawn was not sure how happy he was about David and Jonah bonding. David's family had a reputation at the school. His mother was always loud at school functions and his father had a chequered reputation in the business and investing world that supported many families at RGC. Shawn knew that the father's investment license had been up for review on a couple of occasions.

But you can't tell kids who to like and David and Jonah were becoming best friends on the ice and off. Despite David's lack of attention to conditioning, he was a skilled player and Shawn's number one defencemen. Jonah meanwhile demonstrated his abilities were as effective in Toronto as in Port Muskek. Shawn had never coached a player with such natural scoring ability and Jonah quickly showed that he would centre the RGC first line.

That meant that Jonah and David were usually on the ice together and David became adept at hitting Jonah in full stride with break out passes from their end of the rink. Returning the favour, Jonah always looked for opportunities to set up David's booming slap shot from the point.

In their first game away at private school rival St. Anthony's just outside Toronto, their opponents learned about this new RGC recruit. Early in the game, Jonah took a pass from David as he crossed center ice, undressed the defenceman, and buried the puck in the back of the net. He slipped as he let the shot go and hit the boards behind the goal while stopping. And then the defenceman that he had easily eluded crashed into him, pretending he couldn't stop as he crushed Jonah against the boards.

The ref was moving to separate the two players, his arm up to send the St. Anthony's player off for roughing when suddenly a third body arrived. David Morton threw his gloves down as he hit the St. Anthony's defenceman. He knew this fight was going to get him thrown out of the game. But David was sending a message to Toronto's private school league that if you messed with Jonah Kay you were going to need to answer to David Morton.

RGC was accustomed to being on top of the league standings, but this year was exceptional. By early November, Jonah was leading the league in scoring with twice as many goals as anyone else and the team was undefeated. And David was thoroughly enjoyed playing wingman to his new friend as he introduced him to the private school girls who also loved hockey – both playing themselves and watching the boys play.

David discovered that Jonah's dark good looks and exotic status being from away made him a magnet for girls looking for adventure. David was two years older than Jonah and fully mature physically, if not emotionally. His thoughts were continually fixed on the young women in their social scene. Jonah, now approaching his fifteenth birthday, was rapidly catching up with David's maturity.

The Ketchums remembered their promise to Mary and Samuel and kept a tight rein on Jonah, holding his curfew to eleven o'clock on most weekends and not allowing him to socialize during the school week. When he wasn't away with the hockey team, Shawn was continuously fund raising, out to dinner with parents and alumnae during the week. Evelyn worked with parent groups during the day and would accompany him in the evening if it was a big event. However, she was frequently home while Shawn went out at night after hockey practice.

She started regularly wandering into Jonah's room to see if he needed help with homework. He would usually politely refuse but she would often hang around his room chatting, sometimes asking him about his weekend adventures with girls.

These conversations embarrassed Jonah. He was certainly interested in the girls he was meeting, and his thoughts were increasingly occupied by them. But he was still sexually inexperienced and Evelyn asking about girls somehow seemed creepy.

It began slowly. One night when Shawn was out, Evelyn called out, "Jonah, do me a favour, come in here, will you?" Jonah wandered down the hall to Shawn and Evelyn's bedroom where she was holding two dresses on hangars. "Jonah, you know the coach and I are going to that big fundraising dinner on the weekend. I can't decide what dress to wear. What do you think?"

Jonah had no idea and suddenly felt very uncomfortable. He pointed to the dress she was holding in her left hand and turned to return to his room. "No wait a minute silly, you can't decide until you see them on me. Turn around and I'll try that one first."

Despite his discomfort Jonah found himself becoming aroused at the thought of Evelyn undressing behind him. He knew he should just leave but the excitement was keeping him glued to the spot. He knew that he shouldn't think of her this way, but she was so good looking and so friendly.

"Okay, Jonah turn around and let me know what you think." As Jonah turned, Evelyn was still buttoning the front of her dress. She pirouetted around him and then said, "Okay, remember what that looks like, turn around and I'll try on the other one."

When Jonah turned back to face her the second time, Evelyn's dress was even more open. Jonah was shocked but could not take his eyes away as she slowly closed the buttons. He was embarrassed as he felt himself becoming erect and saw that she glanced down and noticed it.

He felt utterly confused. She was creating the same feelings he would get with the girls he was meeting with David. But she was so much older. That seemed forbidden but somehow even more alluring.

"Well Jonah, do you like the dress?"

The boy mumbled something and left her bedroom, saying

he needed to get back to his homework.

Evelyn continued the flirtation over the next three weeks, grooming Jonah to accept her invitations which became more and more explicit. Shawn was out at least three times a week and Jonah grew to both dread and anticipate the nights that he was away. And then one night it became blatant. Jonah was getting ready for bed and was in his pyjamas when Evelyn entered his room. She was wearing a tight sweater without a bra. Jonah stared at her and could feel himself becoming extremely aroused. Evelyn walked over to him and took him in her hand. He only lasted moments. Evelyn then gave him a kiss saying, "Oh, Jonah, you are such a naughty boy."

And that pattern was then repeated nights when they were alone. Jonah's confusion was multi-dimensional. Evelyn excited him more than he could imagine. She seemed like the most beautiful and desirable woman alive. The girls he was meeting after school seemed trivial in comparison and he stopped going to the weekend dances with David. Evelyn was consuming his imagination.

But despite his fascination with the sexual introduction that Evelyn was providing, he was feeling incredibly awkward about his coach. He had a feeling that the Ketchums were not together much, and he had a sense that he was somehow substituting for the coach in his wife's bedroom. And that felt very weird – and made him very guilty.

His confusion started to show on the ice. Whenever he was near the coach on the ice, he started to feel overwhelming shame. Suddenly he couldn't put the puck in the net and felt like he was skating in molasses. Coach Ketchum assumed he was feeling lost away from home and did not want to pressure Jonah about his performance. But David felt no such compunction.

"Hey Jonah, what the hell is going on? You don't wanna go out with me anymore and you're playing like shit. What's happening man?" They were walking across the beautiful campus heading home after practice. It was the start of

December. The early winter night air that chilled Torontonians felt refreshing to the boy from Port Muskek.

Jonah walked in silence, uncertain what to say and utterly confused with life. He stopped in the middle of campus and then just dropped in the grass, lying on his back, and staring at the sky.

"Man, you would not believe what is going on in that house where I'm living David. You gotta promise you won't tell man, but it's just incredibly weird." And he went on to tell David how Evelyn was coming on to him.

David initially started congratulating his friend. "Oh man, you are so lucky. Evelyn Ketchum is hotter than hell. I can't believe that you are getting it from her." And then he looked at his friend who was speechless staring at him. "But yeah, I get it. That is really fucked-up for you with the coach, huh? Oh shit, Jonah, I can see why you are so upset."

And that is when David cemented his lifelong friendship with Jonah. He went home that night and asked his mother if Jonah could stay over for the weekend. Jonah asked the coach if that would be okay, and Shawn called Mrs. Morton. Shawn did not really trust David's mum, but she promised to ensure the kids came in on curfew that weekend. And Jonah returned from the weekend feeling much less stressed.

Evelyn acted hurt that Jonah had gone away for the weekend but continued coming on to him the next week when Shawn was out. Jonah was now constantly aroused around Evelyn. He knew that sooner or later he was not going to be able to resist having sex with her and knew that would destroy his ability to play for the coach.

After practice he again sat in the grass with David despite the winter temperature. "David you gotta get me out of there. We are gonna be screwing soon if I stay. She's all over me. And I got nowhere else to go. If I say anything they're gonna take away my scholarship and I am gonna end up back home in Port Muskek."

David lay back in the grass. "Jesus Jonah, most guys would

give anything to have a problem like you got. A hot woman like Evelyn Ketchum wanting to do you. Are you kidding?"

Then he rolled over and punched his friend in the arm. "Maybe you tell her that you don't want it anymore, but you got a friend you want to introduce her to." And then David fell into his infectious laugh. "You know Jonah, it'll be difficult, but since you are my good friend, I am gonna look after Evelyn for you. It won't be easy, but that's what friends are for."

Then the two of them were wrestling and laughing in the grass together. "Okay I tell you what. For some reason, my Mum really likes you, tells me that I should be more like you and that you are good for me or something. She makes it sound like you're a pill I should take. How about we convince her that you should move in with us?"

And that's just what happened just before the holiday break. Evelyn was initially tearful when Jonah asked if he could move out. Then she became angry. When Shawn asked whether she thought they should allow Jonah to move in with the Morton's, Evelyn's voice was icy. "That little bastard doesn't appreciate what we've done for him, Shawn. Yeah, just let him go."

And that would have been the end of it. David and Jonah were inseparable as they started living together in the new year. The RGC hockey team won the league and provincial championship that spring and each year that Jonah played. But Evelyn had started something. Jonah could not get Evelyn out of his mind and girls his age paled in comparison. David's mother had girlfriends a bit older than Evelyn who frequented the Morton home – and some were intrigued by the fully mature and muscular young man living at the Mortons.

David knew what Jonah was up to with his mother's friends. "Jonah, I know you're getting it on with my mother's friends. I don't care what you do with those cougars, Jonah, but so help me God, just don't let me hear that you are comin' on to my mum, you understand?"

Jonah groaned. "Oh man, how can you be so gross, David?"

"Yeah, well man, some of her friends that you are messin' with are just as old as she is, Jonah." Jonah shrugged. His attraction to older women seemed natural. Their experience and worldliness excited him. But he was getting worried that he was not feeling the same for girls his age.

When he was with teenage girls that he found attractive, they inevitably awakened memories of his mother, the youthful beauty who had left his life far too early. Those thoughts never surfaced when he had been intimate with Evelyn or Mrs. Morton's friends. But if he was becoming interested in a girl his own age and his mother entered his mind, he immediately knew that relationship was over.

CHAPTER 10

Changes. Summer 2018

S everal months after the International Brands/CannWeed deal was approved by shareholders and regulators, International CEO Norman Ridgely announced his retirement, effective immediately. It wasn't clear whether his departure was previously planned or the result of the stock market response to the CannWeed investment which resulted in a twenty per cent downturn for International Brands shares. It was clear that the International Brands board was not pleased by the billion-dollar reduction in their company's stock valuation that resulted from the CannWeed deal. The word on the street in both Toronto and New York was that David Morton had somehow outfoxed Ridgely.

The board appointed the company's second in command, William Dahlin, as interim-CEO. Confidential sources made it clear in the media that Dahlin's requisite accomplishment to achieve the permanent CEO job was to restore the market's confidence that the International/CannWeed deal would prove to be profitable. And that brought him into immediate conflict with CannWeed's CEO David Morton.

Although Jonah Kay had an office at his law firm in one of the bank towers on Bay Street, Jonah had spent most of his time over the past few years working with David Morton, often on the road raising money or negotiating deals to expand CannWeed's production across Canada and internationally. To facilitate his work with David, he had a small space in CannWeed's trendy offices in Toronto's Distillery District. Within weeks of William Dahlin's appointment as International Brands interim-CEO, Morton had asked his friend to meet him after work in a small bar adjacent to the CannWeed offices.

The day of this meeting with David, Jonah had been conferencing in his firm's offices with tax lawyers and accountants regarding sales of Morton's stock options following closure of the International Brands investment. Afterwards, he enjoyed the walk from Bay Street to the CannWeed offices with the final stretch leading through the Distillery District's heritage cobblestone streets.

It was ironic that the world's leading cannabis company was headquartered in this previously derelict neighbourhood of Victorian brick industrial buildings that had been restored as the Distillery District. The industrial site had been a leading location for whisky production during American prohibition and had provided a steady flow of illicit booze across the US border. And now CannWeed was using their Distillery District headquarters to plan their invasion of the expected soon-to-be legal American cannabis market.

The former distillery offices and production facilities had been carefully refurbished, exposing and restoring period brick and timber. The redeveloped Distillery District was now the home of trendy restaurants, clubs, art galleries, edgy offices, and a favoured spot for weddings. David was seated in a private alcove of High Spirits – a popular, smaller bar where he often went to plot CannWeed strategy. As he approached David's table, Jonah could see his friend was already one or two whiskys into his visit even though Jonah had arrived ten minutes before their scheduled meeting time. Jonah settled into the leather chair, enjoying the reflective mood generated by the bar's exposed period beams and renewed interior brick walls.

Jonah signalled the waiter for his bubbly water without any white wine. He could read David's mood from the bar entrance and knew that he would need his wits about him. David appeared tense and morose.

Jonah opened the conversation. "Some good news David. That tax treatment I told you about last week is going to work out really well for your options. I ran it by our accountants and the tax guys at the firm and they agreed it will work. That's going to save at least ten mil in taxes, I think. When all's done you're going to clear more than two hundred million on the whole International Brands deal."

David allowed a tight grin looking at his friend across the table. "Thanks Jonah. You seem to have more success saving ten million in taxes than I do selling ten million worth of medicinal weed. I can't wait until we're legalized." Then the smile disappeared, and he grimaced. "I spoke to Dahlin today. He's coming up in the next few weeks and I'm not liking his way of thinking. I already miss Norman Ridgely."

Jonah watched his friend take a sip of the twenty-five-year-old Macallan whisky that the bartender kept on reserve for David. Jonah knew each ounce of the whisky was worth about two hundred dollars and could not imagine that the taste was worth that cost. But he also knew, like situating his head office in this expensive heritage district, that drinking the Macallan was part of David's carefully cultivated image of carefree commercial success.

Jonah nodded. "Well, International's stock price has certainly nose-dived since we inked the deal. Do you think he has a mandate from the International Brands' board?"

David nodded. "Oh yeah, he pretty much told me that if he wants to be the permanent CEO, he needs to bring the stock price back up." Another sip drained his glass and he signalled for a refill. "He also told me how he plans to convince the market that the price should go up, and I didn't like it at all."

Jonah was not surprised. The last-minute ambush that he and David had pulled on Norman Ridgely and his bankers had resulted in International Brands overpaying for its interest in CannWeed. William Dahlin had not been directly involved in that deal and would feel at liberty to squeeze his company's investment in the Canadian cannabis company. "What's he suggesting, David?"

"Nothing concrete so far but he told me to prepare options for scaling back the investments we have planned to expand production. He wants to maintain the work in developing cannabis beverages and edibles but wants to consider whether we can conserve cash and avoid buying up more production. I think he expects us to break even or maybe even show a profit as soon as Canadian pot is legalized."

Jonah knew that as CEO of CannWeed, David Morton had ambitious plans for what was now the world's largest cannabis company. From the eight hundred-million-dollar investment that International Brands brought to CannWeed, David had sequestered five hundred and fifty million to pay off debt, pay his investment bankers and reward himself and his early investors. Jonah had just told him that David's profit alone had exceeded two hundred million and his investors were extremely happy about the return they received from the deal.

David was planning to spend about one hundred million developing and marketing marijuana edibles and drinks that he knew eventually would be in demand in the Canadian and eventual American markets. And he was looking forward to spending about one hundred and fifty million on research and facilities to grow more premium pot across Canada and around the world. David's ambition was to make CannWeed the world's biggest producer of high-quality cannabis. He wanted to corner the international high-end weed market.

Jonah looked at his friend. "Any threats from Dahlin?"

David looked at Jonah over the edge of his glass as he

sipped. "Not yet. He wanted to know our projections for sales once the legal market opens. That worries me. If he wants to get the International stock price up by showing he can make an immediate profit from the Canadian market, then our expansion plans will be on hold for years."

Jonah nodded. He and David agreed that CannWeed should run like an early-stage technology company, focusing on product quality and market expansion rather than profitability. They wanted to build an international brand that would be recognized as the provider of premium weed in every country that legalized cannabis around the world. Just like Amazon used its early investors' money to build market share rather than worrying about profit, David did not expect CannWeed to be profitable for several years. He needed the International Brands investment to achieve his growth strategy.

"If Dahlin wants to hold back on spending and worry about profit margin now, then we are going to have a problem, Jonah. Norman Ridgely believed in the vision of quality and scale and knew that was why we needed the investment. Of course, he did not want me and our investors to walk off with four hundred million more of their money than they expected to pay." He smiled at his friend across the table. "That was your doing, Jonah. But I have a feeling that Dahlin may not like what his Canadian CEO is telling him when we meet on his first visit to CannWeed."

Norman Ridgely had insisted that David Morton would continue as CEO of CannWeed after International Brands' investment. But David and Jonah both knew that the American company now controlled the CannWeed board with a majority of directors. If International's new boss did not like what CannWeed's CEO was proposing, David Morton could be readily fired from the company that he worked so hard to build.

Jonah sat quietly staring at the lime floating in his glass. Jonah knew that his friend would be heartbroken to lose

CannWeed. However, Jonah lacked David's blind optimism about the future success of the company. Jonah was not as positive about the start of the legal Canadian recreational pot market that was now only months away. David was sure that if he could provide a quality product then every Canadian would leave their neighbourhood drug dealer behind and become a CannWeed customer. Jonah did not share David's certainty.

Jonah's cousins legally selling medicinal marijuana from dispensaries had casual connections in the illegal pot business and Jonah knew that these illicit dealers were not worried about the start of the legal cannabis industry. Possession of marijuana had been decriminalized years ago in Canada and upstanding citizens were already able to buy high quality product cheaply without concern about police. In setting up the International Brands investments and the structure of its control over CannWeed, Jonah had been careful to protect his friend. David would receive a further large payment if he was terminated as CEO of CannWeed within two years of the deal closing.

Jonah sat quietly listening to David recount his plans for rapid expansion of CannWeed production and how he was going to convince William Dahlin of his growth strategy when David's new boss came visiting in two weeks. As he listened, Jonah was increasingly relieved that David had a golden parachute embedded in the investment agreement.

*****

Jonah felt mounting apprehension as he worked with the CannWeed team over the next two weeks preparing for William Dahlin's visit to Toronto. The first board meeting of the newly merged company would follow the day after Dahlin met with David Morton to agree on CannWeed's strategy.

Jonah appreciated his friend's aggressive approach to planning the future. David accepted that it might take several years for the average recreational marijuana user to leave their friendly neighbourhood dealer and move to the legal marketplace, but he was convinced that eventually that shift would occur and that it would happen faster if he could offer high quality products at a fair price. David's strategy required substantial investment to create new edible and drinkable cannabis products as well as building supplies of better-quality Canadian weed to prepare for the legal market opening.

David Morton also expected that other western countries would soon legalize marijuana. His goal was to develop international partnerships across America, Europe and South America to bring CannWeed brands to those new markets as they opened. David's plan was risky but the eight hundred million investment from International Brands meant that he had the money to accomplish this rapid growth strategy.

As the CannWeed team planned for the presentation to the visiting American International Brands' CEO, Jonah was concerned that David had no intention of presenting an alternate low growth, cash conserving strategy to his new boss. With three days to go until Dahlin's visit, Jonah took David aside at the end of the dress rehearsal that allowed CannWeed's quality and production leaders to practice the pitches they would present to Dahlin.

"David, didn't Dahlin ask for options to hold back on investments until you establish CannWeed's profitability after the Canadian legal market opens?"

David Morton snorted. "Yeah, that's what he said. But let's face it Jonah, you and I both know that would be a pussy approach. We have a potential tiger by the tail. We need to use the International Brands investment to supercharge our growth and get ready to use Canada as a launch pad to show the world how much money can be made when the market is legalized. Ridgely understood this. That's why he kept me on as CEO."

Jonah nodded. "Yeah, but Ridgely's gone, David. We don't know exactly what the International Brands board has told Dahlin he needs to do. But we are sure that he told you to provide him with a low growth, low investment, profitable option. David, it strikes me that you are not really providing your new boss with what he requested from you."

David's smile was broad and confident. "Jonah for Christ's sake, why would I give him something that I wouldn't want him to approve? He doesn't understand CannWeed and the last thing I should do is to suggest a direction for my company that I do not believe in."

Three days later, Jonah was in his small office at CannWeed when David and his two leaders came out of the boardroom where they had been presenting their future strategy to Dahlin and a team of accountants from New York. David immediately left his team, came into Jonah's office, and slammed the door. His face was a glowing stop sign.

Jonah remained seated at his laptop and looked up, closing the lid. "So?"

David spun in the chair across from Jonah's desk, his face practically blazing. "That fucker just changed the agenda of the board meeting for tomorrow. I was going to present our plan for CannWeed to the new board. Now my presentation will be followed by one of his fucking accountants presenting what Dahlin is calling a profitability plan." David snorted in derision.

"That profitability plan will eliminate expansion and keep the money International invested for growth on the balance sheet rather than spending it."

"And he just revised the board agenda to finish off with an in-camera session without the CEO. The CannWeed board has never met without me in the room, Jonah, and now they are going to decide on our future with me cooling my heels outside the boardroom."

Jonah looked at his friend calmly.

"David, you know that you don't schedule an in-camera without the CEO to decide on investment strategy."

"Jonah, what are you talking about? Why else?" Jonah sat quietly without response to his friend's question.

David stared at Jonah's eyes. "Oh shit, Jonah. Do you suppose?"

Jonah leaned back in his chair and clasped his hands behind his head. He thought for a moment, looking at the ceiling. "David let's go and try that new seafood place that's opening in the district. I'll even join you in a couple of glasses of wine if you treat me." Friends of David and Jonah were opening a restaurant in a beautiful old brick building that they had restored less than a block from the CannWeed offices. They had invited Jonah and David to drop in during the pre-opening phase.

"Not tonight, Jonah, I want to go over my presentation for the board tonight and make sure it's airtight." David stared at his friend. They had shared each other's thoughts for twenty years and could communicate without words.

David took a deep breath. "Fuck Jonah. You think that's it, huh?"

Jonah lifted his hands. "I think we should eat some oysters, drink some wine, and think great thoughts David. That's what I think you and I should do tonight."

The next day, Jonah was in the boardroom as corporate counsel while David presented his plan to the new board. There were no questions from the board when he finished. Then one of the nameless team of accountants that Dahlin had brought with him presented a different plan that preserved cash on the balance sheet and delayed investment in cannabis growth until after the Canadian legal market demonstrated profitability.

After that presentation, the new board Chair stared at his notes while announcing that management should leave including the CEO and counsel for the board in-camera session. The Chair looked over at William Dahlin as David and his team prepared to leave. "Bill, the board wants you to stay." He barely looked at David Morton when he concluded, "David, hang around the offices, okay? I'll come and get you when we are done."

David followed Jonah to his small office. "Jonah, they can't do this to me, can they?"

Jonah shrugged. "Well David, they are gonna have to pay you a shit load of money if they fire you. I made sure that was in the agreement. Let's wait and see what happens."

It was only twenty minutes later that they saw William Dahlin leave the boardroom and head down the stairs without waiting for the elevator or coming to talk to David. Jonah knew what that meant. Minutes later, the rest of the board filed out and the Chair came to Jonah's office and asked David to join him. Moments later David left the boardroom slamming the door behind him. The Chair followed David and motioned to Jonah to join him.

It took only moments after the boardroom door closed behind Jonah. The Chair did not even bother offering Jonah a seat.

"Mr. Kay, I just told Mr. Morton that he is finished as CEO of CannWeed. I am afraid that we will not be needing your services any longer either, Mr. Kay. Corporate counsel in New York will take over your role on an interim basis and she will discuss your departure with your firm. Thanks for your service." And with that he turned his back on Jonah and proceeded to pack his briefcase.

CHAPTER 11

The Chair. August 2018

Brynn Allard was eagerly anticipating her annual progress report to her university Chair. The Chair was responsible for assessing the performance of all orthopaedic surgeons working in the university system and had the ultimate authority for appointing and promoting surgeons in his department. The Chair reported only to the Dean of the medical school and the Dean would never overrule decisions made by the Chair.

Brynn's split from Brian was nearly a year past and was becoming less painful. Her family was supportive in the months after the break up, but both her parents were becoming more insistent that "time was running out if she was going to have a family". Brynn was a single child, loved her parents and appreciated their support for her career as a surgeon. She knew that both her parents wanted grandchildren but their progressive prodding was becoming both annoying and hurtful.

Professionally she knew she had made major progress in her career over the past year. Her research for improving the metals used in hip and knee joint replacements had resulted in several prestigious publications in leading medical journals. Brynn's work was achieving wide recognition and she had received generous grants from both government agencies and companies that manufactured joint replacements to continue this research. She was rapidly becoming known as the international authority on enhancing metal surfaces to improve joint replacements.

Brynn had also invested time in planning the new medical school curriculum used in teaching medical students how to diagnose and treat bone and joint pain. Evaluation of how the opioid epidemic got started in North America showed that too many doctors handed out opioid pain killers for back and joint pain because they hadn't been taught in medical school how to appropriately investigate and treat skeletal pain. Brynn and other younger orthopods on the university faculty were now providing increased student teaching on treating bone and joint symptoms. This year Brynn had won the prestigious award given to the one university faculty member that medical students judged to be their best teacher.

Her annual progress report was important since her university Chair had considerable power over Brynn's future. He would determine when she would be promoted toward the rank of professor in the university. This scholarly ranking was not only prestigious – it would also increase her pay. She was certain that this year's performance review, which demonstrated Brynn's success in research as well as teaching in the university, would show her Chair that Brynn deserved to be on the fast track for promotion. She also wanted to gain her Chair's support in convincing St. Barts to allow her to continue doing trauma surgery.

As she waited in the Chair's office for her boss' arrival, Brynn's anticipation for reporting on her accomplishments was tempered by her discomfort. Everything in orthopaedics, including the furniture in the Chair's office was designed for large men. The chair she was sitting in across from her boss' massive desk was huge and Brynn's feet could not touch the ground. With her feet hanging several inches above the floor, she felt like a grade school student waiting to be admonished by her principal rather than an esteemed colleague prepared for a scholarly performance discussion.

As Brynn's feet dangled, the Chair entered the room, with a brief apology for being late. Prepared for a serious discussion of her career, Brynn was wearing a business suit. Her boss was wearing a rumpled surgical scrub suit that showed evidence of his recently completed operation. The Chair had been in his role for more than ten years now and represented both the department's glorious past and its need for renewal. He sported a bushy gray mustache, and the hint of a Scottish brogue. That accent reminded his surgeons that it was only a few years since faculty dinners were initiated by surgeons being marched into the dining room by a bagpiper.

Brynn's painstakingly prepared performance evaluation sat unopened on his desk. She wondered if he had even read it in advance of this meeting. His first words confirmed her doubts that he had any idea about her accomplishments in the past year.

"Brynn, I heard from the team at St. Barts that you broke up with that ER doc." The Chair had met Brian at several faculty events during the two and a half years that Brynn had been dating him.

"He seemed like a pretty good guy and willing to put up with your schedule. Not every guy will be sympathetic to the hours you put in Brynn. Is there any way you can patch things up with him?"

Brynn was initially shocked by his opening comments but then realized that she should probably not be surprised. She was here to report on a particularly successful year as a university surgeon. She was probably one of the Chair's most productive faculty members. And now, rather than reviewing her progress and determining how he could support her accomplishments, this dinosaur was telling her to take back her cheating former fiancé because he would put up with her work hours?

Brynn felt her feet dangling in space and her life and career also lacking solid purchase on the ground. Her boss sitting across the enormous walnut desk would never see her as anything but a misfit girl who needed his advice about how to keep a man happy. Brynn had difficulty breathing for a moment. She dug her nails into her palms to concentrate and decided to change the subject.

"Have you had a chance to review my performance report?"

The Chair flipped open her dossier and spent a minute reviewing her accomplishments.

"You have done pretty well this past year Brynn. I worry however about the toll this may be taking on your personal life. If you are going to have a family, time is running out you know."

Brynn's nails dug deeper into her palms. Hearing comments from her parents about her reproductive longevity was one thing – hearing it from her university boss was definitely out of bounds.

'*But not really surprising*', she thought. Although there were now a few women on the university's orthopaedic faculty, the long-standing tradition in the department was that the Chair's wife was responsible for supporting the surgeons' wives. This tradition promoted the standard that the male surgeons should be constantly working in the hospitals or travelling to lecture at international medical meetings, enhancing the university's reputation, while wives stayed home and cared for families largely alone. Senior faculty wives provided support and counselling to younger women around how to accept the role of a surgical wife. Women surgeons simply did not fit into this tradition.

Brynn decided that the right thing to do was to ignore this less than auspicious start to the meeting and try to enlist her leader in supporting her ability to continue doing trauma surgery.

"Chair, you may have heard that St. Barts has decided that all trauma cases should be managed by trauma sub-specialists. I was removed from the fracture call schedule late last year. You know, I have excellent training in managing trauma. If you look at my articles, I have published extensively in the fracture management literature. I love doing joint replacements but doing only joints can get a bit tedious. Practicing trauma care provides me with clinical variety that keeps me up to date." She paused. He was looking over her shoulder and did not seem to be listening to what she was asking.

"On top of that, trauma care represents almost forty per cent of my income, Chair. Reducing my compensation by that amount without any recourse does not seem fair. There is no question that I am providing quality care to trauma patients. This is just an administrative decision at the hospital, and I could really use your help in getting it reversed."

Brynn could see the Chair start paying attention when she mentioned money. Maybe that was the way to get him on her side. But his next words deflated her expectations.

"I can see how the hospital wants to support those two guys they just brought back from trauma fellowships. I know those guys and they have young families they are supporting. They probably need the money more than you, Brynn. After all, you are just looking after yourself at this point." Brynn thought he might be smirking as he went on.

"And Brynn, doing trauma, with all that nighttime and weekend surgery. Doing all that work after hours – well Brynn, if you ever expect to have a family, maybe you should realize that the hospital is doing you a favour by taking you off trauma call."

Brynn felt at extreme risk for an outburst that might label her as "just an angry bitch" in her Chair's important opinion. Rather than allowing him to see her anger, she thanked the Chair for his time and left his office.

She rushed into the hall outside the Chair's office without

thanking his ancient receptionist for the appointment. She ran down the stairs of the heritage building that housed the faculty offices and did not stop until she reached the street. She emerged from the building into the heart of Toronto's Discovery District. Slick new laboratories and commercialization incubators surrounded her in the gleaming towers that had been built over the past ten years. The heart of Canada's technology and life science future – and right now it didn't seem like she fit in this future.

Years as a straight "A" student, succeeding as a surgeon appointed to one of the world's premier universities, producing internationally recognized research and educational curricula – and what did people want to discuss with her? Whether her university boss or her parents, the chief response to her accomplishments was to ask when she was going to find time to have children. No concern about how she was going to find someone caring enough to share a life and family other than the advice she just heard that she should accept any cheating bastard who would accept her work schedule.

Turning onto the sidewalk, she pulled out her phone to check the time and her schedule while biting her lower lip to restrain the tears she had felt welling in that ridiculous seat in the Chair's office. It was a beautiful late summer day and shaking her head, she decided to walk back to St. Barts rather than taking the subway. She had planned her day expecting to spend another half hour with the Chair but clearly the time would be better spent on a pleasant walk rather than looking for advice from that misogynistic old man.

Walking toward Yonge Street through the Discovery District, Brynn remembered the text she'd received that morning from Dr. Yvette Nguyen, her classmate who was back visiting Toronto. She had not seen Yvette in more than a year since her friend left the downtown family practice office where she had worked after completing residency. Brynn remembered that she had moved far north to work in a hospital located in the town of Moose on the James Bay coast.

Yvette's text told Brynn that she was in town for a continuing education course that was ending this afternoon. She was not returning north until tomorrow and her text said that she wanted to meet Brynn that evening to get her advice about something happening in Moose. Given the reception she had received from the Chair, Brynn was pleased to spend time with someone who did not fix bones for a living. She and Yvette had been close during med school and while they were starting practice in Toronto. Brynn texted her back, suggesting that they should meet in the pho restaurant that they used to frequent just outside Chinatown. She was pleased when Yvette immediately returned her text agreeing to be at the restaurant at seven that evening.

Brynn's final thought as she turned south on Yonge Street to return to St. Barts was that her Chair would be pleased that she was doing something social this evening – although he would obviously prefer her to be cooking dinner for a man rather than meeting a woman friend.

*****

As she joined her friend in the restaurant that evening, Brynn smiled remembering how Yvette failed to fit the immediate first impression that most people formed when meeting her. Yvette was tiny, shorter and slighter than Brynn. She had lovely South Asian features that could inspire a "China Doll" description. However, anyone imagining that depiction when first meeting Yvette would however be immediately disabused of the notion. She usually talked like a truck driver and Brynn knew how tough she could be when advocating for herself or her patients.

Yvette was a first generation Canadian. Her mother left her country following the fall of Ho Chi Minh City and was initially interred in a refugee camp in Hong Kong. Four years later she emigrated to Canada where she met her husband, another refugee from Vietnam, and five years after that she gave birth to Yvette. Yvette's father had difficulty acclimatizing to Canada, suffered from depression, and left his family before Yvette turned two. Her mother followed the classic immigrant pathway, working hard at menial jobs while raising her daughter alone and studying at night to become a human resource specialist. She was now vice-president of human resources at a large insurance company.

Yvette and her mother shared an interesting relationship characterized by the mother's insistence that her daughter should always work harder and that she would likely always be a failure in life. But Brynn had seen Yvette's mother's glowing pride at their class medical graduation.

After graduation, Yvette had completed a two-year residency in family medicine while Brynn took on the longer challenge of surgical training. Yvette never forgot her immigrant roots and started practice working in Toronto's downtown core caring for new Canadians, refugees, and patients with chronic mental health issues. When they would meet prior to Yvette leaving Toronto, Brynn enjoyed Yvette's profanity laced diatribes against the Toronto and Canadian medical and social systems that failed to provide for her patients' needs.

Tonight, Yvette had arrived before Brynn and was sipping from a wine glass. They hugged as Brynn approached the table and Yvette sat down with a contented sigh. "So nice to see you, Brynn, thanks for meeting me." She sighed again, breathing in the aromas of the Vietnamese restaurant.

"And thanks for recommending we meet here. I haven't had pho since I moved to Moose a year ago. I think that I may be the only Viet on the James Bay coast. This meal needs to last me for a long time."

They exchanged small talk about the course that Yvette had attended over the past three days which focused on better management of chronic disease in primary care. Yvette threw up her hands as she described how the course had largely missed what she needed to help her patients. "Brynn these courses are fuckin' designed for rich goddamn docs looking after rich, white, southern Canadians, not my patients. How the hell do I go home and tell my patients to eat a fuckin' Mediterranean diet when in Moose tomatoes cost two and a half bucks each."

Brynn was pleased to see that her refined and delicate looking colleague had not changed her style. They both provided their waiter with their orders from memory without consulting the menu.

Yvette was not surprised to learn that Brynn and Brian had finished as a couple. "I never thought that guy was good enough for you Brynn. And to be honest, he always seemed pretty interested in getting to know the women med students if you know what I mean." She raised her elegant eyebrows. "I heard that he might be fuckin' around. Believe me, you are better off without him."

Brynn shook her head at that comment. "Thanks Yvette. Today I had a meeting with my university Chair who told me I should accept Brian back with open arms and have children with him because he would accept my work schedule. And my parents are constantly reminding me that my ovarian function is inversely correlated with my age." She looked at her friend and threw up her hands.

"Nobody seems to care what I have accomplished. They just want to know when I'm likely to conceive."

Yvette looked at her friend critically. "Okay Brynn, you are forgetting what my mother's like. Ever since I was accepted into medical school my loving mother has wanted to know when I was planning to provide her with a granddaughter." She smiled to soften the next comment. "So girl, I totally understand what you are saying but just don't expect any sympathy at this table. Maybe we both just need a course in how to avoid being over-achieving women and focus on finding a sperm donor."

They stared at each other for a moment and then both

broke out in uncontrollable laughter. Brynn caught her breath first, "Yeah, I am going to add that course to the curriculum I am developing for med students. 'A course for women physicians to learn how to treat bone and joint pain while avoiding over-achievement and ensuring conception." Yvette responded that she would sign up for that course immediately when it was listed.

As they turned to the steaming bowls their waiter had just placed in front of them, Yvette described what she was doing in Moose. "I have a clinic at the hospital and work in the ER and on the wards. And once every two weeks, I take a helicopter or plane up the James Bay coast to one of the smaller communities and do a clinic. Those people along the coast are looked after most of the time by nurses. The nurses say that they work in hospitals in the coastal communities, but they are really just glorified out-patient clinics attached to nursing homes. The nurses are pretty good though." She paused and shook her head.

"Those so-called hospitals provide everything – pharmacy services, nursing, some labs, treatment for about eight thousand people scattered along James Bay. Some of those communities are pretty desperate. Their water supply is shitty and every spring, flooding results in one or more communities having to fuckin' evacuate down south for Chrissakes. You'd think after they evacuated four years in a row the government would help them build some houses away from the riverbank, but they just go back to those same places that stink of mould."

Yvette looked at her friend closely. "Anyway, I shouldn't talk smack about the place. The people are great and appreciate me being there. There is a new administration in Moose that is actually drawn from the local community for the first time ever. Believe it or not, the government used to send up old white guys at the end of their careers to run the hospital and clinics. Those guys hated being there and showed no respect for the people they were supposed to be serving. But things are changin'."

Brynn enjoyed listening to Yvette's passion for her work. At first thought, it might be unexpected that a Vietnamese woman would be dedicated to providing care to Indigenous People. But Brynn knew that Yvette and her mother had always considered themselves as outsiders in Canada, despite both being successful in Canadian society. Brynn could imagine Yvette feeling right at home in Moose.

Brynn smiled, remembering that Yvette would always come to class in Toronto dressed in multiple layers of woolly clothing, complaining bitterly that, "The university needs to pay the heating bills for these fuckin' classrooms. I am freezing." Brynn could not resist asking.

"Yvette how are you tolerating the cold up there?"

Her friend looked at her with disgust. "Shit, it is so cold and damp up there, even in summer for Chrissakes. Whoever decided to live on the shores of James Bay was crazy." Then she smiled back at her friend.

"So, I put on about double my weight in down coats and padded boots up to my knees and people look at me like I'm crazy. And I remind them that I was designed for the fuckin' Mekong Delta, not the Moose River estuary."

"Well, it sounds like you're settling in up there Yvette. What did you want to talk to me about?"

They both took a moment to appreciate the steam rising from their bowls and to sample noodles and savoury chunks of meat with their chop sticks. Yvette sighed with her eyes closed. "Goddamit, that is delicious."

Then she continued. "I need your advice, Brynn. Like I said earlier, there is a new leadership team in Moose at the hospital. Finally, after all the lip service paid to reconciliation in this country, the government has agreed to replace the old rickety hospital and wants to maybe start providing some surgical services including orthopaedic surgery in the new hospital." Yvette lifted a morsel with her chopsticks.

"The admin team asked for my advice about what we need to provide orthopaedics since I am the most recent graduate on staff, but I told them, what the fuck, we need to get a real orthopod to figure this out. So, my question to you, Brynn, do you know anyone who would be willing to spend some time in Moose and figure out how we could offer an orthopaedic program in the new hospital?"

For some reason, all Brynn could think about at that moment was sitting in that big chair in the Chair's office. Her legs would never lengthen to reach the ground in that chair. She would never sit in front of the Chair and expect her boss to see her as a colleague. She knew that he would be replaced as her leader in the next few months, but she also knew that there were plenty of misogynistic old guys eager to take his place.

She looked across the table. "Yeah, Yvette, I may know someone who might be interested in learning more about this."

CHAPTER 12

Risks. August/September 2018

Immediately after he and David had been dismissed by the new CannWeed board appointed by International Brands, Jonah took his friend by the arm and led him directly down the stairs of their building and across the cobblestone street of the Distillery District to High Spirits. He had warned the bar owner that he and David would likely need their private room for the rest of the evening and asked that the room should be stocked with scotch and tapas for their arrival.

Reaching their seats in the reserved room, Jonah's first request was essential to his plan. "Give me your phone, David."

"What the fuck are you talking about Jonah, I need to get my story out there. These fuckers cannot do this to me."

Jonah reached inside David's coat pocket, taking his phone. "David I am your lawyer and for the next few days I am going to protect you from the one person who can do you the most damage." He reached past David to open the bottle of twenty-five-year-old Macallan while switching off the ringer on David's phone. He deposited one cube and three fingers of liquor in the crystal glass that sat on the table between them. "Right now, you are your worst enemy, buddy. You drink this, David, while I make a call or two." The waiter just then stuck his head in the door holding an antipasto plate and Jonah motioned him to put the food on their table.

Jonah buried David's phone in his coat and pivoted away from his companion while making a call on his own cell phone. "Yeah, it's like I thought," he said into his phone, ignoring David's puzzled look. "Get in touch with International Brands comms and work on the statement that we discussed. It will go out before the markets open tomorrow. Let me see it before you approve." Jonah sipped on the sparkling water that the waiter had also placed on their table, then continued providing direction over the phone.

"Let's get our new office opened tomorrow in that space we rented in the district. Yeah, we'll call it "Mindful Innovation". I want two receptionists answering calls and get one of your best crisis comms people in the office, okay? I want every call picked up on the second ring from nine to five. We'll open the office phone line referred to in the press release tomorrow morning and your crisis person will have David's cell phone." Jonah paused, listening, and smiled at David. "Yeah, I've got his phone, I'll drop it off tonight. David is officially off-line for a while but each call to his cell will be answered by your crisis expert as planned. I'll stop by your place to drop off the phone before seven tonight – is that okay?" Jonah nodded, agreed with the party on the line and hung up.

By now David had downed most of the first glass of scotch and was adding a cube and additional liquid. He looked up at his friend. "Jesus, Jonah, were you planning for this? Who the fuck were you talking to?"

With the International Brands/CannWeed deal, David Morton had wound up two hundred million dollars richer. His new wealth had been dependent on Jonah ensuring that David's founder shares in CannWeed were purchased at a substantial premium. Jonah protected his friend's future tax liabilities by negotiating tax advantaged stock options as part of the investment that were approved for tender as soon as the deal closed.

Jonah had also carefully considered David's future. He quietly disagreed with his friend who could see nothing but upside in the Canadian cannabis industry. David was certain that Canadian cannabis legalization would be a lucrative moment in the international expansion of Western society's pot market. He was a true believer when it came to pot's future and was determined to benefit from what he expected would be an imminent gold rush by positioning CannWeed as the worldwide producer of choice for high-quality cannabis.

Although Jonah generally agreed that legal pot use would increase in the future, he was more realistic than David about pots of gold and cannabis rainbows. He did not believe that the legalization of the Canadian pot market (now expected to occur within months) would necessarily be a bonanza for cannabis companies and their shareholders. He was also concerned about CannWeed's potentially uncertain role in International Brands future strategy. He knew that Norman Ridgely was nearly as convinced as David Morton that cannabis infused beverages were going to be a huge growth opportunity for his company. But, at the time of the investment, Jonah recognized that Ridgely's days as CEO of International Brands were likely numbered and that his successor might not be as optimistic about the future of pot drinks.

So in the investment agreement, Jonah protected David against the potential that International Brands might find him expendable. The first layer of protection was a generous cash settlement payable immediately if David Morton was fired in the first two years after the deal. International Brands also agreed in the investment agreement that if David was terminated, the move would be described to the media as mutually agreed upon at the time of the deal and the result of David's desire to move on to new challenges. As well, International Brands committed to covering the costs of establishing a new private company for David with several months' worth of public relations support. This new company would immediately announce David's appointment as CEO when he left CannWeed. And finally, Jonah insisted on David signing an agreement to remain silent about the reasons for his departure except to say that he was delighted to take on new challenges.

Jonah knew that his friend would be both angry and hurt if he were forced to depart from the company he had worked so hard to build. David's emotions would make him prone to explosive media comments that would cast David as angry and petulant. This would destroy the image Jonah hoped to construct allowing David, if let go by International Brands, to claim he had decided to leave CannWeed as soon as the deal was complete.

Now that David's forced departure from CannWeed was a reality, Jonah knew his most important task was to stop his friend from providing intemperate media commentary.

Jonah knew that the generous cash settlement and confidentiality agreement would not be sufficient to keep David quiet. He knew that the first reporter who contacted David would get an earful about International Brands' stupidity and deceit in separating him from the company he founded. Jonah expected that David would slowly settle over time, but for the next two weeks Jonah needed to insulate David from his own worst impulses. Jonah knew that he was about to become his friend's babysitter.

"Buddy," Jonah said to his flushed friend, "you pay me to look out for potential downside and that's what I've been doing. I've had the country's best crisis management firm on retainer for the past few weeks after Dahlin told you he wanted options presented at this board meeting. I figured that he might get rid of us." Jonah leaned forward and put his hands on his friend's forearms.

"David, I know what CannWeed meant to you. But right

now the only thing I care about is getting you through this intact with your reputation untarnished. International's interests are best served by spinning this like it was a planned departure and that's best for you too, David. I know right now that you want to call every media hack you know to blast off on Dahlin and International. But that will make you out to be an angry, vengeful loser who just got fired." Jonah knew that the only thing that counted right now was perception and he had prepared carefully to win the perception battle.

"Tomorrow we have a nice little office opening just down the street in the district as headquarters for a company I have registered as Mindful Innovation. Tomorrow morning Mindful Innovation will announce you as their new CEO and their press release will go out at the same time as Internationals'. Our crisis team will man the office with a couple of receptionists and a senior crisis communicator. I will be overseeing your comms for the next couple of weeks, David. The official word is that you are taking a break for a couple of weeks after stepping away from the incredible company you created through the deal with International Brands. Basically, you are now considering your options to start something new."

David shook his head and lowered his chin onto his chest. Jonah could see the whisky having its effect. "What the fuck am I gonna do Jonah? CannWeed is all I've got and now it's gone." David was too gritty for tears, but Jonah could feel the despair.

"Well, the first thing we are gonna do is get out of here, David. The press will be camped out at your building tomorrow morning after those press releases goes out. We are going to take the scotch and the food and head out the backdoor of this place. I have a car waiting to take us up to Georgian Bay tonight. One of my cousins has a really nice place on Moose Deer Point. He tells me there'll be a fire going, scotch in the bar and steaks in the fridge. His guys will make sure we've got what we need and also ensure no one knows where we are."

"We are gonna drop your phone with our crisis team tonight and then our driver will go up to your condo and get your toothbrush and personal computer and stuff. And then we're off to the lake, buddy." Jonah went to the door of their room and signaled the waiter to get their supplies ready for the car. He could see that the fight was gone in David for the evening, although he knew that keeping him in line for the next few days would be difficult. But he knew the setting they were headed to would help in the transition from CannWeed to Mindful Innovation.

*****

Jonah awoke to the haunting sound of loons calling on the bay. The water was warm from two months of solar baking, and families were preparing to leave after enjoying the brief Canadian summer in the cottages that surrounded the lake. Neighbours were distanced by the half mile of pristine Georgian Bay shoreline his cousin enjoyed. The lake house had every modern convenience with excellent communication connections and Jonah's cousin provided a cook and cleaners from the local community.

Jonah was sitting with his laptop on a deck overlooking the water and was pleased his cousin had not exaggerated the speed of the internet connection. He approved the press releases that International Brands and the new start-up Mindful Innovation were putting out this morning. Jonah had also signed off on the bright new website that the crisis team had developed in the past few weeks for Mindful. The comms team would be posting the press release about David's appointment as CEO on that website at nine-thirty.

Jonah thought briefly about his own situation following his departure from CannWeed. He had received a text to call the human resources leader of his law firm and he knew that he was likely finished as a junior partner at the firm.

CannWeed had been his only client and lawyers without clients did not last long on Bay Street. Jonah shrugged, putting his own plight aside for the moment. He would worry about his future after ensuring that his client and best friend survived the next few days with his reputation intact.

He could hear his friend snoring in the master bedroom. The first bottle of Macallan had barely lasted until their arrival last evening and the second bottle was significantly dented. Jonah knew that he and the crisis team would be alone working social media channels until noon when David would join them. Jonah's plan was to absorb the energy from the story, and he expected that the media would have difficulty spinning it for more than two or three days. Mindful Innovation would simply say that their new CEO was taking a well-deserved break and would be available for media interviews after returning in a few weeks. By then, Jonah needed to ensure that David would be ready for their next step. As he watched the rising sun shimmering in reflection from the bay, Jonah was already considering what that next move might be.

*****

Brynn and Yvette linked up on a videoconference two weeks after their Toronto pho dinner. Dr. Jane Gagne joined them on the video. Jane was a family doctor and the first member of the local community to be appointed CEO of the Wiichihinan Hospital and Health Authority. Brynn immediately appreciated Jane's warmth and enthusiasm as the CEO explained her hospital's plans for the future.

"Brynn thanks for your time. Yvette has told me a lot about you, and I appreciate the chance to explain what we are planning for Wiichihinan Hospital and Health Authority. I hope if you are interested, we might arrange to get your advice about our next steps. If I drop off it's due to the weak signal." She smiled over her shaky internet connection and shook her head. "That's one of the things we need to fix up here." She looked directly at Brynn over the video connection.

"How much do you know about Wiichihinan Health Authority, Brynn?"

Brynn shrugged. "Not much really, Jane. I recently looked after a patient sent down from Wiichihinan after a bad injury up at Port Muskek. He could have lost his leg but everything turned out okay thank goodness. I was impressed by the treatment he received at your hospital."

Jane nodded. "Yeah, that's Samuel Sunderland. He and his nephew Jonah Kataquit are well known up here. Jonah was a great hockey player as a kid and got scholarships to play high school and college hockey. I didn't know you operated on his Uncle Samuel. Maybe his care is a good way for me to explain what we do at Wiichihinan." Brynn gave her the thumbs up to continue.

"Wiichihinan Health Authority grew out of a merger of federal and provincial hospitals and clinics that provided care to our First Nations along James Bay's western coast. The old federal Indian hospital was taken over by the province. It was originally built as a sanatorium and turned into a general hospital when the treatment for TB changed." She looked up at the screen, "Am I freezing up, can you guys hear me? Just nod every once in a while, so I know I haven't been dropped, okay?" Brynn and Yvette gave another thumbs up.

"In addition to the Wiichihinan Hospital, the province took over the small hospitals in a few communities up the coast like Port Muskek. Along with the hospital in Moose, service in those peripheral small hospitals comprises the Wiichihinan Health Authority. Mr. Sunderland's treatment shows how we work. He was taken to the Port Muskek Hospital after his accident. We call them hospitals but the facilities outside Moose are really more like nursing stations with attached nursing homes and one or two beds used for patients about to be transferred to or from Moose or down south. Serious illnesses or injuries like Samuel's get evacuated to Moose and stabilized before going south."

Brynn interrupted. "Like I mentioned, I was impressed by the way your team treated Samuel. First class care."

Dr. Gagne nodded. "Thanks, I'll let them know what you said. Usually, they just hear shit about giving shoddy treatment to Indigenous People. They'll appreciate your comments." Brynn smiled. Jane and Yvette probably shared colourful language discussing hospital issues. Like Yvette, the CEO seemed young for her role. From what Brynn could see on the video, she was dressed much more casually than the suits worn by Toronto hospital executives and wore colourful jewelry that Brynn imagined came from her community.

"Care along the coast is provided by nurses who do an amazing job looking after some pretty complex problems. They can get telephone consults from our docs in Wiichihinan Hospital and the docs visit the communities to do clinics with the nurses once weekly, weather permitting. But ninety-five per cent of care is provided by our nurses." She shrugged.

"I always wonder why we make such a big deal about southern Canadians being unable to get a family doctor. I think we should just start nursing clinics down south as well as up here."

Yvette smirked. "You say that too many times, sister, and the medical associations will put a bomb under your snowmobile." They both smiled. It seemed unfair that southern Canadians in cities with incredible specialist and hospital resources usually had family doctors to look after them. Indigenous People on reserve and Canadians in remote regions were usually cared for by nurses who had no specialist and very limited hospital back-up. Those nurses accepted far more responsibility that the average southern family doctor.

Jane continued. "Yeah, I'll leave the medical politics aside for now, Yvette. Brynn, Wiichihinan Hospital is probably the oldest medical facility in Ontario, if not Canada. It is certainly the only hospital in the province made entirely out of wood. We've been asking for a new building for years. In fairness to the government, part of the problem is getting building materials up here. We just don't have any local supply of cement, and everything has to be brought in by rail from three hundred kilometres away. And that railway track has a history of derailment and closures." She raised her hands.

"But advances in modular construction have finally come to Ontario hospitals. Two or three years from now we will have our new Lego-like buildings bolted together and Wiichihinan will have a new hospital. We are planning to have four operating rooms as part of that new building and that's why I need advice from an orthopod, Brynn. Yvette tells me that you may be the person we need." She looked at Brynn carefully over the link as she continued.

"We need advice on setting up the OR, of course. What equipment is needed and various best practices. But more important is understanding the model of care that we should provide. I believe that planning how we care for people requires the services of someone willing to get out and talk to people in the community. You know that expression, 'Nothing about us without us'? This is our opportunity to demonstrate that we can design service based on what people say they need and want."

Brynn looked at the CEO with interest. Throughout her career she had simply 'fit in' to pre-existing care models, accepting their flaws as part of the way things were. The idea of designing a new way to provide orthopaedic care was fascinating.

Jane checked, "I'm not frozen, right, you guys can hear me?" Yvette and Brynn nodded. "The connection is good today. Brynn you are bringing us wifi luck." She smiled. "So, anyway, as you experienced with Mr. Sunderland, we have lots of industrial accidents and trauma along the coastal communities. We have mining, forestry, and lots of hunting and fishing that guarantees we see orthopaedic injuries that currently get transferred down south after stabilization in Moose. But transportation is always an issue. Bad weather usually increases the risk of trauma and sometimes we end up holding on to people waiting for transport who would be much better being immediately treated in Wiichihinan Hospital rather than going down south. However, at present we cannot recruit orthopods to operate here."

She shook her head as she continued. "Our current approach to send everyone who needs surgery down south does not work for some of our Elders either. When they develop arthritis or other problems requiring reconstructive surgery, they need to travel to Moose and then fly out to Toronto or another southern city for surgery. Many of them are not comfortable speaking English and a trip south can be very intimidating."

Yvette broke in. "Brynn you would not believe the number of Elders along the coast and in Moose who are disabled by severe arthritis but unwilling to travel south for joint replacement. I bet I see two or three patients every clinic who would benefit from you operating on them who are reluctant to go to St. Barts."

Brynn nodded. "I think I'm understanding what you are looking for, Jane. It's kind of a two-fer, huh? What services could be safely provided in the new Wiichihinan Hospital and how do we get orthopods interested in providing those services closer to the patient's home. Have I got it right?" She looked at the screen and saw both Jane and Yvette nodding. And then they both froze mid-nod and the connection failed.

*****

David had spent five profanity-laced days on his computer, doom scrolling through the social media discussing his departure from CannWeed. Jonah checked frequently to ensure that he was not uploading commentary to any of his platforms. After three days of extensive coverage and wild speculation about David's departure from CannWeed and his future, Jonah's strategy of keeping David out of the story had proven successful in deflating the media balloon. But Jonah also recognized that his friend needed a new project to start working on immediately to avoid the waste of his various talents and avoid future intemperate outbursts.

The two men wore sunglasses to protect them from the brilliant, early morning summer sun as they dug into a generous breakfast of scrambled eggs, baked beans, sausages, and thick cut toast that the house cook had prepared. They were sitting side by side on what had become Jonah's favourite deck overlooking the bay as the lawyer started sounding out his friend as to next steps.

"David, I figure with the money from the purchase of your founder's shares, the stock options and now the settlement from your departure, you must have put away more than two hundred and fifty million Canadian from this deal, huh?"

David nodded. Nothing focused his mind more than discussing money. His family had been engaged in the financial industry in Toronto for years and the discussion of accumulated wealth was second nature to him.

Jonah continued. "I know that you think legalization of cannabis is going to be a make it or break moment, David. I understand that part of your anger about your departure from CannWeed is that you won't continue to lead that expansion of the cannabis market that you started and have been planning."

Three days ago, these comments would have provoked an angry tirade. David now just sadly nodded. "You know I've been planning for legalization for the past four years, Jonah. Nobody knows that better than you. It's not just about the money. It would be the satisfaction of building a Canadian company to be an international leader in a brand-new industry. We both worked so hard for that opportunity and now it's just vaporized."

"Yeah, I know you're a patriot at heart." Jonah smiled at his friend. "But David, let's look at this in a more dispassionate way, like an outside investor might assess this moment in time."

David leaned forward with interest. Jonah could sense his resentment was ready for replacement by new thinking. "Okay, dispassionate investor, tell me more."

Jonah pushed his breakfast plate away and leaned back in the rustic wooden deck chair, turning his head to his friend sitting beside him. "David, realistically I think that the federal government will legalize sales across the country sometime in October. That's only six to eight weeks away. And, in the usual Canadian disorganized shit-show, the feds will control whether selling pot is legal, but the provinces are going to be responsible for establishing how you buy it. And in our largest province with the biggest potential market, the Ontario government has decided that their bureaucrats will control sales by running wholesale distribution and limiting the number of licences given to private retailers."

David finished his breakfast plate and pushed his sunglasses up on his forehead to see his friend better. "Look Jonah, I know the government has totally fucked this up like they usually do when they try to micro-manage what should be a free market. But very soon everyone will be going to their local cannabis store instead of finding the dealer in the back alley."

Jonah's eyebrows lifted. "C'mon David, you and I both know that the days of back-alley pot dealers are long gone. After decriminalization the cops stopped chasing dealers for small amounts of weed. Those guys come in through the front door now and you know how entrepreneurial and service-oriented they are. They provide great product, they price fairly, and they serve their customers extremely well. It's gonna be a few years before government licenced stores can compete."

David sipped from his coffee mug, enjoying the peace while gazing over the smooth, luminous water. Early morning on Georgian Bay was usually accompanied by still water before westerly winds rippled the lake in the afternoon. "Jonah, we've been over this. The right approach is to cultivate the best cannabis, using all the genetic innovation we were developing at CannWeed. And create the new products, the edibles and drinks, that will be the future of the new cannabis market. Local dealers won't be able to compete with the new products and quality that CannWeed will bring to the market. That was what the International Brands deal was all about. And now that dream is gone." David uttered those last words without much emotion. Two days ago, the words would have been accompanied by a fist pounding the table, but now his gaze remained fixed on the bay with his hands wrapped around his coffee mug.

Jonah put up his hand in disagreement. "For the next few years, the market is going to be predominantly smoked product, David. Those new products and better weed are at least two years away. I totally agree with your long-term view of where pot is going. After all, the need for patience and a changing retail market is what we sold to International Brands. But that's not how the stock market is responding right now."

David's family was well known around Toronto financial markets, sometimes for the wrong reasons. David's dad had a well-deserved reputation for operating at the shady margins of Canada's securities industry, often associated with raising money for penny mining, oil drilling or early technology stocks. From his family's business, David had first-hand knowledge of how investors' naïve hopes and greed could move stock prices unrealistically higher, only to see the price eventually plummet.

In the years that he had lived with the Morton family, Jonah had learned about the vagaries of capital markets and how fortunes could be made or lost based on strong beliefs that might be entirely right or wrong. In his years as a corporate lawyer raising money and buying and selling stakes in cannabis companies for CannWeed, Jonah had also become knowledgeable about various methods for investing and speculating in corporate stocks.

"How are you reading the market, Jonah? What are you

seeing that I'm missing?"

"Well, the International Brands investment gave a huge boost to CannWeed's stock price and that price has not returned to a realistic value. Based on its current sales and cash flow, CannWeed stock is very overpriced. Even though the press described the International/CannWeed deal as a "merger", you know we structured the deal as an investment by International Brands in our company. CannWeed remains an independent company as far as its stock is concerned, even though the board that selects and directs CannWeed management is now controlled by International Brands."

David threw up his hands in mild exasperation. "Jonah, obviously I know all this. Get to the point."

Jonah smiled at his friend's impatience. "Stay with me, David. International Brands investing in CannWeed at the price we achieved is important because that investment suggested to the market that International is betting on CannWeed's revenues increasing very, very soon. We know the smart, professional investor money got into CannWeed two to three years ago. Now, I'm thinking it's the dumb retail investors – the doctors and the dentists who buy the stocks that are discussed in the media – that are keeping the stock floating at a crazy price level based on what International paid for its investment. Current prices could only be justified by increased cash flow that you and I know will not occur for at least three years – maybe ten years."

Jonah could see his friend nodding. "Yeah, if International was investing based on CannWeed's immediate earnings, they would have paid no more than four hundred million – maybe less. Jonah, you and I know why they doubled their bid to get long-term control of the company. That made sense at the time. But you think retail investors may be thinking that International is expecting a big bump in earnings from legalization, huh?"

David continued. "We figured the stock price would drop for a year or two while cash flow caught up with our expectations, Jonah. That's why we needed the International Brands investment in our war chest to allow development of more and better pot and better products no matter what happened to the stock price. But people who don't know the cannabis market might be thinking cash flow will increase as soon as marijuana retail sales are legalized."

Jonah shrugged. "I think that today's high stock price is absolutely unrealistic. But it offers a great opportunity for big time shorting of the entire industry – all the Canadian cannabis producers – when or just before legalization occurs. Suddenly the dumb money is gonna see that the cannabis emperor's clothes are pretty shabby and sooner or later there's gonna be a rush for the exits. And CannWeed, as the market leader, with by far the highest stock valuation, is at big risk for short sellers tearing it to pieces."

David turned in the deck chair so he was fully facing Jonah. "You're not suggesting we go short on CannWeed, are you Jonah? Aren't we still insiders, despite our departure from the company? If we're insiders, we can't sell CannWeed short, can we?"

Jonah shook his head. "I'm not suggesting selling CannWeed shares short David. Despite your recent financial gains, you don't have the wealth that the big short sellers need to wait out a potential short squeeze. It's just too tough to judge exactly when the market will turn. Selling short would be too risky for you." Jonah paused.

"David, I expect that CannWeed's share price is gonna drop sometime around when weed is legalized. A classic short sale would mean selling borrowed stock we do not own at a high price today before legalization and then actually buying stock to return to the dealers we borrowed it from to sell after the price falls following legalization." Jonah held up his hands, showing that was not the course he was recommending.

"I would not want you to experience the pressure of selling the stock short before legalization and then seeing the stock price unexpectedly rise for several months. We've both seen that happen, when short sellers mistime the market and the stock price rises rather than plummeting. Eventually the short sellers have to accept their losses and buy the stock back at a much higher price that they initially sold it for. That's the classic short squeeze that can cost the short seller a huge amount of money." He looked at his friend and was pleased to see that David was fully concentrating on the topic at hand. This was the most engaged he'd seemed since they arrived at the lake.

"As for as being insiders, we would not have to register any trades we make since we are no longer officers or managers of the company. I took care to ensure that we would not have any restrictions on our market activity after leaving the company. And we would not be benefitting from any insider information. Any information to determine a trading strategy for CannWeed is available in public reporting. It's what we do with that information that may be interesting."

"What are you suggesting?" David was clearly intrigued by Jonah's reasoning.

"Well, I think there's a much safer way for you to bet on CannWeed stock falling around the time of legalization. You know there is a very active market in CannWeed futures on the Montreal derivative exchange. Right now, sixty-day put options are selling for about a hundred bucks a contract. That's only about a dollar a share. You know how these put options work, right, David?"

David shrugged. "Yeah but explain your thinking."

Jonah pushed his sunglasses onto his forehead and turned toward his friend. "Let's say the stock is currently selling for fifty bucks a share on the stock market and you buy a sixty-day put option. Then that gives you the right to sell that share of CannWeed for fifty dollars any time in the next sixty days. The seller of the put option is obliged to buy it from you for fifty bucks anytime in those sixty days."

Jonah lifted his hands to emphasize his next comment. "If the stock price then falls on the stock exchange before your option expires, then you can buy the stock at the lower price and sell it to the option seller for the higher value. So if you buy a sixty-day put option for a buck a share at a stock price of fifty and the price falls to forty before expiry, your option is worth the ten-dollar difference between fifty and forty – minus the one dollar you paid to buy the option. The seller of the put has to give you nine dollars for the option you bought for one dollar. You get nine dollars for investing one dollar. David, that's a nine hundred per cent gain."

Jonah could see David's interest and continued. "And the good thing about using options rather than selling the stock short is that if the stock price does not fall or increases, you simply lose the dollar you paid for the put option. You've seen people get badly damaged if they sell a stock short and they are wrong about when the stock will fall – and instead of falling – the price increases. In that situation, the short seller has to ante up and pay the higher price to cover their short position. That can be hugely expensive and risky. Using put options is much less risky if you think a price is going to fall. And provides pretty much the same upside opportunity."

Jonah leaned forward in his deck chair. "David, what if your new company, Mindful Innovation, quietly purchased ten million dollars of put options? We could spread the purchase through a few brokers to keep individual positions small and quiet. That could be a very lucrative way for you to benefit from our understanding of what's likely to happen to the cannabis market."

David rubbed the side of his face thoughtfully. "Okay, I get it – if we buy a put option on one share for one dollar and then the share price drops ten dollars below the price of the share when we bought the option – before the date when the option expires – then our option is suddenly worth nine dollars, right? The ten dollar drop minus the dollar we paid for the option? One dollar paid for an option turns into nine dollars. Ten million paid for put options turns into ninety million. That's a pretty good multiple, Jonah." He looked out over the bay and then rotated in his chair again to stare at his friend.

"How strongly do you feel about this Jonah? Are you willing to put your own money into it?"

Jonah frowned. "David, I just got fired too, first by CannWeed and then by my firm. Lawyers without clients don't last long – in my case, the firm fired me within two days." Jonah shook his head and smiled wistfully.

"So, I'm out of a job. And I was expecting a big bonus at year end this year from the fees my firm got from closing the International Brands investment, but that bonus went up in smoke when we both got fired. Unlike you, I did not get a settlement. I suppose that I could sue my old firm for the bonus but doing that would make me unemployable in most Toronto legal firms." He sighed. "Pretty soon, David, I need to start looking for a new job. I want to get you through this departure from CannWeed and on to your next adventure. But when you are up and going, I need to think about what I'm going to do next."

Jonah shook his head, looking out over the bay. "My friend, I think that buying ten or twenty million dollars of put options as a safe way to bet against today's CannWeed share price would be a really good move for a guy with several hundred million new dollars in his pocket. The worst thing that can happen is that the put options end up worthless because CannWeed's stock price does not fall before the options expire and you lose the money you paid for the options. In my opinion, that's a good bet for you David – but not a good move for an unemployed lawyer."

David was squinting in the morning brightness and pushed his sunglasses down over his eyes. "How much do you think your bonus would have been, Jonah?"

Jonah shrugged. "About one and a half mil, I figure."

"Well buddy, you have made me about two hundred and fifty million dollars over the past few months. I figure I can bankroll you with a bit of that. If I give you five million, straight out, not a loan, but a gift to show my appreciation for what you've done for me, will you join me using put options to short CannWeed?"

David smiled. "After all, my friend, you are asking me to put some of my newfound wealth at risk in the derivative market. Maybe if you also have some new wealth, you can jump in with me. You know I'll feel less anxious if my best friend's swimmin' in the shark tank with me."

CHAPTER 13

James Bay. November 2018

After her videoconference with Dr. Jane Gagne and Yvette was cut short, Brynn thought hard and realized that she needed a change. She decided that she would try to get a sabbatical from the university and St. Barts to go and work in Moose for four months. She couldn't stand the thought of another conversation with her university Chair to request time away. And she worried that the head of surgery at Barts would simply demand that she should permanently give up her hospital appointment if she was going away for four months. Having worked so hard to get her current position, Brynn was unwilling to give it up for a four-month consulting position in Moose.

She decided to discuss the issue with Keshini Jayawardana, the new St. Barts Hospital CEO, and Brynn was pleased her request for an appointment with her hospital boss was immediately granted. Brynn had not yet met the new leader who had recently been recruited to the hospital from the City of Toronto's management team. St. Barts had a history of budget problems and the hospital board had decided to appoint a leader who could balance a budget. The new CEO had a reputation from her time at the city as a tough administrator who never allowed a deficit.

As the two women sat in the CEO's office, Jayawardana surprised Brynn with her opening comment. "Wow, it's nice to meet a woman surgeon working at St. Barts. Most of the surgeons I've met so far have been guys."

Brynn smiled. After her recent experience with her Chair, it was a welcome change to hear someone in leadership mention her gender in a positive way. She explained that she was hoping to take a sabbatical to spend time at Wiichihinan Hospital in Moose helping to develop an orthopaedic program for James Bay.

The CEO frowned. It was not what she was expecting from her first meeting with Brynn. "I checked up on you when you asked for this appointment and learned that you are one of our best surgeons, teachers and scientists, Dr. Allard. Going up to Moose would be quite a switch for you, huh?"

Brynn explained her interest with the idea of designing a new orthopaedic service for people living on the James Bay coast and described the Wiichihinan Health Authority hub and spoke model of the central hospital with clinics in smaller communities.

Keshini nodded. "Thanks for explaining, Brynn – I am obviously new to healthcare. I guess that figuring out how we provide better health services to Indigenous People is a challenge that all Canadians should support. You know, I learned from my days at the city that we have a large population of people identifying as Indigenous right here in Toronto. St. Barts needs to up our game at addressing the needs of that community and, to be honest, I have no idea how to go about it. I have heard a lot about culturally sensitive care, but I am not sure exactly what that means practically. Do you think you would be able to teach us something after this sabbatical?"

Brynn was delighted to have her CEO's support and spent

the next two months transferring patients to her colleagues and preparing her laboratory for remote leadership during her sabbatical. Her flight to Moose required a connection in Timmins. As Brynn flew north, she could see fall turning to winter in the progressively undeveloped landscape.

Brynn was not expecting much from the accommodation provided by the hospital. The one-bedroom apartment was small and sparsely furnished but had the advantage of being close to the hospital which Brynn appreciated in expectation of cold winter mornings. The spartan living quarters were more than compensated for by the warm welcome provided by Yvette, Dr. Jane Gagne, and other members of the hospital staff as Brynn settled in to learn about how orthopaedic services could be offered in James Bay.

The need for those services became apparent as Brynn started her clinic in the hospital. She began seeing patients from Moose shortly after her brief orientation ended, using offices in the family practice clinic where Yvette and her colleagues practiced. St. Barts in Toronto was an older urban hospital and most of its clinic facilities needed updating. However, the Wiichihinan clinics made St. Barts look like an elegant executive health centre.

Paint was peeling, insulation was stuffed in corners of windows to arrest the winter winds and the thin partitions between examination rooms seemed to amplify conversations across the clinic making doctor-patient confidentiality an abstract notion. The waiting room for patients scheduled to see Brynn was constantly crammed which she understood when she discovered that patients were not given specific times for their visits. They were given "morning appointments" with patients starting to line up before eight a.m. for a clinic starting at nine o'clock or "afternoon appointments" that were also scheduled on a first-come, first-served basis.

During her first week in Wiichihinan Brynn identified more than fifteen patients who would benefit from hip or knee joint replacement, back operations, or a variety of other orthopaedic surgeries. Many of these patients were older and were often uncomfortable speaking English. Their families had brought these Elders into the clinic hoping that they could convince the new surgeon to operate on their family members here in Moose because the Elder refused to consider going to Timmins, Toronto or other southern centres for surgery.

Dr. Jane Gagne dropped into Brynn's clinic at the end of her first week in Moose as Brynn was seeing her last patients on Friday afternoon. "Wow, I'm hearing lots about you, girl. Everyone in the town is talking about the new bone doctor and how nice she is."

Brynn smiled. "I don't think I have ever heard as many 'thank yous' as I've heard in the past few days! People are really grateful that a specialist is seeing them here without them flying down south."

Jane was nodding. "I've already heard from lots of people that they want you to start operating here. What do you think? Are there enough people needing surgery to justify having a surgeon at Wiichihinan?"

Brynn shrugged. "Jane there are so many people I've met in the past few days who would definitely benefit from surgery. I don't know if that's just because there is a huge backlog. But if you had an OR available, you could definitely keep a surgeon busy for a month just with patients I've seen here this week."

The hospital CEO was clearly interested. "Have you seen our current OR facilities, Brynn? Is there any way we could start a program before the new hospital is built? I understand the provincial government is eager to announce delivering some new programs here. I think they believe that the feds will offer offsetting money if we can start providing new services."

Brynn smiled. "I haven't checked out the ORs yet. Should we wander up there right now?"

The two women walked out of the clinic and took the stairs up to the second floor where the operating room facility was located. The OR was originally designed for TB surgery and had been mothballed for several years but the lights were still working. There were three large surgical rooms and Brynn whistled as she entered the first surgical suite.

"Well Jane, this room is plenty big enough to do any surgery." She flipped on the OR lights over the OR table. "The surgical lights are old, but they are still working and they'd be okay." She looked at the ceiling vents.

"The big issue would be to determine whether there is sufficient ventilation for safe surgery. To reduce the risk of surgical infection, you need at least fifteen to twenty air exchanges per hour in an OR suite. That's especially important in orthopaedics because developing a bone infection from unclean air is just devastating."

Jane looked over with interest as Brynn examined the ceiling air vents. "I've heard that the air ventilation is pretty good because the hospital was originally designed for TB patients. I guess that we can check with the engineer to find out for sure."

Brynn walked back to the supply rooms that stored surgical equipment and supplies. "Wow, Jane, you have a ton of stuff back here. These anaesthesia machines are not too old and look, you have a complete set of surgical sutures." Brynn lifted one of the suture packets out of its tray and examined the text on the package.

"Well, that's surprising. The sutures are still within their expiry date." She looked over at Jane. "You must have been exchanging stock as it approached its end date."

The CEO was nodding. "Yeah, we get funded to keep the equipment stocked even though it's not being used. Apparently, when the federal and provincial governments agreed on funding for the province to take over the hospital, one of the conditions they insisted on was that all equipment needed to be kept updated. So, we have ORs that are stocked and ready. All we really need are surgeons. We have general practice anaesthetists who can put patients to sleep, and we make sure that we have some nurses maintaining OR skills by taking annual courses. But no surgeons have operated here for several years." Jane paused and shook her head.

"But I'm going on and on and you're just starting your stay here. Most important, Brynn, welcome to Wiichihinan! It's great to have you here. I'm planning a dinner to welcome you tomorrow evening and have invited Yvette and a couple of the other docs over. What do you think? Can you find time in your crowded social calendar for a welcoming feast on Saturday evening?"

Brynn gladly accepted the invitation and Jane continued. "We are expecting our first snowfall of the year starting tonight and it's supposed to continue tomorrow. It's not far to my place but I'll make sure that we pick you up. I don't want our new bone doctor getting lost in a blizzard."

Brynn walked from the hospital to her apartment through the promised snow that was just starting. Within an hour visibility was diminished and by morning more than thirty centimetres of fluffy powder had fallen. Pursuing her morning run with some difficulty in the uncleared streets, Brynn could hear and see snowmobile riders taking advantage of the first snow of the season. Brynn spent all day Saturday on videoconference with her lab staff in Toronto, reviewing their recent results and planning further work, new publications and grant applications. As usual, she was utterly absorbed by her discussion with her lab team. As she finished the team meeting and started to get ready for Dr. Jane's dinner party, she looked outside for the first time in hours and saw the winter storm intensifying with white-out conditions limiting visibility to a matter of feet. The ground was covered with over four feet of fresh snow that the snow plow teams were working hard to clear from the streets.

Yvette called her shortly thereafter, "Jesus Brynn, I hate driving in this winter stuff. They're just starting to clear the roads. Jane asked me to drive you to her place, but would you mind walking? It's only about a fifteen-minute walk and I just don't want to drive in this blizzard."

Brynn readily agreed and the two trundled out through very snowy streets bundled like mummies and leaning against the wind. It took twenty minutes to arrive at Jane's home where several trucks and four-wheel drive vehicles were parked. Jane lived in a beautiful site overlooking the Moose River, but this was not the night to appreciate her view. Yvette and Brynn walked into her vestibule, stomping snow off coats and boots, joining five other guests who had arrived before them.

Jane gave them both hugs and then admonished Yvette. "Yvette, for cryin' out loud, you didn't make our guest of honour walk, did you?"

Yvette was in the midst of removing several layers of down clothing. Brynn smiled at her host. "Not to worry, we were safer walking than we would have been with Yvette behind the wheel. I know it's dangerous to drive with Yvette on a sunny day in Toronto in June. I was delighted when she suggested that we walk. It smells pretty good in here Jane. I worked up an appetite walking through those snow drifts."

Jane was starting to introduce Brynn to her other guests when her cell phone rang. Excusing herself, she left the group to answer her phone but then immediately returned to the room.

"We've got patients from a multi-vehicle snowmobile accident at the hospital. Susan is on in the ER and tells me that one of the patients has a nasty knee injury. It's actually the Chief's oldest son. Brynn, I hate to ask just before we are about to sit down and feed you. But if we drive you over to the ER, could you have a look at him? We'll keep your dinner warm, and we'll bring you back as soon as you assess the kid. Is that okay? I know that I'm asking a lot."

Brynn shrugged. "Well, this is a big part of what I'm here to figure out, right? What's the best way to manage trauma at Wiichihinan? I am happy to go back to the ER and fortunately haven't had anything to drink yet. Only one request though – I don't mind going back but I don't want to walk and really do not want Yvette to drive me." She looked at the guests she had yet to meet. "Could one of you with a truck take me over and bring me back? I am worried that if Yvette drives, we may end up in the river."

One of the guests smiled as he responded. "Brynn, my name's Andy. I practice with Yvette and do a little anaesthesia on the side. Most important, I have an F-150 just outside. Not to criticize Yvette, but if we wait for her to reapply all those layers she just removed, it'll be springtime."

Brynn and Andy went out into the blizzard while Yvette protested that she needed special consideration to live on the James Bay coast. Andy's truck made short work of the snow drifts returning to the hospital. Entering the ER, Andy went to help assess the injured drivers from the snowmobile pileup. Most seemed stable but one young man was moaning loudly holding his knee.

Brynn had previously met Susan the ER doc while working in the clinic. She had been working at Wiichihinan since her graduation from a southern medical school six years ago. She took Brynn over to the computer where the patient's x-ray was displayed.

"Brynn thanks so much for coming. I just had a look at the x-ray. I thought the knee was dislocated when I examined him. He has a big abrasion over the front of his upper tibia where he hit something travelling at high speed on his snow machine. I think that blow likely dislocated his knee joint. He's the Chief's son, they're both pretty good guys. I'm really glad you are here to look at him."

Brynn examined the x-ray. "Yeah, you are absolutely right Susan. Whatever hit the front of his shin bone dislocated the tibia behind the end of the femur. Have you checked his pulses?"

Susan slapped her forehead and moaned. "Shit, I forgot. That's a classic, right? Dislocated knee results in the tibia slamming back and damaging the artery behind the knee."

Brynn nodded. "Yeah, let's check him out." Brynn

introduced herself to the young man who, despite being in considerable pain, politely thanked her for coming. Brynn took scissors from the nurse, checking her nametag and explaining her concern. "Thanks Suzanne. The x-ray shows a knee dislocation, and that injury can be complicated by a vascular injury that reduces blood flow to the foot." She divided the patient's pant leg and then cut his sock off to reduce moving the leg around. They could see his knee was massively swollen and Brynn also noted that his foot was blanched white and cold. Feeling for his pulses in the foot, she looked at Suzanne. "Do we have a Doppler in the department?" Suzanne nodded and went to get the instrument that allows for sensitive detection of pulses. Just then a large man entered the department shaking snow from his coat and hat and came over to the stretcher.

"Doctor, my name is Arnold Checkwing. You've probably heard that I'm the Chief of the Moose First Nation. Thanks so much for being here. You've probably already met my son James. How's he doing?"

Just then Suzanne returned with the Doppler and handed it to Brynn. "Nice to meet you Chief," said Brynn, nodding her thanks at Suzanne. "James has a serious knee injury – a dislocation of the knee. That's very fixable and will probably require eventual treatment by a knee ligament surgeon in Toronto, but what I am really worried about now is that the dislocation may have damaged the artery behind his knee." After applying ultrasound gel to the skin of James' foot, she placed the Doppler on the top of the foot and moved the device around, listening for the audible sounds of an intact blood supply. Hearing nothing, she moved the monitor to her own wrist, checking that the device was functioning. Her wrist artery demonstrated a reassuring "whoosh-whoosh" of normal pulsatile blood flow. But James' foot was silent.

Brynn stepped back, returning the Doppler to Suzanne, then looked at the Chief and James. "Gentlemen, this can be serious. We need to get that blood supply restored quickly or your foot and leg can get into real trouble."

Both James and his father's faces turned as white as his foot. "Jeez, Doc, what are you gonna do for him?" Arnold asked.

Brynn was nodding. "Well Chief, if we were in St. Barts in Toronto where I normally look after trauma patients this would be straightforward. I would just take James up to the OR, anaesthetize him, pull the knee back into position, and check his pulse again. If the pulse didn't return, I would get one of my vascular surgery colleagues to repair the damaged vessel with a vein graft from the other leg. In terms of how we should manage James's injury here, to be honest, I only arrived in Moose this week. Part of my job is to provide Dr. Jane Gagne with advice about how we should organize better management of this type of injury."

Brynn's driver Andy had come over to James' stretcher and was listening intently. "Brynn, I can anaesthetize James so you can reduce the dislocation. If that restores the blood flow, we can fly him south tonight for knee repair with a good pulse present. And if pulling the knee back doesn't restore his pulse, we can probably get him to Toronto by medevac within about four hours and have them fix the dislocation and the artery."

Suzanne the nurse had been standing quietly, watching Brynn intently. She now motioned to the surgeon. "Can I speak to you for a moment?"

Brynn excused herself and put her head down with Suzanne. "What's up?"

"We just heard from the airport that all flights are grounded due to weather. Wind and snow conditions will likely cancel all flights until noon tomorrow." Brynn stared at the nurse silently processing her next steps. She turned back to the Chief and his son.

"Okay guys, I just learned that the airport's closed, so we need to figure out the best way to manage this here. Chief Checkwing, James – give me a minute to think through how we are gonna fix this."

She put her arms around Suzanne and Andy and led them

to the side of the ER away from James and his father.

"Andy, you can put him to sleep right? He seems like a healthy guy part from this injury." Andy nodded. Brynn looked at Suzanne.

"I heard from Dr. Jane Gagne that some of the nurses here were taking OR courses so that they can help in the OR if needed. Do you know where we can find one of those nurses?"

Suzanne nodded. "Actually, I've taken the course. We'll call to get someone to come in and take my place in the ER and I can help out in the OR if needed."

"Okay, great. Let's think about what we do if James' pulse does not come back after we pull his knee back into place." She turned to Andy. "If I need to open the artery, you can provide a bolus of heparin, right?" The anaesthetist nodded. He knew that heparin would be used as a blood thinner to reduce further clotting in the artery damaged by the dislocation.

Brynn looked at Suzanne. "Do we have 6-0 prolene suture to repair the artery if I need to open it? Or, God forbid, if I need to do a vein graft to the artery?" Suzanne nodded. "Yeah, we've kept all our suture material up to date."

"How about a Fogarty catheter to remove blood clot from the injured vessel?" Suzanne shook her head.

"I don't think we ever had any vascular surgeons here. I have never seen a Fogarty in our supplies upstairs."

Brynn thought hard. "What about a paediatric Foley catheter you would usually use to drain a baby's bladder?" Suzanne nodded.

"Yeah, I know we have a variety of sizes of Foleys and some really narrow diameters. You think you could use that like a Fogarty?"

Brynn was nodding. "Yeah, I hope we don't need it and that the pulse returns after we pull the knee back into place. But if I need to do vascular surgery tonight, we could use a small Foley to pull clot out of the vessel." She turned and walked back to the stretcher to address the Chief and his son.

"Gentlemen, here's the situation. You need to understand

that I'm an orthopaedic surgeon and very well-qualified and experienced in putting your knee back in place. However, I am not qualified as a vascular surgeon – that's a specialist who fixes injured arteries. If a medevac were available tonight, I would pull your knee back into place and send James to St. Barts in Toronto to be treated by a vascular surgeon." She paused to ensure they were following her.

"However, we don't have that transportation option available tonight. It looks like it's me and only me to look after you for the next sixteen hours. And we cannot leave your leg like this waiting for the airport to open. If we leave your leg that long with no blood flow to the foot, you will lose your leg." Brynn hated to be this dramatic, but it was important that James and his father understood what she was about to suggest.

"If you agree, I'll take you up to the OR with Dr. Andy here, he will put you to sleep and I'll pull your knee back into the normal location so it's no longer dislocated. Hopefully pulling the knee back to its normal position will alleviate pressure on the artery and restore your blood flow to the foot."

The Chief was nodding. "And what happens if the blood flow is not fixed when you pull the knee back, Doc?"

Brynn shrugged her shoulders. "Well, in that case, I will do my best to be an excellent vascular surgeon. Guys, I have done a lot of trauma surgery at St. Barts and frequently work with the vascular team. Given the airport situation, that's likely our best bet."

James had been quiet to now. It was obvious that he was in pain. "What would you do if you were me, Doc?" Brynn picked up his hand.

"Well, James, I think that I would trust me to do the best by you."

James looked at his father and then they both nodded. The Chief spoke first. "Jeez Doc, I am glad you are here. This is a lot of pressure on you I guess." He nodded his head and grasped Brynn's hands. "Well, you sure seem to know what you are doing, Doc. Thanks for helping my boy."

Thirty minutes later Andy, Suzanne and Brynn were in the OR on the second floor with James. Suzanne and Brynn had selected various instruments that were being sterilized in the OR autoclave while Andy was setting up his anaesthesia machine.

Just as Andy was placing the mask over James' face to provide him with extra oxygen prior putting him to sleep, there was a knock on the OR door and CEO Jane, Yvette and the other doctors from Jane's dinner announced their arrival, Jane sticking her head in the door. "Shit, Brynn, we called over to see where you were and learned that you're restarting our OR program single-handed. Are you okay, can we help?"

Brynn looked up from the OR table where she was checking instruments that had already been sterilized with Suzanne. "Yeah, absolutely we need your help. We are going to pull this dislocated knee back into place. If that does not restore the blood flow to the foot, Yvette needs to get on some OR scrubs and help me explore the artery."

Yvette clucked her tongue. "The only thing I like less than driving in snow is assisting in the OR. Shit. But yeah, okay, master surgeon, if you want me to assist, I'll scrub." Yvette left to change into a scrub suit.

Brynn felt like she was truly on display. "No pressure at all, here. I got the hospital CEO watching my every move in the OR and the Chief down in the ER waiting to hear whether we can save his son's leg. If this doesn't work out my stay in Moose may be very short."

She looked over at Jane, shaking her head. "This wasn't what I expected from our consultation, Jane. But since you are all here, put on some scrubs. If I need to open his leg, I'm going to need your help holding both legs while I prep and drape. I may need to harvest a vein graft from his good leg so we'll need to include both legs in the sterile field."

Andy was finished injecting the anaesthetic agent that would put James to sleep and allow Brynn to pull the leg back into place. "Okay Brynn, he should be relaxed. You can start."

Brynn stood beside James lying on the OR table, put her hands behind his calf and pulled forward on the top of his shin bone just below the knee. She sighed audibly when the tibia readily pulled forward, clicking into place and eliminating the knee dislocation.

"Well, that was pretty easy. Suzanne, let's check his pulses." Brynn put her hand on the top of James foot. "Oh shit, I still can't feel a pulse. Let's try the Doppler." Again, the Doppler demonstrated a loud "Whoosh, Whoosh" when applied to Brynn's wrist but was silent on examination of James foot.

Brynn looked at Andy. "How's he doing?" The anesthetist shrugged. "He's fine. You're gonna need to explore that vessel, huh?"

Brynn nodded in response. "Yeah." Looking at Andy and Suzanne, Brynn continued. "The dislocation damaged the main artery behind the knee and unfortunately pulling the dislocated tibia back to its normal position has not restored blood flow to the leg and foot. There's probably bad bruising and clot inside that damaged artery blocking blood flow. If we do nothing he will lose the leg. However, if we can identify the area where the artery has been injured and restore the blood flow, he should do fine."

Yvette, Jane, and the rest of the Wiichihinan team were just entering the room dressed in OR scrubs. Brynn turned to them. "Yvette I'm gonna teach you some vascular surgery. You come with me to scrub."

Yvette moaned. "I just did my nails for the dinner tonight, Brynn. You are ruining my weekend."

Brynn smiled at her friend's mock protest, knowing Yvette was trying to keep the atmosphere as light as possible. She turned to the CEO and the rest of her dinner guests. "Jane, you guys stay here and get ready to hold both legs. I am going to have to prep and drape both legs in case we need a vein graft from the good leg." She couldn't resist an ironic smile behind her mask. "Jane, you wanted to know whether we could do major surgery in your OR? Well, we are about to find out."

Forty minutes later both of James' lower thighs, knees and legs were prepped with iodine solution to sterilize the skin and covered with sterile paper drapes. Brynn also sterilized the skin of the injured leg's entire foot to allow assessment of the foot pulses during surgery. Yvette was nervously holding a metal retractor while Brynn worked deep in the muscles on the inner side of James' calf and thigh. "Shit, Brynn, I don't know how you do this for a living. I guess working on the leg is better than operating in the belly on guts and stuff, but this is just so gross."

Brynn was lost in her surgical universe, hearing Yvette and able to chuckle but fully concentrating on moving the calf muscles aside to identify the artery positioned behind the knee that had been damaged by the dislocation. Without taking her eyes off the wound, she released the calf muscle from its attachment to the bone, allowing her to softly slide her surgical scissors along the large blood vessel at the back of the knee joint. She separated the artery from surrounding bruised muscles, exposing it for a distance of about six inches. As the artery came into view, she sighed softly.

"Okay, look here, Yvette. This is where the tibia bone banged into the artery when the knee was dislocated – stretching and damaging the blood vessel." Brynn pointed to the injury with her forceps. "Look you can see the injury and bruising on the artery right here. I can feel a pulse above that point of injury and no pulse below."

"Okay, mighty surgeon Brynn, what the fuck are you gonna do now? This is the grossest thing I have ever done." Despite these comments, Yvette was carefully holding her retractors providing Brynn with a wide view of the damaged artery. Brynn's eyes remained fixed on the vessel. "That's great Yvette. Perfect exposure. Stay just right where you are."

"Look Brynn, just don't expect me to do this every Saturday night, okay."

Brynn's eyes remained glued to the artery while she

prepared for the next step in assessing the artery. Without moving or shifting her gaze she spoke softly to the nurse and anaesthetist.

"Suzanne, give me that soft, plastic vascular loop so I can encircle the artery where it's healthy above the injury. Andy, I am going to control the artery above the injury to prevent bleeding when I open it. You can give him five thousand units of heparin right now before I tighten the loop to close off the vessel." The anaesthetist injected the blood thinner drug that would prevent further clotting inside the artery.

Having gently constricted the artery with the plastic loop to prevent it from bleeding above the injury, Brynn took a tiny blade from Suzanne and made a five-millimetre incision in the artery just above the evident bruising caused by the dislocation. There was a brief spurt of blood and then nothing. The artery was totally clotted at the site where it had been damaged by the knee dislocation and no bleeding was coming back from the lower leg. Brynn knew that the total lack of flow below the injured artery was a bad sign for James' leg. If they could not restore flow through the injured vessel, his foot and lower leg would die from lack of oxygen that was normally carried to the foot by blood flowing through that artery.

"Okay, Suzanne gimme that paediatric Foley." Brynn gently grasped the tip of the soft plastic catheter with her forceps. The catheter was usually used to drain urine from a baby's bladder but was a perfect size to slip into the damaged artery through the five-millimetre incision. Brynn threaded it slowly into the opened artery, pushing the catheter firmly down toward the foot. The Foley was clearly meeting resistance from the blood clot that had formed at the site of injury as Brynn directed it down the tube of the artery with her forcep.

"I wanna be gentle with this move." she reminded herself and Yvette, "I don't want to create further injury to the vessel wall by pushing too hard. If you're not careful, you can rupture the artery and cause even more damage."

"Oh shit, Brynn, you are freaking me out," Yvette

responded, "can you see okay, are the retractors right?"

Brynn continued slowly and softly advancing the catheter. "Yvette, you are just perfect. Don't move an inch." Most of the fourteen-inch soft plastic catheter had now advanced down the artery. "Okay, I think we are past all the clot. Suzanne gimme that five-cc syringe."

The Foley catheter had a balloon at its tip that could be inflated by injecting two cubic centimetres of saline into the balloon through a channel leading from the top of the catheter. The inflated balloon could then be used to gently pull out all the clot that was blocking blood flow inside the damaged artery. Holding the top of the catheter steady, Brynn injected the saline to inflate the balloon and then started gently pulling the catheter back.

James was the only one breathing in the OR as the team focused on the catheter moving slowly back through Brynn's fingers. As soon as she started retracting the catheter, gelatinous blood clot started to extrude from the small hole in the artery that she had used to insert the Foley.

The cause of James' problem was now obvious. The dislocation had traumatized the wall of the artery and resulted in a blood clot forming that was blocking the blood supply that carried essential oxygen to the foot. Gently pushing the tip of the Foley catheter down through the soft clot with its balloon uninflated, and then inflating the balloon with saline was allowing Brynn to pull the clot out of the artery by retracting the catheter.

Brynn carefully deflated the balloon before removing the catheter completely so as not to enlarge the incision she had made in the artery. And as she extracted the catheter through the small hole a pulsating gush of bright red blood flowed out of the vessel and continued to pulsate. This was exactly what Brynn was hoping for – that removal of the clot would restore blood flow to the leg and foot.

"Goddammit Brynn, that looks pretty fuckin' good. Did you fix it?" Brynn remained silent, eyes fixed to the artery as she gently released the elastic band she had previously looped around the top of the vessel. She held her finger over the five-millimetre incision in the artery to prevent blood loss and felt the pulse through the artery past the injury. The vessel was now briskly pounding with each heartbeat. "Suzanne, feel the foot and see if you can find a pulse."

Suzanne put her fingers on the top of the foot and gasped. "It's great Dr. Allard. The pulse is really strong."

Yvette couldn't resist. "Now you listen, Suzanne, she's gonna tell you to just call her Brynn, not Dr. Allard. Even though she's the world's fuckin' greatest surgeon who just saved this kid's goddam leg. Brynn, I love you, you are amazing."

Brynn was still fixated on the vessel. "I'm gonna hold the vessel for the next ten minutes before we close the incision in the artery. I want to make sure that it keeps pumping through that area of injury, so we know we don't need a graft for the damaged artery. Sometimes removal of the clot is not sufficient and the damaged artery will clot again. In that case we will need to take a vein graft from the other leg to replace the area of damage. With the pulse remaining this strong, I have a feeling we are gonna be okay." She turned her head to look at the anaesthetist. "Andy, we should probably keep the heparin going to prevent further clotting until we get him evacuated to St. Barts to fix his knee ligaments tomorrow, huh?"

She turned to Jane who had been quietly watching the surgery along with the other doctors who had been expecting their CEO to feed them. "Jane, maybe one day we could repair his ligaments in this OR as well but right now we don't have the necessary equipment." She looked up at the nurse whose fingers were still on James' foot. "Pulse still okay, Suzanne?"

The nurse nodded. "Yeah, if anything, it's stronger."

With tension receding, Yvette returned to her usual banter. "Okay, master surgeon, I want you to know that I am fuckin' starving to death and Jane has got some amazing stew on the stove at home. Can you think about my stomach while you're working your surgical miracles here? I am going to faint if I don't get some of that stew into me soon. I'm just a small person and I do not do well with hunger."

But Yvette never budged holding the retractors as Brynn carefully closed the small hole she had created in the artery. The pulse in the foot remained strong as she finished closing the wound and then applied a plaster cast that would keep the knee from re-dislocating during air evac to St. Barts when flights resumed tomorrow.

Brynn and the entire team were drained by apprehended anxiety as they returned James to the ER so that his foot pulse could be monitored by the nurses overnight.

However, they entered the ER with smiles on their faces that told James' dad everything he needed to know as he rushed to greet the doctors at the ER entrance. And then Brynn found herself two feet off the floor as Chief Checkwing grasped her about the waist and spun her in circles, hugging her so tight that she momentarily lost her breath. He had difficulty speaking as the tears flowed, but Brynn had no problem understanding his thanks.

CHAPTER 14

The Trapline. November 2018

Days after the big snowstorm that resulted in the injury to James Checkwing's knee, Jonah was pondering recent events as he followed Charlie, the trapper who had rescued Uncle Samuel from the creek bed last year, on his snowmobile. It had been an interesting few months.

After their brief sojourn in Georgian Bay, Jonah and David Morton had returned to Toronto where David did a series of media interviews with Jonah always quietly present along with their crisis comms specialist. David was perfect, never straying from the story that he had decided to leave CannWeed at the time of closing the deal with International Brands but wanted to ensure that the integration with the American company went off without a hitch before leaving. He was very confident about the future of the two companies, especially since the date of cannabis legalization in Canada was rapidly approaching.

As Jonah expected, the lack of drama in the story David was telling resulted in minimal continuing press interest in David's departure from CannWeed. However, media excitement was intensifying covering the imminent start of the legal cannabis market in Canada, now firmly scheduled for mid-October. Retail investors were convinced that legalization would offer a huge new money-making opportunity for cannabis companies and in late August and early September, CannWeed stock was hitting new daily highs on the stock exchange.

The lack of media interest in David allowed Jonah to conclude the relationship with the crisis communication firm that assisted the start-up of Mindful Innovation after compensating the comms consultants richly for a job well done. In the place of the crisis communicators, David and Jonah recruited staff for a small investment team at Mindful. David had accumulated more than two hundred and fifty million dollars as a result of the International Brands investment and the buy-out provided when he was fired. David's family had been financial players for generations, and he enjoyed recruiting the small group of accountants, analysts and traders to manage and grow his fortune.

Jonah had convinced David sitting on the deck at Moose Deer Point that their first investment target should be derivatives of CannWeed stock. Dumb money from unsophisticated retail stockholders was pouring in to CannWeed, with naïve investors convinced that October legalization was going to result in a huge jackpot for CannWeed shareholders. Jonah had convinced David of just the opposite.

"David, I know how excited you are about the cannabis market, but I'm convinced we left the industry at the peak of the market. Let's face it, CannWeed and its Canadian competitors have massively overdeveloped supply. They have tons of cannabis available for the legal market opening and very little of that weed is prime product. Most of it's not as good as illegal dealers bring in every day from Mexico, South America, and the Pacific coast." Here he paused; this was the most important part.

"And where are they gonna sell this massive amount of legal, lousy quality loco-weed, David? Every province in the country will have different regulations and retail plans for selling legal weed. But the one thing that is true in every province is that no one really knows yet how legal customers are gonna buy legal weed. Very few retail stores are licenced. It looks to me like mail order is gonna be the primary retail delivery channel. Would you want Canada Post delivering your weed? The postman telling the neighbours on your postal route that he just dropped off some big bong bags at Morton's place?"

As they started Mindful's small investment team, the first order of business was to purchase put option contracts on CannWeed stock that would rapidly increase in value if CannWeed's stock price suddenly fell. To prevent other investors from learning what they were doing, they kept the purchases quiet and split the contracts with several dealers on the Montreal derivatives exchange as well as other derivative markets around the world. Most of their purchases were individually quite small, no more than one hundred contracts per dealer with each contract representing put options on one hundred shares.

Jonah explained their strategy to their small trading team, all of whom were young men, many recent immigrants to Canada from Eastern Europe. "Guys, David and I are convinced that a giant alarm clock is gonna start ringing just as pot is being legalized. That alarm is gonna awaken everyone from their happy dreams about making a fortuna on cannabis." The analysts listened carefully while their eyes stayed glued to their multiple screen trading computers. Most of them were recruited from the high frequency trading world and became agitated if their attention was diverted from market action for more than seconds.

"We figure legalization is going to happen around October seventeenth, just before the October expiry date for options.

At the start of September, we want to start buying put options on CannWeed for expiry on the third Fridays of September, October, and November. I want you algorithm guys to do some modelling as to how we should distribute the contracts over those three months based on our prediction of CannWeed's stock price. David and I will help you with the assumptions for CannWeed price that we want you to build into the models. We figure the price is likely to start falling just before the legalization date and we want our options to be maturing just after the price begins to fall."

During their conversations at Georgian Bay, David had made it clear that he wanted Jonah to be his partner in this initiative. Jonah's departure from his legal firm had been confirmed within days of his termination as CannWeed's lawyer. While they sat on the deck looking out on the shimmering summer bay, David insisted that he was going to bankroll his friend.

"Jonah let's face it, if it wasn't for you, I wouldn't be sitting pretty on this pile of money right now. You got us the payoff from the International Brands' investment, you arranged the tax deal for the stock options, and you were smart enough to plan for a pay-off if I got fired. I will never forget what you've done for me this past year, Jonah. I know that you missed out on a big bonus when you were let go from your firm. I'm gonna make that all up to you and more."

David had been true to his word. He put Jonah on the Mindful Innovation payroll as counsel at a salary that more than doubled his law firm compensation. And he provided him with a five million-dollar cash signing bonus. Together the two partners played their cannabis hunch aggressively, buying tens of millions of dollars of CannWeed put options as Canada approached cannabis legalization.

Their bet on CannWeed's stock price crashing was remarkably accurate and profitable. As October seventeenth approached, investors suddenly realized that there was going to be no pot of gold suddenly appearing for cannabis stock owners. The lack of a retail market for weed in Canada meant that CannWeed cash flow was going to increase minimally despite legalization. Suddenly, starting just before legalization, the realization hit retail investors that they had badly misjudged CannWeed's potential growth in future sales and cash flow. These investors started selling their CannWeed stock as fast as they had bought it.

CannWeed's stock price peaked in early September just after the Mindful team started buying put options. The stock price dropped in mid-September and the Mindful September options were suddenly very valuable, providing Jonah with his first fortune and substantially increasing David's existing wealth. But in October the real carnage became apparent for CannWeed. The stock price plummeted over the first two weeks of October, as painful reality became evident to the company's investors. Over these two weeks, the stock price dropped from sixty dollars a share to about thirty dollars. David and Jonah had paid an average of about two dollars for each option on shares at sixty dollars that were now worth about thirty dollars. That meant each option was worth the difference between sixty and thirty dollars minus the two-dollar cost to buy it. They had spent two dollars to get thirty in return for each share, resulting in a massive profit over a few weeks. Every million dollars they had invested in the put options was now worth about twenty-eight million. Suddenly the five million David had given Jonah as a signing bonus was worth more than a hundred million. Jonah was richer than he had ever imagined possible, and David had more than doubled his wealth.

Back in the James Bay bush, Jonah realized that he was drifting out of Charlie's snowmobile track as the two drove their snow machines along the creek bed. He stopped thinking about his financial windfall and returned to the reality of winter in the James Bay wilderness. He and David had sold their massively profitable October options just before the options expired a few days after pot was legalized. As the extent of their win became evident, they headed off to High Spirits to celebrate. Jonah took his glass of Chablis without any Perrier in honour of their success and David was enjoying his usual Macallan with ice.

"So, buddy, you are set for life. You have completed your Trifecta, Jonah. You did the International Brands' investment, you protected me when I got fired and then made me an even wealthier man with this option idea. And I'm really happy that you've scored a big win partnering with me, Jonah." David paused for a sip of Macallan. "Well, what are we gonna do next, buddy?"

Jonah swirled the white wine in his glass. "Thinking about next steps, I do have something to talk about, David. I know I just started as counsel for Mindful, but I actually think I need a break. I think you could use some time off as well. We've both busted our butts for four years building CannWeed, then selling it to International Brands. And the past few months getting fired from CannWeed and implementing this option strategy have been pretty stressful. I feel like I need to chill for a while. And I think you should be thinking the same."

"Yeah, I know what you mean." David took a sip of whisky. "I've been actually thinking of looking for some real estate in the South Pacific. I've heard about a premium resort near Bora Bora, and I've been thinking about holing up there for a month and scouting out a place to buy. Whad'ya think Jonah, should we go to the South Pacific together to start up a Mindful Innovation Bora Bora office?"

Jonah shook his head. "No, I've been thinking something different although I totally agree that you deserve time in Polynesia or wherever Bora Bora is. But I think I'm gonna go home for a while."

"What the fuck, Jonah, you gotta be kidding! I'm going to be surrounded by grass skirts, bikinis and palm trees and you're going back to Moose? That place was a dump when I first met you at that hockey tournament and I'm sure it hasn't improved much."

Jonah shook his head again. "No, actually I don't mean Moose. I'm thinking of moving in with Uncle Samuel and Auntie Mary back in Port Muskek. Uncle is still not completely back on his feet, and he could use some help with his various businesses." Jonah looked up at the ceiling.

"I know this may sound like crazy Indigenous spirit stuff to you, David. But I haven't been home except for short visits for about twenty years now. I miss the place. I know its winter starting up there now but I even miss the winter. You deserve the palm trees, believe me. But I think I need some connection to the land or something. And I know it would make Auntie and Uncle incredibly happy if I moved in with them for a while. I kind of wanna see how they're doing. They are both in their sixties and I wanna make sure they're gonna be okay." He put his wine glass on the small table that separated him from his friend.

"I'm sure it's hard for you to imagine just how much I owe those two, David. If it wasn't for them, I would have been lost in an orphanage or a foster home or something. I really owe them some payback."

"Well, Jonah, you sure gotta lot you can pay them back with now." David chuckled and rolled his eyes. "So, I'm going to the south seas and my best friend's going to James Bay. I hear it's beautiful there this time of year. Jesus, Jonah, I can't believe you're really gonna do that."

Mary welcomed her nephew home with delight whereas Samuel observed in his usual way that he guessed Jonah needed a place to live since he got fired from his law firm. But Samuel was not so secretly very pleased to have Jonah move back into his old room.

Samuel was running several businesses that Port Muskek relied on. His woodlot was an important source of heating for the town and his construction company was one of the major employers in the community. Twelve years ago, the South African Helder diamond company had opened a mine forty kilometres from Port Muskek. Samuel's company provided some initial construction work at the mine site and had taken on annual maintenance of the winter road that connected the mine to Port Muskek and the main winter road to Moose. That road was essential for the mine to re-supply all heavy equipment and diesel for the entire year during the time that the winter roads were open.

Shortly after his arrival, Jonah sat with Samuel at Mary's kitchen table while she busied herself with baking to celebrate Jonah's homecoming.

Samuel scratched his chin while musing. "Well, if you are gonna live here rent free with us for a few months, I guess I gotta put you to work, Jonah. We haven't got much lawyering for you to do up here. But I figure I can give you something useful to do."

Jonah smiled. He was pleased to see that the accident hadn't changed his uncle much. His leg was apparently healing well but he still needed to protect it with a cane.

"Jonah, there's a couple of places I could really use your help. Charlie's back working for me fulltime after my accident. I told him that was the least he could do since he decided to drag me outta that creek instead of leaving me there." He lifted his coffee cup. "Your auntie's pies smell pretty good, huh, Jonah?" His nephew smiled in response.

"The boys in the woodlot got things pretty much under control. And Charlie has been great with the construction stuff. We got three new houses built this summer which is important for the community. Everyone's having kids and we gotta get more housing." Samuel shook his head.

"But I'm worried about our road business. The Helder Company says their mine has pretty much been emptied out of diamonds and this will be their last year actively mining although they will be doing reclamation work for a couple more years. We had hoped that they were gonna start another mine just to the east of where they are now, but I guess their exploration showed that eastern site isn't economically viable."

Jonah knew the Port Muskek community thought that the diamond mine had not turned out as well as they had all hoped. Except for Uncle Samuel's construction and road maintenance and some catering business, there were very few people from Port Muskek employed by Helder. The mine had been functioning for more than ten years, but Helder was always complaining that the profits from the mine were not as significant as they had hoped. There were so few people from the community working at the mine that no one really had any idea just how successful Helder was. The company was supposed to have a profit-sharing plan with Port Muskek. However, Helder always provided financial results showing that they were not making much money after accounting for their big initial investment building the mine. So, there were never any profits to share with the Port Muskek Council.

Samuel continued. "Anyway, Charlie's been great keeping the road to the mine open and safe. But now they're talking about needing an extra strong road next winter to get a bunch of their heavy mining equipment down to the James Bay winter road so they can take it out by train from Moose in summer. It really sounds like they are shutting the mine down. Normally I would negotiate a new contract with them for a heavy-duty road next winter. I'm not sure that Charlie will feel comfortable doing that negotiation by himself – he's not too talkative you know."

Jonah nodded. He knew Charlie was entirely reliable in doing what he said he would do, but Jonah also knew he kept to himself – usually doing more grunting than talking. Negotiating a new contract would not be his strong suit.

"There's one other thing you could help me out with, Jonah." The smell of Mary's pies was filling the kitchen and Samuel sniffed the air with appreciation. "After all, if you're gonna hang around here eating Auntie's cooking, you're gonna get fat if we don't give you lotsa work to do."

Mary scoffed from the counter where she was rolling pastry. "Oh, Samuel, just stop it. Look at that boy, there's not a trace of fat on him. He's as lean as the day he left here to go to school in Toronto. Don't you worry Jonah, I'm gonna fatten you up. Sam, you go easy on Jonah."

Jonah felt surrounded by his family's warmth as he sat at his aunt's table. He had almost forgotten how warm he felt being with both of them. He had been away too long. "Don't worry Auntie, your cooking is gonna fill me up no matter how much wood chopping Uncle assigns me." He smiled. "What else can I do, Uncle?"

Samuel was rubbing his chin. "Ever since my accident, I don't want anyone going off into the bush by themselves. I think everyone's safer if they buddy up. That was a really long night I spent in the creek bed under that four-wheeler." He shuddered momentarily. "Anyway, Charlie and Bill went out together to harvest my marten boxes last year and they set up our new boxes with bait in the fall. The last couple of years have been really good on the trapline. Lots of animals in the traps and a really heavy fur set for most of them." He turned to his wife.

"We got over two hundred bucks a skin last winter while I was laid up, didn't we, Mary?"

His wife nodded. "Yeah, that new buyer says his biggest market is in China now. Last year he was buying for more than two hundred a pelt." Jonah whistled.

"Wow, that's really good, Uncle. With all this snow I bet you want to get out and check your traps and re-bait them if you can get two hundred bucks a skin."

Samuel was nodding. "That's what I'm thinkin' Jonah. Anyway, Bill has decided to spend a couple months down south this winter with his cousin in Toronto so Charlie's all alone. Those traps need checking, but I don't want Charlie going out alone. I was gonna go with him but the last time I checked with that Dr. Allard she told me I still need to use a cane and you can't take a cane out on the trapline."

Mary looked up from her pastry. "Sam that reminds me. Did you know that Dr. Allard is here helping out the

Wiichihinan Hospital in Moose for a few months? I was talking to my cousin Betty who works in the hospital in Moose, and she told me that Dr. Allard started there a couple of weeks ago." She looked over at her nephew seeing him lift his head in interest. "Yeah, that's right Jonah. That cute red headed surgeon who looked after Sam. I never understood why you didn't pay more attention to her. She was just lovely." She shook her head and continued.

"And I hear that she is an amazing doctor too. Not only did she save Uncle's leg, but my cousin also told me she operated on the Chief's son James after he had a bad injury to his knee snowmobiling last weekend. Everyone in Moose is saying that she saved his leg too."

Samuel took over. "Yeah, that little woman is a corker. If I were you Jonah, I would get on down to Moose and check out what she's up to." Then he remembered what he was asking. "But not before you go out with Charlie and check my marten boxes. What do ya think Jonah? Can you do that for me?"

Two days later Jonah found himself following closely in Charlie's snowmobile tracks as they drove up the frozen creek bed, stopping about every five hundred metres to snowshoe into the woods to check out the boxes that were marked with fluorescent ribbons tied to their trees. They had already gathered twenty frozen little bodies caught by the Conibear traps set in the boxes. Jonah smiled to himself as he calculated their take for the day. At two hundred dollars a skin, they had made about four thousand dollars so far for their day working in the bush – about a fifth of what Jonah expected to make daily from his investment accounts with exponentially less effort. However, being out in the bush gave him a peace and connection to life and land that he had forgotten. "I've got to get home more often," he said to himself, the words echoing in his snowmobile helmet.

They were close to their last box and the sun was low in the western sky. They would be turning around soon. They didn't mind returning in the dark since no snow was forecast and they would simply follow their own tracks back home with the lights on their machines. Charlie was pleased with the day's haul and demonstrated his exuberance by skidding up on the eastern creek bank at a turn leading to their last box. As he accelerated off the curved bank, he slid down the five-foot embankment, bringing a small avalanche down off the creek bed, exposing the pebbles and rocks under the snow.

The sun's low light was approaching sunset, coming just over the west creek bank. That light, refracted by a scratch in Jonah's helmet visor, created a sudden flash on the creekbank. Jonah was startled out of his reverie and slammed on his brakes, bringing the snowmobile to a sliding stop just past the object he saw lighting up the pebbles of the exposed creek bed.

CHAPTER 15

The Fishing Camp.
December 8, 2018

"**A**re you sure you packed everything?"

Mary was checking the sled behind Jonah's snowmobile for the fourth time. The sled was brimming over with bannock, berry pies, meat and fish pies, containers with different stews, bottles of wine, firewood, and changes of winter clothing.

"Jeez, Mary, you gave them enough stuff for ten men going away for a week. There's just two of them and they gotta return tomorrow for Brynn to catch the Sunday plane back to Moose, remember?" Samuel shook his head. He knew his wife was certain that survival in the bush was dependent on a massive oversupply of rations. And sometimes she was right.

Jonah was packing two more jerricans of gas onto the sled, carefully keeping it away from Mary's food provisions. Then he strapped his cross-country ski equipment onto the sled along with Mary's ski gear which had turned out to be a good fit for Dr. Allard. He looked over at Brynn who was trying to figure out how to adjust her snowmobile helmet over her goggles.

"How are you doing, Doc? Can I help you with that?"

Brynn's slender figure was ballooned by her snowmobile suit, and she was struggling to adjust the various straps attached to her helmet with her mitts on.

"Jonah, I feel like I'm outfitted for a Martian landing. Do I really need all this stuff?"

Jonah looked over at his Uncle Samuel and grinned. "Well Doc, we are going to be travelling on this machine for about two hours to get to the camp and its minus twenty-five. When we are travelling on creek beds, we'll be going slow but when we are in the open, we'll be going faster and believe me you will appreciate the gear. The camp is about twenty kilometres away and we don't want you arriving like a popsicle."

Mary reassured Brynn. "Don't you worry, Doc, Jonah knows what he's doing. Samuel brought him up in this bush and since he's got back, he's been doing lots of exploring."

Dr. Brynn Allard's trip into the Port Muskek bush had been planned the same day that Charlie and Jonah were in the bush collecting marten furs. Mary's cousin Betty who worked in the Wiichihinan Hospital in Moose had called Mary after Charlie and Jonah left for the trapline with a proposal from the hospital leadership.

Since saving James Checkwing's leg, Dr. Allard had become a celebrity in Moose and the people in the hospital were eager for her to experience James Bay hospitality. Several patients from Port Muskek, including Samuel, had been scheduled to come down to Moose for appointments with Brynn. Samuel was booked to see her in follow-up for his leg injury – the rest of the patients were new consults for Brynn. Yvette and the hospital CEO thought that it would be useful for Brynn to visit Port Muskek for the clinic rather than having the people come to Moose to see her. They also decided it might be interesting for her to spend a night in the community to get a sense of the various locations that needed orthopaedic services along the James Bay coast.

Samuel and Mary were well known for offering a generous

welcome to visitors and the hospital CEO remembered that Brynn had treated Samuel in Toronto. So, Dr. Jane Gagne asked Mary's cousin Betty, who worked in the hospital's finance department, to call her cousin and ask if they would host Brynn on Friday and Saturday nights after her clinic in Port Muskek and show her around the community on Saturday.

Mary and Samuel were delighted to welcome Dr. Allard. As Jonah sat in Mary's kitchen after his evening return from the trapline, Samuel told him he had another job for him.

"Jonah, you know we told you that Dr. Allard is working down in Moose for a while? Well, instead of me taking a plane down to Moose so she can check my leg, she's gonna fly up here Friday morning to do a clinic in Port Muskek. There are a bunch of other people from Port Muskek who were supposed to fly down to see her in Moose, so it makes sense for the doc to come up here. I guess the CEO at Wiichihinan wants her to see all our health facilities along the coast." He paused long enough for Mary to place a plateful of hot meat pie on the table in front of Jonah.

"I hear that everyone in Moose is really impressed with Dr. Allard," Mary said with a meaningful look at her nephew. "You heard that she saved James Checkwing from losing his leg after a snowmobile accident?"

"Jeez Mary, you've already told us that four times." Samuel shook his head and continued. "Jonah she's flying up early Friday morning and then she's gonna stay with us Friday and Saturday night before she gets the regular plane back to Moose Sunday afternoon. Mary and I were thinking that after she stays with us Friday night and if the weather is okay, you could maybe take her out to our fishing camp by snowmobile to stay Saturday night. Whad'ya think? That would show her what the bush is like around here and maybe you could show her the bay in winter."

Jonah looked from his uncle to aunt and back again. It didn't take much imagination to guess why they wanted him to show the doctor around.

He shrugged. "I don't know, Uncle. That camp isn't really winterized. It gets pretty cold up there with the winds coming down the bay."

Samuel waved off his concern. "You've been away too long, Jonah. I done some work on that place. I put in a couple of new wood stoves that heat it up in no time and I replaced all them drafty windows. I spent a long weekend ice fishing on the river the winter before my accident and it was as warm as Auntie's kitchen. You remember how to get there, right?"

Jonah nodded. Some of his favourite moments as a child were spent staying at the camp fishing with his uncle in spring and summer and ice fishing in winter. The camp was located close to where the Muskek River entered James Bay and was a wonderful spot for big walleye and northern pike.

"Okay, if Dr. Allard decides she wants a freezing, bumpy snowmobile ride through the bush to arrive in a freezing cabin, I am game to take her. We can see if she wants to cross-country ski when we get there and maybe ski to that lookout over the bay. She looked pretty athletic as I remember."

Jonah could not help but notice the pleased looks that passed between his aunt and uncle as he agreed to take the surgeon on an overnight trip in the bush. He knew that they were playing matchmaker but also knew that it would not work. He decided he had to change the topic and reached in his pocket.

"Uncle, something I want to show you from our trip to the trapline today. Charlie was messing around on his snowmobile up ahead of me and cleared snow from part of the creek bed. Just by accident, I saw this stone sparkling in the pebbles. Have you ever seen anything like this?" Jonah reached his hand to his uncle, showing him a stone more than two inches in diameter. The rock was dull on some sides but sparkled brightly on other facets.

Samuel took the stone from Jonah's hand and rotated it in the light. "Yeah, I think that's what they call an alluvial diamond – just a fancy name for a diamond found in a stream or river. Here, lemme show you." Samuel went over to the refrigerator and lifted a small metal container off the top. "I don't know why I keep these on top of the fridge. Just habit I guess."

Opening the container, he tipped the contents on to the table. Four small stones fell out – much smaller replicas of the large nugget that Jonah had discovered.

"See these, I showed them to the guys up at the mine and they told me they are diamonds that got washed away millions of years ago from the surface of the major source of diamonds – what they call a kimberlite pipe – and flowed down streams leading away from where the mine is now. That's one of the ways that they can identify where a major deposit might be – by tracing diamonds up the streams where they're discovered to see where they originated from."

Samuel paused and rubbed his chin thoughtfully. "You were on that eastern creek system today, right Jonah? Near where I had my accident?" Jonah nodded.

"Huh. I found these small diamonds farther to the west, in creeks that run to the Muskek River from south of the mine. You remember those western traplines I used to bait, Jonah? I found they weren't as productive after the mine opened. Maybe it was mine tailings getting into the water or maybe the noise of the mine scared the animals, but I wasn't getting as many skins so I moved my traplines to the east away from the mine. I haven't seen any of those alluvial stones along those eastern traplines, but I've only been there for a couple of years now." He picked up Jonah's large stone and rotated it, holding it up to the light.

"Those little stones, the guys at the mine told me they weren't worth much so I just kept them and thought I would make a necklace for Mary if I found enough. But this is a big stone, Jonah. That could be worth something I guess."

"That's interesting about the location where you found your little ones Uncle, and where I found this one. Doesn't Helder have another site that they are exploring to the east of the current mine?"

"Yeah, that's right Jonah. They call it the Ultra site and they've been doing some exploration there for the past few winters. You remember they call the site where they're mining now Sierra. We hoped they might decide to open another mine at Ultra, but I guess they have decided that the ore there isn't rich enough to support another mine." Samuel rolled the larger diamond in his fingers.

"I get what you are thinking. This stone may have washed down in streams coming down from the Ultra site east of Sierra. Interesting."

Jonah was silent for a minute. "You know, David Morton's family has lots of connections in mining. Geologists, prospectors – they used to raise money to bankroll those guys. Most of those funds went bust – mining is a tough place to make money – but I know they have a lot of contacts who have explored in the north. Maybe I'll get David to introduce me to one of those prospectors to see if they think this stone tells us anything about Ultra. If Helder is going to be leaving money on the table at Ultra, maybe we should be looking into it."

Thoughts of diamond mines quickly faded as Samuel and Jonah helped Mary to plan for the arrival of their celebrity guest. Friday morning, half of Port Muskek was present at the airstrip to welcome Brynn. As the doctor stepped out of the plane, Mary couldn't resist clapping and a few people in the crowd joined her. Since he and Mary were the only residents of Port Muskek known to Brynn, Samuel stepped forward to welcome her and raised her hand over her head, leading to a new round of restrained applause.

Brynn acknowledged her welcome with good nature. "My goodness, thank you for this warm welcome. I feel like a returning astronaut or a Stanley Cup winner bringing the trophy home."

The nursing station team had taken new x-rays for Samuel the day before his surgeon's arrival, and he was the first patient to see Brynn in her clinic. Jonah accompanied his uncle, who was still using a cane. Brynn took a careful look at the healing bone on Samuel's x-ray and nodded appreciatively. "That's healing beautifully, Mr. Sunderland. It's been more than a year and it's doing about as well as I could hope. Climb up on the exam table and we'll see how much attention you're paying to your physio." She was pleased to see that Samuel had recovered most of the motion in his knee. "That's really good Sam. I'm very pleased. I want you to keep using the cane until I see the next x-ray in about two months, but you can take full weight on the leg." Then she looked over at Jonah.

"I am impressed that you came all the way from Toronto to attend your uncle's appointment. I think it's Jonah, right?"

Jonah smiled. "Well, Doc, I'd travel a long way to say thanks for what you did for Uncle. But I'm actually home right now, living with my aunt and uncle for a while."

Brynn was surprised. "Huh. You remember that I told you I asked my lawyer friend about you since you were always threatening to check me out?" Her smile removed any threat in her words. Jonah considered her warm, green eyes and auburn hair. Too bad, he thought reluctantly.

"She called me just before I moved to Moose and told me she had read that you had stopped being a pot lawyer and had gone to a new company."

Jonah nodded. "Yeah, you remember my friend David Morton that you called the pot king? We've left pot behind and we're starting up a new investing company. We decided that we both needed a break before starting work on something new. I came home to help Uncle for a while since he can't really run all his businesses using a cane."

"Doc I know there are a lot of people waiting to see you," Samuel interrupted. "We're going to pick you up after clinic and take you home for one of Mary's home-made meals. You are gonna stay at our place tonight and then tomorrow if you want, Jonah's gonna take you out to our fishing camp. It's supposed to be a beautiful day. We can explain to you over dinner."

Brynn looked appraisingly at Jonah. "So, you're a back country guide in addition to your lawyer skills and dealing pot, huh? That sounds like an adventure. Okay, I better get on with clinic, but I'll look forward to seeing you later. Thanks for arranging such a warm welcome." And she lit up the room with her smile.

As they left in Samuel's truck, Mary leaned forward from the back seat. "Jonah, that girl is something else. She is so smart and so nice, and she's just gorgeous. I talked to my cousin at the hospital in Moose to find out if she has a boyfriend or anything. She told me that Dr. Allard was engaged but broke that off a while ago. Jonah, you just gotta get to know her."

Later that day, as he escorted Brynn to Mary's dining room table after first showing her to her room, Jonah thought to himself that his aunt and uncle's matchmaking would probably be tiresome over dinner. He was surprised that Brynn Allard proved to be a delightful dinner guest who was genuinely interested in understanding what life was like in Port Muskek. She seemed particularly interested in understanding Uncle Samuel's role as a business leader in the community. Her charm convinced Jonah's laconic uncle to open up on his vision for Port Muskek and its people.

"Doc we've got a bunch of different business lines – some you might call traditional like our woodlot, hunting, fishing, and trapping and some more that you might say are more up to date. I've always tried to keep our connection to this land as the thing that defines us as a people. This can seem like a tough place to live, unless you realize how our people have lived off this land for centuries before and after European settlement. And our next generation needs to know where to catch big fish, how to hunt moose and where the geese come to. That's always going to be part of feeding their families. But more important, it's also part of understanding why we live in this marshy, cold part of the world." He paused to take in a forkful of Mary's fish pie.

"That's why I always took Jonah with me into the bush when he was little before he left to go down south. He's not easy to teach, he's a little slow, but he seems to be pretty comfortable with being in the bush. He came home with a nice haul from our trapline a few days ago."

And that led to a discussion about how marten are trapped, whether the animals suffered and what you do with the pelts once the animal was trapped. Mary was pleased with the surgeon's appetite and fed her seconds of everything on the table. By the end of her second slice of berry pie, Brynn pushed back from the table. "Wow, Mary, you have fed me and filled me. I cannot eat another bite." She turned to Jonah, "So, tell me about this adventure you have planned for tomorrow?"

Jonah had been quiet most of the evening, enjoying seeing his uncle open up to this pleasant young woman. "Well, Doc, my uncle – your patient – thinks that to repay you for all the great work you have done on his leg, we should treat you to a bumpy ride on a noisy machine to a freezing cabin in the woods that has no electricity. How does that sound?"

"Yeah, that certainly sounds like an adventure," she said. "Actually, I'm fascinated to see the bush. Especially after listening to Samuel speak so passionately about how important it is to the people who live here." She smiled at Jonah's uncle. "I've noticed that your uncle is not always that eager to talk about things, but he really got going about how important the land is. And I guess he's convinced you, Jonah, getting you to move back here?"

Jonah smiled. "Yeah, he can be pretty convincing when he wants to be." He turned to look at his uncle who shrugged his shoulders in response.

Jonah turned back to Brynn. "If you are up to it Doc, I'm planning that we take about a two-hour snowmobile ride down toward the coast. Our fishing camp is about two kilometres from the bay, overlooking a bend in the river where it heads south to hit salt water. We can set a fire when we arrive and then maybe ski down to the coast to show you James Bay in winter and give you a chance to stretch your legs after the snowmobile ride. Then we'll have plenty of time on Sunday to get you back in time for your flight."

"Great, I love cross country skiing. And I could use some exercise after Mary's wonderful meal." Mary raised her hands to accept Brynn's appreciation for her cooking.

As she settled in to sleep under Mary's thick comforter in the guest bedroom, Brynn's thoughts remained stuck on Jonah. It was more than a year since her breakup with Brian and she was beginning to feel like she might be celibate forever. She found Jonah's features and lean fitness intriguing. He had upset her with his rudeness when they first met in the hospital – but even at that encounter she had found him attractive. He was certainly a fascinating guy with his success in law in Toronto and now his interest in his home in James Bay. And she was pretty sure that with Mary and Samuel organizing the trip he would be a gentleman.

But then she found herself smiling. Maybe she hoped he wouldn't be too much of a gentleman. It was definitely time for her to figure out how she was going to start dating again. The thought did not enthuse her. She didn't have time to meet people. She had promised herself that she would never, ever again start another relationship in the hospital, and she couldn't see herself on a dating site. She knew people at the hospital would see her on any app she registered on and that would just be too embarrassing.

Recently her family's response to her social situation was becoming unbearable. After a family dinner before she left for Moose, her father casually mentioned that he 'had been doing research on the increasing number of professional women who discover they are LGBTQ.' Brynn had initially nodded her head thinking that was an unusual topic for her prim and proper dad to be investigating until she suddenly realized the intent of his conversation. She quickly reassured him that she was not gay and that he did not have to worry about supporting a lesbian daughter although she jokingly said that

189

she appreciated his wokeness. Almost as soon as she said the words she realized that he probably wouldn't understand what woke meant.

Her thoughts returned to Jonah Kay. He was an interesting guy and she was looking forward to spending the day getting to know him. And although it made her feel a bit shameless, she was pleased they would be spending the night together at what sounded like a rather romantic remote cabin in the woods. And then she fell into a dreamless sleep thinking about James Bay dating.

The next morning, as he showed Brynn how to sit comfortably on the snowmobile behind him while adjusting her backrest, Jonah turned on the communicator in her helmet. "Can you hear me okay, Doc?"

Brynn jolted forward in her seat. "Oh, that surprised me. I didn't know that we would be able to talk to each other. Does this mean you are going to provide running tour guide commentary during our trip?"

"Yeah, I'll let you know where we are and where we're going and when we see something interesting. I am planning on going pretty slow, so we don't scare away all the animals. It's not far to the camp and it's a beautiful day." The air was crisp at minus twenty-five, but the wind was light, and no clouds were evident in the sparkling blue sky. "This is about as nice a day as you get in a James Bay winter, Doc."

"Look, why don't you just call me Brynn? This doc stuff is getting tiresome." Jonah couldn't see her smile through the visor on her helmet but gave her a thumbs up. Then they were off with Mary and Samuel waving goodbye, leaving Port Muskek behind on a snow-covered dirt road.

Jonah opened conversation over the helmet communicator. "Brynn, we are going up this road for a couple of kilometres and then going to head down toward the bay along a couple of different creek beds. Do you see that arctic fox up ahead going into the bush?"

"Oh my god, his fur is so white, he just blends in. I didn't see him until you pointed him out."

Jonah kept their speed slow enough that it was easy to chat over the sound of the snowmobile. Jonah pointed out a hare jumping through the snow as well as a marten climbing a tree as they passed through the bush using the frozen creek as a highway.

"Jonah, that fox and the marten were so bushy. Their fur is amazing."

"Yeah, that's the reason that this area was so interesting to the original European settlers Brynn. Our winters make for thick fur on most of the animals that live here. That fur was what attracted the Hudson's Bay company to open a trading post at Moose Factory way back in the sixteen-seventies. This area was settled by Europeans before Toronto or Kingston or Ottawa, believe it or not, because furs were so plentiful here and furs were what Europeans were looking for in what's become Canada."

The sides of the creek bed dropped in height and they could readily see into the bush that surrounded them. Suddenly Jonah slowed the snowmobile to a halt and stood up on the snowmobile runners to peer into the stunted trees.

"Brynn, take a look about a hundred yards deep in the bush. Do you see branches waving back and forth at the bottom of those spruce trees?"

Brynn was holding his waist as she stood on the runners behind Jonah. "Yeah, what is that Jonah? There are brown lumps on the floor beneath those trees."

"Brynn you are getting a great view of a herd of woodland caribou. That slow back-and-forth motion of their heads occurs as they feed on lichen and moss on the trees above the snow. Most of them have antlers – that's unusual for females in other deer species. Their antlers look like branches until you see their bodies. They are really well camouflaged in the bush, huh?"

"This is amazing Jonah. Yeah, now I can see there must be twenty or thirty animals grazing there."

Another kilometre along the creek bed and the trail rose again to run across open, frozen muskeg. Jonah stopped the machine again and pointed to the sky in front of them.

"Brynn, look up there, that's a golden eagle. Incredible, huge birds. There are only a few of these eagle pairs on this side of James Bay. They need a lot of space for their hunting habitat."

"What's he doing, Jonah? He seems to be circling looking at something, is he hunting?"

"Yeah, he's probably seen a hare running across the muskeg."

They continued on across muskeg and then followed another narrow, frozen creek into the bush. And then, rounding a corner through the woods, the fishing camp suddenly appeared overlooking the Muskek River. The creek they had been following would empty into the Muskek River come spring. "This is our first destination, Brynn."

"Wow, that was some trip, Jonah. Fascinating, thank you. I can't believe the wildlife we saw." She was removing her helmet with some difficulty and Jonah helped her. "Thanks. You are a pretty good tour guide. You managed to show me so many different animals. Those caribou were incredible."

Jonah had removed his helmet and was pulling their sled close to the front door. "Come inside Brynn but keep your gear on until I get a fire going."

Jonah was pleased to see the changes that Samuel had made in the camp. The new firebox and stove as well as the new windows would keep the place much warmer. With the wood left in the building and the wood from the sled, Jonah readily got a roaring fire going and within thirty minutes of arrival the cabin was feeling warm and inviting. Jonah also started a fire in the wood stove and warmed up some stew that Mary had packed for them along with fresh bread. They removed their snowmobile suits and sat at the central table in the building, enjoying the warmth and the smells coming from both fire and food.

Brynn was spooning down the hot stew. "Mary's stew is unbelievably good Jonah. If I lived here for long, I would be a blimp." She pushed back from the table and sighed. "So, Mr. Tour Guide, what do you have planned for me this afternoon?"

"Are you up for a ski?"

"Yeah, that sounds good. I could use some exercise. All I have done since I got to Port Muskek is eat. Where are we going?"

"Well, there is a trail through the woods for about five kilometres that leads to a great look-out where we can look over James Bay. It's only about two kilometres as the crow flies but the trail meanders through the bush. I think you'll like it, it's pretty with all this fresh snow. The snow's deep but I can cut trail. I'll take some binoculars. We may be able to see some seals when we get to the lookout. They usually move south as the ice forms. They're chasing the schools of cod that swim south in the bay as the water cools."

"You're giving me a naturalist's introduction to James Bay, Jonah. This is just wonderful. Let's get out on our skis." Jonah banked the fire and they pulled on layered cross-country clothing from the supply of winter clothes Mary had packed for them. Brynn gasped as she saw a rifle that Jonah strapped over his shoulder from the sleigh.

"Really, Jonah. Is that necessary?"

"It's unlikely that we will see bears this early in the season, Brynn. But as a kid I learned from Uncle that it's always best to be armed if you are near the coast. Polar bears move fast and they can surprise you."

Jonah was an expert skier, but Brynn had no trouble keeping up as he cut trail along the path leading eastward toward the Bay. She gasped as they came out of the bush to the lookout and gazed down at James Bay stretching before them to the horizon. "Oh, wow, that's so dramatic Jonah. How many people will stand here with this view, this winter?"

Jonah smiled. "We're probably going to be the first and the last people here Brynn. With Uncle's injury last year, there probably hasn't been anyone here for more than a year. He's really the only person who comes to this camp."

"Where does the Muskek River empty into the Bay?"

"You can't quite see it from here, Brynn – it's just over a kilometre to the south. But the water in the bay is warmed up by the river tumbling in there. And that warmer water draws capelin and cod, and those fish attract seals."

Jonah was scanning the icefield with his binoculars and grunted. "I don't see any seals, but I now know they are definitely here." He lowered his glasses and reached into his pack, retrieving another set of binoculars for Brynn.

"Brynn, look straight out about two hundred metres from the coastline. There's a lump of white snow piled up on the ice. Do you see it? Right beside a flat, black circle in the snow that's about one metre across."

Brynn focused her binoculars. "Yeah, I can see it. I wonder what resulted in the snow piling up just there. Yeah, I can see a dark area on the ice just beside it. Wait a minute, did that snow pile just move?"

Jonah laughed. "Brynn you are looking at a polar bear lying on the ice. We won't need it but I'm happy we brought the rifle. That dark area is a hole that the seal claws through the ice so they can surface and breathe. Those ringed seals can stay under water fishing for up to an hour. When they come to the surface to breathe is when they are at the mercy of Mr. Polar Bear. The seals will make up to ten holes to reduce the risk of any one hole hiding a polar bear. Look, scan around and you will see lots of black holes the seals have made." Jonah focused carefully on the bear through his binoculars.

"These bears are only able to feed on seals when they can get out on the ice. That guy probably hasn't eaten much all summer. You can see how skinny he is. And now through the winter, he needs to catch one or two seals per week to regain his fat stores. He'll lie motionless beside one of those holes for twelve hours, waiting for a seal to poke his head through. If he walks around on the ice, the seals apparently can hear him.

The sound of his paws crunching the snow and ice transmits well through cold water and seals avoid the hole if they hear a bear."

"This is incredible, Jonah. In some ways I would love to see a seal come up. But it must be pretty gruesome when a seal gets caught by a bear."

"Yeah, the ice turns red within seconds. I've seen bears catching seals up here with Uncle when we were ice fishing a few times. The bears are surprisingly fast hauling the seals up onto the ice. And the seals are clumsy out of the water. It's over pretty quickly."

They watched the bear for another ten minutes and saw no movement as the predator waited patiently for what might be his next meal. Then Jonah pointed to the trail. "Brynn, I don't want you to get chilled standing here. This trail loops back to the cabin. Why don't we get going back?"

This time when they entered the camp, the firebox had created a warm, welcoming space. As they walked in the door, Brynn turned quickly and kissed Jonah on the cheek. "Thank you so much, Jonah. That was just an incredible day. I never guessed you would organize a polar bear waiting for me."

Jonah smiled. "Well, the animals here are amazing, but the bathroom facilities are limited. I am going to heat up some water on the stove and I'll put it in that barrel in the corner that serves as our bathtub. I'll pull a screen in front of the tub, and you can sponge bath in the barrel to wash off the sweat from skiing."

Jonah replenished the stove fire and after several minutes dumped the hot water into the bath barrel. Brynn disappeared behind the bath screen and emerged after washing wearing warm sweats. Jonah gave her a small box. "Uncle told me to give them to you after your bath." Opening the box, Brynn found a pair of thick, rabbit fur slippers which she pulled on with delight. "You guys are so sweet; you've thought of everything, Jonah."

They made short work of another of Mary's fish stews that

Jonah warmed on the wood stove, followed by another berry pie. Night had fallen outside as Brynn sat back on the carpet in front of the fire, adjusting pillows behind her back so she could lean against the couch readily seeing Jonah and the fire through the window in the firebox door. They had enjoyed a bottle of white wine cooled in the snow with dinner. Brynn was finishing her third glass and was feeling very mellow.

"This has been such a day Jonah. Thank you so much. It initially seems so forbidding to be out in this freezing country. But when you get geared up and prepared, there is so much to see and do." She paused, smiling. "Thanks for showing me everything I've seen today. That bear was a perfect conclusion to an amazing experience."

She sipped the wine and looked at him closely. "We've been talking all day about caribou and eagles and the country. You haven't told me anything about yourself. You remember my lawyer friend at St. Barts told me you left the pot company? And now I find you here in polar bear country. What's going on with you?"

Jonah had opened a second bottle of chilled wine and offered a refill which Brynn accepted raising her glass. He sat on the carpet across from the surgeon.

"It's pretty simple Brynn. David Morton and I have been working our butts off for the past few years. And we were lucky with that deal you heard about from your lawyer friend at the hospital. David made a bucket of money on that deal and then we took some of it and multiplied it again in the markets. David was very generous to me, and I suddenly found myself financially better off than I ever imagined. David and I have set up a new investment company together but we both decided that we needed a break before starting." He chuckled before continuing.

"And David is right now somewhere in the South Pacific, looking to buy a Polynesian island or something. And here I am, also near salt water, but just about as far from the south seas as possible."

Brynn sipped her wine and set it on the carpet. "It sounds like you could be taking a break just about anywhere in the world, Jonah. Why James Bay?"

Jonah looked at the damped down flames through the firebox window. "Part of it is I wanted to check on Mary and Samuel. Uncle's accident and injury were a shock to me. He has always been the invincible, reliable guy in my life and him getting hurt just stunned me, I guess." He looked up at her. "I guess that's why I went off on you so badly when I first met you in the hospital."

She raised her glass to him. "Okay, you have been officially forgiven for being an insufferable asshole when I first met you."

Jonah nodded and grinned. "Thanks. I was pretty bad, but Uncle means everything to me." He paused and then continued, "So I came back to see how he and Auntie are doing without having any real plans. I've just been helping out Uncle with his various businesses. He has a big contract with the diamond mine owners that I will help him renegotiate in the new year, but after that I have no real schedule in mind." He looked at the fire again.

"I don't know Brynn, I have been away so long, living a life so different from what I would have experienced if I had stayed at Port Muskek. I've kind of forgotten what this place is like. I'm surprised but I am starting to feel something different about being here, peaceful and at home somehow. Especially when I am out on the land like this."

"How did you ever get to Toronto from Port Muskek, Jonah? I heard somewhere that you went to RGC? How did that happen?"

Jonah provided Brynn with an abbreviated story about getting to Toronto, about hockey, and then described his friendship with David Morton, recounting some of David's more outrageous stunts from high school and university.

"So, you guys have been best friends since high school, huh?" Jonah nodded and Brynn continued. "I know that private school social scene in Toronto from my university days. I wasn't part of it, I'm a boring public-school girl from the suburbs. The private school kids were pretty crazy from what I remember. Lots of partying, drugs, and booze."

"Yeah, David was a real leader in that whole party scene. Which I guess led to his interest in the cannabis business. He and I have worked together since I graduated from law school when I went to one of the big Bay Street firms. The only reason they took me on was to get David's business in the early cannabis days. Even though a lot of the younger lawyers knew me from hockey, those firms don't typically hire Indians into their merger and acquisition groups. We made a lot of money for that law firm and for our investors in CannWeed. And I guess now we will try and do it again with our new company." Jonah got up to put wood into the stove. "Enough about me. What the hell are you doing here, Brynn?"

Brynn adjusted the pillows against the couch. "I don't believe what we saw today and where we are. I'm just feeling very relaxed." She settled back comfortably and smiled at him. "The wine's helping too." She adjusted the pillows against the couch.

"I needed a break. Just like you, I guess. I've done nothing but work through med school, residency, lab fellowship. It's been about ten years of head down working, never really thinking about anything except the next step to get where I am today. And now I've been at St. Barts for three years and doing well – I guess most people would say." She swirled her glass and paused, looking at the wine circling.

"It's tough being a woman surgeon Jonah. Stuff happens that you would not believe. I mean apart from patients' family members accusing you of being a racist student nurse." She smiled at him. He couldn't look away when she smiled. "And I had a terrible break up with my former fiancé. I just had to get away for a while. I have a good friend from med school. You would love her, she's Vietnamese and works at Wiichihinan Hospital." Brynn smiled again thinking of Yvette.

"She asked me to come up and give some advice to the hospital CEO about doing surgery here. St. Barts gave me a sabbatical and here I am." She looked at him across the carpet. "I keep on slipping sideways on these cushions. Would you mind coming over here and sitting beside me to hold me upright?" She smiled again. "You get a really good view of the fire from over here."

Jonah felt that familiar sense of panic as he slid across the carpet to push cushions against the couch and leaned back sitting a foot away from Brynn. "You are not helping me stay upright sitting way over there, Mr. Tour Guide." He shifted closer and felt her leaning against him. "That's perfect. The tour guide is supposed to keep the guests comfortable you know." She turned toward him. "This has been an incredible day, Jonah, thank you so much."

And leaned forward with her lips softly contacting his. His anxiety faded momentarily, and he lifted his arm around her back and softly pulled her to him, his lips meeting hers. And then a surge of apprehension returned like a waterfall and he congealed, every muscle tense.

She felt his tension and him retracting from her. "What's wrong Jonah? Don't worry, you're not taking advantage of me out here in the wilderness."

He shifted away. "I'm sorry Brynn. It has been a great day. But I should show you where your bunk is."

She gazed at him with concern. "What's going on? Did I insult you or something?"

Jonah stared at the floor. Embarrassed and distressed. "No, no, no. No insult, Brynn. It's all about me really. Just stuff that happened to me when I was a kid." He looked at her with downcast eyes. "I guess you could say that I have some problems with intimacy with some women."

Brynn blurted out. "Are you gay?" Jonah shook his head. At that moment his thoughts were consumed by the memory of kissing his mother's beautiful but cold face as she lay rigid in the nursing station – he simply could not imagine kissing

Brynn with that memory of his mother filling his mind.

"No, no. Like I say, I had some stuff happen to me as a kid. I can't really talk about it." Jonah pushed against the couch to stand, full of confusion and wanting to be elsewhere. "I'll get some blankets on this bunk over here for you. I'll sleep on the couch so I can keep the fire going."

Brynn was embarrassed as well as disappointed. This guy was so intriguing, so different. He had somehow attracted her even when he was rude when they first met at St. Barts. Today had been so good, so interesting, and easy going. She had not really known what to expect from this evening, but things had seemed close yet casual until she turned to kiss him. She really didn't know what she was planning with that kiss – it was just spontaneous, maybe related to the wine and the general feeling of relaxed pleasure she was feeling. Maybe she just wanted a cuddle, some closeness, just a little warmth? She didn't know, it had been so long since she had enjoyed anything physical.

But was she just going too fast, being too forward? She mentally berated herself for making a first move that was being rejected so firmly. She had thought that he might be interested in the same way. But then decided that she had already embarrassed herself and there was no harm trying again. Maybe he just needed encouragement. She considered the wisdom of trying again and decided to throw caution to the wind.

She joined him standing and helped him to adjust the blankets on the bunk. Then she moved close, putting her hand on his arm. "You are going to be uncomfortable on the couch, Jonah. There's plenty of room here on the bunk for both of us." She looked at him directly. "I guess I can promise to behave."

He shook his head, looking away and lifting his arm out from under her hand. "The couch is closer to the fire and believe me, we need to keep that fire going." Brynn realized he was extinguishing her fire more thoroughly than a bucket of water.

"How about pancakes and bacon for breakfast, Doc?" Oh, God, now he had returned to that stupid doc business. She had really destroyed this evening.

"Yeah, that sounds good Jonah." She reached for her pack, wondering how to regain her dignity. "I brought my tablet with me, so believe it or not, I am going to crawl into the bunk and read for a while. That light won't bother you?"

Jonah loaded the stove with wood, waited until it caught and then damped it down by adjusting the flue. "That's fine, Doc. I will have coffee ready when you wake up." The tension in the room was merciless as they both adjusted their blankets.

"Thanks for a great day, Jonah."

"No problem, Doc."

CHAPTER 16

The Convention. January 2019

T he Prospectors and Miners Convention, or PMiC as it was known to guests at the King William Hotel in Toronto, was the largest annual mining conference in the world. PMiC had been an important date in the international mining calendar for the past fifty years and now major deals were regularly closed at the event with billions of dollars in mining investments, mergers and acquisitions being planned, negotiated, and signed.

New methods for measuring seismic strain in the earth's crust were being featured in the conference program this year. This developing technology was important to the new generation of prospectors who spent more time analyzing wave patterns on computers than wandering through the bush with hammer in hand. In addition to large scale plenary sessions on new prospecting and mining technology, convention delegates attended sessions on corporate social responsibility, the ethics of mining in impoverished countries and demonstrating respect for equity and diversity. But the heartbeat of the conference echoed from the days when prospectors were kings, coming to the conference to announce and often lie about their latest discoveries, looking for financing from both savvy professionals and gullible fools.

Tales from past conventions were legend and included fist fights in bars between company presidents as well as murder at the top of the King William elevator where two promoters of competing Northern Ontario penny mining prospects settled their differences with pistols.

The size of the convention and the increasing number of delegates had moved the actual PMiC conference down the street to the larger convention centre. Delegates were now housed in all the hotels surrounding the convention hall. But the movers and shakers of PMiC, the major mining company leaders and the international bankers and investors who provided the jet fuel that kept the mining industry aloft, booked their rooms at the King William Hotel years in advance, keeping the same suites which provided both hospitality and quiet corners for deal making. Before the morning convention session began, the hotel lobby was filled with a diverse crowd, a few dressed in prospector's jeans and flannel shirts, mining executives in studied corporate casual and the money men identified by their expensively tailored suits and silk ties.

David Morton was pleased to take in the frenetic energy of the mining business buzzing in the lobby. Three weeks of South Pacific palm trees and warm waters had restored his equilibrium but by four weeks he was bored and by six weeks he was leaving. His family had a long history of financial action derived from PMiC, mainly serving as penny stock "pumpers and dumpers" who would promote and sell stocks for junior miners. These small miners and explorers usually took their investors' money down fabled mine shafts that were not always drilled and rarely ever productive. David was at the meeting to renew contacts and to consider creating a mining investment interest for Mindful Innovation. He had booked meetings with several prospectors and junior miners who wanted his help raising money. Mostly David felt a need to be back in the action.

He was also planning to catch up with Jonah. His buddy had messaged him while David was still in the south seas, asking David's help to connect to a prospector with experience in the northern Canadian diamond industry. David's father had raised plenty of money for junior diamond miners and one investment had actually resulted in a mine which was about to start production in the Northwest Territories, several years after the initial results suggested that it might be productive. David was looking forward to seeing his friend later at lunch. This six-week sojourn to the South Pacific was the longest he had been apart from Jonah since high school.

David was standing in one of two long, shuffling coffee lines, desperately needing a morning dose of caffeine. He had been entertained the night before by a couple of old-timers who wanted his help with promotion of a possible new gold find in Kazakhstan. The night had gone long, and David's head was throbbing from the cognac they had consumed after dinner. He was looking down at his phone screen when he heard a vaguely familiar voice standing next to him in the adjacent line-up of customers headed toward the second barista taking orders.

"Where is our session this morning? Do you know what meeting room? Is your PowerPoint set? You're going to do just fine."

David looked at the woman standing beside him and immediately recognized the auburn hair. "Hey, Doc, how are you? Remember me?"

Brynn looked over, then turned back to her phone, signing off her call. "Okay, I'll see you in the room in ten minutes. We can go over your slides before the meeting starts." She lowered her phone, placing it in her jacket pocket, and looked at David with surprise, suspicion and then recognition.

"Of course, the pot king. It's David, right?" David smiled, pleased to be recognized by this beautiful woman. She was wearing a scarlet dress, topped by a green blazer.

"Yeah, that's right. You're the surgeon from St. Barts that looked after Uncle Samuel, right?"

"What, he's your uncle too?"

David smiled. "No, no, but I'm good friends with his nephew, Jonah Kay. What are you doing here, anyway? This is a mining conference." He held his arm up expansively, taking in the crowd milling about in the King William lobby, ready to head underground to walk to the adjacent convention centre for the first morning conference sessions.

Brynn nodded. "Yeah, I realized that these aren't orthopaedic surgeons. Most of them are too well dressed." She smiled at David. "You miners are meeting over at the convention centre I understand. We have a much smaller hip surgery meeting here at the King William conference centre. My team is presenting some research results at that meeting."

Then Brynn seemed to think of something and she looked down, biting her lip, obviously deliberating about her next comment, and then continued. "Hey, are you around all day? There's something I want to talk to you about." She paused again and David could almost see the thoughts spinning around her brain as her teeth grasped her lower lip. "It has to do with your friend, Jonah. I'm in our meeting until about four thirty this afternoon. Could we meet up after?"

David was intrigued. He wondered what she wanted. "Dinner?"

Brynn shook her head. "No, sorry, I am taking my team out for dinner after the research presentation. And then I'm flying back to Moose tomorrow." David was surprised at the mention of Moose. What was she doing there?

David shrugged. "You do not know how many women would fight for the chance to dine with me." He smiled, taking some of the braggadocio off the statement. "How about a drink in the lobby bar before you go out to dinner – say about five?"

Brynn nodded and then obviously thought of something. "Okay, great. If you talk to Jonah, you don't need to tell him we are meeting." She looked at him with green eyes that reflected the green blazer. "Okay? Promise?"

David leaned back. "Whoa, that sounds interesting. Sure, lips are sealed. Whatever it takes to get a drink with you. Let's say the King William lobby bar at five, okay?"

Brynn nodded as she stepped up to give her order. She waved goodbye to David as she turned to go with her cup. "See you at five, lobby bar."

David watched her walk away. He remained impressed by Uncle Samuel's surgeon. And then he wandered off with his morning coffee, going to meet with prospectors searching for rare earths in Canada's north and looking forward to lunch.

David had reserved a suite in the King William for entertaining and negotiating and had ordered lunch to be delivered to the suite where he was meeting Jonah at noon along with a prospector geologist who had been staked by David's family on several occasions in the past. David respected this prospector who he knew to be both knowledgeable and reliable. Reliable in the prospecting business meant that he did not knowingly lie about his discoveries, although he was as prone to exaggeration as anyone else in the mineral finding business. His name was William Myrtle but everyone in Canada's mining industry knew him as Diamond Bill.

Bill was in his late fifties and his face showed evidence of a lifetime spent outdoors. He was dressed in a faded blue blazer and threadbare gray trousers. David smiled to himself, knowing that, despite his ragged appearance, Bill was now probably worth hundreds of millions of dollars based on his diamond find in northern Canada. Bill just didn't care much about clothing or any of the other trappings of wealth. He was well versed in the modern technologies of scanning and computer searching for valuable mineral deposits. However, his preference was to spend time working on the rock collecting samples while staying in fly-in wilderness camps with horseflies and bears as his only companions.

David welcomed Bill and offered him a drink from his room's bar. The prospector took the top off a beer bottle while David poured a glass of white Bordeaux from the chilled bottles that the hotel had delivered to his room. "How's that diamond mine coming along, Bill? Opening soon?"

William nodded. "Yup, just months now." David liked that the prospector was a man of few words. He had always found it easier to raise money for new projects when he could spin the story for investors, leaving the prospector to nod at the appropriate points of the story and otherwise remain silent.

As Diamond Bill settled into a chair at the dining table that had been set in David's suite, there was a knock at the door and David welcomed his best friend. They hugged in the doorway, agreed they were both looking well and entered the dining area where David introduced Bill to Jonah. Jonah went to the bar and poured one third wine and two thirds Perrier into a glass and sat between Bill and David. Bill wasted little time with introductions as two waiters let themselves into the suite delivering broiled salmon for David's lunch meeting.

William took a forkful of fish and wiped the back of his hand across his mouth. "David tells me you want to show me something from James Bay, Jonah."

David smiled at Jonah. "Diamond Bill here gets right to the point." Then he turned to the weather-beaten prospector.

"Bill, Jonah called to ask me to find someone reliable he could talk to about something he has discovered in James Bay. Jonah, Diamond Bill here spent twenty years surveying and prospecting in northern Canada before he identified a major find that is just about ready to start production. My family bankrolled a lot of that prospecting work."

Jonah was interested. "That's a new Helder mine, right?"

William nodded. "Yeah, we staked it and did the original exploration. We then sold out most of our stake to Helder."

David couldn't help interjecting. "Bill made a lot of money selling those stakes. And did pretty well for us investors at the same time." He leaned over and punched William lightly in the shoulder.

Jonah was nodding as he sampled the salmon. "Thanks for

introducing us, David. Bill, I want to show you something and talk about where I found it. Can I trust that you will keep this information confidential?"

David spoke up before Bill could answer. "Jonah, I forewarned Bill that this is a confidential meeting and he agreed to those terms. Bill is one of the few prospectors I know that you can trust to stay quiet about something." The prospector gestured that he understood, and Jonah reached into his briefcase and pulled out a small pouch which he opened and emptied on the dining table. Both David and William leaned forward in their chairs to look closely at the four small diamonds that Jonah had brought from Uncle Samuel's fridge top collection for Mary.

William reached into his pocket and took out a jeweler's loupe which he fitted onto his eye. He also removed a small forceps from his pocket which he used to pick up the closest stone and rotate it under the light while he examined it through the loupe. After a ten second examination he repeated the evaluation for the other three stones.

"Yeah, nice stones. Good quality – but small." He took a bite of salmon and chased it with a swallow of beer from the bottle. "Are they alluvials?"

"Where did you get these, Jonah?" David asked. Jonah shrugged.

"Wait a minute and we can discuss that," Jonah said. "Yeah, these are all alluvial diamonds found in creek beds. But now have a look at another alluvial." He took another pouch from his briefcase and rolled out the much larger stone that he had discovered in the creek bed following Charlie's snowmobile.

David gasped. "Jesus, Jonah, that is huge." Diamond Bill picked it up with his fingers, the stone was too big to lift with the forceps.

Rotating it in the light while he peered through the loupe, William whistled quietly. "You can't tell until it's cut and polished but that is a mighty fine stone. I didn't bring my scale, but it must be close to ten carats uncut."

Jonah looked from David to William and back. "What if I told you those first smaller stones were discovered in a creek bed downstream from a kimberlite pipe currently in production. And that second bigger one was found in another creek downstream from a second pipe that hasn't been developed."

William was nodding his head. "Well, the only mine in production in James Bay right now is the Helder Sierra mine, so I assume the first smaller stones are alluvials from Sierra. I'd also say I want to know where that second pipe is."

He continued, leaning back, and looking to the ceiling. "You guys probably know this – but just hear me out about how you assess a potential new diamond discovery." David smiled to himself. Diamond Bill was taciturn until he started talking about his favourite topic – finding diamonds.

"Kimberlite pipes are vertical volcanic rivers that erupted from the earth's mantle tens of millions of years ago and carved their way up to the earth's surface. The incredible pressure and heat of the mantle one hundred miles underground at the bottom of the kimberlite pipe sometimes resulted in carbon deposits being transformed into diamonds and those stones then being transported toward the earth's surface with the volcanic eruption through the pipe. These kimberlite pipes are full of volcanic rock, fragments of the earth's mantle and interesting stones like garnets and sometime diamonds." He paused to ensure that David and Jonah were following. Jonah nodded and William continued.

"In my early days prospecting you looked for kimberlite pipes by identifying the garnet in the rock or in some cases finding alluvial diamonds in streams like these little fellas." He pointed to the smaller diamonds Uncle Samuel had collected south of Sierra. "Then it got easier when we discovered that the ore typically found in kimberlite results in aberrations in the earth's magnetic field. You can now fly over a region measuring the ground magnetic forces and look for variations than can be detected by the magnetic sensor mounted in the plane. Once you identify magnetic aberration, you gotta get down on the ground and look for stones like garnet that identify a pipe. A pipe is usually only a few hundred metres across in diameter, so it really is searching for a needle in the haystack, even with the aerial magnetic scanning." He paused for a swig of beer from the bottle and shook his head.

"There are about six thousand pipes that have been discovered around the world. Diamonds have been discovered in about sixty of these pipes, only about one per cent. And the only way that you know that diamonds are present is to take out samples of volcanic rock from the pipe and crush the rock and see if you find diamonds. That is a very long run for what is usually a short slide, gentlemen. It's expensive to set up a mining exploratory operation. That volcanic rock is hard to drill and until you crush the core you have extracted and look for the gems, you really don't know if you have a viable discovery. With fewer than one per cent of pipes demonstrating sufficient diamond reserves to make a mine economically viable, figuring out what a pipe is potentially worth is an important judgement call for the prospector and miner. When you sample fifty cores you are sampling way less than one thousandth of one per cent of the pipe volume, even just at the surface, and if you don't find diamonds, then you're probably going to give up on that pipe with only a tiny, tiny part of the deposit sampled." He sighed and shook his head.

"That's why alluvial diamonds can be so important." He passed his hand over the diamonds on the table. "If these were alluvials downstream from a pipe, their presence would be an important indicator that we should take lots of cores to assess whether we should start a mine. The alluvials tell me that the pipe likely has diamonds and that we should take plenty of samples before deciding whether it has value." He picked up the bigger stone and examined it again carefully, then looked at Jonah.

"This is going to be a very nice stone if it's cut right. Where is it from?"

Jonah lifted his hand. "Before I answer that, let me ask you a question." He put his hand over the four smaller diamonds. "If I told you that these stones were found downstream from one pipe," and then passed his hand over the much larger diamond, "and this stone came from a second, different deposit; which pipe would you want to explore first?"

Diamond Bill looked at David and then back at Jonah. "I think you know my answer to that."

*****

The lobby bar of the King William Hotel was a throwback to the hotel's origins as a grand railway hotel - a wide, brightly lit marble bar counter with thousands of bottles reflected in glistening mirrors behind the bartender, polished wood panelled walls, low lights, chandeliers, and plenty of leather booths around the perimeter. David Morton had called down and reserved a quiet corner booth for two, pre-ordering an appetizer tray for the table and arriving ten minutes before five. He wasn't waiting long with his scotch before Brynn was brought to his table by the hostess.

"How was your meeting?" he asked as Brynn slid into the booth.

"That's nice of you, David, to order some snacks," said Brynn, picking up a large olive, popping it in her mouth and chewing slowly before placing the stone in a napkin. "Sorry, I am starving. We presented this morning, describing some exciting results about new metal treatments we have developed to encourage bone cells to grow better against metallic joint replacements. There were a couple of companies attending the meeting who support this research. They like what we are doing and the results we are getting. It'll help them make better hip and knee joint replacements and maybe increase their market share." She paused, carefully selecting a slice of salami from David's snack tray and folded it around a wedge of cheese before placing it whole into her mouth. "Oh, that's really good salami, David, yum." She dabbed a napkin against her lips.

"Both companies wanted to negotiate support for new studies, and I spent lunch time talking money for research rather than eating." She thought for a minute. "Actually, the only thing I have consumed all day was that latte I was ordering when I met you this morning. No wonder I am starved." She popped a mini quiche in her mouth and smiled at David. "There, that's better."

The waitress arrived with the glass of Pinot Grigio that Brynn had ordered before sitting. Taking a sip, Brynn sighed and smiled. "Okay, now I feel human. How was your day, David?"

David shook his head. "Well, I met your friend Jonah Kay at lunchtime. I have known that boy since we were in high school, and he never ceases to amaze me."

Brynn looked up from the appetizer plate with interest. "I didn't know he was in Toronto. Last time I saw him was in Port Muskek just before the holidays."

David raised his hands off the table. "Wow, I've been gone for just six weeks, and you've moved to Moose, and now you are seeing Jonah in Port Muskek. You guys are moving fast! Are you telling me you're like – seeing Jonah? Like are you two hooking up on James Bay? And now you don't know he's in Toronto?"

Brynn leaned forward. "Well, that's why I wanted to talk to you, David. I have been so confused since the last time I saw Jonah and when I saw you in that coffee line this morning it just hit me that I needed to talk to you. Jonah told me that you guys go way back to high school together. I understand you don't know me, and I wouldn't normally do this, but I am so puzzled by Jonah. I'm kinda embarrassed talking to you this way, but I just don't know what to think."

David looked at her carefully, taking a sip of his scotch. "Okay Brynn I may know what this is all about. Why don't you just go ahead and ask me what you want."

Brynn explained that she and Jonah had spent a wonderful day together that seemed to be going in the right direction until Jonah suddenly clammed up, saying that he had "intimacy problems" stemming from something that had happened when he was a kid. She ended slowly, shaking her head.

"I'm embarrassed sitting here with someone who doesn't know me talking about my love life. Really, what I mean to say is the deficiency in my love life." She looked across the table, directly into David's eyes. "A little over a year ago, I had a terrible break-up with my former fiancé, and I'm really starting to wonder if maybe I'm going to be doomed with men. Being a surgeon seems to put a considerable crimp on meeting guys who might be appropriate to spend my life with." She shook her head while plucking another olive from the plate, thoughtfully chewing it and then again returning the stone to a napkin.

"And now that I'm working in the James Bay community, I expect to run into Jonah from time to time. I'm sorry if I am putting you in a tough place asking about your friend, but can you help me to understand Jonah a little bit? He seems like such a good guy, but he totally confuses me."

David looked down at the table and sighed softly. He liked this woman. She would be such a good match for Jonah. Where should he start?

"Brynn, I'm not surprised by what you are telling me, and I'm glad that you are reaching out for your sake and his. I love Jonah, he is my closest friend, but he has some real issues that you should know about." David sipped from his crystal glass and stared at the ceiling, wondering how to approach this.

"I guess the first thing you have to know is what happened to Jonah's mum. She was sexually abused in one of those terrible Indian residential schools as a kid and it had an awful impact on her. Jonah never knew who his father was. Then, when he was only five years old, he discovered his mum dead from an overdose of some sort."

Brynn gasped. "Oh my God. I didn't know. That's why he was brought up by his aunt and uncle?"

"Yeah, that's right. That's why he's so close to Mary and Samuel. They took over as his parents when he lost his mum. They are wonderful people. I have known them nearly as long as I've known Jonah and I love those two."

Then David paused and looked down at the table again. "Jonah is an amazing guy, a fantastic friend. I want to see him happy." He looked at the ceiling again before continuing. "He would be upset if he knew I was talking to you about this Brynn, but I like you and you would be so good for my buddy."

He looked up at Brynn. "About nine years after his mum died, Jonah was given a scholarship to move to Toronto, attend RGC and play hockey. He was a star athlete and student. But then things got pretty weird."

David described Jonah's seduction by the coach's wife, and how Jonah eventually moved in with David's family to escape Evelyn. And then how his mother's friends had discovered him. Brynn listened without saying anything, occasionally shaking her head.

David concluded. "Throughout high school and university so many great girls we knew were interested in Jonah. He's obviously a good looking, smart guy and he was a star in hockey throughout school. Everyone knew him, liked him, and admired him. And he was kind of exotic in our crowd, you know? Different from other guys." He shook his head at memories of potential relationships that would have been ideal for Jonah Kay.

"But Jonah would always avoid girls that seemed just right for him. And I knew that he was quietly still making it with my mother's friends, then with some of our university profs, and once he started in law, with some senior lawyers and judges. Some older women just fall for him, and I guess it's sort of become a habit for him now."

"Well, I suppose if that's what he wants, but I don't really get it." Brynn suddenly felt squeamish. "I have to say, this sounds kinda' weird to me, David. What do you guys call them – cougars? But whatever turns you on, huh? I'm glad you are telling me this. It sounds like I should forget about Jonah."

"Brynn, believe me, Jonah doesn't like where he's at. He wants to raise a family; he wants a partner he can relate to. He has really only had affairs with older women. But what he really wants and needs is a relationship with someone like you. You would be so great for him." David's eyes were almost pleading for his friend as he looked across the table and then continued.

"We've talked about it a few times – it's not easy for him to discuss. He tells me when he is attracted to someone his own age, she will make him start thinking about his mother who was really young when she died. I've seen pictures of her. His mum was really very pretty. I guess he just gets flashbacks to her death or really intense thoughts about her he can't tolerate. Those images must be terrible because he discovered her after she died." David looked down at the table and shook his head.

"And those thoughts somehow associate his mother with the young woman he is attracted to. It sounds terrible and he says he just can't get rid of these terrible images once they start. I know he's had therapy or something – he hates talking about it. It's really hard for him."

Brynn looked thoughtful and took another olive. "Now that I've been at the hospital in Moose for a while, I've heard about this kind of thing – although never quite as dramatic as what you are describing. The docs and nurses up there talk about intergenerational trauma. Damage to the children of abused residential school survivors that gets passed down to subsequent generations. That intergenerational trauma apparently not only accounts for mental health issues, but also for chronic health issues like diabetes where people make bad health choices based on what happened to their parents and even their grandparents in those schools."

Brynn shook her head. "I don't know David. I made it pretty obvious that night on James Bay that I was interested in him – I came on pretty strong. And he let me know in no uncertain terms that he was not interested in me. It was actually embarrassing. Whatever happened to him as a kid sounds terrible. Believe me, I feel bad for him. But it sounds like Jonah has a lot of work to do before he's ready to date someone who's not twenty years older."

David sat back in their booth and sipped his scotch. He looked at Brynn and thought about her intelligence, her energy and her unusual commitment to working in James Bay. About how perfect she would be for Jonah. And realized that he had no idea how to help either of them.

CHAPTER 17

Toronto. January 2019

As David and Brynn sat in the King William bar, the subject of their discussion was lying peacefully in a hotel suite less than a kilometre away. After his lunch meeting with David Morton and Diamond Bill, Jonah had walked over to the Distillery District to check in on the team at Mindful Innovation. The investment group was delighted to see him in person rather than on the phone from Port Muskek and they spent the afternoon reviewing the success of their derivative bets on CannWeed stock and other strategies that the traders had been considering.

The team was energized by their success in the options trades and delighted to pitch other investment ideas to Jonah. Jonah reassured them that both he and David would be back in the office soon to consider the trading strategy that would define Mindful. The traders had told Jonah that the "Mindful" nickname was edging out "MI" as the affectionate term for Mindful Innovation being used by the team. They liked being members of the Mindful trading team.

After the afternoon with the team, Jonah walked back to

the hotel district where he had been invited to a suite. In response to his knock, the door to the suite was opened by Hillary Vanstone, the International Brands corporate counsel who was visiting Toronto from New York, helping the local team to complete the realignment of CannWeed into the International Brands corporate family. She was spending three or four days a month in Toronto and had messaged Jonah that she would enjoy seeing him.

They both agreed it would not be wise to be seen together in public and Hillary had invited him to her suite promising to order room service. But both corporate talk and dinner were forgotten when Jonah arrived. An hour later Jonah was staring at the ceiling while Hillary napped curled on his arm.

She stirred, looking up at him. "Well, that's the nicest thing that's happened to me since I started coming to Toronto, Jonah. This city is too cold for me, but you just warmed it up considerably."

Jonah smiled. It had been over a year since he had originally thought that he and Hillary might hookup the night of the deal dinner at Azo. It had taken longer than he had initially imagined but was worth the wait. Hillary was about twenty years older than him, experienced as well as passionate and Jonah was anticipating spending the night with her.

They checked out the room service menu on their phones. Jonah remembered Hillary's very controlled appetite when she limited herself to a Niçoise salad. Jonah decided that he deserved a steak based on what he had accomplished today.

Wrapping themselves in robes after dinner arrived, they discussed her work re-organizing CannWeed. She complimented Jonah on the deal that he and David had achieved. "I'm not sure to this day what happened at the end of that negotiation, Jonah, but you allowed Morton to make out like a bandit."

Jonah decided it would not be appropriate to tell her how he and David had multiplied their money further with their CannWeed put options. Confidentiality and discretion were advantages of derivative deals and Jonah decided that their success was best kept quiet.

It did not take long after dinner for them to return to the bedroom. Forty-five minutes later Hillary was napping again, and Jonah was thinking carefully about why he was here in her room.

*****

After the Toronto scientific conference and meeting with David Morton, Brynn had one more stop before heading to the airport to fly back to Moose. The CEO of St. Barts had asked for a report on her experiences in James Bay, so Brynn had made an appointment to meet with Keshini Jayawardana the morning of her flight back to Moose.

Keshini seemed frustrated when Brynn entered her office just as the CEO was hanging up her phone displaying obvious exasperation.

"Wow, doctors!" she fumed as she turned her chair away from her phone to stand and greet Brynn with a smile. "I am sorry. Please, forgive my bad manners, come, and sit." She led Brynn to two chairs set up across the office from her desk. "Welcome home. I understand you are only here for a brief stay so thank you for making time to see me."

The CEO continued as the two women sat. "I shouldn't tell you this, but I am so frustrated, and actually I could use your help as a surgeon to help me understand the issue I am dealing with." Keshini tented her fingers in front of her face, obviously considering how much she should say. Then having made a decision, she looked directly at Brynn.

"Can I trust you to keep this conversation strictly between us?" Brynn nodded, wondering what she was getting herself into.

"That call I was on when you came in was with your colleague, our esteemed chief of surgery. I understand he is very well respected by his peers for his skills in the operating room." She looked at Brynn, testing her assumption and Brynn nodded, feeling adrift in uncharted waters. The CEO continued.

"However, despite his surgical skills, he has no understanding of how medicine needs to become more consumer oriented." Brynn could imagine smoke coming out of Keshini's ears as she spoke. The CEO was not a good poker player – her emotions were definitely evident on the surface.

"I am offering to finance and organize a new system for surgical consults for our entire hospital. Consults would be received digitally through a portal that is well-tested, replacing our current reliance on faxing consults. It would allow patients to track their consults and learn when they might expect to see the surgeon and would eliminate lost referrals caused by lost faxes. The portal automatically sends the referral to the surgeon with the shortest waiting list and thereby immediately reduces waiting times by about twenty per cent. And it would allow the hospital to understand each surgeon's wait list and how many patients are waiting for surgery at St. Barts. That data would give me a real asset to use with the government to get more money to provide more surgery." Keshini shook her head.

"So, I cannot see anything but good for our surgeons with this project. They would get a slick referral service that's easy for the family docs to use, paid for by the hospital and a chance to get more publicly funded surgery paid for by the government. And, if GP's don't want to refer patients using the technology, they could still fax the surgeon's office." She almost rose from her chair as she leaned forward toward Brynn. "So, you tell me Dr. Allard, why does your respected leader absolutely refuse to support the implementation of this technology?"

Brynn smiled to herself. There was so much to say about this issue, and it was not really what she wanted to talk about. But maybe if she helped the CEO to understand, it would help her with what she really wanted to discuss.

"Well, Ms. Jayawardana." The CEO interrupted. "Call me Keshini. I know Jayawardana is a mouthful."

"Okay, Keshini, let's start by discussing why women surgeons make about twenty-five per cent less than men despite working the same hours? Part of the reason is that family docs refer female surgeons cases that are likely to require talking to the patient instead of an operation. Surgery pays much better than talking. Most family docs understand that the few women surgeons in practice are more willing to talk to their patients than male surgeons. It has been shown in plenty of studies that referrals to men surgeons are different and pay more on average than referrals to women surgeons."

The CEO shook her head. "Well, that's not fair. That is a good reason to implement my digital referral system that directs the next referral to the surgeon who has the right skills and the shortest waiting list."

Now Brynn smiled at her boss. "That's true unless the current system of faxing directly to the surgeons' offices benefits the surgeons who get those faxes." She paused while considering the wisdom of her next comment and decided to throw caution to the wind. "Like our chief of surgery. Do you think maybe he likes his long wait list? Do you think maybe he doesn't want to change a system that has plenty of patients lining up to see him?" And smiled again at the CEO.

Keshini looked carefully at Brynn. "Hmm, okay, yeah I get it. It's pretty obvious that our chief does not want the hospital looking over his shoulder at how he manages his waiting list. And I can see maybe he doesn't want a nosy new CEO named Keshini to mess with how his practice functions."

Now she smiled back at Brynn. "Maybe some of the changes I want to make require a new generation of surgical leaders. And maybe some women leaders." She continued, lifting her hands in submission to her inability to effect change with her current leaders. "But that's not why I asked you to come in to see me, Brynn. I want to know how you are doing at Wiichihinan Hospital."

Brynn sighed. "Well, I've learned so much in the months that I have been there. First and foremost, the eight thousand or so people who live along the James Bay coast receive much worse service than other people living in Canada. The docs and nurses who work there are committed and skilled at what they can do. But realistically, people need to fly out to get seen down south if they want to see most specialists and that just seems wrong."

Keshini leaned forward again. "I can't imagine that you will get specialists to spend their careers in James Bay. Would you do that as an orthopaedic surgeon?"

Brynn shook her head. "Of course not. My home, my practice and my lab are here. However, I would be very willing to spend three months in Wiichihinan every couple of years if I could get a group of surgeons together who were willing to do joint replacements on a three-month rotation. And while we're there, we could also handle most of the trauma surgery. We could also try and recruit general surgeons, gynaecologists, and urologists to rotate and spend some time at Wiichihinan. If the CEOs of our university hospitals supported surgeons spending some time there, I think that we could interest some of my surgical colleagues."

Keshini was obviously considering Brynn's comments closely. "Would their operating rooms be safe for providing more surgery?"

Brynn was already nodding. "Even in the old hospital, the ORs are okay. As long as the air exchange in the ORs is adequate and infection control principles are followed, we could do most operations there. Total joint replacements are probably the most demanding surgery to do in their old ORs because of the risk of getting an infection during the operation. We got the engineers to check the air quality and they have boosted the air flow so they are meeting the standard of greater than fifteen air exchanges per hour. The engineers are also willing to put HEPA filters into the air supply to make the air even cleaner if we go ahead with surgery. And there's a new hospital planned for the near future. We could design the ORs to suit the needs of the surgeons who would be operating there."

Keshini leaned back in her chair. "Okay I am going to play devil's advocate, Brynn. What difference does it make if the people get their total joint replacement at Wiichihinan Hospital or at St. Barts as long as Dr. Allard is the surgeon? Why can't they come here rather than you going there?"

Brynn lifted her hands. "Yeah, that's exactly what I would have said before I spent the last months doing clinics in Moose and up the coast to Port Muskek. The Elders in those communities who need to have their joints replaced for arthritis are often reluctant to come to Toronto. Many of them speak Cree as a first language and are uncomfortable when they are forced to speak English. A trip to Moose is a big deal – going to Toronto would be very intimidating. They prefer to avoid surgery and use a wheelchair to manage their arthritis rather than fly out to Toronto for an operation." She put her hands back in her lap.

"Keshini, you have to understand the impact of the trauma that has resulted from centuries of colonialism and those residential schools. It's not just the kids who were individually abused there. It's many generations of Indigenous People who were taught by us Canadians, our government, and our churches that their Indigenous culture, language, and values were primitive and needed to be extinguished. And now they are reluctant to seek help from government services that abused them so badly in the past. Maybe one way we can all make up for that abuse is to talk with them about how we can provide better health services. And one of the things I hear constantly in my clinics is the desire to get treated closer to home with the support of their community surrounding them."

Keshini was silent for a moment. "You know Brynn, my Sri Lankan community has fought to have our needs recognized and it's still not easy. Lots of immigrant communities can make the same claim that they need culturally safe care."

Brynn waited, wondering how far she could go in response. "Yeah, but remember Keshini, your people came here. The people in James Bay were here long before any other Canadians. And we made promises to them signing the treaties that took their land, including a promise to provide healthcare, rudimentary as healthcare was when treaties were signed. We have broken so many of those promises. If we are really serious about this big word 'reconciliation,' then maybe we should start thinking about health services being delivered differently." Seeing that her CEO was listening, Brynn continued.

"I mean most immigrants to Canada come to urban areas where services are well established. Public schools and healthcare are planned to be the same for fifteenth generation Canadians and new Canadians. I know that health equity is an important issue in our cities. But the offer of care in your own community simply does not exist for people living in James Bay."

Keshini was thinking deeply. "I told you when we first met Brynn, that I was pleased that you were going to Wiichihinan because I wanted to figure out how we could better serve Indigenous People living in Toronto. Now I am wondering if I can help you provide better options for people in James Bay?"

Brynn was nodding. "Thanks for asking Keshini. I am not ready to provide an answer yet. The first principle would be "Nothing about us without us," as Jane Gagne, who's the CEO of Wiichihinan, constantly reminds me. We need to do more consultations along the coast, especially with Elders in the communities. However, the one thing I have heard consistently is that offering surgery in Wiichihinan Hospital would be appreciated. To accomplish that local delivery of care, you could put St. Barts in the mix along with another couple of hospitals. Let's say you and two or three other hospital CEOs in Toronto agreed to recruit two or three new surgeons who would commit to spending three months a year in Wiichihinan Hospital. If we developed a group of surgeons who would spend most of their time in Toronto but some time offering surgery in Moose, we could respond to what people living on James Bay seem to want in terms of service."

Keshini was thinking hard. "Are you certain this plan would be well received?"

Brynn shrugged her shoulders. "I need make sure with the engineers that those ORs are safe. And I need help from Jane Gagne and her staff to do focus groups with Elders along the coast to make sure what I am suggesting would be acceptable. But I'm pretty sure this would be very well received."

Keshini was nodding. "Okay, let me know what you are thinking over the next couple of months. There's one other thing I want your advice on." Keshini turned in her chair to signal moving on to another topic.

"The Dean of the medical school has appointed me to the search committee to select a new Chair of orthopaedic surgery. Does the surgeon in that role have an impact on someone like you Brynn? What kind of person should we be looking for?"

Brynn thought back to her last humiliating interaction with the Chair and his advice to reconcile with her ex-fiancé rather than discussing her surgery and research career. She again considered how honest she could be with Keshini and decided this was an opportunity not to be missed. "Keshini, the first thing I would say is that surgery is inherently misogynistic. Appointing someone who understands how difficult it is for a woman surgeon to succeed would be fantastic."

The CEO nodded her head. "I guess I shouldn't be surprised. All the professions are changing with their understanding of diversity whether it's gender or race or culture. But not fast enough. I can tell you some tales about racism that I have experienced from people who would swear that they were totally supportive of diversity."

Brynn shrugged. "That's why the Chair is so important. He, or maybe even one day she, sets the tone for what's important for the department. I don't want preferential treatment compared to my peers. But the current Chair treats me like a child at the principal's office rather than a professional colleague seeking career advice."

Keshini stood up in response to her assistant knocking on the door to signal her next appointment. "Brynn, I appreciate your advice and candor. I am pleased that you are doing this consultation work in Moose. Stay in touch about whether you think we should be providing a surgery service in Wiichihinan Hospital. And I may reach out to you for more advice about who should be your next Chair."

*****

As Brynn waited for her return flight to Moose, David Morton pondered why he was so looking forward to seeing his ex-wife Corinne who was meeting him for lunch. He knew that Jonah would be pleased. The two men and Corinne had been friends since Jonah first arrived in Toronto and Jonah had stood up as best man at their wedding. David was experiencing increasing regret for the serial infidelities that resulted in his divorce from Corinne. And he recognized real excitement while standing to welcome Corinne as she approached his table in the upscale Yorkville eatery. It was a place to see and be seen and heads turned as Corinne confidently sauntered toward her ex-husband.

David remembered the anger and bitterness that characterized his wife as their marriage ground to failure four years ago. At that time, David was focused on growing CannWeed and increasingly neglectful of the feelings of people around him. But, as she sat at David's table, Corinne was much more relaxed and composed, reminding him of the carefree young woman he remembered before his recklessness had damaged her expectations of marriage. And he was instantly reminded of why he had originally fallen in love with her.

She smiled, leaning across the table to kiss his cheek. "Welcome back. Did you buy a Polynesian island?"

He grinned in response to her question. "No. You know, I got bored. I saw lots of properties, but I think it's too soon for me to retire to the south seas. It's actually good to be home, despite the winter weather. It's great to see you, Corinne. You look lovely. How's the business?"

Corinne rotated in her chair to order a glass of white wine from their server, giving David a moment to admire her renewed fitness.

"I can't say that we've grown as fast as you drove CannWeed, David. But the business has expanded nicely." While married, Corinne had worked for a national public affairs company, managing their Toronto office. After divorcing David, she started a new company with a colleague from the firm and David was hearing that their new start-up was creating a buzz. "We're focusing on social media and influencing – the older, more traditional companies don't really understand it very well, and we're carving out a nice space." Corinne looked around the airy restaurant and recognized that David had reserved a particularly nice table overlooking the indoor stroller path. "Thanks for organizing this, David. It's good to see you."

The waiter had delivered her drink and Corinne paused to sip from her wine glass. "One reason I was pleased you called, David – I understand that you and Jonah may need public relations advice for Mindful Innovation. I know you had help from that crisis comms firm after you left CannWeed. I assume that Jonah managed that for you. Very professional." She smiled at David who was admiring her confidence pitching him. "If I know you, you will be looking for outside investment in Mindful Innovation and that means you'll need help with your presentation and messaging. My firm could provide you with a fresh and unique brand image."

The waiter returned to take their food orders and David recognized that he was intrigued by the thought of working with Corinne. Their marriage had ended in despair, and he felt increasingly guilty about how he had treated her. Now, the thought of working with her to develop Mindful's branding was very interesting.

Corinne continued her explanation of her firm's potential as they sipped their wine. How creating interest with younger investors would require a different approach. She had several clients in crypto funds and was finding that tailoring online programs to promote these novel ventures was more effective for attracting investors than traditional media approaches. She explained that, as David decided what fields Mindful was going to explore in fund development, and what investors he was looking to attract, she could tailor his message using a variety of approaches.

David sat listening to her talk. Their last conversations had been adversarial and painful. Now it was enjoyable just listening to this beautiful woman talking with enthusiasm and energy.

As she paused, David lifted his glass. "Here's to your success Corinne. It's wonderful to hear how well you are doing. Jonah and I will certainly be talking to you as we figure out where we want to take Mindful. Are you sure that you wouldn't mind working with your ex? I would understand if that couldn't work for you."

David remembered the warmth of her smile as she responded. "Well, I don't know. I would say let's just keep talking and see where it goes, David."

They paused as salads arrived, napkins were unfolded, and lettuce was anointed. "It must have been a shock for you leaving CannWeed behind, David. How are you making out?"

David put down his fork, wiping his lips. "It could have been a disaster for me, Corinne. However, our buddy Jonah was incredibly effective in so many ways. Somehow, he was always at least two steps ahead of everyone, myself included, and he made sure that I ended up better off than I had any right to expect. The guy is incredible. I owe him everything. And now I am looking forward to some new adventures with him as a partner in Mindful. I think the whole experience with

CannWeed has taught me some lessons." David paused and found words coming without thought. "I am really sorry about what I did Corinne. I was a self-absorbed asshole – acting like a horny teenager rather than a married man."

Corinne sipped from her glass. "Nice wine David." She swirled the liquid thoughtfully. "I won't say you are forgiven, but I appreciate you saying that. You hurt me in the worst ways possible and it has taken me a long time to get over what you did to me." She paused in thought. "But I still like you David Morton, even though just two years ago I also hated you."

Then she lowered her face and looked up at him with her eyes peeking over the rim of her wine glass. "And before you ask me if I am seeing anyone, I'd say that would be an inappropriate question to ask someone who is pitching you for your business."

CHAPTER 18

Sierra. January 2019

The Helder Company's Sierra mine was about forty kilometres from Port Muskek, but most of the year it was accessible only by air. The mine and the Port Muskek First Nation were separated by the deep muskeg that gave the community its name. Anyone trying to walk on that swampy, porous surface during spring, summer or fall would quickly find themselves stuck after sinking to their hips in undetectable sinkholes in the muskeg. Four wheelers driven by amateurs who did not recognize the nature of the landscape could literally disappear hours after getting stuck.

But winter brought a remarkable transformation to the James Bay coast. By December, the muskeg froze solid enough to support pick-up trucks and by the end of January the frozen muskeg would safely support heavy transport trucks. However, the road still needed to cross several streams, two small rivers and a number of lakes to get all the way from Post Muskek to the mine. Every year, Uncle Samuel's company cleared and maintained the road over the muskeg and built ice roads over the lakes and rivers to complete the highway to the mine that was safe for trucks to use by early February.

Samuel had been responsible for the road from the time that Helder started building the Sierra mine. People working at the mine flew in and out by fixed wing plane and helicopter. But heavy supplies – diesel for generators, building supplies and mining equipment – were all transported during the two months that the Sierra winter road was open.

Uncle Samuel had learned the tricks of winter road and ice road construction from the experts who maintained the essential winter highway that led from Port Muskek to Moose, connecting all the James Bay communities in winter. Charlie had served as Samuel's foreman from the first road contract that Sam landed for Helder and the two of them knew every inch of the route to the mine and the various challenges presented by the terrain. As soon as the muskeg froze, Charlie and the fifteen to twenty men Sam employed on the road for six months would be clearing the brush that had grown over the muskeg during summer. Samuel had convinced Helder to invest in the most up to date equipment over the years by reminding them that losing one heavy transport truck through the ice would cost much more in insurance premiums than paying Sam to manage the road professionally.

Samuel not only had snow cats and heavy road equipment. He also had a military amphibious troop carrier that made early forays onto the ice much safer, inflatable safety suits for men working on thinner ice, ground scanning radar to measure ice thickness as well as the portable generators and snow blowers that allowed him to rapidly build snow bridges over streams and rivers. Samuel was proud of his safety record. Although his amphibious troop carrier would occasionally go through the ice in early winter, no worker or non-amphibious vehicle had ever experienced a breakthrough or fall into water.

Unfortunately, this lucrative work that provided good winter jobs for Port Muskek was coming to an end. The Helder Company had recently announced that the Sierra mine was depleted of economically viable diamonds and that no other worthwhile deposits had been discovered in the region where the company held mineral rights. The company was planning to stop production at the mine by spring and expected to remove its valuable heavy equipment over next year's winter roads. Helder's mine boss had notified Samuel that next year the road would need to be stronger than usual and asked him to submit a bid for the reinforced highway.

At present, it was still too early in the season to travel the entire road in the comfort of a pick-up although snowmobile travel was safe. Sam's team needed to visit the mine and examine the equipment that would be transported over the road to estimate costing for the contract to build the heavier highway. Although Samuel was game to take the snowmobile trip to the mine with Charlie, neither Mary nor Jonah would consider him making that journey. So, Jonah and Charlie set off for the Sierra mine on their snowmobiles shortly after Jonah returned from the PMiC meeting in Toronto.

Charlie's crew had already cleared the muskeg and had built snow bridges traversing the waterways. The lakes had been plowed of snow by the troop carrier to reduce the insulation over the ice allowing it to thicken faster. The ice was not yet ready for heavier vehicles, but Charlie's team had completed scanning radar showing the ice would safely support snowmobiles.

Charlie and Jonah shared helmet communicators during the ride to the mine, but Charlie had attended the Uncle Samuel school for small talk, and little was said on the trip. It was a sparkling brilliant blue winter day with temperatures hovering below minus thirty at noon. The trip took over two hours with multiple stops along the way to check the crew's progress and allow Jonah to reacquaint himself with Charlie's team.

The last time Jonah had visited the Sierra site was eight years ago during a quick winter visit home during law school. He and his uncle had driven up to the mine on the completed road in February and Jonah was impressed with Samuel's winter road expertise and equipment. When they had arrived at the mine on that visit, it was alive with activity. Two shifts of miners were operating the site twenty-four hours a day, seven days a week. The miners were airlifted in from the south through Timmins and worked two weeks on and two weeks off.

The Port Muskek community was disappointed that they did not get any of those well-paid mining jobs. Most of the work at the mine was done by southerners and locals from Port Muskek were left doing only doing road maintenance and catering. The lack of mining work for local residents was a constant source of friction between Helder and the Port Muskek Council with the mine operator insisting that local workers were not adequately educated or trained to safely work in the mine.

As they drove their snowmobiles onto the mine site, Jonah groaned. Sierra was already showing evidence of reduced activity. Three modular dormitories had originally been constructed for the miners. One was being dismantled and another was taped off and obviously no longer used. Removing those modular buildings along with the expensive and heavy mine equipment was the reason that the road contract needed re-negotiation for next winter.

Jonah and Charlie stepped off their machines outside the mine offices, stretched and removed their helmets, savouring the crisp air. Bob Starfield, the mine manager, had seen them coming and opened the door to the portable office to welcome them inside. In his mid-thirties with short blondish hair arranged around a bald patch above his forehead, wire rim glasses, jeans and a flannel shirt covering an incipient pot belly, Bob could have been sent from central casting to play a mining engineer. He was well known to Charlie who had been working on the road since the mine's earliest days.

Bob had started at the mine as an engineering coop student nine years ago and had risen through the ranks to assume his senior management position three years earlier. He had not met Jonah before today and welcomed him warmly, encouraging Jonah and Charlie to remove their snow suits and join him in the small boardroom where hot coffee and baked goods were on offer.

"The catering team from Port Muskek makes the world's best danish pastries," Bob commented, passing the plate across the boardroom table. "Jonah nice to meet you. Please give my best regards to your Uncle Samuel. We were so sorry to hear about his injury. What a terrible thing to happen. How's he doing?"

Jonah enjoyed the warmth of the coffee and rotated his neck recovering from the snowmobile helmet he had been wearing the past two hours. "Uncle says hello as well Bob. He of course wanted to come up to see you, but my auntie put her foot down. Uncle still thinks he is a young buck who can manage any challenge, but I think his accident has made him listen to Mary a bit more. Don't you agree Charlie?"

Charlie raised his eyebrows in agreement as he bit off a corner of a danish. Jonah looked out the frosted window in the boardroom, watching the men outside dissembling the modular dormitory. "Wow, it looks different from the last time I was here Bob. That was about eight years ago, and this mine was a beehive. You were working around the clock, and everyone seemed excited about the quality of the mine and some other opportunities around Sierra. It's hard to believe that the mine's already exhausted and ready to close."

Bob nodded. "Yeah, I can't say that I remember meeting you then Jonah, but I sure remember those early days. I started here as a coop student and when I got hired on permanently by Helder, I figured that I might spend at least the first half of my career around here. There seemed to be nothing but opportunity back then and now we're getting ready to close down the site and restore the mine." He shook his head.

Charlie grunted again. "This place sure didn't last as long as we all hoped. Lotta jobs being lost in Port Muskek."

Jonah looked closely at the mine manager. "What about you Bob? Are you going to manage the restoration? What do you do after that?"

Bob shrugged. "Jonah, I'm a miner and miners like to dig stuff out of the ground, not put the dirt back like it was when we started. I had hoped this Sierra mine would have kept going for a few years more and that we would have opened at least one more mine in this region." He raised his hands up, acknowledging that, "Unfortunately, that's not my decision to make."

Jonah nodded. "Yeah, I don't picture miners planting shrubs where they dug up mine tailings, but I guess somebody has to do it. Will you stay with Helder after the mine is fully shut down?"

Charlie chuckled. "I guess Lenore will have a say about that, huh, Bob?"

Bob blushed. Turning to Jonah he leaned back in his chair. "The best thing that's happened to me since I came to Sierra, Jonah, is that I met Lenore who runs the catering company based in Port Muskek." Jonah smiled in recognition. He knew Lenore. She was a year or two younger than him, a good-looking, smart girl he remembered from visits home during high school.

Bob continued, "Helder wants me to consider opening a new mine for them in East Africa where they have some positive results in exploration. But Lenore is not too keen on moving to another continent, especially so close to the equator. She tells me she's built for snow, not tropical heat." He shook his head. "That's another reason I'm sorry we're shutting down."

Jonah took a sip of coffee. "So, what happened here anyway, Bob? How come the mine is closing so fast and how come you haven't found any other sites to explore?"

Bob leaned forward putting his forearms on the conference table. "Well, that's an interesting thing about being the manager of a diamond mine, at least when you work for

Helder. My job is to dig the volcanic ore out of the kimberlite pipe in a safe and effective way and feed it into the machinery that grinds the ore, mills it, and then separates the wheat from the chaff, the diamonds from the rock. I run the big drills and shovels, the big trucks, and the machines that turn big rocks into fine gravel. And then I pass that gravel over to the South Africans from Helder who fly in monthly to determine the value of the diamond product we are producing. Nobody gets into that final sorting room except those guys who have worked all their lives for Helder. Helder makes it a point to keep local people like me separated from their guys that do the valuation. We dig up the rock and they fly in for about a week every month to figure out the value of what we dug up."

"And that's why we don't trust Helder in Port Muskek and why we think the government shouldn't trust them either." Charlie turned in his chair so he could face both Bob and Jonah. "Jonah, there's no independent assessment of what the mine is producing. We just have to accept whatever the Helder guys tell us is being discovered in the mine. All the agreements Helder has with Port Muskek about profit sharing only work if the mine turns a profit. And according to Helder, they're just barely covering all the expenses that it cost to develop the mine. Listening to Helder, there ain't never no profit."

Jonah thought this probably represented more words at one time than he'd ever heard from Charlie.

Charlie looked at Bob. "I used to think that you were in on this sweet deal with Helder, Bob. But Lenore tells me that you are outside the inner circle. She told me that you just drill and crush rock and leave the diamonds up to the South African guys."

Jonah whistled. "You mean there is no independent accounting of the value of gems that get discovered here? How does the government know how much resource tax Helder should be paying?"

Bob smiled. "Jonah, your question is the start of understanding the diamond business. Unlike an ounce of gold, or a pound of copper, or a barrel of oil, when you have evaluated one diamond's value, you know the value of one diamond. You can't put a price on diamonds based on the number of stones you find, the weight of the stone or anything else that can be independently evaluated. The value of a diamond can be determined only after it's cut and polished. Part of the value is size – what we call carats of course. But how much you will pay for that stone is also decided by colour, shape, brilliance, and clarity. And guess who ascertains those important qualities?" Bob looked at Jonah expectantly, leaning back in his chair.

"Let me guess. Those South African guys who fly in monthly to check out what you have dug up?" Jonah lifted his eyebrows. "Huh, I can see why it's hard to figure out just how well Helder is doing with this mine."

Bob nodded. "The diamond business is all vertically integrated. Helder has the mineral rights, owns the mine, identifies and evaluates the gems, sends them to one centre in Europe and one centre in India – both of which Helder owns – where cutting and polishing is done." Bob paused. "And now here's the tricky part."

Bob leaned forward in his chair, again resting his arms on the table. "Helder not only wins from ensuring that diamonds are forever in the hearts of young lovers." Charlie grunted and shook his head. "The company also benefits from making sure people think that diamonds are rare and scarce. So, diamond companies not only control production, they also control sales to consumers. It makes more sense to warehouse stones ensuring prices reflect scarcity than it does to release a flood of diamonds onto the market when they are mined. Excess supply would result in volatility in pricing that would not be good for diamond miners. Diamond companies release diamonds from their warehouses very carefully, ensuring that the price only goes in one direction."

Jonah absorbed what he was learning. This all made sense from Helder's perspective. "So, Bob, you're saying that, unlike a gold company that must declare the weight of the gold ingots it produces at its mines, Helder could understate the value of diamonds produced here, pay little or no tax and then have the diamonds sit in their European vaults until they consider the time is right to sell. Wow, that is a pretty good deal for Helder."

Bob held his arm out. "Yeah, you're getting it Jonah. And that also applies to unexplored properties like the Ultra site close by here."

Jonah was intrigued by the mention of Ultra. He wasn't going to mention the large alluvial diamond he had found in the stream bed a few kilometres east of Sierra. But he was interested in why Helder had decided to close their mine and take away their equipment without further work at the eastern site they called Ultra. "Bob, I appreciate your candor here. Why has the company decided not to establish a new mine at Ultra?"

Bob looked uncomfortable. "Well, now I feel like I am telling tales out of school." He looked over at Charlie. "Charlie knows that it would be great for Lenore and me if we did build a new mine at Ultra. We could stay and raise a family here without thinking of moving to Africa." He paused, clearly debating what he should say.

"My mining team drilled the ore and ground the big rocks into little rocks when we explored the Ultra site. But we did not do the analysis of the diamonds that were found there to determine whether a mine would be viable. So, I really do not know what the analysis showed. Helder is a privately owned family run company, and they have no requirement to disclose any results of exploration to shareholders or stock markets. Basically, the results of the exploration at Ultra remain a mystery known only to the executive team at Helder."

Jonah was puzzled. "But Bob, let's face it, if the mine was going to be productive and valuable, it wouldn't make sense for them to walk away from a potential fortune in diamonds, would it?"

Bob smiled. "Jonah, you are forgetting what I told

you about keeping diamonds scarce and storing them in warehouses until the time is right. Warehousing diamonds includes keeping them in the ground until you're ready to sell them. Helder has ninety-nine years of mineral rights over the land around here, including Ultra, contracted with the Ontario government and the Port Muskek First Nation. And there is no clause in those agreements that says, 'use it or lose it'. Right now, Helder is bringing that East Africa mine into production. I hear that it's a pretty rich site. Helder's number one principle is to keep diamonds scarce and not flood the market. So maybe, just maybe, they are just keeping the Ultra site in reserve until East Africa is depleted." Bob looked at the ceiling.

"The Helder Company is more than one hundred and fifty years old, Jonah. They are definitely planning everything for the long run."

Bob shook his head. "Jonah, I just met you and I'm definitely saying more than I should. But to be honest, I don't see much future with Helder anyway." He looked at Charlie. "I just don't see Lenore in East Africa, what do you think Charlie?" Charlie just shrugged and Bob continued.

"I don't have any idea what the analysis of the exploratory drilling at Ultra showed. But I thought at first the South African guys seemed pretty excited. And then they went silent and then suddenly the company announced the mine was not economically viable and that they were closing. Are they just mothballing the site, keeping the diamonds in the ground, knowing that they can come back in the future after East Africa has been mined out? Will they come back and open Ultra when other sources of diamonds get depleted? I don't know. Is it possible? Maybe."

Then Bob took a final bite of the danish that had been on his plate the whole time he was talking about diamond mining. "Hey, listening to me ramble on is not what you guys came here to do. Jonah, I know that you guys gotta do an assessment of what needs to be carried out over the winter road next year. Why don't we get dressed up and go around the mine and look at the equipment? We have some weight estimates and also some idea of what vehicles are going to be necessary to carry this stuff down to Port Muskek and then on to Moose. We have already talked to the guys who build the James Bay winter highway from Port Muskek to Moose. They've already provided their estimate of what it's going to cost us to beef up the James Bay winter road. We figure that once we get the equipment to Moose, we can take it out by train down south to Toronto and then ship it by boat – probably to the East Africa mine."

Bob looked out the conference room window where a large conveyor and grinder could be seen. "We've done most of the estimates of what it's gonna cost to close things down. I figure you guys will look at everything we need moved, take away the information and come back with a proposal for what the reinforced road to Port Muskek is going to cost."

Then a thought struck him.

"Do you suppose that you could return in six weeks with a proposal? I know that you'll need to run it past Samuel. But in six weeks, Jaco Helder is going to be here. He's a member of the family and has taken over as western hemisphere company lead. He wants to review our plans for shutting down the mine and we can likely get him to approve your road contract at that time. It'll save me sending your proposal away for review. If you present the terms of your contract directly to him, he's likely to approve the whole damn thing without trying to nickel and dime you. Does that make sense?"

Bob looked at Jonah and Jonah looked at Charlie who grunted. Jonah looked back at Bob, "I think that meant Charlie is okay with us coming back in six weeks to meet Jaco."

CHAPTER 19

A New Chair. February 2019

Weeks after returning from the scientific conference in Toronto, Brynn found herself in clinic with a friendly woman named Dorothy who did not stop smiling even when Brynn was examining her sore hip. Dorothy had arrived in clinic with her twenty-year-old grandson who pushed her wheelchair and translated for her.

St. Barts provided care to a diverse community in Toronto and Brynn was accustomed to talking to her patients through an interpreter. Many of the Elders she was meeting in James Bay, especially those who came from smaller communities outside Moose, brought their family members to translate. Dorothy was unable to walk because of severe arthritis in the hip. Looking at her x-rays, Brynn knew that a safe and routine operation could get her walking with no pain within days.

Her grandson translated as Brynn held Dorothy's hand while talking. The woman had carefully tended, long braided hair, and smiled shyly as Brynn questioned her. "Dorothy you must have a lot of pain with that arthritis. Are you able to sleep with the pain?"

After translation, Dorothy said a few words and her grandson responded for her. "Grandma sleeps in a reclining chair now, doctor. She says that if she bends her hip just right the pain is not too bad at night."

Brynn smiled back at Dorothy and turned to the grandson. "How does she get out of the house? She would have real difficulty walking with that hip."

He nodded. "Yeah, she spends most of her time in the recliner now and really only gets into her wheelchair to go to the bathroom. She's taking most of her meals in the recliner."

Brynn shook her head sadly. Dorothy was just past sixty and was in good health apart from her hip. "You know, she would do so well with a hip replacement. I could do her surgery in Toronto very easily. We would keep her in our hospital for about a week after surgery so she would be walking well before flying home. People who live in Toronto usually go home the same day as their surgery or the day after, but we would keep her longer, so she was comfortable before we sent her home."

The grandson sounded convincing as he encouraged his grandma to let this nice doctor do her surgery in Toronto. Dorothy looked shyly at Brynn and then hid her smile behind her hand as she responded to her grandchild briefly.

He shook his head. "Doc, she says the pain's not so bad." He looked up at Brynn from where he was kneeling next to his grandma's wheelchair trying to convince her. "I know she is in a lot of pain, and I'm sure she would be much better after surgery. I googled the results of hip replacement to try and convince her." The young man was obviously trying hard to influence his grandmother.

"Doc, I heard that when she was a kid, she was taken away by the Indian agents and sent to that James Bay school, just like all the kids back then. And you have heard the stories about how bad that school was." He looked at Brynn and shook his head again. "She's never left our community since then. You seem really nice Doc and don't get me wrong, this isn't against you. But many of our Elders who went to that school are really scared about leaving home to go to a white man's hospital. It just reminds them too much of when they got scooped up and sent away to those white man's schools."

Brynn had met so many older people needing surgery who would rather live with their disabilities rather than go south for an operation. Anecdotal stories of disrespect for Indigenous people in southern hospitals were also influential in these Elders' decisions to avoid surgery.

Horror stories about patients being loaded onto planes immediately after surgery and being sent back to Wiichihinan Hospital without advanced warning had come to represent what Elders thought would happen to them if they left for surgery in southern hospitals. The significant proportion of seniors along James Bay who were not comfortable speaking English also meant that many Elders would not travel south without accompanying family members to translate and advocate for them. And the government funding for transportation did not always cover the cost of flights for family members.

Returning from the clinic with Dorothy fresh in her mind, Brynn sat with Yvette and Jane Gagne in Jane's CEO office explaining what she was learning.

"There are people in these communities who are literally shut-in year-round using wheelchairs and walkers. I've visited most of those communities now and they are not at all accessible if you need assistance walking. Basically, you are relying on family and friends for anything that requires leaving your home. A safe and easy joint replacement operation could literally change these peoples' lives." Brynn shook her head, looked at her two colleagues and continued.

"Southern hospitals are trying to change their approach to Indigenous patients with cultural sensitivity training and education. But let's face it. Patients from these communities who have gone south for surgery have been treated with disrespect in the past, especially if they didn't speak English. And, with the history of the residential schools I've learned about since coming here, Elders from James Bay only need to hear one negative story about care received down south to say that they'll stay at home and make do forever with their walker or wheelchair."

Yvette responded in her usual fashion. "Fuckit Brynn. The government should pay for family members and advocates to go down south with these patients who need care. And they should have special facilities designed by Elders down south where they could stay before and after surgery. This country is always talking about reconciliation. We gotta put our goddamn money where our mouths are and look after these people." Yvette concluded with an angelic smile.

Jane Gagne was thinking hard. "Yvette, why should we create special programs to transport people away from here to get straightforward care down south? We have a perfectly good hospital here at Wiichihinan and right now we have an expert surgeon on our premises." She looked at Brynn. "Brynn, you tell me there are a bunch of people you've met who need joint replacements. You know our ORs here at Wiichihinan hospital. You are here for several more weeks. Could you start doing total joint replacements for these people during the rest of your stay here at Wiichihinan? That would prove to the government that it's possible for us to do surgery here."

Brynn was nodding. "You know Jane, I was thinking about that all through the clinic I was doing today. I saw at least six or seven people I could operate on tomorrow." She leaned back thoughtfully in her chair. "After we did that emergency knee surgery for the Chief's son, I talked to the engineers about air exchange in the ORs. They revved up the blowers and HVAC systems to get more air exchanges that will provide a safe level of clean air. They also ordered some HEPA filters that they could install in the system if we wanted to do surgery. I know that the companies I work with in research would provide the hip and knee joint replacements at a good price if I ask them. We have anaesthesia capability with a couple of our GPs." She paused for a minute smiling at Jane and then turned to Yvette.

244

"And we know that Yvette here is an expert surgical assistant."

Yvette suddenly sat upright. "Hey, wait a minute, Brynn Allard. I am perfectly willing to help you plan to improve care for our patients. That does not fuckin' mean I'm gonna get my hands dirty doing it." She shook her head.

That short conversation led to the start of Wiichihinan's joint reconstruction program weeks later. Brynn confirmed with the hospital engineers that clean air flow to the operating room was now at standard and the two Toronto companies that worked on research with Brynn had been pleased to fly in a full inventory for hip and knee replacement. Suzanne Cormier, the nurse from the emergency room who had scrubbed with Brynn for the Chief's son's surgery eagerly agreed to lead the nursing team that would work with Brynn in the OR.

The physiotherapist at the hospital was delighted to see the start of a proactive approach to patients along the coast who were languishing in wheelchairs. The physio designed a postoperative program in hospital and at home following discharge. And Brynn was not surprised when Yvette joined her at the OR sink as she was scrubbing her hands for her first case.

"Damn it Brynn, do you know how much time I spend on my nails? And now I just stripped off all that polish I spent so much time applying to help you in the operating room. I wouldn't do this for anyone but you Brynn. I fuckin' hope you realize that?"

The initial cases went without concern or complication and word was soon out in all communities along the coast that the surgeon who had saved the Chief's son's leg was now fixing hips and knees in Wiichihinan Hospital. The weekly local newsletter featured Brynn and the first two patients in a front-page write-up. As Brynn sat down for her regular meeting with Dr. Jane Gagne, the CEO lifted the paper to show her.

"Okay, Brynn, you have created quite a stir. You have shown people everywhere in this community what we can accomplish for our Elders. People are really excited, and they're asking what the heck are we going to do when you leave?"

Brynn was smiling ironically as she looked across the CEO's desk at the news article. "It's incredible to me that doing a joint replacement in Canada would be front page news. That just shows how big the task is to provide adequate care in this community." She leaned forward in her chair.

"Jane, the challenge of health care delivery in Canada is not economic like it is in many countries. Rich people and poor people in Canadian urban centres get access to the same services and surgeons. Jane, you know you can't easily buy access to faster or better surgery. However, the treatment you receive is determined by the geography of where you live and the issue that we are discussing here is a perfect example of that concern. Without false modesty, I can say that patients here at Wiichihinan are now getting access to one of the best joint replacement surgeons in Canada. But how can we organize that type of care, in orthopaedics and other types of surgery, given the difficulty of recruiting surgeons to work here? That's our challenge."

Jane smiled at her. "Yeah, Brynn I know the challenge. Your job is to help me figure out the solution."

Brynn thought before responding. "My time here has taught me about the needs of the community and how much we can help. But it's also taught me about the satisfaction that comes with treating people in this community." She pointed to the paper. "For example, getting your name in the paper for doing a pretty straightforward operation." She smiled. "Seriously, people are very appreciative which is a benefit of working here. And, unlike down south, no one here is telling me what I can and can't do."

Brynn lifted her hands for emphasis. "For example, at St. Barts, they've told me I cannot look after trauma patients. If we were to get some basic fracture management hardware and equipment, I could do surgery for broken bones at Wiichihinan Hospital during any time I am here. You remember Samuel

Sunderland, that man from Port Muskek that I looked after at St. Barts after he rolled his four-wheeler in the bush? He would have been looked after much faster and better in Moose if there was an orthopaedic surgeon working at Wiichihinan hospital when he broke his leg."

The CEO looked at the picture of Brynn on the front page of the Moose newsletter which lay on her desk in front of her. "Well Doc, you have already made an impact with your presence here at Wiichihinan. Whatever you suggest we should do in the future will be listened to very carefully, I promise."

The next morning Brynn and Yvette were scrubbing at the sink outside the OR while the anaesthetist put Dorothy to sleep on the operating table. When they had heard about the hip replacements being offered at Wiichihinan, Dorothy's family had convinced their grandmother that she should have the surgery and advocated to get her on the list of the first group of patients that Brynn would operate on. When Brynn visited her patient in her hospital room the night before surgery, Dorothy was surrounded by at least ten family members who had driven down the winter road to support their grandmother having her hip surgery.

As Brynn entered her room, Dorothy's physiotherapist was trying to get her patient to stand with the assistance of a walker. Brynn waved to Dorothy who was trying to push herself out of her wheelchair with the physio's assistance. She saw the grandson who had translated for her in clinic. The young man smiled at the surgeon and introduced Brynn to his uncle who seemed to be the leader of the family here to support Dorothy. The uncle had the weathered face of someone who was at home in the bush.

"Doctor, thanks for coming to see us. My name is Jerry. I'm Dorothy's oldest son and as you can see, she's an important person to our family." The people in the room gathered behind Jerry, smiling their thanks to Brynn.

"Jerry it's good that you and your family are here to

support Dorothy. I know from talking to her with her grandson here how frightened she is about having this surgery." Brynn watched the difficulty Dorothy was having trying to stand upright in the walker. "You can see how much trouble she is having standing. That is because her hip has been bent up at ninety degrees in her wheelchair and recliner chair for so long. We will straighten that hip out when we operate tomorrow but it's going to take a few days after surgery for Dorothy to get accustomed to her new joint."

The physiotherapist was attempting to straighten Dorothy's hip while the woman was standing but stopped when she saw the pain in the woman's face. "Dr. Allard, her hip is really stiff and just does not straighten out at all. She has obviously been sitting with her hip flexed up for a long time."

Brynn nodded. "We will make sure we release that flexion deformity in the OR, but you're right. That bent position has been there forever. After surgery we will need to get her standing with the walker right away so that she is able to keep the hip as straight as we accomplish in the OR." She looked around the room at Dorothy's family.

"We will keep Dorothy here for a few days after surgery so she can learn to walk properly again. I am glad that you all came with her to keep her company and help with her therapy. After the surgery tomorrow I will come by and let you know how the operation turned out."

Jerry stepped forward and held his hand out to Brynn. Before speaking he turned his head back to look at his mother and when he turned back to thank Brynn, she could see the shimmer in this rugged-looking man's eyes. He grasped Brynn's hand in his two much larger hands. "I can't tell you how much we thank you Doc." Brynn could hear the rest of Dorothy's family murmur their thanks behind Jerry. "If she can start walking again, you're gonna make a lot of people happy."

"I'll see you here tomorrow after Dorothy's surgery around eleven o'clock Jerry." Before leaving the room, Brynn walked over to Dorothy who had settled back into her wheelchair. "I promise we will take good care of you Dorothy." Her patient smiled up at her.

By eight thirty the next morning, Brynn and Yvette were well underway in the operation to replace Dorothy's hip. Brynn was dealing with the difficulty she had expected in exposing the damaged joint. Dorothy's years of sitting with her hip flexed in the wheelchair made it difficult for Brynn to get access to the deformed anatomy.

Helping Brynn with the surgical exposure, Yvette exclaimed as she pulled the leg back, trying to pull the joint straight so that Brynn could see the front of the hip. "Shit, Brynn, this is hard work. I'm not sure I'm gonna be strong enough to help you enough with this case."

Yvette couldn't see Brynn smiling behind her mask. "Hey, not to worry Yvette. There are two kinds of orthopods. Some rely on strength and spend their time grunting and sweating and pulling on things. I don't have that much more strength than you, but I find that you can get the same results by being smarter rather than stronger."

Just then Brynn finished dividing the contracted hip capsule over the front of Dorothy's damaged joint using her electrocautery instrument. Opening that tight fibrous tissue immediately released the restricted motion resulting from years of wheelchair and recliner sitting. Suddenly Yvette felt the leg easily respond to her attempt to pull it straight.

"Holy shit, Brynn, what did you just do? My job just got a lot easier." She pulled on the leg again which was now much more mobile as she held the metal retractor exposing the hip. "You really know what you are doing girl. I'm impressed."

Two hours later, the two women were pouring themselves coffee having completed Dorothy's operation. Brynn was looking at the x-ray done in the recovery room after surgery. Yvette looked around her at the computer screen showing the x-ray. "Shit, girl, that x-ray looks pretty good. You happy?"

Brynn nodded. "Yeah, that was a tough operation, but it came out real good. I'm lucky I had such a good surgical assistant." She smiled at Yvette. "I'm going up to the ward to let Dorothy's family know everything went well. Can you get the next patient positioned on the table while I talk to her family, Yvette?"

"Don't you worry Doc. See one, do one, teach one is my motto. You just relax here in the coffee room, and I'll do the next case." And Yvette curled up her arm, showing off her tiny biceps.

Brynn entered a crowded but silent room where Dorothy's entire family was anxiously awaiting news of her surgery. She checked the digital clock on the wall as she walked in. It was minutes before eleven, just as promised to Jerry and his family last evening. Jerry was the first to see her coming and leapt to his feet, welcoming her just inside the entrance with the rest of his family crowding in behind him.

Brynn smiled and gave everyone a thumbs up and the room exploded with relieved cheering. The next moment Jerry was spinning her around in a bear hug while thanking her with tears in his eyes. Brynn remembered Chief Checkwing lifting her in thanks after she had finished his son's knee surgery and realized that this was her second operation at Wiichihinan that had received a bear hug spin. She also reflected that she had never received that kind of thanks visiting many patients' families after surgery in Toronto.

Her realization that practice in Wiichihinan was different was accentuated the next day when she returned to see Dorothy on morning rounds. Before entering her doorway, Brynn heard applause and praise coming from Dorothy's room. The physiotherapist was working with Dorothy, getting her up standing straight on her new hip using a walker. It was the first time that Dorothy had been upright with both feet on the ground in many years and the family members who had stayed with their grandma overnight were delighted to see her standing.

Jerry stood beside his mother, helping the physiotherapist to stabilize her on her walker. "Hey Doc, good morning, look at my mum! She's already standing on your new hip."

Brynn approached Dorothy gingerly and lifted her hospital gown forward to check the dressing on her hip for signs of bleeding. Seeing the wound was dry, Brynn looked up at Dorothy and asked, "How are you?"

Suddenly Dorothy let go of her walker to stand unassisted on both feet with her hands held aloft in triumph while her family cheered again. Jerry was close by to assist if needed but Dorothy turned to put her arms around her surgeon as Brynn stood up. "Thank you, thank you, Doctor." And her family started clapping as Brynn realized again that surgeons received different rewards for providing care in James Bay.

Brynn had a total knee operation scheduled for the afternoon and was completing her rounds when her cell rang. She was surprised to see her St. Barts CEO, Keshini Jayawardana's name on her screen,.

"Hey, Brynn, you got a moment to chat?"

"Of course."

"How are things going up there in winter land?"

"Really good Keshini. Can I still call you by your first name?"

The St. Barts CEO laughed. "Yeah, of course you can. I'm so glad I caught you. You know I told you that the Dean asked me to serve as the hospital CEO on the search committee to identify a new university Chair of orthopaedics?"

"Oh yeah, I remember you mentioning."

"Well, it turned out your name came up in the discussion about choosing a new Chair. There were a bunch of old white guys who applied for the job and then there was a new guy in Toronto who came back from England a while ago. He's Canadian but took on a Chair at Oxford for a few years and then returned to our other trauma hospital about a year and a half ago. His name is Subi Rajarathinam. His name sounds Tamil like me, but he was born in Canada."

"Yeah, I've heard he's a good guy, but I haven't really met him. Keshini, what do you mean my name came up in the discussion? What's this about?"

"Well, Brynn, I hope you won't get mad at me. I was listening to all these old white men who wanted the job go on about that the most important goal for the new Chair would be to protect the traditions that made the department great. That just sounded like keeping things exactly like they are now. And then Subi gave his pitch to the search committee about why he wanted the job and he talked about increasing diversity of the faculty, serving patients differently and the importance of making faculty appointments better for young women surgeons. So, after all the candidates had described why they should be Chair, when it came time to discuss who we should appoint, I couldn't help myself from speaking out."

"What do you mean, you couldn't help yourself speaking out, Keshini? What did you say and what has it got to do about me?"

"Brynn, I told the committee about you and about how frustrated you are with the attitude of the faculty and Chair about women surgeons. And I mentioned what you are doing in Moose and the whole committee thought that was very cool. I said how you wanted to figure out a different way to provide services to diverse communities like James Bay and that's what Subi was talking about as well. And I said if we didn't appoint some fresh blood and fresh ideas to the Chair role, we were going to lose people like you."

"Oh my god, Keshini, I hope you didn't make me sound like a malcontent or troublemaker or something. I do want to return to Toronto to practise, you know. My lab is at the university after all."

"Yeah, well, don't you worry Brynn. The Dean was leading the search committee and when we made our final decision to appoint Subi instead of one of those old white guys, the Dean told him that he wanted him to develop a diversity plan that would start with policies dealing with gender equity as well as new models to serve diverse communities. And he suggested strongly that orthopaedics should consider developing a new collaboration with the Wiichihinan Hospital."

"Wow. I have some ideas about that, Keshini. That's fantastic."

"Yeah, I figured you might." The CEO chuckled. "Anyway, Subi is super excited that this will be his first task as university Chair. I volunteered St. Barts to play a lead role in developing a collaboration with Wiichihinan and the Dean wants to be involved in that planning to figure out how he can extend this to other faculties and programs at the medical school as well. So, Brynn Allard, tell me how we are gonna get this going."

And that was the start of a series of videoconferences that brought together a young Vietnamese doctor representing the Wiichihinan medical staff, the hospital's Cree CEO, two Tamil-Canadians and a woman orthopaedic surgeon. They decided their first task would be developing a joint replacement and trauma program that would link St. Barts, other Toronto hospitals and Wiichihinan hospital with a rotating staff of surgeons from Toronto. Keshini committed that St. Barts would hire two new surgeons who could rotate with Brynn and other surgeons spending time on site in James Bay. During their time in Moose these surgeons could operate on both elective and trauma patients and would see patients in clinics along the coast.

By the end of their third meeting the plan was crystallizing. The Dean joined them on this third call. He surprised them with his opening remarks by acknowledging the land they lived and worked on as being the traditional lands of many First Nations. He congratulated them on their progress but suggested that before finalizing the plan they should likely talk to the First Nations Chiefs and Councils they were planning to serve because, as he put it, "Really, if we are creating a service plan for Indigenous People, we should really consult directly with the community. You know that old saying, "Nothing about us without us."

There were murmurings of agreement on the line and then one voice cut in.

"You just don't fuckin' get it, Dean. When you speak to our First Nations here in Wiichihinan Health Authority, they're only gonna have one question. And that question will be, 'What does Dr. Brynn suggest?' Dean, in this community, Brynn is just a fuckin' rock star."

Usually, Yvette would have had the last word. But Dr. Jane Gagne, the Wiichihinan CEO quietly challenged her. "Hey Yvette, I know your heart's in the right place and we both know how Brynn has opened our eyes to what we need in our community. But the Dean is right. Lots of white people – mainly men – have decided in the past what's needed for Indigenous People across Canada. And some of those wise, well-meaning white men have decided that we need things like residential schools to 'modernize' our communities."

Jane paused but the other participants on the videoconference were not saying a word until she finished her thoughts. She looked at the screen showing her colleagues' faces and continued. "I don't want to sound ungrateful or unappreciative about what Brynn has done and what she is helping us to propose here today. However, there are some echoes of the past in what we are talking about – a bunch of white people coming to Wiichihinan to treat people in our community with white man's medicine. I think that is going to be a big improvement over what we are doing today. But we need to discuss this with our communities – especially with our Elders who are going to see the major impacts of this approach. And we need other commitments, I think, as this program gets going."

Again she paused, assessing the faces on the screen. "First of all, like the Dean suggests, we need to take this plan to all our First Nations and give them the opportunity to make this their plan, not your plan. That will take some time and may be frustrating to people who do not understand how our decision-making works. But I think it's essential for us to start this program the right way." Jane again looked at each of the faces on the screen.

"After all, I am sure that Egerton Ryerson thought that he was doing a great service for us Indigenous People when he supported the idea of residential schools. Let's take the time to ensure that we do not repeat the mistakes from the past."

She turned in her chair but kept her eyes fixed on the screen. "And one other thing." She took a sip of coffee. The Dean thought to himself, '*Wow, she is really good. She has us hanging on her every thought. That mention of Ryerson had us all cringing.*'

"Dean, we need you to work with all the Ontario medical schools to increase training for our people in medicine, nursing, physio, and all the allied health services if this is going to work. The first principle we are adopting here is that we are going to try and treat our people closer to home when possible. The second equally necessary step is to start planning for a day when that treatment will be provided by people from our communities. And that means identifying and training people a lot earlier than we do down south – in early high school really. Wiichihinan will certainly commit to that training process with you, but we need help from Ontario universities to develop programs that will increase self-sufficiency."

Jane leaned back in her chair. "If we can start this surgery program with these thoughts in mind, I think this can be very, very special."

The Dean filled the thoughtful silence that followed Jane's remarks. "Well, Dr. Gagne, thanks for that. I can promise you that our university will listen to your advice on how we should do this. And we should probably start by getting several more people from James Bay on this planning team."

CHAPTER 20

The Mindful Games.
February 2019

It was a couple of weeks after Charlie and Jonah's trip to the Helder Sierra mine that the teams gathered in Moose for the first Mindful Games. The Games were entirely David Morton's idea. With his appreciation for Jonah's role in creating his newfound wealth, David told his friend he wanted to recognize their partnership with a philanthropic venture they would design together. They had discussed the project briefly after meeting with Diamond Bill at the Prospectors and Miners Convention in Toronto and had decided that Mindful Innovation should consider investing in sports facilities, activities and events for children and youth living in James Bay communities.

As a starting point, they decided to organize the first of what they hoped would be an annual hockey tournament that would bring together James Bay hockey alumni to play with and provide mentorship to the current crop of James Bay players. Jonah had consulted with the hockey organizers in Moose and along the coast. They determined that there was one free date at the Moose arena before the annual March tournaments began. Jonah paid the arena to reserve the ice for two games – one between the alumni team and a northern all-star team selected from the best players from communities north of Moose and a second game with the alumni playing a team of Moose all-stars. He also booked every available motel and guest room in Moose and then immediately invited all the James Bay hockey "grads" he knew who had gone on to play for colleges and junior teams as well as two famous Moose graduates who were now retired after starring in the National Hockey League.

Attracting the two retired stars on very short notice was essential to gaining attention for these Mindful Games. David closed the deal by offering the two retired players a private jet trip to Moose – one from the player's home in California and the other from the New England area – as well as a generous honorarium. The retired players cancelled other plans to take a luxurious and well-paid trip home in support of what everyone realized could be a very good initiative for kids in their home communities. David and Jonah explained to all the alumni that they wanted their advice on how they should invest in the future of sport for James Bay communities, emphasizing their desire to encourage girls' sports.

Jonah had been on skates regularly during his time in Port Muskek and was looking forward to teaming up with David Morton for the first time in several years. David was being granted honourary alumnus status to play. But Jonah was immediately worried when he and Uncle Samuel picked David up at the Moose airstrip where his friend's leased private jet had landed the night before the first scheduled game. David was noticeably short of breath and sweating just lugging his equipment to Sam's pick-up.

"David, are you sure about this? You could sit out of this year's games and get ready for next year," Jonah suggested as the two men climbed into Sam's truck. He could see his uncle looking at David with concern.

David shrugged and illuminated the truck with his grin as Sam drove them to the motel where he and Jonah were sharing a room for the weekend. "Don't you worry. I'll play myself into shape on Saturday and I'll be back in top form by Sunday."

David's confidence in his conditioning was misplaced and he barely lasted his regular shifts through the first period of the game against the northern stars on Saturday. Fortunately for the alumni, the retired NHL defenceman was only a couple of years removed from professional competition and had had maintained game fitness playing for a seniors' team. He was able to double shift to allow David prolonged bench time while reassuring Mindful's CEO, "Don't worry David, you pay for these games and I'll play in them."

The alumni team's talent was too much for the northern stars despite many of the older players' lack of conditioning and the alumni won comfortably. But the main purpose of the weekend was accomplished after the game when both teams as well as the Moose players scheduled to play Sunday were served dinner in the same high school gym where Jonah and David had dined during the Moose Tournament years ago. The younger all-stars were eager to meet with the alumni visitors – especially the NHL stars – and lapped up the stories of how the alumni had left James Bay to play in a variety of Canadian and American hockey towns.

The Elders who organized hockey leagues along the coast joined the meal and were eager to provide advice to David and Jonah about how Mindful Innovation could support hockey as well as other sports as well as what facilities were needed. The dinner began around five p.m. and by nine thirty the crowd was still noisy and enjoying the evening. As people started to drift away and the alumni began thinking about resting for the next day's game, two of Jonah's alumni teammates approached him and asked if they could chat.

The two needed no introduction. They were both Sunderland cousins, Uncle Samuel's relatives related to Jonah by Sam's marriage to Auntie. Jonah had followed their careers from Toronto. They were a few years younger than Jonah and after their James Bay careers had both played junior hockey in southern Ontario but failed to reach the pinnacle of making the professional leagues. However, their junior success had earned them Canadian college scholarships and Jonah knew that they had also starred in college hockey.

Jonah was sitting at a table with David who was deep in conversation with Elders about development of a girls' league that would provide an all-star travelling format similar to the boys' league. Jonah turned to his cousins who had pulled up chairs beside him.

"It's great to see you guys. I lost track of you when you finished playing college hockey. What have you been up to?"

One of the two was obviously the usual spokesman for the pair. "We both got a full ride through undergrad with our scholarships earned playing junior and then paid for grad school by coaching as well as playing hockey for the school. I've spoken to a lot of the kids here tonight about how that works and how valuable those junior scholarships can be for guys who are not good enough to get to the top level. We all know how impossible it is for someone to make it to the NHL." He shook his head thinking about the talent needed to play professional.

"Anyway, I got a business degree and then my MBA and Franklin here did undergrad and graduate work in computer science. We graduated five years ago and after a couple of years working for other companies decided we would start our own business." He nodded to his cousin. "You explain what we are doing, Franklin."

Franklin nodded his appreciation to Jonah. "Thanks for giving us a few minutes of your time Jonah. This is not hockey related but we could really use some advice. I specialized in encryption and cybersecurity in my graduate work and that turned out to be a really good choice for today's business world. As you know, cybersecurity expertise is in big demand and we've had no problem getting all kinds of work since we set up our company three years ago." His cousin nodded in agreement.

"Recently we scored a big federal contract to improve security on the satellite internet providers the government is supporting for broadband access across the north. Most of it is focused on education but there are also some companies who rely on satellite broadband – mainly in mining."

Franklin's business-oriented cousin took over. "And that is what we want to discuss with you Jonah. I think that we need legal advice but we really don't know where to turn. Can we discuss this with you confidentially to get your thoughts about who we should be talking to?"

Jonah shrugged. "Why don't you start telling me about what is concerning you? Everything you tell me will be held in confidence and if you get to a point where I'm out of my league, I'll tell you to stop. I'm sure that I will know someone back down south who will be able to help in my old firm or another Toronto company."

Franklin and his cousin looked at each other, took deep breaths and started to describe their experiences at Helder's Sierra mine.

*****

David and Jonah got back to the motel room they were sharing just before eleven. The two had showered at the arena after the game and were now stretched out on their single beds wearing sweats.

"Just like old times, us rooming together, huh, Jonah? Reminds me of college." David paused to take a large sip of his favourite Macallan beverage. Jonah had noticed the five bottles that accompanied him for the weekend. "That was a great start today, huh, Jonah? I think Mindful is going to be able to help a lot of kids. What do you think about starting a foundation to handle this?"

Not hearing a response, he tossed a pillow at Jonah who

was staring at the ceiling across the room. "Hey man, are you listening to me? Are you asleep already?"

Jonah threw the pillow back, sitting up in the single bed. "Sorry David, I was just thinking about something a couple of my Sunderland cousins told me after dinner. Yeah, we got lots of great advice today. A foundation is a really good idea. I'll think about how we should set it up, who should be on the board and a few other technicalities. It would be good for us to set the terms of what we want to accomplish and then pass the money over to the local sports organizers to decide how to spend it. That's probably better than us trying to figure out how to do it. They are the experts after all – they've been keeping these kids playing for years now with minimal support. It'll be fun to see what they do with our financial help." Leaning against the wall, he watched David filling up his glass from the Macallan bottle. The bottle was already half empty after just thirty minutes in the motel room.

"How are you feeling David? You were bushed out there today."

David shook his head before responding. "Yeah, good thing that NHL'er was able to cover up for me. I thought I was gonna barf when I was taking every shift in the first period. He told me that he would take extra shifts tomorrow against the Moose kids. Thank god he agreed to come or I might have embarrassed myself."

Jonah spun his feet onto the floor and faced his friend. "Well, when I get back to Toronto, you and I are gonna spend some time working out together." He smiled at David. "I think you got pretty soft with that trip to the south seas. We'll register together in that gym in the Distillery District and find a trainer we can both use. And if we are going to keep playing for the alumni in these Mindful Games, maybe we should join one of those year-round hockey leagues in Toronto as well."

David looked at him suspiciously. "If I'm gonna share a trainer with you old buddy, I will definitely be visiting the porcelain throne after workouts. Shit, I can't wait for that.

Yeah, I haven't been working out much the past six months. You're right, it's time to get going again. Now that CannWeed's gone, I've got no excuse not to work out." He looked disconsolate and took another large sip of scotch.

Jonah considered his words. "You know, David, you are drinking more than I've ever seen before. I know that it calms you down and I could see why you used that Macallan to relax while we were building up CannWeed – those were some crazy times." They looked at each other and both smiled wistfully. "But David now that those crazy days are over, it seems to me that you're drinking even more than you used to. Should I be getting worried?"

David took a long look at the glass that was already halfway to his lips and then looked over at his friend. "Oh Christ, not you too." He put the glass back on the table unsampled.

"What do you mean, David, not me too?"

"Ah shit, just before I flew out to Moose, Corinne and me were having dinner and she told me that I'm drinking too much. Now I've got both of you on my case."

Now David had Jonah's full attention. "Corinne? Wait a minute, having dinner with Corinne? When did that start?"

David smiled. "Ah, the all-knowing Jonah Kay doesn't quite know everything, eh? Yeah, well Corinne and I have been seeing each other quite a bit since I returned from the South Pacific. She's still pissed off at me but is telling me that if I keep apologizing on a daily basis, she may forgive me one day." He looked up at Jonah, started to lift the glass of Macallan and then set it down on the table again without drinking. "She really is a great woman, you know, Jonah? I was such a shit. I can see that now. I'm not sure that she could ever trust me again, but I am trying."

"Hey, that's wonderful news. You know, I've always loved Corinne. She's way too good for you, David. I think she blamed me for some of the shit you gave her, even though I always told you that you were screwing up a good thing. Man, I'm happy you guys are at least talking again."

David looked at him with a sly grin. "Actually, we may have gotten past just talking."

Jonah threw up his hands. "Holy smoke, I have to get back to Toronto. I can see I am losing track of things. Seriously, are you guys hooking up? That is kinda strange, but also strangely great. Dating your ex-wife? Interesting." He shook his head. "You never fail to amaze me, man. Corinne is so terrific. I hear she's started her own company, is that right?"

"Yeah, she is seriously intense in social media and public relations. You know how she has always been deep in fashion and connected to a lot of people in Toronto and New York who are in that fashionista world? Those connections seem to be paying off for her."

"So I gotta get you in shape and off all that Macallan for your new babe who's also your old babe. I gotta catch up with you David but seriously, this booze has gotta stop."

David put the cork back in the Macallan bottle and looked at his friend. "I hear you, I hear you." Then he paused as another thought hit him.

"Hey, speaking about women, after our lunch with Diamond Bill, I had a very interesting talk with Uncle Samuel's surgeon, that Dr. Allard, during the Prospectors Convention. She seems like she is really into you, man. I met her in the King William Hotel by accident – she was there for some medical meeting. She's a very impressive woman, Jonah. Different than Corinne, not into that fashion scene, but gorgeous and seems really nice. She told me that you guys had some kind of misfire when you took her out camping in the middle of winter. It sounded like she wanted you to warm up her sleeping bag and you turned her down or something?" David looked at his friend carefully.

"I figured it was your old fucked up response to women our age coming back to bite you again. She told me that you said that you had difficulty with intimacy. Man, I have heard that from a lot of women who wanted to jump your bones without success. Anyway, she was asking my advice about you so I told her a little bit about your mum and about Evelyn. Then she thought that you were just a grossed-out guy chasing cougars I guess, but I told her that you were actually pretty decent – even though I don't understand you."

Jonah leaned back against the wall. "Yeah she is actually pretty amazing. Auntie and Uncle entertained her when she visited Port Muskek and I took her out to Uncle Samuel's fishing camp. We were getting sort of close and I just froze up like I always do, David. It's embarrassing and frustrating." He paused.

"But you know David, seriously, I think I have a different understanding about what's going on with me since I've been back in Port Muskek." He picked up his hockey stick from the floor next to his bed and started to rotate it in his hands mindlessly as he thought about what he was about to say to his friend.

"You know, I've told you before, when I've been in Toronto, I have tried to work this shit out with a couple of different counsellors – a psychologist and a psychiatrist. They both listened to my story and then told me that I am suffering from Post-Traumatic Stress Disorder and obsessive thoughts related to how my mum died and to Evelyn. Like I know all that, but that doesn't help me get rid of those thoughts that stop me from getting close to someone my own age." He sighed. "I have done hours of mindfulness training and meditation, but when I get close to someone like that Brynn Allard, I still just freeze up. My thoughts lock onto memories of how my mum died and then it's over. I have always figured that it's my fault, something weird in me that I have to get treatment for or just accept." He spun the stick in his hands and looked at David. Then he suddenly reared back from his seat on the side of the bed and unexpectedly vaulted forward, smacking the stick against the floor, splintering the blade.

"Fuck, David! Since coming back to Port Muskek, hearing about all the psychological damage that has resulted from those residential schools and what happened to my mum and other students at those schools, well I'm thinking about this in a different way." Looking over at his friend, he saw David staring at him with shocked attention.

"Wow. Say more, Jonah."

"Well, since I've been here and thought about and seen the impact of colonialism on my people and the impact on me personally, I'm starting to feel more angry instead of fucked up like I've felt for years. I mean, can you imagine, my mum getting raped as a fifteen-year-old by someone supposedly in charge of her wellbeing at that terrible school? No wonder she couldn't be a decent mum and no wonder she died the way she did."

He pointed the broken stick blade at David in emphasis. "And then Evelyn at RGC, taking advantage of me the same way that someone took advantage of my mother at the residential school. Look, I know that what happened to me at RGC is a long way from what happened to my mother at that James Bay Residential School. But let's face it, I was abused just like my mother. And it totally pisses me off that I have not been able to have a relationship and start a family because of the way that I was abused by that woman and because of what happened to my mum."

David leaned over toward his friend. "Holy shit Jonah, that's the most I have ever heard you say about this. I mean you told me that when you got it together with a girl, it would make you think of your mum and that didn't happen with older women like Evelyn. But I have never heard you describe it all just like that."

"Yeah, I know, David, I know. To be truthful, up until now I have always thought that it's just my fault. I guess that being here and seeing how settler Europeans have fucked up my people so badly is helping me understand myself more than years of counselling in Toronto. I am also sort of figuring out that it may be more helpful for me to feel pissed off than it is to feel fucked up." He continued to spin the splintered stick in his hands. The intensity on his face slowly faded as he stared at his best friend.

"If I wasn't determined to get you off that shit, I'd take a big glass of that Macallan right now. But I figure that we both need to sort out a better way to fix whatever is ailing us." Jonah turned back, lay on the bed, and fluffed his pillow. "Now we better get some sleep or those kids from Moose are gonna eat our lunch tomorrow."

David looked longingly at the Macallan bottle before fluffing his pillow and rolling over. "Okay, let's make sure we join that gym so I can look forward to playing in next year's tournament without puking."

CHAPTER 21

James Bay. March 2019

T he Helder Diamond Company had been led by a series of hard men throughout its hundred and fifty-two-year history. Jaco Helder was one of the new breed, however, who effortlessly hid his hardness under a veneer of business sophistication. Born in Cape Town thirty-two years ago, Jaco had been introduced to the company in his teens and had worked at many of the African mines where Helder still discovered most of its diamonds.

After his introduction to diamond mining, Jaco had been educated at the best Boston business schools and was expert at finance and marketing. His uncle who was currently serving as Helder's CEO recognized his intelligence and ambition. Jaco and two of his cousins knew that they would be competing for the Helder CEO job in about ten years' time. The three cousins knew they were constantly being assessed as future CEOs in all the jobs they were assigned in the company.

Over the last twenty years, the Helder Company had accommodated to the reality that prospecting for diamonds was now a less significant factor in the company's success. Modern geologic technology had reduced much of the expensive guesswork in identifying likely spots to dig diamonds out of the ground. Although kimberlite pipes containing commercially viable quantities of diamonds were still exceedingly rare, computerized aerial electromagnetic scanning had made the job of identifying potential diamond mines easier. Before this change in technology, the hard part of Helder's business was finding diamonds. Jaco's business school training was focused on the company's future challenges of financing mines and selling diamonds in a changing market.

The introduction of laboratory-cultured diamonds in the 1990s had altered the market for stones mined from the ground. The remarkable hardness of diamonds meant the stones were important in industrial applications as coatings for drills and grinders as well as in jewelry. Forty years ago, smaller diamonds from Helder mines could be sold as industrial abrasion coatings. But the increasing ease with which diamonds could be grown in the laboratory meant that this industrial market was now supplied by cheaper laboratory-cultured diamonds. Helder, along with other international diamond merchants, had managed to keep their mines supplying most of the world's jewelry markets by emphasizing the brilliant, white clarity of mined diamonds. To protect sales, the big diamond miners refused to sell high quality mined stones to jewelry manufacturers that also used cultured diamonds.

The complexity of diamond marketing had doubled down with the release of the 2006 movie "Blood Diamonds" which portrayed the terrible social conditions associated with diamond mining in conflict ridden parts of Africa. The understanding that diamonds mined in Africa could support genocidal conflict added an ethical aspect to diamond marketing. Stones discovered at the Sierra mine near Port Muskek were laser etched with a maple leaf to document their origin from Canadian mines. Identification of these ethically sourced diamonds increased the value of Canadian gemstones by about twenty per cent.

Jaco knew that the future important challenge in the diamond business would not be related to the discovery of diamonds. Increasingly, commercial success would be determined by convincing young lovers that they should not only invest in diamond jewelry but should also spend the extra money to purchase "natural, brilliant, white stones" rather than cultured diamonds. This required that the diamonds must come from ethical, well documented sources and also meant that larger mined stones were increasingly important for the business. Smaller, "casual" jewelry diamonds as well as industrial stones were now usually laboratory produced rather than dug out of the ground. A mine's profits were increasingly dependent on finding a significant proportion of large stones that could be sold for greater returns in the high-end jewelry market.

Despite these challenges, the demand for high quality diamond jewelry continued to grow, accelerated by the expanding middle class in China and India. Although the successful advertising tagline that "A Diamond is Forever" was initially focused on the American market, diamond engagement rings and jewelry were increasingly important in Asia as well.

Jaco knew that discovering a successful mine and bringing it into production required a five to fifteen-year long cycle of prospecting, ore sampling, financing, and mine development. Helder borrowed most of the money needed to bring a mine into production which was why shortening the time from starting a mine to selling its diamonds was an important factor in determining the company's profits. A diamond sitting in a vault waiting for sale continued to accumulate the interest costs of the loans negotiated to dig it out of the ground.

Despite the financial pressure to sell mined diamonds as quickly as possible, Helder's first commandment was to maintain the scarcity of the product to guard its value. The choreography of matching diamond production to the world demand for mined stones required exquisite timing and forecasting skills. Borrowing money to take diamonds out of the ground that could not be sold immediately was a drain on company profits. Supply needed to be constrained to stimulate rapid sales, keep prices high and minimize interest costs. Helder's success was determined by its ability to bring new mines online just as the supply of high-quality stones was lagging and demand in the market was peaking. The company would always consider delaying development of a potentially lucrative mine rather than flooding the market with new product.

Although Helder remained tightly controlled by its South African founding family, young Helder leaders were trained and educated in international schools in the USA, Canada, and Europe. Voice coaches were well paid to eliminate evidence of the South African accents that would associate Helder with that country's turbulent history. Jaco Helder sounded like he had grown up in the Northeastern United States. He had recently been placed in charge of Helder's North American mines and markets. Although Helder's Chinese sales were growing rapidly since Jaco's cousin had established a position on the Shanghai Diamond Exchange, the American retail market remained the most profitable part of Helder's business. Jaco's appointment as North American head meant that he was favourably positioned for future consideration as Helder's CEO.

Sitting in the portable building that Helder used as an office at the Sierra mine site, Jaco was thankful that this would likely be the last time that he would visit James Bay for many years to come. Growing up in Africa, he felt more comfortable in tropical heat than Arctic cold. He also understood African politicians better than Canadian leaders. In Africa you always knew which local decision makers you could influence and even purchase. That was more difficult in Canada.

Jaco found that dealing with the local Indigenous leaders was profitable but mildly frustrating. Prior to the mine's development, First Nation leaders in Port Muskek had agreed to Helder being granted ninety-nine years of mineral rights in return for a profit-sharing agreement that required Helder to report its own profit without audit or meaningful oversight. And then the Council was surprised to learn that Helder consistently reported zero profit from their mine. Their naivete was good for Helder's bottom line but also contributed to periodic outbursts of anger from the Port Muskek community that usually resulted in short term blockades of Helder's supply lines.

Sitting in the small Sierra office boardroom, Jaco was wearing a black goose-down vest over a matching turtleneck, dark woolen trousers tightened with elastic fiber and light Baffin boots that were rated comfortable at one hundred degrees below zero. Like most Helder executives, he was lean and tanned, close shaven with short cropped blonde hair. It was part of the Helder culture for leaders to look after themselves. He was eager to return to New York after approving the last plans for mothballing the Sierra site.

His executive jet could not land on the Sierra airstrip and had touched down at Timmins, a few hundred kilometres from the Sierra mine. Jaco had taken a propeller bush plane from Timmins to Sierra, arriving the night before. He spent the morning after arrival going over plans to close the site with the local mine manager, Bob Starfield. Starfield had asked him to stay that afternoon to approve the last contract necessary to conclude the mine's closing plans, a deal with a local road contractor to build a fortified winter road next year to enable removal of their heavy mining equipment.

Normally Jaco would have told Starfield to close the deal himself. But Jaco knew that the used equipment from Sierra was going to be needed at Helder's new East Africa site the year after it was removed from its current location. Helder would save millions by foregoing purchase of new equipment if they could transport that gear to Africa, with arrival just as the new East Africa mine was going into full production. Establishing a mine with used equipment was not common practice but Jaco had determined that effective use of equipment throughout its full lifetime of service was going to be important in Helder's hyper-efficient future. If Jaco delivered that equipment to Africa on time from Canada, his ability to operate efficiently in the complexity of Helder's international business would be obvious to the family and his uncle. His visit to this cold and miserable part of the world was worth it to ensure the mine manager's closing plan was comprehensive and dependable.

Jaco was also paying attention to the mine closing because he expected that Helder would be back in James Bay in about ten years' time. By then, he'd probably be CEO. He'd seen the initial exploration results from the Ultra mine a few kilometres away from Sierra. These results were a closely guarded corporate secret and Jaco was one of the few people who knew that the Ultra mine exploratory drilling had demonstrated a high yield of large stones. Big diamonds classified by their likely finished weight as one point five carats and greater generally constitute about twenty-five per cent of a mine's output but eighty per cent of the value a mine produces.

Jaco knew that Helder was simply keeping the value of the Ultra site in its "underground bank" while the company produced and sold the diamonds from the East Africa mine they were about to open. It was part of the complex dance of diamond marketing to keep Ultra diamonds in the ground while the East African stones were sold at top dollar.

Jaco's job was to close the Sierra mine without fanfare nor negative media attention. This would ensure that Helder would be welcomed back with open arms by naïve Canadian officials ten years in the future when he would announce as a new CEO that Helder wanted to renew exploration of the Ultra site.

While waiting for the winter road contractor to arrive, Jaco ate lunch in the boardroom with Bob Starfield. Jaco was puzzled that Starfield had not immediately accepted Helder's offer to manage the opening of the East Africa mine. "What's going on with you Bob?" he asked as they sat to eat. "I heard you haven't accepted our offer to go to Africa after you get this place closed down. Most engineers would jump at that chance."

Bob was always surprised that Jaco sounded mildly American rather than reflecting his South African roots. He shook his head ruefully and looked down. "To be honest Mr. Helder, my fiancée lives in Port Muskek and she's not too keen to move to Africa. So, I guess I'll get the Sierra site closed and then look for something else in Northern Ontario."

Jaco shrugged. "Okay, well, if you change your mind, let me know Bob. You've done a good job for us here." He picked up a fork full of limp salad and thought to himself that nothing he had ever eaten here was fresh. Everything seemed frozen. How the hell did anyone live in this godforsaken place?

"Bob, who are these guys we are meeting this afternoon and why do you want me to hang around to meet them? After listening to your closing plans this morning, I'm satisfied you have everything well in hand. I've got a lot of stuff waiting for me back in New York. Why did you want me to delay my flight to meet these guys?"

The mine manager rubbed his chin nervously. "I'm sorry to delay you Mr. Helder. This is the last contract we need to get approved for our equipment removal plan. I know once we get the heavy mining equipment back down to the main winter road from Post Muskek to Moose, there won't be any trouble in getting it to the railhead. They have lots of experience hauling heavy stuff along that road to Moose. But from here to Port Muskek, we didn't really stress that part of the supply route when we opened the mine ten years ago and brought the equipment in. It was before my time, but we assembled much of that heavy mining gear on site."

He put down his fork and raised his hands, showing his concern. "Now we want to remove that equipment without dismantling it completely and that means really bulking up the road. The guys doing this road contract are good, but I expect the contract they will bring in today will be more costly than Helder expects. I want them to pitch their contract to you directly so you'll understand the challenges they'll be facing getting all this equipment down to the main James Bay winter road."

Jaco realized how limited Bob was. So concerned about the local issues and missing the big picture. As if Jaco would care about a few hundred thousand bucks more or less. He had much bigger things to think about. But he couldn't show that sentiment to the mine manager. "Okay Bob. We'll listen to them." And took another bite of limp salad.

"The other thing is Mr. Helder, you may want to get to know one of the guys who is coming this afternoon. His name is Jonah Kataquit. Down south they call him Jonah Kay. His uncle runs the road construction for us and some other businesses out of Port Muskek. The uncle had an accident more than a year ago and Jonah came back from Toronto to help him out. He's been practicing as a lawyer for one of the big Bay Street firms in Toronto and I think he may be influential with the Port Muskek Chief and Council in the future. If Helder ever decides to come back here to explore the Ultra site, he could be a good guy for you to know."

Jaco looked at Bob suspiciously. "What do you know about Ultra, Bob? Why would you think we would be coming back?"

Bob realized his mistake in mentioning Ultra. The official word was it would never be economic to explore it. "Oh, I'm sorry Mr. Helder. I just mean that the company has mineral rights for years to come, that's all."

Just then they heard a truck pulling up to the office. Jaco glanced out the window to see five men get out. Three were dressed like they were locals in flannels and heavy pants, one man was wearing an expensive, long down coat and one a grubby ski jacket. Bob went out to greet them. Jaco heard a brief conversation and then the three local men entered the boardroom and closed the door. The two other guys had stayed outside in the waiting room for some reason.

Jaco was introduced to an old guy named Samuel Sunderland who sat down closest to him with another weathered man named Charlie sitting beside Samuel. Jaco nodded when introduced to the third visitor, Jonah, who was sitting farthest away from him beside Charlie. Jaco figured the young guy must be the lawyer Bob wanted him to meet. He didn't seem very imposing. Looked like a local native with long black hair in a ponytail, some bead jewelry from a necklace over his chest, flannel shirt and heavy, loose trousers. He was holding two file folders but was clearly subordinate to this Samuel guy who seemed to be the boss. Jaco promised himself that he would get this contract settled in an hour and start the trip back to New York.

Jaco smiled at the three men sitting to his left who seemed appropriately impressed to be meeting a high Helder executive. Turning to the boss man, Samuel, Jaco started to thank him for coming when Charlie interrupted, directing his comments to Bob Starfield, seated to Jaco's right.

"Hey Bob, got any of them peach danishes Lenore makes?"

"Sorry, Mr. Helder. Lemme just see what we've got." Bob left his boss speechless as he put his head through the boardroom door and asked his assistant to do a pastry check.

Jaco started again. "Mr. Sunderland, we appreciate you and your team coming today..."

Bob's assistant stuck her head through the door. "We got some apple danish, Bob. That okay?"

Charlie grunted. "No peach?"

The assistant picked up a tray and brought it into the room. "Nope, looks like only apple and maybe some strawberry, Charlie."

Charlie shrugged. "That'll have to do." The assistant laid the tray down on the table and Charlie picked up two danishes and stacked them one on top of the other, taking a big bite from both pastries.

Jaco looked at Charlie without saying a word as the man

slowly savoured the pastry with eyes closed.

Samuel turned his head to look at Charlie and then turned back to look at the Helder executive with a slight grin. "Charlie sures loves Lenore's pastries." And then sat silent.

Jaco wondered whether they thought he was running a bakery. Feeling frustration rising, he shook his head slightly to refocus and started again. "We appreciate you being here today, Samuel. I'm eager to hear what it'll take to build up the road next winter so we can take out our mining equipment."

Samuel shook his head slowly from side to side. "It's too bad this mine is closin'. It'll mean a lot of lost jobs in Port Muskek."

Jaco had learned how to express empathy with the help of several leadership courses and summoned all his training as he put his hands face up on the boardroom table. The table was crowded with the five men sitting around it. The room was small, and the fluorescent lights flickered. As he spoke Jaco's thoughts escaped to his return to Helder's elegant New York office.

"Sam – may I call you Sam – believe me, no one is more disappointed than me and the Helder team that we have to leave this mine. The site just didn't turn out as rich as we thought it would be. It's also very expensive to work here with all the miners needing to be flown in and supplies coming in mainly during the months that the winter road is open. And we haven't been able to find any other areas within our mineral rights that would justify another mine." He shrugged his shoulders and shook his head to show his regret. "That's just the way the mining business works, Sam. You never know what you've got until the mine is producing. We are as upset as you are that we need to leave."

Samuel looked sad. "Yeah, it's too bad the other site east of here didn't work out. Whad'ya call it – Ultra – or something like that?"

Jaco was surprised that a simple road worker would know the name for the Ultra site. "Well, we explored that area pretty thoroughly, Sam, and it just won't fly."

Sam pushed his chair a few inches away from the table and leaned back. "Yeah, the Port Muskek Chief and Council were hoping that if you started another mine, we might be able to convince you to hire some people from our First Nation to work at them good mine jobs. You know, instead of just doing roadwork and catering. Too bad."

Jaco ensured that his concern was evident on his face. "You know Sam, those mining jobs can be dangerous. Our first duty is to the health and safety of our workers and our assessment was that people from Port Muskek just didn't have the skills to get trained as mine workers."

"Yeah, we heard that. We just thought with more of the kids getting high school degrees now that you might consider hiring some young men and women if the new mine opened. But I guess that ain't gonna happen, so I suppose there ain't no use talking about it."

Charlie had reached for a third danish and took a big bite.

Samuel looked at Charlie and turned to smile at Jaco. "Charlie sure loves them pastries, eh?"

Jaco could do nothing but smile back.

"I guess Charlie won't be getting any more of them pastries when the mine closes," Sam added.

Jaco thought he could use this to steer the conversation back to the contract. Sitting in this godforsaken place talking about baked goods was a total waste of his time. "Well, we can make sure that we include some pastries in next winter's contract for the beefed-up road." He looked at Bob and smiled again. "Bob, let's make sure we write some danishes into that contract we're going to discuss with Samuel." He looked at Charlie. "It's peach ones that you like, right, Charlie?"

Charlie grunted. Samuel leaned back to the table shaking his head. "Well, I guess it's too bad for everyone, but there ain't gonna be no contract and there ain't gonna be no road next winter as far as I can tell. So, I guess we gotta get Lenore making pastries for something else."

Jaco's smile disappeared. "What are you saying? I thought you're here to present me with a revised contract to build a stronger road next winter so we can get our heavy equipment out." He looked at Bob, feeling anger mounting. "Aren't these the guys that do the winter road work, Bob?"

Bob was nodding but starting to look pale. "Yeah, Mr. Helder, these are the guys. They've built the road to Port Muskek every year since the mine opened. What's going on, Sam? Are you joking or playing with us or something?" Bob looked distraught, wondering what this was about. Was Samuel trying to jack up the price of the contract? He wished that Sam had warned him about this before they got in front of Mr. Helder.

Jaco looked intently at Samuel, knowing that this damn fool was about to pressure him for extra money for the road. He didn't really care what the price of the road would be. But it was part of the Helder culture that the company never got squeezed. Especially by some damn natives who thought they had Helder in a corner. He took his time staring at Sam who wouldn't meet his gaze. Jaco held out his right hand in front of Bob, reminding him who was in charge of the negotiation.

Then Jaco spoke directly to Sam.

"So, Samuel, I guess you think that because we have mine equipment here that needs to be transported, that you have us in a good place to squeeze us, huh?"

He let the silence hang in the air. Sam continued to stare at the table. And then Jaco leaned forward suddenly, slamming his fist on the table. "Well, lemme tell you, mister, nobody fucking dictates terms to Helder. If you fucking guys don't want to build our road, we'll find someone who does."

Charlie wiped crumbs from his mouth and nudged Samuel. "You see, Sam, I told you he wasn't gonna be happy."

Samuel nodded, lifting his eyes to stare at Jaco. "Yeah, I know Charlie. Why don't you explain to Mr. Helder here why we can't build his road?"

They could see Jaco's face reddening. Charlie picked up the

last half of his third danish and thoughtfully chewed it before he turned to Jaco. Then he took time carefully wiping crumbs from his mouth before speaking. Jaco's face was becoming slightly purple as he waited for Charlie's explanation. Having finished the danishes, Charlie leaned back and lifted his hands from the table as if to launch into a prolonged discussion of road engineering.

Then, he uttered two words.

"Global warming."

Jaco exploded. "What the fuck do you mean global warming? It's not like next year is going to be that much warmer than this year."

Charlie grunted. "I don't know where you got your weather degree, Mr. Helder, but I can sure see the weather changing almost every winter." He shook his head sadly and turned to Jonah sitting next to him. "You've been away for a while Jonah. You see a change, right?"

Jonah nodded without commenting. He was watching Jaco closely. The Helder executive was clearly exasperated and turned to his mine manager.

"Starfield, I don't know where you found these clowns, but they are either incompetent or trying to extort me or both. This is a waste of my time." He stabbed his finger at Bob Starfield who looked like he wanted to vanish. "I'm not going to sit here a minute longer. I want you to find me some engineers down south and a construction team that will get the road ready to extract our equipment next winter. We've got plenty of time to get a new team in place. I don't care what it costs." He looked at Samuel and repeated jabbing his finger for emphasis. "You just fucked up a chance for a pretty good contract, mister." Jaco started to stand to leave.

Then a quiet voice stopped him. "Mr. Helder, I think that you should sit and listen to me for a few minutes." Jonah had learned through years of negotiating for David Morton that sometimes softening his voice was an effective technique for business discussion. Helder paused, then sat back down and leaned forward slightly to better hear Jonah.

"You need to take my Uncle Samuel very seriously when he tells you that we will not be able to remove your equipment from the Sierra site next winter. You may be able to find some other road construction company that does not know this geography and its unique features as well as Uncle Samuel and Charlie. Remember, they are the only two people who have ever built the road between Port Muskek and the mine." He continued in a soft voice, barely audible and forcing Jaco to lean forward further to hear him.

"However, if you do decide to contract another company to build this road remember that about half of the route is on Port Muskek First Nation's land. Linking up to the main winter road to Moose requires you to build the road across our territory. And we would treat our responsibility for the safety of workers on our land just as seriously as you take your responsibility for workers at the mine. You mentioned earlier to Uncle Samuel that worker safety prevented Helder Company from hiring people from Port Muskek to work in the mine. Well, I am sure that Port Muskek Council would insist on carefully assessing the skills of any road workers that you would hire to work on our land. That assessment would take some time and would definitely not allow road construction across our land next winter. Uncle Samuel and Charlie have an enviable safety record. We would not want any mishaps if another company attempted to build the road."

Jonah shook his head. "If my uncle tells you the road is not going to happen next winter, I think you should listen to him very carefully, Mr. Helder." Jonah looked at Bob Starfield who was looking nauseated. Bob had no idea what Samuel and Jonah were up to, but it was clear that they had planned this out.

Jonah turned his gaze back to Jaco and continued. "Mr. Helder, the people of Port Muskek and Helder have been partners at this site for more than ten years. And partners always look out for each other's interests. Right now, I think

Helder interests may need some help from us." Jaco was silent and now sitting deep in his chair, carefully listening to Jonah's quiet words.

"Jaco – you don't mind if I use your first name?" Helder nodded and Jonah continued. "You know those Helder guys that you fly in every month to count and examine the diamonds? I know they come from South Africa or Europe or from New York and they figure out how much the diamonds are worth that Bob is digging up, right?"

Jaco leaned forward looking intently at Jonah. "What are you talking about? What's that got to do with the road?"

"Well, Jaco, those guys are usually here for a week or so and there really isn't much to do at this mine. The satellite connectivity here is pretty good so of course they all get hooked up to internet and some of them sign on to some pretty messed up websites. Including some porn sites."

Jaco began to redden again and looked like he might pound the table a second time. "Just what the fuck are you talking about?" He spun in his chair to face an increasingly distressed Bob Starfield. "Starfield, did you know that these idiots were coming here to waste my time about porn sites on the internet?" But Jaco made no attempt to leave. Jonah clearly had his attention.

Jonah turned in his chair so he could look across Charlie and his uncle to address the Helder executive more directly. "A couple of my cousins work in cybersecurity for the satellite internet provider you use here at the mine, and my cousins were concerned about the sites that have been accessed by your guys when they stay here. You know, those eastern European porn sites can compromise all your cybersecurity, right? These porn cybercriminals put phishing software into your guys' phones and computers to access financial data and passwords. My cousins, they started paying attention to your internet access here and found that a lot of passwords for your internal servers were compromised."

Jonah was starting to speak less softly and Jaco slumped

back in his chair again. "My cousins felt they were responsible to find out what files might be compromised on the Helder servers. I'm glad they behaved so responsibly, because they found some important stuff was probably exposed by those stolen passwords." He looked at Jaco, nodding slightly.

"We understand that these guys who fly in figure out the value of the diamonds that Bob here pulls out of the ground. We know that it's not a straightforward thing to estimate how much a gem is worth when its raw and just separated from the ore. We know that you have to imagine how much the gem will be worth when it's cut and polished and that requires the special expertise that these guys bring when they fly in. We know that Bob here can't figure that value out by himself and we figure that information must be a pretty important Helder trade secret."

Jaco was silent, not understanding what this internet bullshit had to do with the winter road. Nonetheless he felt a vague sense of foreboding.

Jonah continued. "My cousins used the passwords that your guys had exposed and located the documents covered by those passwords. Then they came to me for legal advice about what they should do. You know, they didn't want to get anyone in trouble or freak anyone out at Helder unnecessarily. You'll be glad to know my cousins also patched the password leaks after they discovered them. Everything on your network is secure again and my cousins are managing all your cybersecurity without a hitch now that they fixed these leaks. They also restricted those dark sites your guys were using."

Somehow, Jaco did not look comforted by the reassurance Jonah was offering. He didn't say a word as Jonah continued.

"We wanted to find out whether we should notify Helder about the leak, whether it was important. When the guys came to me with these documents," Jonah held up a file folder and Jaco seemed to blanch, "I got a guy who is sitting outside who knows the diamond business to look at the spreadsheets and that's when it started to get interesting. Charlie, why don't you bring in David and William. It's rude to have them sitting outside while we're talking about them."

Charlie opened the door and ushered in David Morton and William Myrtle. They sat on the right side of Bob Starfield surrounding the two Helder men in the small boardroom.

Jonah provided introductions. "Jaco, this is David Morton, CEO of Mindful Innovation, my boss. And this is 'Diamond Bill' Myrtle. I bet you've heard of him?" Jaco nodded. He had never met William Myrtle but everyone in the diamond world knew about Diamond Bill and his big strike in northern Canada. Helder had bought out Bill's claims and was nearly ready to open that mine.

"Diamond Bill provides us with advice at Mindful Innovation, so we got him to look at these documents we found." He again waved the file folder at Jaco. "And Bill knew right away that these documents behind the compromised passwords were the monthly reports that the outside South African guys provided when they flew in, telling Helder how much value Bob had dug out of the ground that month."

Jonah looked at Bill. "Yeah, that's right Jonah," Diamond Bill said as he turned to Jaco. "It was pretty obvious that Jonah's cousins had uncovered your monthly evaluation reports. I told them they should just turn the reports over to you and tell you how they got the documents. But this lawyer here," he hooked his thumb at Jonah, "wanted to take it one step further."

Jonah leaned forward in his chair. "Before we got anyone in trouble, I wanted to be sure what we had, that nothing had been changed or corrupted, and then it came to me. I knew that we had copies of the original monthly reports in the band council office to compare with these documents in the compromised folders." He stopped speaking and leaned in to stare at Jaco, lifting one of the two file folders in front of him as he spoke. And suddenly Jaco felt all the eyes in the room fixed on him.

*****

Brynn was thinking about her upcoming trip to Toronto for her first meeting with her new university Chair when she sat down with Yvette and Jane Gagne in the Wiichihinan CEO's office. She wasn't sure whether her plans were more exciting or anxiety provoking, and she needed to discuss her ideas with her two James Bay colleagues.

"Before I finalize my recommendations for the new Chair, I want to make sure you agree with what I'll be telling him." She glanced from Yvette to Jane who were waiting for her comments and then continued.

"You know that Wiichihinan Health Authority serves about eight thousand people here in Moose and in the communities along the coast. If you look at the rest of the Canadian population, eight thousand people would typically require about forty hip and knee joint replacements a year and that number is increasing by about five per cent per year as our population ages. But we know that in James Bay we have a backlog of Elders with a need for joint replacement who don't want to travel south for surgery. We've learned over the past few weeks that they will probably come to Wiichihinan Hospital for an operation. So, I am estimating that if we start an orthopaedic surgery program at Wiichihinan we need to do about eighty total joints per year for the next two or three years to eliminate the backlog and then probably settle back to about fifty operations a year."

Jane nodded. "Based on my conversations with the Ministry of Health, they will definitely pay us for up to one hundred total joints per year if we start an orthopaedics program here. So, the hospital can certainly commit to doing eighty joints a year."

Yvette added. "And I have the agreement from medical staff to provide anaesthesia and surgical assists in the OR. Our docs are really excited to start offering surgery at Wiichihinan. They're hopeful that this orthopaedic program will encourage other surgeons to come here to work as well."

Brynn was consulting notes on a piece of paper as she discussed the plan. "From what I have seen, there are usually one or two people with fractures that get flown out for treatment every week. If we combine the fractures and the total joint replacements and other surgery like arthroscopy that will undoubtedly be necessary when we have an orthopod doing consults fulltime in Wiichihinan clinics, we will have enough activity to keep an orthopod engaged while he or she is up here. I figure most surgeons will be willing to come for two or three months at a time." Brynn looked up from the paper she was consulting.

"Who knows, when they learn how appreciative everyone is here, maybe eventually someone will stay fulltime and then we could change the model to support that person when they need time off. But for now I am going to suggest to our new Chair that we will have enough work to support a rotating team of up to six surgeons who will each spend one or two periods of at least two months here over the next two years. After two years, we can review and modify. Agree?"

Jane was nodding her head. "Yeah that sounds good from the perspective of the surgeons, Brynn. But is the Dean still okay taking this plan to our First Nations Councils for approval? And still committed to a pre-professional training program to produce more health professionals from our communities?"

Brynn smiled. "Yeah, you convinced him Jane. From my telephone conversation with the Dean, I don't actually think he's really all that excited about the surgery. He seems more interested in making this an example for how reconciliation can work through education and training. And your comment on our last videoconference about Egerton Ryerson probably thinking he was acting in the best interests of Indigenous People really got the Dean's attention."

Two days later she was sitting across from her new boss Dr. Subi Rajarathinam in his university Chair's office. Even though the new Chair had only been in his role for a few weeks, Brynn was pleased to see that the old, massive oak furniture that had defined his predecessor's office was gone and replaced by light coloured, modern furnishings that were both more welcoming and more human in their proportions. Rather than staring at her over an enormous desk, Subi sat with her in comfortable chairs away from his small computer desk. Brynn's feet were firmly planted on the carpet.

"Brynn thanks for coming down from Moose to see me. You have another two weeks in your time up north, right?" Brynn nodded and the Chair continued.

"Well, my boss the Dean is very eager to get this collaborative program started with Wiichihanan Hospital. I understand that you have a concrete proposal for me?"

Brynn nodded and described the concept of a two-year plan to rotate surgeons who would do total joints, fracture surgery and other general orthopaedic operations. While she was describing the proposal that she had discussed with Jane and Yvette, Subi was taking notes and nodding.

"This sounds very doable, Brynn. Keshini Jayawardana, your CEO at St. Barts has agreed to recruit two new surgeons who would participate in this program. I understand that you would continue to participate?" Brynn nodded. "So, we would only need to find three more surgeons to complete our commitment. And I think that for the next two years at least, I will commit to working in James Bay two months a year. I have always been fascinated by the north, even though my DNA is likely better suited for the tropics." He grinned at Brynn, putting aside his note pad.

"Leave this with me, Brynn. With the Dean's support we can get this planned and organized in the time that you have left in Wiichihinan. In fact, one of our senior joint replacement surgeons heard about the project and called me saying he's ready to go tomorrow. It would be great if we got him to start before you leave so that you guys can overlap a bit." He crossed his legs and sat back before continuing.

"Brynn, you know it's important to the Dean that we get

this plan approved by the local communities?"

Brynn nodded. "Yeah, we can keep the program going as a temporary continuation of what I have been doing, Subi. That will give the First Nations Councils time for consultation and discussion – especially with Elders in the communities. I think that with the Dean's commitment to take a long-term approach to training local healthcare workers, those councils are going to be enthusiastic in their support."

Subi returned her nod. "On our last call, that CEO Dr. Gagne was very impressive talking about the importance of local approval and a commitment to training. But Brynn, more important for us right now, I want to talk about your career." The Chair reached over to a coffee table to pick up a folder.

"I was reviewing your performance report from last year. It's incredible what you have accomplished in research as well as in education. I must tell you; you are definitely the brightest rising star in our faculty. And what you have done in Wiichihinan is really remarkable."

Brynn looked down at her hands. This was a different approach than the last Chair had taken in discussing her performance.

Subi continued. "The Dean wants orthopaedics to take a lead in addressing diversity in surgery. With your leadership in developing the Wiichihinan project and with your success as a leading academic surgeon and a woman, I want you to think about leading our department's approach to improving equity, diversity and inclusion. Would that interest you?"

Brynn pondered for a moment and then shook her head. "Subi, I am delighted that you are making this a priority for the department. Women surgeons in particular will be very pleased that you are going to start addressing some of the issues we face. But with this new program up north, running my lab and picking my practice up on returning to St. Barts, I am not sure that I would want all the committee work that would be part of addressing diversity. I will support you and the person you choose to take on a leadership role one hundred per cent. But that job is probably not for me."

Subi nodded. "Yeah, I get it. Well, listen, my job is to help you to be successful. Is there anything I can do to help you succeed, Brynn?"

Brynn thought for a moment, remembering her last trip to this office. "Well, there is one thing you could really help with. Could you speak to Keshini and tell her that I should start doing trauma surgery again? It's important that I maintain my expertise doing fractures if I am going to look after trauma at Wiichihinan. They took me off the trauma service at St. Barts several months before I left to go up north."

Subi smiled. "Keshini has told me how much respect she has for you and I know that you are very important in her plans to renew the Department of Surgery at St. Barts. Given everything you are doing for the university and our department, I can guarantee that you will be back on fracture call when you return to Toronto, Brynn. I can commit to that right now."

On her way out of Subi's office, Brynn thanked the new young assistant who had replaced the former Chair's ancient gatekeeper. She walked down onto the street to emerge into the late winter sun lighting up Toronto's Discovery District. Looking up at the imposing hospital, university and laboratory buildings that encircled her, Brynn suddenly felt very much at home in her surroundings.

*****

Under the flickering fluorescent lights in the Sierra mine boardroom, Jonah held up one of two file folders that were on the table in front of him. "You know those reports you send monthly to band council, Jaco? The ones that show the value of the monthly diamond haul minus the expenses of running the mine? Those reports that show there is never any profit, never anything to share with the band in our profit-sharing agreement? You know these documents, right, Jaco?"

Jaco felt sick and wanted to leave. But he was hemmed in on all sides. And he needed to know how much they knew and what it was going to cost him to fix this. Trying to level the playing field, he decided that the best defence was offense. "Yeah, I know the reports you are describing. We've been doing them for ten years. What's the big fucking deal now? What the hell are you going on about? We're here to talk about a road." The people sitting around the table observed that Jaco was not threatening to leave. He needed to know what was in Jonah's file folder.

Then Jaco felt increasingly nauseated as Jonah continued. "Well, Jaco, Diamond Bill here compared the reports you provided to band council with these Helder documents, and it all becomes pretty obvious. Every month the amount of diamond value reported to Helder by these guys flying in to examine your newly discovered stones was more than you report to band council. You guys are the only ones who know what a stone is worth. We have to take your word for it. And it looks like every month you've been under reporting to us. Probably cheating us out of almost ten million dollars a year based on what our share of the profit was supposed to be." He passed the file folder to Charlie who reached around Samuel to give the documents to Jaco.

"Have a look at these pages, Mr. Helder. Every monthly report Helder receives from its experts is stapled to the equivalent month's report that you have provided to Port Muskek Council. I included about a quarter of what we discovered but each month in the last ten years is about the same as what you see on these examples, Jaco. Each month you understate the value of what this mine is producing."

Jonah looked around the room at Charlie, his uncle Samuel, David Morton, and Diamond Bill. "That means we should have received almost half a million a month on average, about ten million a year according to our profit-sharing arrangement. Can you imagine how many new houses we could have built in Port Muskek with that money? The new hospital and school we could build?" He looked at Jaco, who was increasingly pale as he leafed through the pages in the file folder he had been handed. Then Jonah turned to David Morton.

"Jaco, I introduced you to my boss, David Morton. David has quite a bit of experience with reporting to the government and declaring profit for tax purposes. After he heard all about this, David raised another concern. Jaco, when you reported the mine's financial statements to the government for tax purposes, which monthly reports did you use?"

They all looked at the diamond executive who had shrunken into his chair. David Morton examined him closely and turned to Jonah. "I think Jaco's silence tells us what numbers they used when reporting to the government, Jonah. When you have two sets of books like Helder seems to maintain, you use the same copy for the tax man that you use to inform your profit-sharing partner. Is that about right, Mr. Helder?"

Jonah continued David Morton's discussion. "As a lawyer, if I were aware that you had made false statements to the tax authorities, I would be required to let the tax people know. At present Jaco, David's suggestion regarding your company's tax filings – which in the past two years since you starting leading the North American branch of the company would have been submitted over your signature – remains conjecture to us. But it would be straightforward for us to open discussions with Revenue Canada to determine whether Helder has defrauded the Canadian government."

Jaco was thinking quickly. He needed to shut this down. Immediately.

"You guys are exaggerating – you just don't understand the diamond business. It's impossible to be exact on what a stone's gonna be worth on the market so we're just conservative on what we report until its cut and polished, that's all."

Jonah motioned to Diamond Bill. The diamond expert leaned his forearms on the table before talking. "Mr. Helder I've seen lots of estimates in my time in this business and never seen consistent under-estimations like you have reported to Port Muskek Council. If you low-ball the value of a stone initially and it eventually sells for more, then you can always adjust the price for your profit-sharing partners or for the tax man. But Jonah showed me ten years of reporting that Port Muskek got from Helder. I saw no evidence of any upward revenue adjustments."

Jaco was now thinking as he was talking. "Listen, these are probably just calculation errors. So maybe we can review this and see if we should make some adjustments to provide more money to the Council? No need for us to get the tax man involved though. That'll just slow us down in making retroactive payments to Council." He looked desperately at Bob Starfield and held up the incriminating file folder. "Bob we can look at these documents and you and I can make some estimates for adjustments, huh?" He looked around the table. "You guys will trust Bob on this, right?"

Jonah took over. "Jaco, let's just explore that a bit. Let's say to cover the discrepancy between your corporate estimates and what you reported to Port Muskek Council, you might make a donation to council. And that might start us thinking we should keep this between us in this room." He looked around and everyone was nodding back at him. "But Jaco, what about the trouble we took in bringing this to you rather than the tax man? We are saving Helder a lot of money, some very bad public relations and maybe even criminal investigation for fraud."

Jaco licked his lips as he stared around the table at these five men who were ruining his day and possibly his chances at eventually becoming Helder CEO. "I do appreciate you bringing this to me and Bob." Bob Starfield shuddered at the second mention of his name. "We can certainly make this worth your effort." Jaco was thinking hard. "We could maybe think of some amount over and above what we pay to council." He looked around the table. "Like maybe another million."

Jonah nodded. "So, we are talking about Helder providing a

million for each of us? Five million in total?"

They could see Jaco sweating despite the cool temperature in the boardroom. "No, no, for Chrissake. I meant a million for the five of you." The five were staring at him without speaking. "Okay, I can go to one point five, that's three hundred each. That's as far as I can go."

Jonah nodded again and looked over at Charlie. "You got that Charlie?" Charlie nodded.

"David?"

And Morton nodded, holding up his phone as Jonah continued. "Okay, Mr. Helder, we now have you recorded offering us a bribe to keep this away from the taxman." He enjoyed Jaco's unspoken response to his comment.

"Realistically, none of us would be willing to take your bribe, Jaco. In fact, it's quite insulting and we will ensure the record and transcript of this meeting shows that we turned down your bribe." He looked at Charlie and David, both of whom checked to ensure their recordings were still running and nodded back to Jonah. "But the records in the folder I gave you, plus these recordings…" He looked at Charlie and David who both held up their phones, "Would be an interesting story for our authorities. I can imagine massive fines for Helder and probably jail time for decision makers who knew about this. Especially executives who offered bribes to cover up the evidence."

Jonah paused for effect. Jaco was silent. His veneer of sophistication was floating in a puddle at his feet. The five men almost felt sorry for him. Then Jonah continued.

"Charlie, David, please turn off your recordings. Mr. Helder, Bob, please put your phones on the table." As the two men delivered their cell phones, Samuel checked them to ensure they were not recording.

"Jaco, you'll be pleased to know we have a different proposal for you. We don't want you to pay anything to council. We do however expect you to sign on to a new joint venture with Council and with David's company, Mindful

Innovation. You will have a twenty per cent share in the new venture which will be controlled by a partnership between the Port Muskek First Nation and Mindful. If Chief and Council agree, I will serve as CEO of the joint venture. And the purpose of this new three-way partnership will be to start a new mine at Ultra."

He looked carefully at Jaco. "Jaco, it's much more important for Port Muskek to get new jobs working at the Ultra site than it is to get retroactive payments from your company. Rather than getting money as you close down Sierra and all the legal ramifications that might entail, we would prefer to extend our partnership to development of a new mine at Ultra." He paused to provide his next comments with the deserved emphasis.

"Walk-away, retroactive payments to Port Muskek would become public very quickly and would undoubtedly attract attention from authorities regarding the financial statements that you have previously filed for tax purposes. Instead of opening that can of worms, we would like to start afresh at our new mine." Jonah held up his second folder.

"These new incorporation documents describe that Helder will transfer its mineral rights and equipment to the new company in return for its twenty per cent ownership. Mindful Innovation will provide the capital for the new mine in return for a thirty-one per cent share and the First Nation will transfer its profit-sharing agreement from Helder to the new joint venture for a forty-nine per cent interest. I have already explored this option with Council leaders, and they are excited about the potential for a new mine and new jobs. This is described in a joint venture proposal you will find in this folder."

Jonah looked at Bob who was obviously shaken by the disclosures that had just taken place in front of him. "Bob Starfield, we will be offering you the job of mine manager at Ultra. And Diamond Bill here has agreed to help us with regular assessment of the stones."

Jonah stood up. "Gentlemen, I expect that we should be leaving to let Mr. Helder consider his options." He reached across the table to deliver the second file folder to the Helder executive. "Jaco, these documents define our new joint venture. I need these executed by Helder in the next week. My email address is available on those documents and your counsel can get me any time." He then pointed to the first folder with the incriminating documents.

"We will keep the originals of all the false reports you provided to council, along with the accurate estimates your experts provided to Helder, carefully secured along with the transcripts and recordings we made from our conversations today.

"As long as we get this joint venture established in the next week, these reports and our conversation will remain safeguarded within our new partnership." He looked around the table. "Right, guys?" He was greeted by nods as his four companions stood to depart.

A snowstorm was beginning as Charlie started the truck outside the Helder office and backed slowly out of the parking space with Samuel beside him and William, David, and Jonah in the back of the spacious pick-up. David turned to look at Jonah sitting beside him.

"Well, buddy, I am reminded yet again never to play poker with you." He looked at his friend and smiled. "I think I am going to like working with you in the diamond business just as much as I enjoyed our partnership selling pot."

CHAPTER 22

Mindful Messaging. September 2019 to January 2020

As the three of them sat in the Mindful Innovation office in the Distillery District, Jonah was intrigued to see the chemistry developing between Corinne and David Morton. The three had been friends since early high school and Jonah had watched their initial romance evolve, served as David's best man at their wedding, and then sadly looked on as their marriage fell apart with David's infidelity. They had divorced just as David and Jonah began working together full time on CannWeed.

Jonah had attempted to stay in touch with Corinne after the couple split. But she feared that Jonah might have been complicit with David's various acts of betrayal and said she couldn't trust Jonah. Although Jonah had constantly supported Corinne during the marriage and tried to let David know that he was destroying a good thing and a good person, he understood Corinne's suspicion.

When he had last seen her about two years ago, Corinne

seemed angry and resentful. Jonah was taken aback when David told him that he was talking to Corinne again while the two men were rooming together in Moose for the Mindful Games. But he was not entirely surprised when David suggested that they should consider Corinne's public relations company developing a marketing plan for their new diamond company.

Helder had signed on to their new joint venture with Port Muskek First Nation and Mindful Innovation within the time limit that Jonah had imposed on Jaco. Shortly thereafter Jaco had been replaced as Helder's North American top executive by another of the Helder cousins. The new North American leader immediately let Jonah know that the company was slowing development of their East Africa mine because he was re-evaluating the initial exploratory drilling results at Ultra. They agreed that Bob Starfield should immediately start further test drilling at Ultra to complete assessment of the site. Three months later, Diamond Bill had analyzed these new exploratory results and reported that this second set of test cores showed a high content of large gemstones.

The new Helder boss was excited by Diamond Bill's analysis. Calling Jonah from the New York office, he announced that the new drilling results meant that Helder was immediately stopping development in East Africa to concentrate on this exciting new Canadian supply of ethically sourced large diamonds. He also told Jonah that Helder was willing to change its gemstone cutting, polishing and marketing operations to focus on the diamonds they expected to produce at the Ultra mine.

"Mr. Kay, if this mine is as rich as these new results suggest, we will transform our polishing and cutting operations in Antwerp and Mumbai to give priority to this new source of Canadian stones. We will of course share in profits from the raw diamonds according to our twenty per cent interest. But we want these Ultra diamonds to have a prime position in our international marketing. We think this product will be very special."

Jonah and David found themselves in a remarkable situation. Mindful Innovation had agreed to provide the upfront investment costs of the mine but, with Helder transferring all the equipment and facilities at Sierra to the new joint venture at Ultra, the start-up costs were lower than at most new mines. Uncle Samuel and Charlie had already transferred most of the lighter equipment between the two sites and would complete the transfer of heavier equipment with a short beefed-up road between Sierra and Ultra this coming winter.

Samuel's crew was also planning to build a permanent road between Port Muskek and the Ultra site for mine staff to commute daily by company bus from Port Muskek. Although building a year around road to the mine would be relatively expensive, it would save money quickly by eliminating costly air flights and reducing long stay shift premiums for miners. As Bob Starfield started training miners in Port Muskek, men and women from other James Bay communities were arriving in Port Muskek for the employment opportunity offered at Ultra. Samuel was already building both dormitories and more houses for miners in his home community. Mindful Innovation was providing the funds for the road, housing and hiring future miners for training in Port Muskek.

Lenore was delighted that Bob Starfield would be the manager of the new mine and was providing Charlie with regular trays of peach danishes. The last time Jonah had seen Charlie, Jonah pinched his belly and told him that he looked like he was putting on weight. Charlie said little in response but Jonah saw Charlie pinching himself as he walked away.

David had suggested to Jonah that he wanted to brainstorm how they were going to strategically position their new company. Port Muskek Council had agreed that Jonah should lead the corporation which would be owned forty-nine per cent by the Port Muskek First Nation and thirty-one per cent by Mindful with the remaining twenty per cent owned by

Helder. David had suggested that since Corinne's new company was focused on developing marketing strategy for luxury brands, she could possibly help them to understand how the new company would fit in the world diamond market.

"Jonah, I don't know if Corinne's company is right to develop our whole go to market plan. But you and I don't know the jewelry business. I'm worried that Helder's experience with stone preparation and marketing will leave us with limited understanding of our potential revenues. Remember our joint venture only relates to the production of raw diamonds, not the gem value after stone preparation and retail marketing. Helder gets twenty per cent of the value of the raw diamonds but I don't want those South Africans making all the decisions about how we prepare and sell these stones. We've seen from the Sierra mine experience that we need the knowledge to hold Helder strictly to account. Mindful needs to be involved in the marketing strategy for these gems to ensure we understand what Helder is doing."

Jonah looked at his friend carefully. "David, I agree that we need to be involved and knowledgeable about gemstone finishing and marketing. But you told me that you and Corinne are working on a new relationship, or something. I don't know what you call it when you start dating your ex-wife. Whatever it is, are you sure that we should be talking with her about work issues? Is it wise to be mixing business and social life like that? Couldn't that compromise you and Corinne in some way?"

David winked. "Actually, since we talked in Moose, things are going well between Corrine and me. But that's not the reason I want you to meet with her. You know how smart she is, and I have heard really good things from her clients about the fresh insights her firm is bringing to marketing and raising investment funds – especially with social media. No commitments, Jonah, I just want the three of us to have an introductory discussion for you to hear her out."

David looked down at his hands and then continued. "I don't know whether I am older, wiser or what, Jonah. But

I'm realizing what an idiot I was treating Corinne and my marriage with such disrespect. You know that she and I grew up together in high school and college. I just have a connection with her that I've never really felt with anyone else. And somehow, partnering with her in building our new company just makes sense. I respect her, I want to learn from her. I wouldn't say this to anyone else, Jonah, but I just feel that Corinne and are I are fated to be together somehow."

Jonah immediately felt the change in Corinne when he joined her and David in the Mindful conference room. Far from the bitter woman he remembered from their last encounter, the executive sitting with David was brimming with confident elegance. Jonah couldn't overlook that she and David still made a charming couple.

After exchanging pleasantries, Corinne opened the conversation with a suggestion, looking from one man to the other. "Why don't I summarize your current situation as I see it and you can respond to my analysis. Does that make sense?" Jonah and David glanced at each other and both nodded.

"Thanks. Well, as I understand from what David has told me and from reviewing the initial reports that this wonderful 'Diamond Bill' character has provided, you guys are probably sitting on one of the richest diamond discoveries ever made. You have the mining process well under control. Preliminary exploration is completed and this coming winter you will transfer the rest of the equipment that you need to completely open the mine. Full production will start by spring of 2020." She paused to see that the two men were agreeing and then continued.

"The amazing thing about this story is that the Port Muskek First Nation has the biggest ownership share and will receive a huge financial contribution if this mine is as rich as our friend Diamond Bill expects. Port Muskek will not only have the largest share of profits from raw diamonds – people from the community will also have the best jobs at the mine. You are currently training people from Port Muskek and other

James Bay communities to safely take over the mining work. Mindful Innovation is hiring these workers and financially supporting their training. You are also paying for the biggest building spree Port Muskek has ever experienced and your Uncle Samuel is ensuring that this construction is being done with local workers. By the way, Jonah, please give my regards to Mary and Sam." Jonah nodded. Corinne had met his aunt and uncle when they visited to watch hockey games during high school and Mary had been close to Corinne. Corinne continued with a smile.

"The value of these diamonds will also benefit from this First Nations ownership. The brand will have high consumer acceptance reflecting the ethical sourcing of the gems and the benefit that Indigenous People will achieve from the stones." She paused, looking at Jonah. "How am I doing so far in reflecting your view of reality, Jonah?" He nodded again and she continued.

"The stones will be fed into Helder's very efficient production line for cutting and polishing diamonds. I understand that Helder has agreed to provide those services within their twenty per cent cut and that's a good deal for the First Nation and Mindful Innovation. It would take a major investment for you to develop the infrastructure that Helder will provide as part of their contribution to this company. But I understand that you have had some experiences with Helder and don't trust them entirely to report on the value of your finished stones at the retail level." She glanced at Jonah, raising her eyebrows, and stopped her pitch.

"Okay, Jonah Kay, I remember that far-away look. It makes you look very mysterious, but it tells me that you may not agree with everything I've said." She smiled at him. "Out with it, Jonah, what are you thinking?"

Jonah leaned back to stare at the ceiling and then sat forward looking at his friends. "It's not that I disagree Corinne", he said, raising his hands. "Okay, we are just brainstorming, right?" Corinne and David both nodded. "Then let me tell you a bit of a story and you tell me if I am crazy." He took a breath, gathering his thoughts and started.

"Do you know where the first European settlement was established in what is now known as Ontario? Before Ottawa, Toronto or Kingston were settled?" Seeing no response from Corinne or David, Jonah continued.

"Well, in 1673, the Hudson's Bay Company founded a community at the mouth of the Moose River that they called Moose Factory. That first James Bay trading post was started there because my ancestors were expert at trapping fur bearing animals, especially beavers, and Europeans rapidly became obsessed with beaver fur – using it in their hats if you can believe it. So, my people started trading beaver pelts that had traditionally been used for warm clothing in our communities in exchange for items provided by those original settlers – metal cooking pots and sewing needles, thread, and rudimentary firearms – items that improved the efficiency and comfort of my ancestors' lives. Our oral history as well as settlers' accounts of that time also record that my ancestors taught those early settlers how to survive on our land. Where to hunt and fish, how to avoid scurvy and especially how to survive our winters."

He looked at his companions. "I may bore you a bit with this history lesson but hear me out. I think this may be relevant to our discussion."

Corinne shook her head. "No, this isn't boring. I had no idea that a James Bay settlement was established that long ago. This is interesting and could be part of the branding story we develop. Keep going Jonah."

"As trading beaver pelts with the settlers expanded, the Hudson's Bay Company used small, wooden sailing ships to bring trading goods through the Arctic ice and down to James Bay every summer. Those little boats then turned around and returned to England full of beaver skins before freeze-up. Settlers brought us the metal goods that made our lives somewhat easier, and we provided the settlers with furs and much of the food and knowledge they needed for survival. For years after settlers arrived, that relationship between Indigenous People and European settlers provided the economic value that made this land significant to Europeans as well as the support the settlers needed to live in this harsh environment. Without help from Indigenous Peoples, those settlers could not have survived and wouldn't have seen anything of economic significance in this sometimes forbidding land we call home." He paused to ensure they were following him.

"Many years after our relationship started in James Bay the beavers were gone in the Hudson Bay and James Bay regions – the animals were over-harvested and their population depleted. The settlers moved on westward, chasing beaver as far as the Rocky Mountains and then onward to the Pacific coast. And my people were left with our original lifestyle and no means to purchase the European goods that we had come to rely on. So, in many cases we started working for the settlers, rather than supporting them as equals. Then, as more settlers arrived, we were hammered by the European diseases that we had not experienced before – smallpox, TB – and our communities started to shrink and lose their self-sufficiency." Jonah shook his head.

"After that initial relationship when settlers relied on my ancestors, things went downhill fast for my people. Disease, depopulation, and disregard from the descendants of those settlers that we had originally helped to survive. Europeans moved on to find further sources of economic value in this country – the agricultural riches of wheat production on the prairies, extraction of minerals and petroleum, the manufacturing centres of southern Ontario. My people were left on reserves through treaties and federal legislation that was declared without us having adequate legal representation. Then the Canadian government instituted a thinly veiled approach to genocide through the policy of residential schools that tried to eliminate our language, our culture, and our future as a people."

Jonah leaned forward on the table. Corinne and David could sense his intensity. "Somehow, we have survived these attempts to eliminate us. Birthrates in our communities have rebounded and Indigenous communities are amongst the fastest growing in this land. Reconciliation for the years of attempted genocide has become the official policy of our federal government. And global warming is changing the nature of Canada's geography and increasing the opportunity to expand development in the north. It's become obvious that Canada's need for further natural resource extraction in the north and west will depend on a new relationship with Indigenous Peoples who control access to those resources."

Corinne was taking notes on her tablet. "I'm loving this, Jonah. Don't stop."

He nodded. "We are in the early stages of transforming our narrative from grievance to self-reliance. As we graduate more lawyers, doctors, nurses, and businesspeople from our Indigenous communities, our story will only get more resilient. And I think that our company can contribute to that narrative of strength." He sat up straight, looking from Corinne to David.

"That's why I'm thinking our company should be named Tapwe Diamonds."

David responded first. "What does Tapwe mean, Jonah?"

Jonah nodded. "Tapwe is a Cree word that means truth or real. I think this could be a wonderful description for remarkable diamonds that come from mines owned by this land's Indigenous People. I think this will fit with the ethical marketing approach you are suggesting Corinne."

Corinne looked up from her tablet. "Yeah, let me think about this Jonah. It sounds intriguing for our story." She looked at both men. "Tapwe is a beautiful name. It has a very evocative sound."

Jonah raised his hands in a cradle in front of his face, deep in thought. "This thinking is at early stages but hear me out." He turned to his friend. "David, I think that we need a way to verify what Helder tells us about the marketing of the jewelry that uses our stones. The idea that we just turn over the raw diamonds to Helder to cut, polish, and sell reminds me of the situation at Sierra mines where they reported false information about what the stones were worth. I also want to create much more value for the Port Muskek community and, if we can, for other Indigenous communities across the country." He saw that his colleagues were puzzled by this last comment.

"I can see you're not following me. Okay, here's what I'm suggesting. Tapwe Diamonds could have two sales channels for our diamonds, one here in Canada that we would develop and run, and the international channel run by Helder. At our mine, we would train and employ as many people from Port Muskek and other communities along the James Bay coast as possible. We would also insist that Helder helps us develop a cutting and polishing centre in James Bay that prepares finished stones for our Canadian market. Are you with me so far?" He looked at his companions who nodded.

"I want Tapwe to vertically integrate and cover all aspects of our Canadian sales channel, partly because this will contribute to jobs in First Nations communities and partly because it will force us to learn the jewelry business and ensure that Helder cannot cheat us. And one more thing." Corinne and David waited for him to finish.

"I want to re-establish the relationship between settlers and Indigenous People that was beneficial for both parties during those first years of European settlement of our land. If Tapwe controls mining, cutting, polishing, jewelry manufacture and retailing I think we have a chance to do something interesting."

He looked at David. "We know that these diamonds will be produced at a very reasonable cost since exploration and sourcing mining equipment were essentially completed before we took over the company. The Indigenous ownership also gives us tax advantages." Jonah paused and then continued with urgency.

"How about if Tapwe sells a line of large, beautiful diamond jewelry at retail outlets on reserves across the country. At stores that employ Indigenous sales staff and managers? With all jobs in that integrated supply chain going to Indigenous Peoples and importantly – deals that no settler can resist?" He paused and looked at Corinne.

"How does that sound as a strategic vision for Tapwe Diamonds, Corinne?"

*****

The Prime Minister was adjusting his cufflinks for the black-tie dinner he was not looking forward to attending at the National Arts Centre when his wife stepped in front of him to adjust his tie.

"Darling, I was just watching this crazy YouTube video from a new jewelry company operating a mine up in James Bay. Have you seen their social media? It's quite sophisticated."

"Yeah, I saw something about it." He shook his head. "Sorry, I'm having trouble thinking of anything right now except the briefing I had today about some new flu virus that is locking down a city in China. It started around Christmas and of course the Chinese probably suppressed initial information – I was only briefed about it today." He smiled, thanking his wife for the bow tie fine-tuning. "What's that jewelry company called? It's got an interesting name."

"That new virus sounds frightening. Anyway, the diamond company is called Tapwe Diamonds. Here, look at this video. The CEO is from the local community in James Bay. I have to say the camera just loves him."

The PM finished with his cufflinks and picked up his wife's tablet as the video began. He agreed that the guy doing the pitch was striking in appearance wearing a beaded shirt with his hair in a long ponytail. The PM admired effective communicators and this guy was superb with perfect pace and timing. His eyes on the screen somehow controlled the narrative.

"Do we know this guy? He's really good."

His wife nodded. "His name is Jonah Kataquit and he's from Port Muskek but educated in Toronto apparently. Everyone's been talking about him since this video and other social media exploded just a few days ago."

Corinne's firm had won the contract to work with Tapwe Diamonds and started a campaign focused on Canada as a starting point. Corinne thought that Jonah was the best spokesman they could have, and he was all over social media, talking about the Port Muskek First Nation owning Tapwe, describing how mining and production would employ workers from James Bay communities. The PM paid special attention as the camera closed in on Jonah and his eyes linked to his audience.

"*The Tapwe mine will produce the world's most beautiful diamonds and we are reserving much of the output from this mine for settlers in our land. We want to recreate the relationship that defined our peoples for the first years after European settlers arrived in James Bay – when you relied on us and we improved our lives together. That relationship got lost as this land developed and settlers forgot about how my ancestors helped the original Europeans to survive. We want Tapwe Diamonds to benefit both Indigenous Peoples and settlers. This company will remind us of how we once respected and helped each other.*" The PM noted the guy's timing was impeccable as he paused for breath.

"*Settlers will share the benefit that our First Nations will enjoy from this incredible mine. We will reserve some of the largest and most beautiful stones for you. And you will be surprised by the remarkable deals you will enjoy despite the quality of these gems.*" The Prime Minister looked at his wife. "He's good. I really like this."

The video continued. *"In Canada, Tapwe Diamonds will only be available in new retail stores we are currently opening from east to west. You will be able to examine the beautiful jewelry we will offer online, but purchases and fitting will be completed at Tapwe shops in First Nations communities across the country that will staffed by local Indigenous Peoples."*

As the PM looked on in admiration, Jonah finished the pitch that was rapidly earning views all over social media. Corinne had curated a variety of messages for various platforms and Jonah was everywhere, now immediately recognized by users of every app. His message was also starting to gain attention internationally.

The message varied depending on the platform, but Jonah ended each of his videos by reminding Canadians, *"Settlers relied on Indigenous People when they first arrived in this land. Now, at the happiest moments of your lives, we want you to rely on us to offer you a beautiful Tapwe diamond that will provide you with a lifetime of truth and memories."*

The Prime Minister and his wife were already late for the Art Centre dinner, but she understood when he paused to call his Chief of Staff as they got into his car. The PM directed that they needed to get this Tapwe jewelry CEO in for a conversation. And his wife was not surprised when the Chief of Staff responded that the meeting was already scheduled.

*****

Wifi had improved dramatically in Port Muskek since Chief and Council engaged Jonah's cousins to connect the community to satellite internet. Mary and Samuel had been amongst the first to install a satellite router and were amazed by the blazing download speeds they were enjoying. This was one of many changes that had occurred as Tapwe Diamonds started investing in Port Muskek.

Sam's company was busy constructing prefab buildings being used as classrooms by Bob Starfield's team who were upgrading skills for local people interested in working at the Ultra mine. Dorms were also being built, along with new homes, to house men and women from other James Bay communities who were interested in moving to Port Muskek to work at the mine. In getting Ultra up and running, Bob's biggest problem was finding and training new workers from James Bay communities. Chief and Council and Mindful Innovation together were governing all decisions about the company's start-up and were insistent on local employment.

Jonah's connection with Chief and Council remained tight as Tapwe invested funds provided by Mindful Innovation. Jonah was living with Mary and Samuel as Tapwe developed its corporate principles and policies with frequent meetings of the First Nation's leaders and Jonah as Tapwe CEO. Jonah knew that the governance of Tapwe Diamonds would evolve and was taking time explaining the start-up process and corporate requirements to Chief and Council. Mindful Innovation was funding the improvements being made on the reserve along with paying local people training for mine work. These Mindful investments provided Jonah with immense credibility in Port Muskek.

It took time for Jonah to convince Chief and Council that Tapwe needed a Canadian retail division rather than just marketing all gems through international channels for the highest available price. Jonah stressed the importance of the company learning about marketing and retailing diamonds to ensure that they were not reliant on Helder although he could never mention the fraud that Helder had perpetrated on the community at Sierra. Given the massive investment that Mindful was directing to Port Muskek, the local political leaders eventually agreed with Jonah's concept for Tapwe marketing through retail stores situated across the country.

One evening after dinner, Mary and Samuel sat together in the kitchen enjoying their new tablet connected to the satellite router. Jonah was away for a few days down south but had suggested his aunt and uncle might want to watch the social media messaging being used by the new company. Clicking from platform to platform enjoying the clarity of the videos they were watching, the two sat without comment, watching Jonah describe Tapwe's vision for its owners and customers.

Samuel found it hard to breathe as he listened to his nephew who had already accomplished so much more than Samuel could have imagined for his community. As a video ended, he looked at Mary and saw her eyes glistening.

"Oh, geez Sam, if she could only see him now. She would be so proud." Mary caught her breath with some difficulty. "I miss her so much, Sam."

Sam felt his eyes moisten as he silently nodded, taking his wife's hands in his across the table.

CHAPTER 23

Casa Loma. March 7, 2020

O riginally occupied in 1914, Casa Loma is one of North America's few remaining castles. The ninety-eight-room stone edifice is situated in five acres of lush gardens in mid-town Toronto on the ancient shores of Lake Iroquois. Twelve thousand years ago, that lake suddenly drained when the end of the ice age melted the ice jams that had dammed outflow from the Great Lakes for millennia. Lake Iroquois was about thirty metres deeper than today's residual Lake Ontario, its ancient shoreline extending several kilometres north of the current water's edge with most of today's downtown Toronto deep under water.

Casa Loma's dramatic location on the shore of that prehistoric lake is situated at the top of a hill that rises from the city centre. Standing on the edge of the property overlooking Toronto, it's easy to imagine Lake Iroquois suddenly again filling with water and flooding the city. Before the First World War, a Toronto financier built the magnificent castle with profits made investing in Toronto's original electrical system. He was ruined financially in the

Great Depression, forced to auction the castle's contents, and eventually surrendered Casa Loma to the city for unpaid taxes. The property now attracts tourists to its beautiful gardens and the castle's restored interior glory provides one of the city's best sites for extravagant entertainment.

When Corinne and David decided that they would end their divorce and re-marry, they initially planned a quiet, private ceremony. But the fact that their second nuptials overlapped with Tapwe Diamonds' launch was too good an opportunity for Corinne the marketeer to pass up. David had decided that his future happiness would be best served by generally agreeing with his fiancé's decisions and also recognized that a lavish public wedding would be an excellent opportunity to promote a new jewelry company. With the financial gains of the past year, Mindful Innovation could well afford to sponsor an extravagant celebration and Casa Loma seemed the obvious venue.

Corinne and David's renewed relationship was the talk of Toronto society. Corinne came from a patrician family with generations of prosperity gained from manufacturing and blue-chip investing. David's family was, by contrast, on the margins of Toronto's higher social caste. David's father and grandfather were known as highfliers – promoters of a variety of splashy initiatives in mining, oil and gas discovery, entertainment, and technology start-ups that generally made more money for the investment sponsors than for less fortunate investors. Corinne's family had been displeased when she began her relationship with David, but she committed to him in high school and David eventually charmed his detractors.

When David's bad behaviour resulted in the failure of their marriage, Corinne's parents were quick to suggest the relationship had been doomed by Corinne marrying below her family's standing. Her parents simply sighed at her announcement that she and David were getting back together, knowing that Corinne was now far beyond their influence.

Jonah was just happy that the two of them were reuniting. He readily agreed to serve as their best man for a second time but first ascertained that Corinne did not blame him for the failure of their first marriage. When he asked Corinne about any residual resentment, she smiled and hugged him, reassuring Jonah that she was happy to have him back in her life. She held his hands before continuing, "My relationship with David has really benefitted from the opportunity to work with you guys on Tapwe Diamonds, Jonah. I feel David respects the expertise I provide on how we market the company and these wonderful jewels. There's a partnership now Jonah, and that wasn't there in our marriage before." Then her eyes flashed.

"And I swear to God, Jonah, if he ever cheats on me again, I will do major surgery on him. And you too if you know about it and don't stop him." She stared fiercely at Jonah for a moment before they both broke into laughter, hugging again.

Corinne's public relations team took over the wedding planning as part of the promotion of Tapwe Diamonds. Continuing with the social media themes that distinguished the company's launch, influencers on a variety of platforms as well as Canadian traditional and digital media were invited to attend, cover, and promote the wedding and its relationship to Tapwe Diamonds. Bob Starfield, Diamond Bill and Helder worked overtime to deliver a number of beautiful large stones that would be worn by the bride and select models and influencers attending the wedding.

With many million dollars' worth of diamonds being displayed on the wedding night, security planning was tight. The exemplar of Tapwe Diamonds was the stunning six carat, round, brilliant stone mounted on Corinne's engagement ring. After much discussion and comparison of various gems, Diamond Bill and Helder experts suggested that Corinne's ring should showcase the alluvial diamond that Jonah had discovered in the creek bed while working the trapline with Charlie. Jonah appreciated that the stone that started his interest in the Ultra mine would be the gem that introduced Tapwe Diamonds to the world.

Three hundred and fifty people from a variety of communities – with James Bay, Toronto, and New York all well represented – were invited to the wedding ceremony. The formal service was to be held in Casa Loma's Great Hall, a magnificent space complemented by sixty-foot ceilings and stained-glass windows. Five hundred people in total were invited to the reception and dinner that would follow the wedding ceremony in the Library, Dining Room, and Conservatory spaces. After the wedding seating was removed, a dance floor would be set up in the Great Hall.

Corinne's team organized a DJ to start the evening and secured the Bold Rez Kids, a group from Moose that combined hip hop with traditional Cree music, to perform into the midnight hours. The wedding day was scheduled for early March and the south-facing Casa Loma covered porches overlooking the city were outfitted with heaters in expectation that guests would step outside to cool off from dancing.

Jonah was pleased that his friends were resuming life together and also realized what a wonderful promotion this very public event would provide for Tapwe Diamonds. Since taking over leadership of Tapwe he had been dividing his time between the mine, Port Muskek consulting with Chief and Council, Moose where Tapwe Diamonds was establishing a Canadian centre for diamond preparation, Toronto where he was building the corporate infrastructure for the firm and New York getting to know his new Helder partners. The Helder team was training people from James Bay to work at the diamond cutting and polishing centre that Jonah had insisted would be located in Moose. People from Port Muskek and other James Bay communities were being trained by Bob Starfield's managers to take over most of the mining jobs at Ultra.

Corinne's team impressed Jonah as they assumed marketing duties for Tapwe Diamonds. Her young marketing specialists knew the importance of consolidating social media messaging to promote new luxury brands and suddenly all channels were filled with Toronto and New York style leaders discussing, showing, and wearing the remarkable, ethically sourced gems being discovered in Canada's north. These early presentations of Tapwe jewels were usually accompanied by Jonah's video posts. Jonah was on North America's talk channels for several weeks, telling an irresistible story that combined history, terrible injustice, resilience, and amazing diamonds.

Appearing in Los Angeles on late night talk, Jonah was a dramatic guest with his beads and lustrous ponytail falling over a pale silk shirt, explaining to Jimmy how the twin challenges of harvesting beavers and winter survival created a relationship between his people and early European settlers on his ancestors' land. Describing his own experience on a marten trapline that resulted in the discovery of the first Ultra diamond, Jonah reached into his jeans to reveal Corinne's ring for the first time. While slowly rotating the enormous, glittering gem under the bright lights for the cameras, Jonah described how Tapwe Diamonds would be marketed in Indigenous-owned shops across Canada establishing new relationships with settler Canadians. That clip of a unique spokesman describing an unusual social enterprise and stunning jewelry was so intriguing that it dominated channels across North America for weeks after the show aired.

Jonah was planning to attend the wedding alone.

When he was in Toronto and New York, he was continuing his affair with Hillary Vanstone, corporate counsel for International Brands. He would have asked Hillary to attend the wedding with him but International Brands was still suffering financially and regretting their deal with CannWeed. Jonah understood that Hillary was reluctant to have their relationship become public given the role he had played in the International/CannWeed investment. So Jonah planned to attend the wedding without a guest.

Samuel and Mary were leading the James Bay guest list

for the Casa Loma wedding. Mary naturally considered this an opportunity to foster a relationship for her nephew and told David Morton that he must invite Dr. Brynn Allard and seat her at Jonah's table. Mary remembered the great hopes she had for Jonah and Brynn when they left on the trip to Samuel's fishing camp and her disappointment when they seemed distant on their return from the cabin the next day. But Mary was nothing if not persistent, and she was certain in her bones that this doctor and Jonah would be perfect together.

Plans and invitations for the wedding and the Tapwe launch were being organized by Corinne's company. Instead of a head table, they were planning a Tapwe Table that would seat Port Muskek leaders along with Moose dignitaries, Toronto financial backers and Helder executives. David, who would never disappoint Mary, directed the wedding manager to seat Dr. Allard at the Tapwe Table next to Jonah.

The next day David was at the end of a meeting with Corinne's team when the event manager cornered him. "Mr. Morton, I talked to that Dr. Allard you want seated at the Tapwe Table. She said she would come but would need to bring a plus one who is visiting her from Moose named Dr. Yvette Nguyen. She says she will only come if Dr. Nguyen can sit at her table."

David shrugged. "Have you got the list for the Tapwe Table? It's getting pretty crowded. This has become the event of the year, and everyone wants to sit at our table." The young event manager smiled. That was exactly what she wanted – responsibility for organizing the party that everyone wanted to attend. This unique intersection of Toronto, New York, and Indigenous communities along with the wedding of two high profile beautiful people and amazing jewelry – she could not imagine a better celebration to deliver.

She showed David the table seating. Jonah was placed next to David, followed by Mary and Samuel. If he put these two women doctors together, it would break the boy-girl alternating seating plan on the groom's side. David scratched his head and then saw the solution. "Okay, put Dr. Allard next to Jonah and then move Charlie beside her and then Dr. Nguyen and then Sam and Mary. That'll work." He smiled to himself hoping that this Dr. Nguyen was a conversationalist since he realized Charlie was better known for grunting than talking.

*****

The wedding was scheduled to start at seven p.m. and the Great Hall was at capacity by six forty-five. At five minutes to the hour Jonah and David strode to the altar from a side room, joining the Anglican priest from the girls' school who had married Corinne and David eight years before. Having spent some time in earnest discussion with the bride and groom, the cleric was reasonably certain that he would not be back for a third try. Corinne had a great sense of timing and at seven minutes after seven the assembly music ended. Seconds later a piano struck the opening chords of the Fleetwood Mac classic "Songbird".

Corinne stepped into the aisle from behind a curtain, joining her father who would accompany her to the altar, just as the soprano standing on a balcony overlooking the Great Hall started the song's second line, "For you, the sun will be shining". The gasp of the congregation was audible and palpable. The bride's slender gown was silver rather than white given this was her second stroll down the aisle. As she walked slowly toward David, the congregation's eyes were glued to Corinne as a series of spotlights ignited the diamonds that Helder had prepared from the first stones discovered at the Ultra site.

Everyone had seen various posts showing her engagement ring. But this was the first showing for her double stranded necklace comprised of more than one hundred stones with diamonds ranging from three carats in the front to smaller one carat stones in the back. A broad bracelet around her right wrist was created from a double strand of similar flat mounted stones and her jewelry was completed with a tiara decorated with hundreds of diamonds. The spotlights were focused on the tiara and Corinne seemed somehow to be floating above the floor of the Great Hall, elevated by the radiance reflected from the sparkling stones arranged over her forehead. Her father stepped aside as the two reached David and Jonah, just as the singer reached the final "love you... like never before." David smiled in appreciation as he held out his hands to his bride, captivated by the drama Corinne was bringing to the ceremony. Gasps were again heard through the Great Hall as he parted her veil, gently tilting her head back and detonating the brilliance reflected from her tiara and necklace.

Diamond Bill had estimated that she was wearing over fifteen million dollars in diamonds apart from her ring. Corinne knew that she would be returning all jewelry except her engagement ring after the ceremony but was thoroughly enjoying modelling these beautiful gems. As she turned to the altar to marry David for a second time, she recognized that this time it was a marriage of equals who would truly partner each other – just like this partnership launching Tapwe Diamonds at their wedding.

*****

Following the ceremony, Jonah stood to the side watching the myriad photographers capturing the bride and groom – but especially the bride. In addition to the "official" photographers, a significant portion of the congregation wanted to photograph Corinne and her jewelry as well as getting selfies with her for their sites. This was part of the plan to launch Tapwe Diamonds and the event manager had allocated over an hour for photos to be taken.

After watching the picture taking for a time, Jonah was happy to leave his friends in the chaos which David was patiently tolerating while Corinne moved between various backdrops around the Great Hall, spotlights following her providing brilliant reflections from her jewelry. Jonah saw Uncle Samuel at a table in the Drawing Room reception adjacent to the Great Hall and went in to join him. As he entered the room, he noticed that Samuel and Mary were sitting at a café table with Dr. Brynn Allard, a small Asian woman and Charlie. Brynn was wearing a forest green frock, partially obscured by the table.

As he approached, the smaller woman between Brynn and Charlie jumped off her chair and ran to Jonah squealing in delight with hands clasped in front of her. She clapped her hands looking at Jonah, then reached up providing him with a hug and a kiss on the cheek. Jonah was taken aback, especially when she released him and turned back to Brynn, giggling.

"Jesus, Brynn, he is even better looking in person than he is on YouTube." Yvette returned to Jonah, grasping his hands, "Say something about Canada's history in that incredible deep voice you use on social. Your voice makes me crazy – you have to do more podcasts. I'll download anything you ever say." She then literally jumped up and down, clapping her hands in glee before running back to stand beside Charlie, grabbing his arm in excitement.

Jonah was speechless, looking at Brynn who had risen from the table coming to greet him. "Hi Jonah, you have now been introduced to my friend, Dr. Yvette Nguyen, who is in town from Wiichihinan Hospital. As you've noticed, she is quiet and retiring, but I'm hoping she can get over her shyness and enjoy herself tonight." She smiled and turned to Charlie. "Charlie, I told you that your job is to keep Yvette out of trouble tonight." Charlie grunted in response and Yvette sat on the chair beside him, telling him breathlessly how much she wanted a tiara like Corinne's and that if she had a tiara like that, she would wear it all the time and would sleep in it forever. As she continued, Charlie listened carefully and occasionally snorted while he sipped his beer.

Brynn turned back to Jonah. Samuel had started to get up

from the table to come over to Jonah, but Mary grabbed his arm and firmly pulled him back to his seat. "Just leave them alone for goodness sake, Sam."

Brynn leaned her elbows on one of the cocktail tables set up in the reception area and looked up at Jonah. Now that she was standing he could appreciate her dress, seeing how the green complemented her eyes and hair. "Things have certainly changed for you since we last met, Jonah Kataquit. The last time I saw you, you were dressed in a snow suit introducing me to caribou and polar bears. Now you're in a tux and known as an international raconteur explaining James Bay to the world and pitching these amazing diamonds you have discovered. That's quite a transition."

Jonah smiled down at Brynn. "Well, I hear you've accomplished some big things too, Doc. When we were in Port Muskek you were explaining how frustrated you were that some of our Elders could not travel south for surgery. Now I understand that you've started doing surgery at Wiichihinan and that other doctors are coming up from Toronto continuing what you started." He looked at her thoughtfully. "Things are going to change in James Bay, Brynn. With the new mine, the new company and its commitments to jobs and profits staying with the local people, there is going to be a lot more money for new homes and facilities. And the changes you are bringing to our local hospital and healthcare are going to be an important part of a better life for people in James Bay."

Just then the Master of Ceremonies announced that the bride and groom would be arriving in the dining room in ten minutes and could guests please find their places for dinner? Jonah had already discovered where the "Tapwe Table" was located on a dais at the front of the Library and led Brynn, his aunt and uncle and other head table guests to their places. They had just settled into their seats when the screech of a bagpipe filled the high-ceilinged spaces of Casa Loma and the newlyweds were led in by the piper to circulate amongst their guests on their way to the Tapwe Table. Corinne's team had arranged models and influencers to follow the bride and groom, a procession of very stylish women and a few men wearing the beautiful jewelry produced by Tapwe Diamonds.

Conversation at the Tapwe Table sparkled during dinner and toasts to the members of the wedding party filled the time between the courses of the wonderful meal being served by Chef Bruno Patolli. While dining, Jonah wanted to learn how Brynn planned to get surgery established at Wiichihinan. He listened intently while she described how the university and her hospital in Toronto were now committed to developing collaborative clinical programs as well as education and training with the James Bay hospital.

Samuel caught Brynn's attention, sitting three seats away from him. "Doc, I'm feeling my leg's ready for dancing, especially since you're here in the room if anything goes wrong. Whad'ya think, Doc?"

Brynn reassured him, "Sam it's been over two years since your injury and that bone is solid. Just remember that your moves on the dance floor will advertise my surgical skills for better or for worse."

Samuel smiled at Brynn, silently tilted his head toward Charlie who, sitting to Brynn's right, had wordlessly listened to Dr. Yvette Nguyen throughout dinner while steadily consuming beer. Brynn returned Samuel's grin. She knew Yvette's poor tolerance for alcohol. With Yvette finishing three glasses of wine with dinner, Brynn hoped that Charlie would be patient enough to listen to her friend rambling on throughout the evening.

The security detail was vigilant during dinner, watching all the guests with their jewels. After the meal, the team started moving discreetly between the tables, collecting the gems to return them to the vaults as dessert was being served. Corrine insisted on returning her bracelet, her necklace and her remarkable tiara before the dancing started following dinner.

When the music began, the guests began filing back to the

Great Hall where a welcoming, polished wooden floor had been installed during dinner.

After the bride and groom's first dance, the Toronto and New York guests were surprised as the James Bay contingent dominated the dance floor. House parties during long James Bay winters were often dance parties and traditional dancing was an important part of local culture.

The DJ got the room limbered up, but the party began in earnest when the Bold Rez Kids started their first set just before midnight. Jonah had been dancing together with the Tapwe Table celebrants. He always enjoyed watching Charlie on the dance floor. Despite his usual laconic approach to life, Charlie was electrified when he danced and tonight, his connection to the Rez Kids was readily evident. Yvette was keeping up with him step for step. Brynn and Jonah stood aside to watch them bringing their moves together in repetitive rhythm, holding everyone's attention in the centre of the floor. As they moved to the side watching Yvette and Charlie, Jonah found himself holding Brynn's hand.

He glanced at Brynn while she gazed in delight at the two dancers, feeling his usual anxiety surfacing. He was enjoying the evening with this beautiful woman. She was stunning in her green dress and distinguished by her confidence and optimistic good humour. But he felt increasingly overwhelmed by her youth and beauty – he could feel the familiar agitation welling up. David and Corinne were so excited to be starting a new partnership and Jonah could almost taste the regret that he could never have what they were enjoying.

The Bold Rez Kids were combining hip hop with traditional music and the crowd was responding with contagious energy to the beats. Jonah managed to control his anxiety by surrendering to the music, partnering Brynn as the infectious rhythms took over. At about one fifteen the band signalled a break. Jonah and Brynn came slowly down to reality, realizing their considerable thirst. They stopped at the bar for bottles of water and glasses of wine and Jonah led

Brynn onto one of the covered porches that had been outfitted with heaters. Most people were staying inside to sample the late-night dessert table and the two found themselves alone at one end of the second-floor terrace, leaning on the surrounding railing and gazing across the city below to the lake.

As they quenched their thirst, Jonah noticed Brynn's shiver and removed his coat, draping it over her shoulders.

She turned her head to look up at him. "There you go, keeping me warm again. Just like when we visited the fishing camp." She smiled and then sighed, tentatively lifting her eyes to his face. "I obviously misread things at the camp after dinner, Jonah. I came on pretty strong and I'm sorry for making you uncomfortable that evening." She looked over the city, sighing again. "This is so beautiful. What a night."

Turning back to face Jonah, she saw his jaw clenched, his face clearly troubled.

"Jonah, I'm sorry. Did I say something that hurt you?"

At that very moment Jonah's thoughts were overwhelmed by memories of his mother lying cold on her bed and he had to force himself to respond to Brynn. "Oh, god, Brynn... it's me that's sorry. The emotion of this day... the happiness... happiness I am feeling for David and Corinne."

He dragged his hand across his eyes and momentarily gazed at her, then shook his head and stared at the floor. The lights coming through the porch windows illuminated her profile as he warily lifted his eyes to hers.

"I am so happy... happy for my friends," Jonah started. "They had... had some hard times, but I think they are good now. David knows now... knows how special Corinne is. I think he's learned... learned his lessons. But it is just... so... so difficult... for me... that I can never have... have what they are celebrating."

He looked back down and Brynn could see that his jaw muscles were quivering with tension.

Jonah realized that he needed to somehow recover his

equanimity. He was ruining a night of celebration. He forced his diaphragm to relax and attempted to speak more normally while examining the floor. "Brynn, I'm... I'm an idiot to be wrecking the evening... for you, for you... like this. I'm so sorry. Like I told you... told you at the fishing camp, I had some issues when I was a kid and, like I said... like I told you... Brynn, I have real difficulty with intimacy. On a night like tonight, it's just so hard... so hard to accept the problems that I'm left with."

To his surprise, she softly put her hand under his chin to tilt his head up so that they were looking directly at each other. "You know Jonah, I had a wonderful time with you on that trip to the camp and skiing to see the bay. I thought that we were getting close and to be honest, I wanted to get closer. I thought maybe you felt the same." She paused and looked at the city and then back to him. "I was pretty hurt that night. You turned me down pretty hard. But I didn't know then what had happened to you in the past."

Jonah started to apologize but Brynn put a finger against his lips. "David explained to me what happened to your mother, Jonah, and also what happened with that principal's wife." She shook her head. "It's no wonder intimacy is threatening to you. The things that happened to you were just indescribably awful. After learning about those events, I think I can understand something about how you might feel." She thought carefully about her next words.

"It's amazes me how you have overcome that terrible trauma in most aspects of your life, Jonah." He started to shake his head in disagreement but she held his face with both hands while looking directly in his eyes. "Jonah, it looks like we will be spending time in the same places for a while, here in Toronto and up in James Bay." She continued to hold his face and softly ran her hand over the tense muscles clenching his jaw.

"I think I would like to see you, Jonah. Maybe, who knows, maybe we can get to know each other a bit better over time, no pressure. Those issues must be very difficult to face alone." She looked at him from inches away and smiled.

He felt himself breathing more slowly. He exhaled deeply, putting his hands against hers on his face. "Thanks Brynn." He took another deep breath and words came easier. "I guess my thinking has changed a bit since the time we talked at Uncle's fishing camp. Being back in my community for the past few months has given me a different perspective on what happened to me and my family."

He paused, then slowly continued, again staring at the floor. "For so long, I've felt that something intrinsic to me is broken, totally screwed up. But now I am starting to understand this didn't start within me – it's something that was done to me and my family by racism and genocide. I guess that I'm slowly changing from feeling that I'm responsible for being damaged to getting more angry about it."

He looked up, shaking his head. "Wow Brynn, these are bitter thoughts to be sharing on such a happy occasion. Forgive me."

Her smile broadened and she turned her head back to the Great Hall where the band had returned and were starting to wail. "Jonah I can't think of a better prescription for bitter thoughts than these amazing Rez Kids."

Her face was so lovely. Jonah cautiously allowed himself to respond to Brynn's energy and confidence as they left the balcony. She took his hand in hers, leading him back to the dance floor.

ACKNOWLEDGEMENT

I learned about the devastating impact of intergenerational trauma while serving as Ontario's Deputy Minister of Health. At the time I was dismayed by my limited prior understanding of this issue despite having practiced medicine in Ontario for more than twenty-five years. I thank countless Indigenous leaders, community members and healthcare providers for their patience in teaching me that our history of residential schools and colonialism represents an ongoing, current threat to mental and physical health for Indigenous Peoples in this country.

Similarly, despite working with talented women surgical colleagues daily, I had little awareness of the impact of misogyny on their lives and professional careers.

Hence my interest in and regard for Jonah and Brynn whose remarkable successes are achieved despite challenges that a white man is fortunate to avoid.

This book could not have been written without the contributions of two "Learning Circles" that met virtually to discuss fundamental issues pertinent to this novel and advise on relevant passages of the book.

The first "Learning Circle" included people who live or have lived in James Bay communities, attended residential school, and understand the impact of intergenerational trauma. This wise group of advisors also described their encounters with

First Nations health and social systems.

I humbly thank them for their generosity in committing time to this project. Any mistakes made in describing the lives of people living in the fictitious northern communities represented in this novel or in describing the devastating ongoing effects of residential schools, colonialism and intergenerational trauma are solely mine.

The second 'Learning Circle" was comprised of internationally esteemed, academic women surgeons.

Again, I thank them for their time and honesty in describing the pervasive misogyny they have experienced in academic surgical practice. These experiences are both heart-breaking for individuals and devastating for surgical scholarship since this sexism threatens the accomplishments of women surgeons and reduces the appeal of a surgical career for women.

Members of both "Learning Circles" will remain anonymous. As a cis-gendered, able, white male I reiterate my sincere thanks for the contribution these people provided to my understanding of the issues addressed in "Jonah K."

ABOUT THE AUTHOR

Dr. Bob Bell

Robert Stuart Bell, MDCM, MSc, FRCSC, FACS, FRCSE (hon).
Emeritus Professor, Department of Surgery, University of Toronto.

Dr. Bob Bell received his medical degree from McGill University in 1975. Following three years working as a GP, Bell returned to surgical residency at the University of Toronto and received his fellowship in Orthopedic Surgery in 1983.

Bell then spent two years as a surgical fellow at Harvard University and the Massachusetts General Hospital in Boston. While in Boston, he gained clinical expertise in arthritis and cancer surgery.

Recruited to the University of Toronto's Faculty of Surgery, Bell worked as a cancer and orthopedic surgeon for 19 years. During that time, he trained more than 30 surgical fellows who are now surgical leaders on five continents and published more than 200 peer-reviewed scientific papers.

In 2005, Bell was appointed as President and CEO of University Health Network (UHN), Canada's largest research hospital. Toronto General Hospital, one of the hospitals in UHN, was recently named the fourth best hospital in the world by Newsweek magazine. During his nine years as CEO of UHN, Bell led a substantial expansion of clinical and research programs.

In 2014, Bell was appointed Deputy Minister of Health in Canada's largest province of Ontario. For the next four years, Bell was responsible for the operations of a health system serving 14 million people.

After resigning as Deputy Minister in 2018, Bell has focused on writing fiction, consulting, charitable activities, and providing commentary on Canada's publicly funded health system. This commentary can be found at www.drbobbell.com and @drbobbell.

Jonah K. is Bell's third novel.

Bell and his wife Diann divide their time between homes in Toronto and on Georgian Bay.

All profits from this book will be donated to the Indigenous Health Program at University Health Network.

Bob Bell can be followed on Twitter @docbobbell, at www.drbobbell.com and can be contacted at docbobbell@gmail.com.

BOOKS BY THIS AUTHOR

Hip: A Novel

Andrei Kovalov has created a biolayer coating that provides amazing results in dog hip replacements. This super-B.I.G. implant with the biolayer has been approved for human use, and investors will pay Kovalov more than $25 million for his invention.

However, Kovalov has destroyed evidence showing that several dogs treated with the super-B.I.G. developed bone cancer from his biolayer. Patrick Maloney, a lowly surgical fellow, has observed cancer in a super-B.I.G. specimen and is concerned when the evidence of cancer disappears after he reports his findings.

Since international leaders in the famed Boston hospital where he works will benefit from the super-B.I.G., Patrick is told to curb his suspicions. With his career on the line, Patrick must choose whether or not to ignore his misgivings—and risk hurting the woman he loves.

This cautionary tale describes the conflict between profitable surgical innovation and the weak approval processes for surgical devices. Patrick knows he must uphold the oath to protect patients from harm. With extremely powerful forces aligned against him, will Dr. Maloney be able to honor his oath? Will his promising career be destroyed? Surprising answers follow.

All proceeds from this novel benefit sarcoma cancer research at The Princess Margaret Cancer Foundation.

New Doc In Maple Ridge

Rave reviews for the new medical thriller, "New Doc in Maple Ridge"! All proceeds will benefit community primary care research at University Health Network, fourth best hospital in the world according to Newsweek magazine!

"New Doc in Maple Ridge is a wild ride that takes the reader from a small-town ER to the battlefields of Afghanistan, to the underworld, to the courtroom, with high-spirited stops along the way in the bedroom. A real page-turner, grounded in the unparalleled, extensive experiences of Dr. Bob Bell." Deb Matthews, PhD, Former Ontario Minister of Health

"After decades performing life-saving surgery, Dr. Bob Bell uses his surgeon's attention to detail to craft a brilliant story populated by some of the most extraordinary characters you will ever encounter! I dare you to put this book down once you have started the remarkable journey with Dr. Ed Brinkley."Paul Alofs, Former CEO Princess Margaret Cancer Foundation & Author of "Passion Capital"

"Surgeon, hospital CEO, and provincial deputy health minister.... Dr. Bob Bell has done it all, so no surprise that his new novel is steeped in medical authenticity. The tension builds from the first page, when the new doctor in town saves a boy from choking on a peanut. Whether it's treating a mobster's STD, or reliving military action in Afghanistan, you feel that you are right there." Phillip Crawley, CEO/Publisher of The Globe and Mail

Dr. Ed Brinkley concluded his career as a battlefield surgeon following highly classified tours of duty in the Middle East. He arrives in Maple Ridge, Arkansas to start over as a small-town GP and to settle down in a new home. Things are looking up for Ed when he meets the lovely Linda Davis, managing partner of Arkansas' leading law firm.

But Ed refuses an unethical demand from Tony Malto, a local gangster who tries to bully the doctor, triggering traumatic memories from Ed's past.

Ed's response to Malto's intimidation takes the reader on a page turning flashback to Afghanistan and on to Biloxi, Mississippi as Ed fights back to protect the woman he wants to love.

Manufactured by Amazon.ca
Bolton, ON

29412485R00188